THE BALLINGTONS

A NOVEL

BY

FRANCES SQUIRE

Published by Left of Brain Books

ISBN 978-1-396-32092-7

First Edition

Table of Contents

PART I	1
CHAPTER I	1
CHAPTER II	13
CHAPTER III	29
CHAPTER IV	33
CHAPTER V	39
CHAPTER VI	46
CHAPTER VII	56
PART II	62
CHAPTER I	62
CHAPTER II	70
CHAPTER III	73
CHAPTER IV	80
CHAPTER V	85
CHAPTER VI	93
CHAPTER VII	98
CHAPTER VIII	103
CHAPTER IX	111
CHAPTER X	124
PART III	131
CHAPTER I	131
CHAPTER II	137
CHAPTER III	143
CHAPTER IV.	150
CHAPTER V	160
CHAPTER VI	165
CHAPTER VII	175

CHAPTER VIII 188

CHAPTER IX 194

CHAPTER X 203

PART IV 216

CHAPTER I 216

CHAPTER II 223

CHAPTER III 234

CHAPTER IV 237

CHAPTER V 243

CHAPTER VI 254

CHAPTER VII 262

CHAPTER VIII 273

CHAPTER IX 283

PART V 297

CHAPTER I 297

CHAPTER II 306

CHAPTER III 317

CHAPTER IV 320

CHAPTER V 329

CHAPTER VI 336

CHAPTER VII 344

CHAPTER VIII 351

CHAPTER IX 358

CHAPTER X 366

CHAPTER XII 374

PART I

CHAPTER I

A GIRL went up to the piano and stood half-turned toward the group of guests in Mrs. Ballington's drawing-room while an accompanist played through the prelude of a Rubinstein song. The girl was dressed in white, with no ornament except an old-fashioned Roman sash; but she stood very straight, and her hair had a rebellious wave that showed fire under the brown, and her neck and arms were like flushed marble. Presently she turned toward the listeners and began to sing. Her voice had the sweep and vibration of a 'cello and she used it daringly. As she sang she seemed to expand from a fledgling college girl into some elemental spirit, the grandeur of whose passion awed while it thrilled the listeners.

"Charming!" Mrs. Ballington said, with a sour look through her lorgnette at the wandering lights in the girl's dark eyes. She had been chagrined for weeks past at her son Donald's devotion to this country doctor's daughter. Her chagrin flamed into exasperation at the girl's unembarrassed flaunting of herself—such was Mrs. Ballington's phrase—in the Ballington parlor as though it already belonged to her.

Donald did not speak, but Agnes Sidney caught the look of adoration in his eyes as she left the piano and went over to his younger brother Tom. Tom withdrew his elbows from his knees and looked up from the floor. "No, you don't get me to sing any coon song or play the banjo!" he said briefly. Agnes came to a stop and began to laugh.

"I don't want to talk, either. I want to be impolite and still," he went on severely. "You ought to want to be still, too, after singing like that."

Another college girl, who had come with Agnes, at this moment joined them. It was her first opportunity to escape from perfunctory conversation with the third man of the Ballington family.

As she drew Agnes down beside her on the lounge near Tom's chair, the light from the chandelier fell upon her heavy hair, changing it from brown to bronze. Her face was not beautiful, but it had a power and a kind of sardonic sweetness which compensated for beauty. A pair of straight black brows marked her face, and impenetrable gray eyes looked out from beneath them. Miriam Cass was five years older than Agnes and was as well-known in the scientific and art life of Winston College as was Agnes in its social life.

"Then will you play your flute for us?" said Agnes. "That was what I was going to ask you."

Tom moved impatiently, whereupon the newcomer inter posed, smiling, "Mr. Ballington thinks the flute is too precise and soulless an instrument after your Rubinstein, Agnes."

Tom looked up with a return of his natural good humor. "Precise?" he exclaimed. "You never heard me play! Soulless, is it?" He paused and looked across the room at the man who was sitting imperturbably where Miriam had left him. "Ferd! You're the man to play the flute. It shall be my Christmas present to you."

Agnes sat up eagerly, glad of an excuse to look at the man of whom she had been thinking while she sang. He, too, was looking at her, as it chanced. The flush of her face and neck deepened as their glances crossed.

Ferdinand Ballington rose at once. Agnes noted afresh, as she watched his leisurely approach, how he differed in looks from his cousins, Donald and Tom. Ferdinand's eyes were blue, but, unlike the mild Ballington eye, bright and intense. His brows and lashes were dark and there was a cold steadfastness in his regard.

"Are you going to let them call you soulless, Mr. Ballington?" said Agnes, as soon as he reached her side.

"I have begun to think that I have a soul," Ferdinand answered quietly.

Agnes felt a tingle of excitement as she asked with a half-smile, "Why haven't you talked to me before this evening?"

"I have been waiting to do so ever since I saw you. I saw you the moment you entered the room."

"Well," replied the girl, arching her brows, "I saw you while I was singing and I wondered if you liked the song. You kept so still."

He made no reply.

She was embarrassed at his silence and nervously pressed the inquiry, "Did you like the song?"

"I would listen as long as you could sing. There is a spell about you."

Agnes was oppressed by the unvarying gaze of her companion's eyes. "I would be glad if I could bring out the spell that is in great music. I wish I were great enough to do it," she said.

There was a dignity in her way of receiving the compliment which checked him. He considered a moment, then drew a chair near her and sat down, beginning in a less personal tone to question her about her musical studies. They soon passed to other subjects and only the girl's heightened color and eager attention intimated that she was peculiarly interested in her new companion.

A kindred interest would have explained Tom's brightening up as he found himself with Miriam Cass.

Presently Miriam withdrew her arm gently from Agnes and turned entirely to Tom. "You don't want to talk," she said humorously, "so I am going to look at these photographs."

"Oh, yes, I do, now!" Tom answered frankly.

Miriam's hands were already upon the basket of photographs, which she lifted from the table near by and placed upon her knees.

"You won't be interested in these," volunteered Tom. "They are mostly our relations and the hideous houses they lived in and their funeral flowers."

Miriam laughed and began taking them out carelessly.

Tom stopped her suddenly. "Wait a minute. That one is worth looking at. It is Uncle Tom's Old farmhouse. I was named for him. That was the finest old place between here and Albany. Ferdinand owns it now." He leaned over and pointed at the picture, lowering his voice confidentially. "You see that beautiful avenue of cedars, winding up to the house? You couldn't have duplicated that anywhere. Oh, well—" he broke off. "Let's look at the next one."

Miriam, however, continued to study the picture, and Tom impatiently picked up another from the heap. He glanced at it and flung it back into the basket.

The action aroused Miriam and she innocently took it up and looked at it carefully. "Who is this?"

"Old General Mott," Tom replied shortly.

Agnes caught the name and turned toward them.

"Beatrice Mott's father!" she exclaimed; "I want to see it."

Her energy made the group who had petrified around Mrs. Ballington near the piano look across the room. Agnes was studying the picture. "Does his daughter look like him?"

"Very much," said Ferdinand. Then he asked with interest, "Is Fred Sidney any relation of yours?"

Agnes looked up. "Yes. He is my cousin. I've been very anxious to see the Motts ever since Fred and Beatrice were engaged. Their engagement was so sudden—"

An embarrassed pause followed the words, and Tom's face hardened.

Without looking at him, Agnes dropped her eyes again to the picture in her hand. It was the likeness of a burly, bold-featured man with lines of laughter about eyes and mouth, a determined chin, and an expression of vigor and contentment. He wore a military uniform.

To relieve the constraint which General Mott's photograph had produced, Miriam held up the picture of the Ballington farm. "You have a beautiful home, Mr. Ballington," she said to Ferdinand.

"Yes," he replied. "I think a good deal of it. I intend to make a fine place of it in time."

Tom was called away during Ferdinand's remark to summon the carriage for one of the guests, and when he came back he found that the leave-taking had become general. With some relief he noticed that, at last, Agnes and Donald were together. He knew that Donald had planned the whole evening with reference to her coming, and he had wondered why his brother had not taken advantage of his opportunity. Agnes was saying good-night to Mrs. Ballington, who responded with grudging civility. Miriam was already in the doorway. Tom caught up his hat and joined her, divining that Donald had looked forward to an uninterrupted conversation with Agnes as he accompanied her back to the college. Miriam walked rapidly and she and Tom were soon well in advance of Donald and Agnes.

As the latter went down the path Donald at length broke silence in an unnatural voice. "Are you really going tomorrow?"

"Yes," replied Agnes. "I have stayed over two days, now, and I must go home."

"Could you not make your home here?" he asked very low.

It had come sooner than she expected. She did not reply. They reached the end of the linden walk. Here Agnes stopped, and, partly to regain her composure, turned for a last look at the house. She saw Ferdinand Ballington standing alone on the piazza, looking after them. Perhaps he saw her stop and look back, for he turned immediately and went into the house.

"Don't you understand me?" said Donald earnestly. "Will you be my wife?"

It was her first proposal, and a direct one. Agnes instinctively quickened her step to catch up with her companions. There was a longer pause. She heard Tom's laugh on ahead, and was soon near enough to see the responsive humor in Miriam's face as it was raised to his. It was a relief to hear their words distinctly.

"How could you expect your mother to tolerate Benvenuto Cellini?" Miriam was saying.

Agnes brought her mind away from Tom's enthusiastic visions of statues in bronze and salt-cellars in gold, to answer her lover. "Donald," she said at length, struggling to utter what was plain to herself, "I'll tell you how it is. I know I must marry some time, but I can't bear to think about it yet. I want to be free." She opened her hands with a sudden gesture of wings.

"Love doesn't make slaves—true love," said Donald.

"Yes, it does!" She was started now, and ran on glibly, half in earnest, but with the growing dramatic instinct. "It does. At least for a woman. A woman gives up so much for the man she marries: her name, her individuality, all her chance of personal ambition, her health often, and sometimes her life."

She stopped, artistically elated with her speech. She could not conceive of herself without health, and she certainly did not intend to give up her life for anyone.

"*Yes*," said Donald, with solemnity in his voice. The one word awed her.

"But I will confess," she went on, after a moment, "there are times when I think I should like to marry now. You know what my home is, how hard papa works and how shut up mamma is. As your wife—of course I can't be oblivious of it—I won't deceive you, that's one thing I won't do I—it would give me an opportunity—"

He interrupted her, anticipating. "You should do for your parents whatever you might wish," he said seriously. "I can understand the desire, and it would be my happiness and my honor to gratify it."

Agnes was silent in acute mortification. She was ashamed, for she saw that he had put a generous interpretation to her words. She had been thinking only of herself.

"Thank you," she said at last.

"I went up to Kent and called upon your parents a fortnight ago," continued Donald. "I went there on purpose to give them an opportunity to see me. I was tempted to speak to your father of this matter, but I thought I ought to ask your permission first. Oh, Agnes!" He choked and stopped. After a minute he resumed again. "Think what our life together might be! If God would give me this blessing, my cup would run over. Everything else I have. There are the ten talents. Oh, my dear girl, help me to make them the twenty!"

As she still remained silent, he spoke again. "I feel free to say your father liked me. I went to church with him and had supper at your good home. If you had been there my heart would have been full. I know I am not clever, but I would be content to have you so. Just let me love you! We would grow nearer each other as the years went on."

Still Agnes said nothing. Her sensations were confusing. This was not the wooing of which she had read and dreamed—this solemn talking about God and the church. Yet she felt the kindliness of his reference to her home and her parents, and a transient tenderness made her exclaim with sudden shame, "You are too good for me! You deserve a good woman."

He caught her hand which hung by her side. "Oh, Agnes! What better woman could I ever find? Say 'yes' to me, dear. Do say 'yes.'"

"Will you let me wait a little?" she asked, feeling repugnance to pledging herself, yet rebelling against the return to her village life without some chance of escape.

"Take as much time as you wish," he answered. "God forbid that I should hurry you. But you will write to me, will you not?"

"Yes, I will write."

Then he allowed her to change the subject. When they reached the college grounds they found Tom and Miriam waiting for them at the gate, and they all walked up the long path together.

"I used to wonder what was inside this place when I was a boy," remarked Tom, as they neared the steps. "I asked my Uncle Tom once, and he said it was a deer park. So it is," he added, turning a frank smile upon the two girls.

Miriam laughed, but Agnes scarcely heard the sally. Neither did she hear Tom explaining to Miriam that Uncle Tom was Ferdinand Ballington's father, though not a soul would know it.

After the good-nights were said, Agnes and Miriam hurried through the dimly-lighted halls of the dormitory. Trunks were standing by certain doorways, but the corridors were deserted. Miriam's room was the first one they reached.

"Won't you come in?" she asked, inserting the key and throwing open the door.

Agnes entered and walked over to the open window. Miriam lighted the gas. "Fräulein is awake still," Agnes said as the sound of a brilliant run in sixths came over from Music Hall.

After a moment, she turned and glanced around the room. It was stripped of all its ornaments except Miriam's finished and unfinished models in clay which stood or lay along the top of the long bookshelves. As Agnes looked them over, Miriam regarded her with pleasure. She let her eyes pass from the well-poised head down the figure, noting the girl's pose. There was a glint of good-natured satire in her expression as she said finally, "Well, which one of the Ballington company do you think the most interesting? I select the dowager."

Then, with a deepening amusement at the puzzled look Agnes gave her in reply, Miriam went on: "How much longer do you suppose she went on talking about Mrs. Mortimer Tompkins' Napoleonic bedquilt after we left her? Wherever do you suppose Tom Ballington got his good humor from, and his taste?"

"His taste is making the family a good deal of trouble," commented Agnes; "when he is supposed to be attending to business, as often as not he is down at the library poring over books on metal work. He has a private collection of outlandish things that have cost him a good deal more money than he ever has made."

"It's a strange thing," said Miriam in reply, "that conscientious men like Donald Ballington, utterly regardless of centuries of warning examples, keep on trying to make pigs' tails out of whistles. He'll be sorry someday that he doesn't let his brother do what he is born to do."

Agnes laughed. "Tom does pretty much as he wants to. He isn't the martyr in that family. From what I hear, he and Beatrice Mott made a record for gayety in this city."

Then her expression sobered. "I hurt Tom's feelings tonight," she continued regretfully. "I oughtn't to have mentioned Fred's engagement to Miss Mott. There was an old love-affair between her and Tom. Did you notice him while we were speaking of her?"

"No." The monosyllable was accompanied with a reminiscent look. Miriam added, "I was struck with Ferdinand Ballington's expression. Evidently he doesn't like Miss Mott."

"Ferdinand Ballington?" Agnes spoke with quick surprise.

"Do you know," Miriam continued reflectively, "I believe his old homestead is the place with the clipped trees—out by the lake. You wouldn't recognize it from the old picture."

"And he says he's only begun the improvements he intends," Agnes returned with animation. "He told me quite a bit about it, and how he and little Miss Margaret Ballington live out there all alone."

"Why do you like Ferdinand Ballington?" asked Miriam, gravely.

Agnes flushed. "Do I?" she said tentatively.

"Yes. See here, Agnes,"—Miriam touched her friend's arm with unusual initiative—"he is a selfish man. A mate on one of my father's vessels had eyes like his. He stood by and saw a man drown once and said afterwards, 'The damn fool never learned to swim. I told him he'd wish he had.'"

"You don't think, do you, that if people look alike they necessarily are alike?" Agnes questioned anxiously.

Miriam disregarded the question and went on. "Ferdinand Ballington is the kind of man to say 'The damn fool never learned to swim.' I know that head perfectly." Her hands were modeling imaginary clay.

Then her manner changed into a caricature of Ferdinand's. "You may think you have been brought up by parents who are an honor to the human race. But they're not. None of the real New Englanders are. They're troglodytes back in the stone age. Ferdinand Ballington is the flower of humanity. Evolution points to him. All the Christians are going to disappear.

Not adapted to this world. I hope he will enjoy society when all we decent warm-blooded simians are extinct." She added the last sentence with a reversion to her own tone.

Agnes did not respond and Miriam added presently, "They are queer business partners."

"Who are?" Agnes asked.

"Ferdinand and Donald Ballington. I like your friend," she said courteously.

And then she rose, as Agnes had done. "It was nice of you to take me with you tonight. I stayed over only because Professor Dimmock thought he would be at liberty to show me some new microscope slides—alligator egg. It would have been lonely enough here."

Agnes looked at her friend still more curiously. Miriam always had been odd, she knew, but that a girl should deliberately stay at college a day after Commencement just to see alligator eggs was abnormal. It was queer, too, that Miriam should speak respectfully of Donald and cavalierly of Ferdinand Ballington, when the latter seemed to have so much more in common with her. Ferdinand was fluent upon the scientific subjects which interested Miriam, while Donald was a plain business man. Miriam had spoken of Christians with esteem, too, and Agnes noticed this with some relief. Perhaps all the gossip about Miriam's heterodox religious opinions was unfounded. Because a girl studied with Professor Dimmock was no proof that she must share his dangerous doctrines.

As Agnes turned to say good-by, a wave of emotion swept over her. It was not the first time she had felt it for Miriam during the three years they had lived so near to each other and yet so distinctly apart. In spite of all their differences something drew her to the older girl. She had sought her persistently, though with little success. Now Agnes said abruptly and unexpectedly, "I wish you liked me, Miriam."

"I do," Miriam replied readily. "I have always liked you, Agnes." But she dropped her eyes.

"Why haven't you ever shown it then?" persisted the girl. "I have made you many advances. Why do you think I tried to read the 'Origin Of Species?' I've wanted you more than I have any other girl in school, but I've—I've always been afraid of you."

Miriam kept her face down. At last she said with her slow smile, "Well, we'll make it up next year. You needn't be afraid of me then."

"No, we can't make it up next year. I—I'm not coming back."

"Not coming back? Your senior year?" Miriam looked up keenly. Then she remembered that there would probably be a marriage, instead, so she dropped her eyes and added, "Something more interesting, of course."

Agnes was repulsed, but she continued, "I just heard the other day. The fact is—" Her voice broke. Suddenly she dropped on the bed, put her head down in the pillow and began to cry.

"What on earth do you mean?" asked Miriam, looking down irresolutely at her companion. She felt tempted to go over and put her arms around Agnes, but Miriam was not demonstrative, so she stood still and waited.

Presently Agnes sat up, much ashamed of herself for giving way to her feelings before her self-controlled friend, and explained why she could not go back to college. An aunt, crippled with rheumatism, had come to live with her parents. She could not use her hands and part of the time she had to be nursed. Dr. Sidney was not able to afford a trained nurse and his daughter was needed at home.

Miriam heard her through, and then, coloring a little, requested that she might lend Agnes the money to carry her through her last year.

Agnes was startled. She recalled a school-girl rumor that Miriam sold clay models to enthusiastic New York millionaires. "I didn't know you were rich," she said.

"Oh, not rich! But I've a share in one of my father's vessels. It brings me in something, and I've nothing to spend it on. Dress doesn't suit me."

Agnes was touched, but she could not be prevailed upon to accept the offer. When Miriam urged the loss of the observatory work of the senior year the girl replied with sudden frankness that she didn't care much for that or for any other course of study; that her regret was for the athletics, the chorus, the orchestra, the dramatic club.

Miriam had long secretly ridiculed Agnes for her devotion to what she considered superficialities, and it was therefore quite as much to her own surprise as to her friend's that she found herself urging Agnes to take the money and come back even for these things. It suddenly struck her that the college would seem very lonely and dull without the vivid touch of light and color Agnes lent it, and at the same instant she was conscious that the standards she hitherto had set up for herself seemed false. Life was much wider and richer than she lived it, and as she looked at her friend vague longings and regrets awoke in her.

Presently Agnes met her gaze with a kindred longing in her own eyes. "Miriam," she said earnestly, "I wish I had a mind like yours. I never wished it so much. It is what you have found lacking in me, and the lack is why you never have responded to me."

"You have a good mind," answered Miriam, choosing her words. "It is a better one than you deserve, for you don't use it. You have gained results all your life by relying on your temperament. And why not—why not?" She laid her hand on Agnes' shoulder as she spoke, and held her off at arm's length, regarding her critically.

Then with a good-by on her lips she drew the girl toward her.

Agnes divined her intention and put out her hands with a desperate gesture. "Miriam, no one knows what may happen before we meet again. I want your love, and I want to earn it. You are the thing I want most in the world. That is the truth. You could make out of me almost anything you wished. I will work for years to be what you honor and admire. You are different from everything else I have known. If you turn me off, there's nothing left for me but a country life which I'm not fit for. This is my last chance."

She spoke with difficulty, but with tearless eyes, and then turned away to the window. The truant ivy leaves that were climbing over the window-ledge were cool beneath her hand, and the air was sweet with locust bloom. The turf stretched away like black velvet in the night, and out of the shadows came the sound of water falling from the fountain-jet back into the basin. The elms—those palm-trees of the north—swayed their Gothic, arches softly to and fro, and through them she could see the lights and spires of the city in the valley. As she stood waiting and fearing a reply, the girl experienced a longing to stay on there forever. The fairest life she knew was fading behind her.

Miriam made no reply.

Agnes stood erect at last and turned back to her companion. "I shouldn't have said that, Miriam. What I said about you is true, but it isn't my only chance. I know I'm not worth you. I know—"

A slow wave of color crept up Miriam's cheeks. "Wait, Agnes!" she interrupted, with the first uncertainty Agnes ever had seen in her. "It sounded egotistic to say it, but—" she made a swift gesture to the casts along the wall—"there is my life! One cannot serve God and Mammon. I want to become a sculptor. I haven't time and I thought I hadn't inclination for the emotions. But tonight I have begun to feel that if I succeed in my work it will be at the cost of sacrifices."

"Sacrifices?" repeated Agnes, uncomprehending.

"Yes. I have no other relation than my father, and I never shall marry."

"Do you disapprove of marriage?" asked Agnes wonderingly.

"No," replied Miriam seriously, "but if some women are to do their best they must give it up. I believe I must. There is room in the world of homes for us and if we keep true to ourselves we ought to make the homes more beautiful."

She put up her hand gently and touched the bust of Hermes on the shelf. As Agnes looked at her she was conscious of a greater distance between them than she ever had realized before.

"Do you feel that in justice to your work you cannot make friends either?" she asked impersonally.

Miriam's hand left the Hermes, and her smile came back. "I feel that I may not have many friends," she replied, "and there is therefore a world of meaning in that word to me. It means what home means to other women, the strongest tie I ever shall have."

Then she put out her hands, drew Agnes to her until their faces touched and said in a tone Agnes never had heard before, "I need you more than you need me. Henceforth we will be friends. What I can do for you, I will do. Whatever you may achieve or become, count on my help, such as it is, on my unswerving help."

CHAPTER II

THERE is a limit even to the patience of Job," remarked Mrs. Sidney, and she looked up significantly from her sewing at her daughter.

"Oh, I'll write it before long," returned Agnes, putting the last hairpin in her Aunt Mattie's hair. "I'll write it before I go over to the sewing society. There, Aunt Mattie!"

Agnes did not look at her mother as she spoke. During the two weeks at home she had been struggling to keep up her collegiate dignity, but it was not easy to do this with her mother, who knew her every weakness, looking on. Mrs. Sidney faced the world squarely and she was a master-hand at stripping off from others their rags of pretence. The zeal with which she called her daughter to account for those slips which Agnes willingly would have hidden even from herself was taking the heart out of the makeshifts which the girl bravely put up to deceive the outside world. Agnes felt herself sinking back into her life-time relation with her mother and she did not find it half so agreeable to be helped along the road to perfection by being admonished of her faults as in the college way of being lured onward by visions of attainment. She put on her acquired manner at rarer intervals and even then, shamefacedly, feeling ever in her mother's shrewd smile a pitiless comment upon her effort. On this particular occasion, she sought to divert attention from herself by centering it upon her aunt. She turned the invalid's chair so that the occupant could see herself in the glass. Aunt Mattie eyed quizzically the angular figure which faced her from the mirror. She took in the grim face surmounted by a pompadour roll which Agnes had substituted for the usual tight top-knot, and then she exchanged a humorous smile with her hair-dresser.

"When Donald Ballington was here," went on Mrs. Sidney, undiverted, her strong face lighting up with satisfaction, "he told me he didn't play cards. I thank the Lord there is one pure young man left."

"There's a younger brother—Tom," remarked Agnes, loosening some strands of her aunt's hair still more, and apparently studying it critically. "Did you ever see him?"

Mrs. Sidney's face settled into sternness. "Your cousin Fred told me of Mr. Thomas Ballington. He is the one who has been carrying on such a flirtation with Beatrice Mott. He hasn't given it up yet, either. I'm very much afraid he's sowing wild oats."

"Oh, Fred was jealous of Tom," said Agnes carelessly. Then her expression brightened. "I'm glad Beatrice and Fred are really engaged. She will give him a great deal he never has had."

Mrs. Sidney answered with considerable feeling, "We don't any of us know Beatrice Mott, and Fred has known her only a few weeks. Her father is a very worldly man. Fred would have done better to stick to Mary Bucher, whom he's known all his life. This running back and forth out to the Motts' lake house is upsetting him at the bank, too. Young girls ought not to interfere with young men's work like that. I'm going to tell Mr. Bucher he'd better put a stop to it."

"Oh, don't, mother!"

"I think I shall." Mrs. Sidney looked over at Agnes, where she stood fingering some wild flowers her father had brought in that morning from the country. Are you going to write that note now?" she asked without changing her tone of voice. Agnes knew now that her reply to Donald no longer could be postponed. Mrs. Sidney continued, "No girl has a right to shilly-shally as you are doing. Don't tell me it's because you don't know your own mind. It's coquetry, and it's very dishonorable. If you don't want Donald Ballington, you must tell him so, and let him be looking for somebody else. There are plenty of girls who would be glad to have him."

"You talk as though a man started out to get a wife as if he were going to buy a hat," said Agnes petulantly. "And if that is the way you look at it, I'm sure I don't fit him."

"Why didn't you refuse him right away, then?"

"Well, I don't know why I didn't. I thought maybe there was a doubt—"

"He that doubteth is like the surge of the sea, driven and tossed," interrupted Mrs. Sidney. "Do learn to know your own mind, Agnes. There's a tendency in your father's family not to know its own mind. You'll have to guard against that. And when you've made up your mind, don't be ashamed to say it. I believe you do love him, but you aren't willing to admit it." Mrs. Sidney eyed Agnes over her glasses while she spoke.

"I don't!" Agnes turned suddenly, then dropped her eyes under her mother's gaze and continued, apologetically, "I just can't take to him. I can't bear the way his lip trembles when he talks. And his hair lies down so sleek."

"When you're married you can rumple it up for him," suggested Mrs. Sidney, giving her daughter a cheerful smile, to which Agnes disdainfully responded.

"Yes, you can rumple it up," repeated Aunt Mattie, with a canny glance in the mirror at her own pompadour.

"You respect Donald Ballington, don't you?" persisted Mrs. Sidney.

"Oh, yes, I respect him."

"Respect is the best foundation for—"

The three looked up, for the office door had opened and a tall, slightly-stooped figure stood on the threshold, hat and driving gloves in hand. The face looking down at them was strongly but sensitively featured, weather-beaten by wind and sun, but nevertheless speaking of the study. The eyes were deep-set but clear. The crisp wave of the hair and beard was plentifully sprinkled with gray.

"Am I interrupting?" he asked, looking at them with a smile.

"You never interrupt, papa," returned Agnes with a genuine ring of love in her voice. Her next sentence took on a decided tone of proprietorship in her father. "You don't think respect is enough to marry on, do you, papa?"

The doctor passed his hand across his forehead and answered tentatively, "No."

"And you wouldn't advise a girl to marry a man she didn't love, would you?"

"No, I would not."

Dr. Sidney turned to his wife. "Did you get those bandages down to the Richards', Kate?"

"Yes, I did, but I don't know how I got the time. You seem to think I can be in six places at once, Stephen."

"You are equal to six women in other respects," returned the doctor, his kind eyes lingering on his wife's face. "I won't be back till late, Kate. I've got to drive way out on the plank road."

Mrs. Sidney dropped her sewing instantly and started to get up. "You must eat something first."

"No, I won't wait."

"It won't take me five minutes. Agnes, you—"

"I'll have supper at the Block House. I've got to stop there."

Mrs. Sidney sat down with a look of relief and the doctor turned to the office. Before he closed the door, however, he paused and looked again toward Agnes.

"And if no one comes whom you want to marry, you always can count on one man to love you," he said. Then he nodded to them and shut the door.

"Stephen furnishes every drop of medicine that goes into that Richards house," exclaimed Mrs. Sidney impatiently, as soon as the door closed. "He's paying the nurse, too. I told him I'd never take another thing there as long as I lived. I believe he sends them things just to irritate me."

"Stephen lives to irritate," remarked Aunt Mattie dispassionately. Mrs. Sidney looked at her, perceptibly vexed. "Mattie, it wasn't necessary for you to say that. I know just as well as you do that Stephen never did anything to irritate anybody in all his born days. I couldn't say as much of you."

Then she turned to Agnes. "It's all very well for you to have your father to love you," she said meaningly, "but he won't live forever. I want you to consider carefully what you write Donald Ballington."

There was an old-fashioned desk standing in a corner of the room. When Agnes sat down before it she saw a marked newspaper placed where she would see it. The paragraph indicated read as follows:

Hannah More, who knew whereof she spoke, was once heard to make the remark that she would advise every woman to close with the offer of the first God-fearing man who wished to marry her.

Agnes shoved the newspaper aside and began to write. After some painful work upon several sheets, she drew a sigh of relief and began again upon new note-paper. Presently she stopped, reflected, rose and consulted a Shakespeare in the book-case. Then there was more writing, a pause now and then for thought, and then copying.

Mrs. Sidney kept watch of her daughter's face, and what she saw there was so gratifying to her hope that she worked silently and did not interrupt her. She only once attempted conversation. Then she said, with the pleasure she always found in making plans, "When you have a home of your own, I'll let you have that desk. It's solid mahogany. Charlie Brace made it for your grandmother. He was the best cabinet-maker in Burlington." Agnes looked indifferently at the desk.

"I want to see your letter before you seal it," Agnes, said Mrs. Sidney when the writing was done.

Agnes rose and held the envelope before her mother's eyes. It was addressed to Miriam Cass, and she stood waiting superciliously while her mother glanced at it.

"Here is the one you want," she said, handing out the first sheet she had written and feeling somewhat embarrassed at her mother's silence. Mrs. Sidney adjusted her glasses and read a kind but short refusal of Donald's offer of marriage.

Mrs. Sidney handed the letter back to her without a word, and, rising, began to pack her hampers for the sewing-society. The odor of lavender penetrated the air as the large figure moved about among the baskets. This mood of her mother's always awed Agnes. She did not understand it, and it was years before she learned that after Mrs. Sidney had passed a certain limit of disappointment her lowered eyes no longer held flames, but tears, behind their brilliant blue.

When Agnes came back to the sitting room Mrs. Sidney was putting on her bonnet to start for church. Her face showed the disappointment she felt in the outcome of Agnes' love-affair, but Mrs. Sidney never wasted time with a matter which was once decided and out of the way. "I'm going to carry over all the sewing," she said, at once. "That ought to go first, because they'll be wanting to pack the missionary box right away. You'll have to bring the things to eat. And be sure you bring the plated ware. Don't bring the solid silver. And be sure you count it. Now, I'm going, Mattie. You'll find your supper on a plate in the refrigerator, and Agnes shall bring you over some coffee from the church. I'm sorry you won't come over to the concert."

She picked up her hamper and started toward the office door. Here she stopped short and spoke to her sister-in-law again. "If there is anything in a hurry, Mattie, you can telephone Quinn. Run along, Agnes, and open the outside door for me."

Some fifteen minutes later Agnes followed her mother down the familiar street to the church, walking under elms which met overhead and which lent to the old town a dreamy, half-religious atmosphere.

As she entered the church and went up the stairs, the odor of coffee greeted her. In the front parlor a dozen women were packing the garments for the home missionary into a dry-goods box, while Mr. Carter, the pastor, stood by, pencil in hand, making a note of the contents. Other ladies were setting the table in the back parlor, and further on, in the kitchen, Agnes saw her mother's flushed face bending over a big boiler of coffee on the stove. A few elderly men, early comers, were straggling about the room waiting for supper.

"There aren't any forks on this table in the corner, Agnes," said a sweet-faced girl who already had been quietly at work for some time. "Did you bring any?"

"Yes. They're right out in the kitchen pantry. You can get them. I want to garnish this bowl."

Mary Bucher went at once for the forks.

While the girls were setting the table, a party of young people came tumultuously into the dining-room. Among them was Agnes' cousin, Fred Sidney. The first thing one noticed about Fred was the family resemblance to Dr. Sidney. His face lacked the weather-beaten experience which was so noticeable in his uncle's, but it had a sweetness and innocent grace, while underneath these qualities was a steadfastness that saved him from weakness. His was not an aggressive nature, but it had that fineness of temper that would enable it to resist and endure pressure indefinitely. He carried his youth excellently well as he approached the girls—without rawness and without timidity.

"Good evening," he said, shaking hands with them quaintly. "We came early on purpose to have a good time with you two downstairs in the lecture-room before supper. Will you come down?"

"Indeed we will come down!" exclaimed Agnes joyously, and the group left the room, elated with their reinforcement.

Down in the lecture-room the chairs were not yet placed for the concert which was to take place that evening. The piano stood in front, and near it on a table were several other instruments.

"Is that your guitar, Hattie?" asked Mary, turning to a red-checked girl in plaid.

"Yes. I'm one of the old people. Sport and I are going to play some old folks' duets, aren't we, Sport?" She elbowed the young man named Sport, and giggled.

Sport turned a dazzling smile to the rest of the group. "Who else is going to perform?" he chuckled.

"I'm going to play," said Mary without embarrassment. "And Agnes is going to sing."

"Yes, and Montfort is going to declaim," added another voice.

"Meantime," said the young man called Sport, "let us have a cozy dance before we are interrupted. Will you play a waltz, Mary?"

"I don't believe I'd dance if I were you," returned Mary, glancing uneasily at her companions. "Perhaps Mr. Carter wouldn't like it."

"Father doesn't object to dancing at all," spoke up a young man who wore his hair ferociously low on his forehead. He looked down at Mary from over a very high collar, and remarked in addition, "The Bible upholds dancing. David danced. And—some others danced."

"Perhaps the bears danced while they were eating up the children," suggested Hattie Pierce.

"Do you think your mother would mind, Agnes?" asked Mary, still hesitating.

Agnes had anticipated this question. Her mother's opinions about amusements were a continual mortification to the girl, and she blushed when thus pinned down to them. "If Montfort thinks his father wouldn't mind, I should think that is all that need be considered."

She walked over to the piano while speaking, sat down, and began to play a waltz. It always had been a rueful satisfaction to Agnes that she could at least play the piano at dancing parties.

"It's too bad Agnes can't dance," she heard Mary say to Fred as the two went out on the floor; "I'd offer to play for her, but—"

Agnes' cheeks crimsoned and she held up her head proudly. What an irony of fate it was that her mother should be so fanatical while she herself was so full of music and motion.

After a time she was conscious of a lull in the scraping of feet and brushing of dresses. She turned on the stool, and saw standing in the doorway a portentous figure. It was Mrs. Sidney, with a pitcher of coffee in her hand, whose steam was like the smoke of a disregarded offering ascending to an irate divinity.

As she looked from one to another of the dancers, a storm gathered rapidly in her face. "Fred Sidney!" came the explosion at length. "Mary Bucher! Hattie Pierce! Montfort Carter! Agnes!"

There was an ominous pause. Mary was the first to stir. She detached herself from Fred's arms.

"Dancing!" continued Mrs. Sidney, and a second gust of terror swept over the room as she spoke. "Dancing in the prayer-meeting room! Montfort Carter, what do you think your father would say?"

"Father doesn't object to dancing at all, Mrs. Sidney," began Montfort weakly. "Father approves of dancing. David danced."

Hattie Pierce choked down a hysterical giggle.

"David danced before the Lord," said Mrs. Sidney grimly. "He wasn't dancing round dances." She advanced into the room, and looked around her. "Let me see, who is here?" she went on, "Who is that young man?" and she pointed to "Sport."

"This is my friend, Mr. Hitchcock," answered Hattie, pinching her "friend's" elbow. "He was kind enough to come here to take part in the 'Old Folks' Concert' tonight."

Young Mr. Carter had been regaining his self-possession, and seized this opportunity to speak. "Would you object to telling me why you think it is right to sing in this room and not to dance here, Mrs. Sidney?" he asked blandly.

Mrs. Sidney turned to Agnes without noticing him. "Have you been dancing?" she asked sternly.

"I don't care to dance," said Agnes, moving toward her mother.

"Agnes Sidney, have you been dancing?"

"No, she hasn't, Mrs. Sidney," interposed Mary Bucher. "She only played for the rest of us."

"Only played for the rest of you! Mary, I'm surprised at you for excusing her in that way. Was Saul guiltless of Stephen's death because he only held the clothes of them that stoned him? Montfort! Don't you leave this room!"

"What is it you wish, Mrs. Sidney?" In spite of himself, Montfort felt that he was but a toy in her hands, and he fumed inwardly.

"You go upstairs and tell your father that I want to see him down here."

Montfort left the room, and Mrs. Sidney sat down to await his return. Agnes made a nervous attempt to take the pitcher of coffee from her mother and escape with it, but Mrs. Sidney silenced her.

"We didn't mean any harm, Aunt Kate," said Fred, coming over and sitting down by his aunt. "Don't make too much of it."

"This comes of your learning to dance, Fred," and Mrs. Sidney shook her head at her nephew. "The responsibility is upon you older ones. You should have been setting a good example to those boys and girls. Look at them! They are just like sheep that will jump over any fence after their leader." The sheep spoken of were now huddled together at the opposite side of the room, and did not look capable of vaulting any kind of a fence.

At this moment Mr. Carter appeared at the door with Montfort behind him. The minister looked uneasily about the room, and then at Mrs. Sidney with deprecating politeness. He was wondering, as those of his profession so often are obliged to wonder, how he could arbitrate in this awkward affair without offending anybody.

Mrs. Sidney rose. "Mr. Carter, I came down here to send my daughter on an errand," she said, "and I found these young people dancing round dances in the prayer-meeting room."

"I see. Yes."

Mr. Carter let his eyes rove while he was speaking. They rested upon the red tie of Hattie's friend who was kind enough to come and play at the concert," and the sight of this outsider offered a moment's respite. "Ah! How do you do, Mr. Hitchcock!" he said, extending his hand.

The interruption lasted only an instant, however, and Mr. Carter then felt bound to take some stand upon the question. At this critical moment the side door of the church opened and two gentlemen came into the hall together. They were Judge Pierce and Deacon Snow, both of them advocates of new-fangled ideas, and Mr. Carter felt his position still more ticklish as he observed that they were waiting in the hall to listen. Mr. Carter prided himself upon being a liberal minister. He liked to refer to the bigotries of his parents and tell how he had outgrown them. It is worthy of remark that his own liberality was along those lines that were in fashion among his contemporaries.

Now he had just begun to say, "Montfort had been telling me—" when he noticed the somewhat contemptuous smile upon the face of Deacon Snow. He drew up his little figure and completed his sentence with more assertion— "That his friends and he were indulging in a little harmless dancing." He glanced furtively toward the hall again, but to his dismay the two men were passing out up the stairs.

"Harmless dancing!" exclaimed Mrs. Sidney, facing him. Alas! She had no intention of following them. "Harmless dancing in the prayer-meeting room, Mr. Carter?"

"Well! Mrs. Sidney, the past generation was perhaps a little too stringent. Perhaps there isn't so much harm, after all, in letting the young people dance a little at a church sociable. The Congregational Church at Winston has a theater in it. But, at the same time, if you object, Mrs. Sidney—"

"I do object, Mr. Carter. And Jesus Christ would object. Would you see any harm in the money-changers turning the temple into a booth for merchandise?" She controlled her speech and waited for an answer, looking at her pastor with righteous indignation in her eyes.

"Would you have me drive them out with a scourge?" questioned the minister, spreading out his hands. "Are you not, perhaps, judging Jesus Christ by one incident, rather than by the trend of His—er—customs? Jesus was meek and gentle."

"He knew how to be meek," returned Mrs. Sidney carefully. Then she dropped her voice to a deep tone. But He knew how to be terrible." She straightened herself and loomed before them like a prophet in wrath. "I'm getting tired of hearing of Jesus' meekness. Do you think it was the few wisps of string in His hand that drove the money changers out of the church? You couldn't—there are some people who couldn't have driven them out with a flail. It was the moral power of the man. No, I wouldn't have you take a scourge to the children, but I'd have you show some moral stamina. They don't know what you mean. Let your yea be yea, and your nay, nay."

Mr. Carter's fair face flushed, but he smiled through it all. When Agnes was younger, she used to wonder if he wore that smile when he was asleep.

"Have you anything to say to the children?" asked Mrs. Sidney peremptorily.

He hesitated, and then said, turning to the awe-stricken group behind him, "Well, children, since Mrs. Sidney objects—er—suppose we have no more dancing in this room."

He bowed to Mrs. Sidney and withdrew.

Outside the door, however, he turned and added to his son, "You can take your friends over to the parsonage when you wish to dance, Montfort."

Agnes took the pitcher and hurried away. She was glad of an excuse to leave a scene which humiliated her. Why would her mother make such a spectacle of herself? She had seen Deacon Snow's smile, and she knew what a tirade of ridicule would descend upon her mother as soon as the "children" were left alone together; so she decided to remain at home for the evening instead of returning to the concert. She was disappointed in her plans, however, for a message came from her mother about an hour later, summoning her back to the church.

When she entered the lecture-room she saw the people gathered together for the concert. Her mother was sitting alone near the front of the room; for the story of the dancing had circulated, and no one seemed to care or to dare to show friendliness to Mrs. Sidney after the way she had talked to the minister.

"Why! Here's Aggy!" said Judge Pierce, who stood near the door, taking admissions. He drew his mouth down into an "O," and looked at Agnes with the genial surprise which he always seemed to feel upon meeting his daily companions in their accustomed places. "Well, Aggy, I was brought up to disapprove of round-dancing, too. Your mother is only one generation behind the times. She'll come around in the course of time. I think she's cavin' in a little, now," he ended, in a confidential whisper. Agnes passed on coolly.

The sight of her mother sitting alone caused Agnes' irritation to swerve away from the original object and fix itself upon the other people present. Her loyalty to her mother was further strengthened by the Judge's prophecy that Mrs. Sidney would soon "cave in," a condition of affairs which suddenly struck the girl as so undesirable that she was seized with a determination to back up her mother in her misguided but gallant ways. As she made her way down the aisle she saw Mary Bucher leave the minister, to whom she had been talking, and cross the room to sit down by Mrs. Sidney. A throb of gratitude to her friend caused a flush to rise to Agnes' face. She took her seat beside the two with a manner which she meant to be impressive. However they might feel toward her mother, who wouldn't feel proud to sit down by herself, she wondered. She had not yet learned that the fluctuation of emotion which Mrs. Sidney aroused in the townspeople at large was only a wider example of the effect produced by the operation of the maternal vigilance upon herself at small.

She no sooner was seated than Mr. Carter arose and began to speak. He gave a perfunctory account of the missionary box which had been packed that afternoon.

"We have undertaken the whole support of this home missionary and of all his family," he said plaintively. "They are naked and ye clothe them not. They have called for a hundred articles, and ye send them twenty."

He consulted a paper in his hand and began to read. "John Darke, male, five feet ten, has sadly needed two suits, under clothes, hat, shoes and stockings. He also asks very modestly for an umbrella." Mr. Carter looked up and volunteered the interpolation, "I am sure you will all feel that he certainly ought to receive the umbrella." Then he continued reading, "He has received only one suit, hat and shoes. No under clothes and no stockings."

"Maude Darke, female, five feet four, waist twenty-six inches. Required, two suits, underclothes, nightclothes, hat, shoes and stockings. She has received only nightclothes." Again he looked up and remarked, "I may state that she has received really more nightclothes than are necessary, but unfortunately this does not relieve her other wants."

At this point Mrs. Sidney's sides began to shake. She leaned toward Agnes and had it on the tip of her tongue to whisper something.

She thought better of it, however, and Mr. Carter went on. "Frank Darke, male, four feet ten. Required, two suits, underclothes, hat, shoes and stockings. I am pleased to say"—and Mr. Carter beamed—"that Frank Darke is thoroughly provided for."

There followed the requirements of four Darke girls, and then Mr. Carter drew apart his coat-tails and sat down, happily unconscious that he had presented the tragedy of seven isolated lives, dedicated to labor, self-denial, and humiliation, as a farce.

"Why doesn't the concert begin?" Agnes whispered to Mary. Her question, however, was answered by Mr. Carter himself, who was on his feet and speaking again.

"As was announced on Sunday, there was prepared an 'Old Folks' Concert' for this evening, for the benefit of the home missionary fund," he began, and he dropped his eyes to the programme. 'The first number upon the programme is a piano solo by Mr. Forest Gregg."

There was a pause. Several in the audience turned their heads, but no one came forward.

Mr. Carter continued:

"If Mr. Gregg is not present, we shall be obliged to pass on to the next number, which is a declamation by Mr. Montfort Carter."

Again the pause. Again a rustle among the audience. Mrs. Sidney's face began to settle into grimness.

"The third number on the programme is a flute solo, by Mr. Hitchcock," said Mr. Carter, looking innocently around the now smiling audience.

As was expected, there was no response.

Agnes felt herself growing hot and red. Mary leaned over and whispered to her:

"They've all gone home. I tried to make them stay, but they wouldn't. There's no one to do anything but you and me."

"I am very sorry we should be so disappointed in our programme," began Mr. Carter, looking not ill-pleased as he cast a glance at Mrs. Sidney's side of the room. "I greatly fear we shall be obliged to dismiss the audience. Judge Pierce, you will please refund the admission fees at the door."

"Read the programme through, Mr. Carter," said Mrs. Sidney's positive voice, breaking into the hum that followed.

"Yes, read the programme through. Let us have what we can," spoke up a sing-song voice from across the aisle where Mr. Bucher sat. "No one wants to have his money refunded."

"The next number is a song, with guitar accompaniment, by Miss Hattie Pierce," continued Mr. Carter.

There was no response, but before he resumed Mrs. Sidney rose. The austerity of her face was replaced by a good-humor. "Well, if we were advertised as an 'Old Folks' Concert,'" she said, walking toward the front, "we might just as well have an 'Old Folks' Concert.' I don't believe in putting our hands to the plow and turning back. I guess Hattie Pierce won't object to my using her guitar."

She took the instrument off the table and began to tune it. The uncomfortable smile of the audience changed to one of relief. Somebody cheered her, and the applause grew till everybody in the room was clapping.

"I didn't know your mother played the guitar," whispered Mary to Agnes.

"She used to when she was a girl, but she does it only once in a long while now." Mrs. Sidney began her accompaniment. After playing it a second time her fingers somewhat lost their clumsiness, and her sonorous alto took up a song of her youth:

"We met; 'twas in a crowd,
And I thought he would shun me;
He came; I could not breathe,
For his eyes were upon me.
He spoke; his words were cold,
But his smile was unaltered.
I knew how much he felt,
For his deep-toned voice faltered."

When she finished and was eagerly encored, a flitting tenderness softened the corners of her lips and the creases about her eyes while she laughed at what she called the "silly words," but she sang again.

Agnes watched with satisfaction the frozen pleasantry on Mr. Carter's face, and beyond him she caught a glimpse of Montfort peeking through the window to see what was the meaning of the clapping inside. She set herself at work determinedly to assure the success of the evening, and when her mother's encore was done, she said with enthusiasm, "Now Mr. Bucher must play the flute. Come, Mary, bring your father up in front. Here's a flute."

After some urging Mr. Bucher consented and played several airs, ending with "Hail Columbia," which he executed with a spirit that Agnes had not believed possible from him.

"Ask Mr. Carter to whistle," Mary whispered to Agnes, as she rose from the piano-stool. Agnes pretended not to understand. She did not want to share the evening's success with the pastor. Mary gained courage, however, made the request herself, and offered to accompany him.

What it was that happened when Mr. Carter whistled no one could quite explain. But the little minister underwent a transformation. His whistling was like a flute for softness, with the melancholy and richness of the 'cello, and when it was done the afterglow of the transformation still lingered about the shabby personality, touching it with that grace and kindness which pleasure brings to the most insignificant.

Mary smiled with delight as Mr. Carter sat down by Mrs. Sidney and received her hearty congratulations. "Now I'll play," she said to Agnes, "and then you sing. That will keep the best for the last."

During Mary's solo, which was a time for whispered conversation, Agnes caught her mother's eye. She nodded reassuringly, rose, and went forward with resolution. Her song was to have been the chief feature of the evening, as originally planned. Now she was prodigal of her music. The people in the back part of the room began to come forward, and at last, when she turned on the stool and looked laughingly around her, many were gathered in groups about the piano.

"Let us have some chorus-singing!" she cried, keen to their sensitive mood. "Let's begin with 'America'!"

She struck the chords. Mr. Bucher took up the flute again and played with her, and all joined in.

Kent still talks about that Old Folks' Concert. Old eyes glistened, faded cheeks grew rosy, voices trembled with emotion that had long lain dormant. A host of memories were summoned from the sweet and glowing past, and thronged into the meeting-house on the wings of familiar and beloved airs.

At last Agnes took her hands from the keys and sat still. It seemed to her that the whole room was full of the perfume of lindens. She saw a man turn on a broad piazza and pass away out of sight while she watched him.

She shook her head, laughed a little to throw off the vision, and turned to the others. Mr. Bucher was wiping his eyes, and Agnes caught the look which Mary Bucher in entire self-forgetfulness was giving Fred. The other singers, too, were looking at one another, confused, ashamed of their feeling, when the door of the lecture-room was thrown open from without.

Mary, who was half facing it, suddenly flushed scarlet and rose. Those sitting near her turned around.

"Why, Beatrice Mott!" exclaimed Mary, speaking in too low a voice to be heard by any save those near her, "where in the world did you come from at this time of night?"

A young woman, who seemed a blaze of color, had entered the room. The door swung shut behind her and her bold figure seemed to start out from the bare, cheerless wall of the church parlor.

The newcomer surveyed the group before her with scarcely-disguised amusement. Church sociables were truly appropriate gatherings for these stagnating town-folk. There was a latent distrust and disapproval of her, in turn, on the part of the church people, but Agnes stood up with a throb of interest and started after Fred toward the girl in the doorway.

Beatrice was standing still waiting for him, but she looked as though she were still in motion because of the forward inclination of her superb head and shoulders. The black hair and red tam-o'-shanter, the oriental brilliance of her face, her smile which arrested attention because of the whimsical short upper lip, and the rich red scarf flung backward across the shoulders, made up a picture Agnes never forgot. Wild stories were afloat about Beatrice Mott, and Agnes acknowledged with a thrill of excitement that the newcomer looked as though one and all might be understated.

CHAPTER III

"WHY did Beatrice Mott throw over Tom Ballington and engage herself to Fred?" Agnes asked herself many times during the days that followed the church sociable. The vivid figure that had appeared in the doorway of the lecture-room at the close of the concert persisted in her memory. How had Fred gotten up courage to offer her his poverty? She was rich, fond of excitement—above all, restless. Fred was quiet and without ambition. During the days that Beatrice stayed in Kent Agnes watched the pair with puzzled anxiety, trying to arrange an equilibrium between Fred's stillness and the energy of Beatrice. She gave it up finally comforting herself with the reflection that extremes were said to get on better together than two of the same type.

When Beatrice went back to the lake she took Fred with her and urgently invited Agnes to accompany them. When Agnes reluctantly declined, Beatrice added with a sidelong glance of her black eyes, "Some Ballingtons might come out from Winston!"

"Tom?" asked Agnes, confused, looking from Beatrice to Fred. Then she reddened, avoided Donald's name, and concluded, "Do you know Mr. Ferdinand Ballington?"

Beatrice laughed. "Know Ferdinand Ballington? Nobody knows him better." Then she withdrew her scrutiny from Agnes and smiled at Fred as she continued, "But he won't be down. I want you to remember him, Fred. He's the one man in the world you never need be jealous of."

Fred looked flattered at this frank recognition of his proprietorship and Beatrice turned back to Agnes. I was talking about Donald's coming out," she said. "I'm going over to get your mother to let you come."

Agnes had longed for this invitation, but she had little hope that her mother would consent. As she had expected, Mrs. Sidney promptly declined when Beatrice spoke to her, and, what was worse, gave her reasons. She told the young heiress good-humoredly, but without mincing matters, that she would not permit her daughter to visit at a home where young girls wearing red tam-o'-shanters were permitted to come without escort in evening trains to town.

Agnes left the room in embarrassment while Mrs. Sidney and Beatrice were talking. She was mystified when, a little later, Beatrice came after her, threw a strong and supple arm around her shoulder, and said heartily, "I tell you, I like your mother. She's the jolliest person in Kent. My General ought to know her. They would like each other. Don't you mind, Agnes! We'll make it up in August. Then I'm coming to Kent to stay weeks."

Agnes often thought of this promise during the early summer, for by a coincidence it was in August that Mrs. Sidney was to go out to Iowa to stay until her elder daughter, Helen Mabie, should be up again from her coming confinement. This would remove parental supervision, for Agnes never thought of her father as a check, and would give to her more liberty than she had enjoyed at college.

"I believe you want me gone!" Mrs. Sidney said abruptly one day, stopping in her preparations and scrutinizing Agnes.

The girl never had stated this nakedly to herself, and she at once denied it, saying she was glad only for Helen's sake.

"If I thought you would neglect your father, I would never stir from the house," Mrs. Sidney went on. "He must have his regular meals, and you must get up and give him a lunch when he has to go out at night. I've done it for twenty years and he would break down without it. I want you to listen to what I am saying, Agnes. You don't know what a heedless girl you are. But I believe you have some love in your heart for your father, and I count on that!"

"Papa and I will get along all right together. We generally do," answered Agnes.

"Yes, because he always lets you have your own way. But I've always been here to do the unpleasant things, and it's an ungrateful position, I can tell you. Your father never crosses you himself, but you should hear him talk to me at night. Then it's 'Kate, you must see that Agnes does this,' and 'Kate, you must take care that Agnes does not do that.' He's troubled, too, about Beatrice's wanting Fred to leave the bank. You'll find it a very different thing when I'm not here to bear the brunt of everything."

"Yes, I imagine I shall."

"I won't be here to do the mending while you smile and pet your father," Mrs. Sidney went on. "It's very easy to bring in bouquets of flowers after somebody else has swept and dusted and put things to rights. I'll work all day and nobody thanks me. But your father and you will bow and scrape to each other over a pansy."

"Sometimes I wish you wouldn't do so much work and that we could have a breathing spell from gratitude," Agnes exclaimed crossly.

Mrs. Sidney turned toward her. "How ungrateful you are, Agnes! What must the Lord think of such a speech?"

A grim smile came to Aunt Mattie's lips as she sat with her hands crossed watching the two. "If He has any sense of humor I think He might be entertained by this conversation, Kate," she remarked.

"Mattie!" said Mrs. Sidney to the widow, "I don't like the tone of your voice. You are teaching Agnes irreverence. You may find out, when it's too late, that the Lord does laugh. 'He that sitteth in the Heavens shall laugh. The Lord shall have them in derision.'" She closed her lips and moved about in silence for some moments.

But as Agnes was leaving the room, she looked up and spoke once more in a prophetic voice: "Experience teaches a dear school. I guess you'll miss mother before she comes home again."

Before Mrs. Sidney left she made each of them promise various things. Aunt Mattie promised to keep sharp watch of Stephen's health, and, when Agnes went out evenings, to sit up until she returned. Dr. Sidney promised that he would not contribute over a certain amount to the church collections; he was to make a point of passing in and out of the room when Agnes received callers; above all, he was not to overdo in night practice. As for Agnes, she had many instructions. She must not forget to comb Aunt Mattie's hair and to help her dress and undress; she was to keep the boys in the lane from playing in the barn; she was to keep the lamps trimmed and filled, and the best linen packed away.

"Only if we entertain I will use the best linen, then," the girl excepted.

"You mustn't think you can invite in the town to eat your father out of house and home," said Mrs. Sidney at once. "I don't like all these new friends of yours. I like to know the parents of your friends. And be careful about this, Agnes! You must study your father's appetite, and not your own. I think I've seen a tendency in you to make a god of your belly."

"Why, mamma! You know it is you who are always asking people in and cooking good things."

"When it's proper I should," Mrs. Sidney answered tersely.

Above all, Agnes was to look after her father. She listened nonchalantly to her list of duties, and felt relieved when her mother was done. She helped Mrs. Sidney pack her satchel very graciously, and went with her parents to the station.

Mrs. Sidney left in the evening. She would not reach her daughter's home in Iowa till the following afternoon. It was a long journey for the woman who had spent her life time in her country home, but she started out with characteristic resolution.

Dr. Sidney saw his wife into her compartment and then returned to Agnes. They stood on the platform till the train rolled away, then turned to where Peggy was waiting. Agnes was surprised to find her father so quiet, and more surprised at the depression of her own spirits. As her father helped her out from the buggy at their doorstep, and she glanced up at the house, it looked empty—foreboding.

"Here is the key," said Dr. Sidney. "I told Mattie not to sit up for us."

Agnes inserted it in the office door and went in. She lighted the lantern, went out through the kitchen door, walked down the garden path beneath its grape arbor, and joined her father in the barn, where he was unharnessing Peggy.

"So you have begun to take care of me," he said, looking pleased. "Hold the lantern on this side."

When the task was over and they went inside, Agnes brought a glass of milk to her father, gave him a lighted lamp, and kissed him good-night. "You call me in the morning, if I don't wake up in time," she said.

Then she went to bed, and in the quiet of the dark began to plan all she would accomplish during her two months' regime in the home.

CHAPTER IV

AGNES found the housework irksome at first. Aunt Mattie could not assist in the manual part, owing to the deformity of her hands. She could, however, do the marketing, answer the telephone, and attend tolerably well to the office. To be sure, in this latter capacity she "had no knack," as Mrs. Sidney once said impatiently. She would weakly permit the patients to go away when the doctor was absent, whereas Mrs. Sidney had been known to keep them waiting cheerfully three hours for the physician. In the course of a week, however, the housekeeping began to show some system, and if Beatrice Mott had not come to Kent the summer might have passed with fair success.

The first effect of Beatrice's arrival was to stimulate Agnes to an unwonted effort for appearances, but before the guest had been in town a week Agnes not only lost ambition, but fell away from her ordinary ideal of order. Beatrice came in at all hours, sometimes scant in dress, sometimes overdressed, always graceful and picturesque. When she had time to wonder about it, Agnes used to ask herself why this disorderly girl could attract, with strands of hair disdaining the loose coil, her silk jersey raveling, and her French stockings showing holes in the heels as she drew them in and out of her pomponed Turkish slippers. The unconsciousness with which Beatrice at one time bore her dishabille, at another a mass of color and ornament, lent distinction even to her shiftlessness. People in her company were apt to let themselves go, too, feeling something large and friendly in her unrestraint. Fits of tireless energy alternated in her with days of languorous indolence. She would watch Agnes lazily for half a day, following her around from room to room and talking her thoughts aloud while Agnes worked. Then suddenly she would beg to wash dishes, to comb Aunt Mattie's hair, to sweep, to clear the table. "Why don't you work quicker?" she would cry to Agnes, shaking the napkins on the floor and rushing to the kitchen with single dishes, which she bestowed upon chair, table or stove.

So far as the ordinary eye could observe, Fred took his sweetheart's moods with equanimity, but Agnes, who had read from childhood his silences, nervous acquiescence, and sensitive smiles, knew when he was troubled. She knew that he frequently was hurt by Beatrice's free manners and consequent notorious popularity. More than once Agnes had detected in him the Sidney brightness of eye which accompanied suffering of the mind. She found herself secretly questioning whether Beatrice Mott were heartless or only willful and thoughtless.

One morning Beatrice came in breezily as Agnes was making her father's bed.

"Agnes!" she began at once, dropping her tam-o'-shanter on the high part of the bureau and dropping herself on the low shelf before the long glass, "Tom's written to me again!" and she pulled an envelope from her pocket as she spoke.

Agnes looked up attentively and saw a pleasurable excitement in her companion's face. It was the spark to her resolution to have a talk with Fred's fiancée. Her nervousness lest she should injure instead of help her cousin's cause made her speak more aggressively than she had planned. "Beatrice, you ought not to allow this. It's not honorable."

Beatrice waited a moment, then burst out laughing. "What a saintly engagement you and Donald will have!" she exclaimed, and went off in another peal of merriment.

Agnes' color heightened as she turned to her work again. "Your hair is coming down," she remarked in her mother's tone.

Beatrice reached around, tucked in her hair and pinned it carelessly. Then she went on: "Agnes, you don't know anything about life. You've been mewed up in this town or in that Presbyterian boarding-school ever since you were born. I've traveled all over and have had a good many experiences. If I want to have a little fun, there's no harm in it. It's just for variety. There hasn't been a single thing going on here for three weeks but congratulations and tally ho's and tennis-parties and billing and cooing. This Sunday school life uses me up. I've got to have a change. Tom Ballington and I don't care a snap for each other, but we can have more fun carrying on than any two people who ever have lived. We make an artistic success of it. You know if we cared for each other 'twouldn't be any more fun to flirt with him than it is with Fred. There's always a strife between Tom and me to see which can flirt with more originality. He's the smartest thing that ever lived. He never does it twice alike. He keeps me up to my best level all the time. Now, Fred is as good as gold, and

I'm going to marry him, but I do wish he didn't say the same things over and over. He hasn't real originality, Fred hasn't, but he's the best man I ever knew."

Agnes listened to this artless exposition with indignant dismay. It was followed by some moments of silence. Then she said gravely, "Beatrice, if three weeks of Kent are intolerable to you, how dare you think of passing your life here?"

"Who? I? Pass my life here?" Beatrice's startled tone changed to one of stifled amusement. "I suppose I could join Fred's church and Mary Bucher's Dorcas society. My dear,"—she rose and went over to place her hands on Agnes' shoulders—"speaking about Mary Bucher, she's in love with Fred as much as she can be. Now I shouldn't mind how many letters he got from her. I'm perfectly willing he should go in and have a good time with her. They are as safe a pair as Tom and I are. Fred has been too soft and I have been too tame with him. We'll make the dullest kind of a couple if we don't look out."

Agnes reached up and took Beatrice's hands down from her shoulders. As she looked down at them she noticed how pale and weak her own hands looked beside the darker, heavier hands of Beatrice. "See here, Beatrice," she said, "I want Fred to be happy. You don't know how little he's had in his life, as I do, and you don't know how these flirtations of yours pain him. He isn't narrow. He's—high-minded." Agnes forced herself to say what she feared would incense Beatrice, but the last words were lost on the girl.

The allusion to Fred's meager share of happiness turned her mobile emotions into a new channel, and it was one which must have been familiar to them. As she stood perfectly still, struck by Agnes' voice and looking down at her, her face quickly sobered and she was betrayed into a look that was new to Agnes, but which carried with it unmistakable self-revelation.

"Beatrice!" cried Agnes involuntarily, infinite relief and joy in the exclamation. She knew now that Beatrice loved Fred.

With a stiff military wheel Beatrice turned away to the window. The look in her eyes, the gravity of her silence, embarrassed and awed Agnes.

After what seemed a long pause, without turning around, Beatrice spoke in a voice as unfamiliar as her manner. It was rough and wavered curiously. "Nobody but an ass would have wanted to keep up that nonsense with Tom. You don't have to tell me Fred has had a lonesome life. A boy who has earned his own living since he was twelve years old! He looked like a starved dog trying not to beg the first time I saw him."

Beatrice dashed the tears from her eyes, and began to tear up Tom's letter viciously, first lengthwise, then across. "Don't you go getting a wrong idea of Tom. He does this because he feels mean about a story that's gone around that he jilted me. He's a straight fellow. He'd rather have people think that I had jilted him. So he says it himself. There isn't any truth in it either way."

Beatrice threw the fragments of Tom's letter in a miniature snow-storm through the window. "As soon as I've married Fred everything will be all right. He is not going to do a tap of work for five years. I'm going to take him out of the bank where he handles other people's money year in and year out, and give him enough of his own to keep him busy spending it. We are going abroad, and when we come back we shall have a town house as well as the country place here. Fred says he wants to earn his own livelihood, but I tell him I haven't had anybody to take care of since I was born, and he's never had anybody to take care of him."

Agnes was beginning to see the explanation of Beatrice's feeling for Fred. There was an imperative need in her large nature of giving. She was not satisfied, as her father was, to give money. She must give herself. Fred was the one who had most appealed to her on her generous side, while he satisfied her pride by being a distinguished object upon whom to lavish the best she had to give. On the whole, Fred filled a larger place in Beatrice's heart than any other man could.

Agnes' relief on this score, however, now transferred itself into uncertainty about Fred. Was Beatrice as necessary to him as he to her? Agnes was skeptical about his accepting as much as Beatrice wished to give him.

"A man doesn't want a woman to take care of him. He wants to take care of her," she said gently.

"Nonsense!" returned Beatrice, her mind still intent upon the future. "Look at your father and mother."

Agnes was startled. Beatrice's analysis of the relative position of her father and mother in the family shocked her. She always had thought of her father as the corner-stone of the home.

"My father has always cared for and supported his family. He has done the man's part," she said with emphasis.

"Well, you must excuse me for speaking plainly, Agnes," returned Beatrice promptly, "but I don't think much of this matter of earning money. Your mother has done a good deal more. She has run the home, and I guess the church and a share of the town, and taken such good care of your father that he has been able to do the work of two doctors. Now, has your father really supported the family? I say, nonsense! I'm glad you brought this up. I'm going to use it as an argument to Fred. We'll be just such a couple as your father and mother. Good-by!"

With this prospect of ideal domestic life before her mind, Beatrice whirled round the room in a vortex of spreading skirts. On her way she caught up her tam-o'-shanter and pinned it on her head. "I can hardly wait to get married when I think of the gorgeous family we two are going to make!"

As she reached the door she paused on the threshold, looking over her shoulder impishly. "You didn't know I had so much sense, did you? Neither did my General. He said he was surprised I had brains enough to let Tom go and take Fred."

Then she darted out, slamming the door behind her.

Agnes followed, dizzy with her guest's evolutions of mind and body. When she reached the outside door Beatrice was already disappearing round the corner a block away. She looked after the retreating figure, saying to herself, "It's all right! She has a warm heart after all! And she loves Fred. All she wants for herself is to be able to do for him."

She waited a few minutes in the yard before returning to her work, looked up into the heavens where it seemed as if a soft, gray swan were brooding over the world, listened to the twittering of the birds, watched the sunshine filter down through the elms and checker the walk with light and shade, felt the fall coming in the air. Her happiness was passing into loneliness. She wished her father would come home, and when she went into the house at last she let her work go while she hunted up Aunt Mattie and asked her to come down and sit in the kitchen while the dinner work was getting under way.

There was a touch of tenderness in the relation of the two girls henceforth. Even under Beatrice's most volatile moods Agnes was yet aware of it. It salved her conscience for spending more and more time in the whirl of social life whose center was Beatrice. There were pricks of conscience, indeed, but the time was drawing near when Beatrice must go and when Mrs. Sidney was to return. It was the only chance she ever had had for a good time unchecked by surveillance, and Agnes told herself, with a thrill of lawlessness, she would let herself make the most of it.

CHAPTER V

IN due time the telegram came announcing the birth of Helen Mabie's second son. Agnes sat in the sitting room, writing a letter of congratulation to her sister, when Aunt Mattie came into the room. Agnes looked up as she entered and was struck with the frowsiness of her aunt's hair.

"Aunt Mattie!" she exclaimed, reddening, "how long is it since your hair has been combed?"

"Two days," replied the gaunt figure briefly.

"For pity's sake! Why didn't you remind me?"

Agnes gradually had slipped into shiftlessness in her household duties. Aunt Mattie's hair, instead of being arranged in the morning, had been twisted up at any time of day or evening when it happened to be convenient, and finally had been neglected altogether. Agnes had fallen into the way of economizing labor by letting the kitchen fire go out, and making meals of cold meats and vegetables, served with iced tea or lemonade. Some steaks and chops which her father had brought home and handed her occasionally had spoiled in the refrigerator. Aunt Mattie, in trying to clean the ice box one day, had found them and thrown them out. When Dr. Sidney at last had expressed a wish for warm food, Agnes took a new start. She soon back-slid, however, into warming canned stuff once a day over a quick wood-fire, shifting the one hearty meal of the week upon Mrs. Macy, who came every Monday to wash.

Now, with a shock at her forgetfulness, she sprang up from the writing-desk to attend to the hair-dressing.

"I do hope you'll forgive me," she said as she untwisted the tangled coil. "I'll never forgive myself."

Her aunt did not reply at once.

Then she said, choosing her words, "When does this young lady leave town?"

"What young lady?" Agnes felt her heart sink.

"The one who made my hair look like a Chinese pagoda."

"In about a week, I think."

There was a pause.

Then Agnes added, "Why?"

"Because I think all these picnics and parties worry your father. He looks thin and tired. I think he needs regular hours and warm meals."

"You mean I ought to stay at home and attend to him, instead of—" Agnes broke off. She was glad she was behind her aunt, for she knew it would be mutually disagreeable should their glances meet.

"Yes, my girl. That's what I mean."

"Well—you're right. I shan't go any more."

She left her aunt and walked away, deterred by the instinct of self-preservation from further talk. Her compunction was aggravated by the realization that Aunt Mattie, like her father, waited till a situation was unendurable before blaming the guilty. She finished her letter, and then, contrary to her engagement to spend part of the morning at the Buchers', began to dust the room.

When Dr. Sidney returned to dinner. he found the table bountifully spread. There were fresh blossoms in the room, and a quiet, but sweet daughter, in a clean dress, presided. Agnes watched her father and was struck to the heart in reading the surprise and pleasure in his face, though he scarcely tasted the daintily-served food.

When she had done her dinner-work she went to her piano. Then she realized that it had been many days since she had practiced. The music was scattered over the top of the instrument as it had been left since her last party. "What a looking place!" she exclaimed to herself, shocked at the appearance of the room, and instantly picturing her mother's consternation could she by any chance become aware of the state of things. "It looks just ready for the ostriches and satyrs to dance here."

As she gathered up the loose sheets an envelope addressed to "Agnes" fell from between the leaves. It evidently had been placed upon the rack and inadvertently covered up. She recognized her father's handwriting, and tore open the envelope with fingers that trembled. Inside a folded sheet of paper was a five-dollar bill, and written on the sheet these words—"To the sweet singer. From Father." The paper was dated four o'clock in the morning four days back. Agnes dropped her music with a sob, and sank into the nearest chair, covering her face with her hands. It had been Dr. Sidney's custom to put missives from time to time on her piano, and they occasionally contained money. One circumstance only was now in the girl's mind, and it dominated her thoughts. She at once connected the bill with words of hers complaining about singing in the Presbyterian choir without pay.

After a little while, she stopped crying and resumed her work. Presently she found another envelope with a paper dated two days later, which read:

Will my dear daughter, when she has a little time, see if she can arrange the enclosed words to music, and sing them some Sabbath day in church?

There was enclosed another sheet containing the words of a hymn.

Through the remainder of the afternoon until time to prepare supper, Agnes worked on the music for her father's hymn. Generally she preferred secular songs to sacred, and she had wondered rather peevishly why her father persisted in composing hymns when he could write poems which were clever and light-hearted. Now, some hitherto-concealed spring of action in his nature attracted her notice. What was it that drew that gifted mind to center itself upon religious thought? Why was it that through all he said or wrote or did, there sounded the motif of another world? With what invisible friend was he communing during the early morning hours which he spent at his desk or during which he strolled about in his garden, as she sometimes had seen him do through her window?

Agnes knew that Dr. Sidney had returned and was keeping his office hours, but she did not attempt to speak with him then, knowing that patients were coming and going. She went about her supper preparations as noiselessly as possible, and when the meal was ready she went to her father with a grace that was new since morning. Her presence seemed especially sweet to the doctor as she bent over him where he lay on the lounge and kissed his forehead.

"I found your letters on the piano today, papa. Thank you so much for the money. I shall sing your words on Sunday."

As Agnes' gaze met that of her father there occurred one of those flashes of understanding which have it in them to avert the tragedy of a life. It was as though to one who had given his life for an ideal too exalted for his world to comprehend there suddenly had appeared his beloved disciple, aroused from sleep and come to watch with him.

Neither Dr. Sidney nor Agnes spoke as they went in together to supper. Before it was over Dr. Sidney excused himself and went back to the lounge.

Agnes was not quite through with the dishes when Beatrice and Fred came in. She heard the sounds of merriment in the hall and met her guests with an unusual dignity. They remained only a few minutes and asked Agnes to go with them to a mesmerist's exhibition the following evening. The girl had little heart for amusement, but she accepted the invitation, as it was to be Beatrice's last day in Kent. The two went off, talking and laughing. As Agnes closed the door behind them she heard Fred trip on the gravel walk, heard Beatrice's mocking laugh, a little scuffle and then receding voices.

She finished her work quietly and returned to the parlor with a book and a letter from Miriam Cass. Suddenly she heard her father's footsteps. He was walking back and forth in the sitting-room beyond. As he passed and re-passed the door of the parlor, she was struck with the pallor of his face, the weariness of his movements. He did not notice her until she spoke to him.

Then he turned, a flash of surprise on his face. He joined her at once. "I thought I heard you go out with a party of young people," he said.

"No. It was only Beatrice and Fred."

He paused in his walk, stood before her, and said, looking down, "I am glad you did not go away without speaking to me."

Her heart smote her, for she rarely had been at home of late.

"You look worried, papa," she said. "Is there any trouble on your mind?"

He walked across the room, paused, and said with peculiar earnestness, "I am convinced that something will happen to your mother. I wish I could go for her. But I have not the strength."

Agnes was alarmed. "What do you mean, papa?" she asked, hastily putting down her book and half rising. "Mamma is well. She writes that she is perfectly well. Have you heard anything?"

"No. I have that feeling." There was uncontrollable anxiety in his voice and manner.

So the soldier, struck in battle, as he falls, sees with his darkening eyes the sword that hangs over some unconscious head far away. The blow falls there. He passes into peace.

Agnes made an effort to smile. "There is nothing to make you feel like that, papa."

The weary steps began again.

"In the second drawer of my desk," said Dr. Sidney presently, "there are some notes which I have written from time to time. Most of them have been taken down early in the morning before the rest of the house was astir. Perhaps some time you will care to read them. Not now! They may bring you closer to your father's thoughts; when you grow older and have aches of your own in the head and the heart (for they will come), they may help you a little. There are many things I have wanted to say to you, but youth has its rights, and I always have believed that the soul must first hunger and thirst after righteousness before it can be filled. That day will come."

"Yes. I know."

"There are qualities in my sweet daughter's disposition," he said, smiling a little, "which I notice now and then, and recognize as having come from me. They are not bad qualities, but they need others along with them, and I hope that with my weakness she may develop something of her mother's firmness of character."

Agnes tried hard to keep back the tears that scalded her eyeballs. "Don't! Don't, papa," she cried. "I didn't get any weakness from you. I tell you—never from you!"

He came back and sat down near her, and held up the volume of Cowper which he had in his hand. "These are poems by a man who was heart-sick over all the pain and sorrow in the world. It unsettled his mind at last. He once took a wounded hare and tended it, saying that one creature out of all the myriads should be cared for."

Agnes did not reply at once. Presently she exclaimed, "What is it all for, papa?"

"Many a man has wished for the understanding heart," the doctor returned thoughtfully. "But there is a better gift. David knew it when he prayed 'Create in me a clean heart, O God!'"

After a moment's silence, his face changed and he began to speak with unusual rapidity, following out the new train of thought. One always was conscious of a dramatic intensity beneath his somewhat austere manner, but tonight it transformed him. His language gradually took on the glory of the Hebrew prophets. Many silent thoughts of his life welled up into words. He seemed to forget Agnes' presence, to be communing with the spirit of the unseen world. Agnes felt an awe of her father stealing over her as she realized how thin was the veil that divided him from the eternal. It was flashed upon her that his face always was turned away from time with its accidents towards the light and the profound brooding love which awaited him yonder. It was as though some gentle denizen of boundless ether were caught here and struggled, patient and undiscouraged, to wear its fetters through and soar again.

When he ceased, it was with the same suddenness with which he began. The two sat for some time in silence. The silence seemed to grow into an immensity of crowding intuitions and suggestions. Some of them the girl felt that she must tell her father, but when she tried to speak, she did not know how.

"Papa, something has happened to me," she stammered at last. "I never felt before how unreal the things are which I have most longed for. I wish I could live in your world with you."

The look which accompanied what she said, as well as the words themselves, told the doctor of the understanding that had come to her.

"You will live in that world more and more," he said, the brilliance of his eyes settling into the usual quiet luminousness. He took up his volume of Cowper, but did not open it at once. Presently he added, "And though in a different way from what you think, I doubt not with me." Then he opened his book, an expression of peace upon his face.

As his daughter's eyes lingered upon him an answering peace came into her heart, but it was accompanied by a feeling of foreboding wherein solemnity and aspiration and renunciation were mingled.

They spent the remainder of the evening in silence.

At last the doctor rose, walked to the piano, and opened the hymn-book on the rack. Agnes smiled and complied at once with his unspoken request for her to sing. He selected a verse here and there, as was his custom, and she sang them.

Last of all he turned to his favorite hymn, following the words through in his Cowper as she sang:

"God moves in a mysterious way
His wonders to perform;
He plants His footsteps in the sea,

And rides upon the storm."

He stopped her before she went on to the second stanza.

"That first stanza is one of the finest ever written," he said. "The rest is not equal to it. The grandeur is gone. Sing that one over."

And she sang it again.

When she turned on her stool, she was arrested by the radiance of her father's face.

"We soon shall have your mother back," he said, and he bent down and kissed her, adding, "The Lord has better things in store for you than you know."

CHAPTER VI

MRS. SIDNEY, in a blue and white gingham dress, was washing dishes in the kitchen of the Mabies' country home. From time to time she moved about the room to pick up a stray dish. At last they all were clean except one plate, which contained the remains of tidbits that had been sent to Helen during her illness.

Mrs. Sidney stood in indecision with this plate in her hand, when Pleasant Mabie came into the room. He came in on tiptoe, and shut the door noiselessly, for he had been well trained as to how to deport himself in a house with babies. A small mongrel dog with a clipped tail came close at his heels.

As she saw who it was, Mrs. Sidney suddenly held out the plate. "Here, Pleasant!" she said briskly, "eat this! It's real good. I want to wash the dish."

Mr. Mabie took the dish awkwardly and ate the contents.

Then Mrs. Sidney washed the plate, and after putting away her pans, went into the dining-room. Here Helen Mabie was sitting in a rocking chair, her sleeping baby in her lap. Three little children ranging from five to two were playing with a box of toys on the floor.

"Where's grandma's baby?" said Mrs. Sidney in a full buoyant tone, patting the smallest of the three on the head as she passed.

"What's Kitty doing?" she asked, looking at the older girl, who was standing, toys in hand, and who looked as though she had been interrupted.

Kitty's manner was theatrical, and she threw out her arms, as she answered that she was burying her doll, with a passionate abandon which would have done honor to Niobe.

"Helen," said Mrs. Sidney, "that's the smartest child ever saw. You'll be a proud woman someday. I hope you'll appreciate her."

"My kindergarten journal says it's better not to let children know about death," returned Helen musingly.

"Nonsense!" said Mrs. Sidney, rocking; "I don't approve of any new-fangled ideas that start children in life on a false basis. I've meant to speak to you about that kindergarten paper of yours before. You'd put in your time better if you'd read your Bible, and use your common sense."

"It gives me a good many valuable suggestions, mother."

"What suggestions has it given you?" asked her mother.

"Well, teaching by object-lessons. It gives a definite picture to the mind."

"Of course it gives a definite picture to the mind," answered Mrs. Sidney disdainfully, "and that's the reason Isaiah walked naked before the children of Israel, and the reason Ezekiel lay on his side for four hundred and thirty days. That's no new idea. No, sir! What mothers need is to read their Bibles. You can't expect to bring up your children in the way they should go, without the help of God. I've been sorry to see that you've given up church-going. You can't expect God to bless you if you go on like this."

Helen turned her face away, and looked wistfully out through the window. "We are all so tired on Sunday," she said gently. "And it's such a long way to town. The horses are tired, too."

"Pleasant got in to see the seven Blondin sisters, though," said Mrs. Sidney, looking sternly at the kitchen door, "and you went to hear that Italian man sing. You didn't either of you feel too tired, then."

Helen looked through the window some moments longer, and then turned her delicate face toward her mother, with a look of care-worn tenderness which would have come more naturally from the mother to the daughter.

"Mother," she said, with a swift smile whose sweetness had pierced Mrs. Sidney's heart years ago when she saw it in a darker, sterner face, "something of the pines and rock-ribbed mountains of Vermont was born in you. I think it is easier for you mountain people to be good than it is for us out here on the plains. Sometimes I wish..."

Her thin hands clasped each other tensely, as she looked out again over the wide level view to be seen from the window. But her voice sank, the hands came apart again, and she did not finish her sentence.

"Is our God only a God of the hills, then?" said Mrs. Sidney, lowering her knitting and eyeing Helen over her spectacles, a posture which lends authority to far less convincing gazes than those of Mrs. Sidney. "You aren't thinking of encouraging Pleasant to go out to that mining town in the Rockies, are you?" she added keenly, before her daughter could reply. "If Pleasant could get into a worse place, he'll be sure to do it!"

"Oh, no. I wouldn't want to go there."

"Did you tell Pleasant so?"

"Yes."

"Well, I'm glad you did. I don't like the look of that mining town. And I don't like the look of the hills either, with all those prospecting holes dug along like so many graves. It looks as if nature had broken out with a malignant disease."

Helen smiled again. This time it was her mother's smile, open, cheerful, free from subtlety, free from charm.

"I was always glad," went on Mrs. Sidney, "that Moses talked about the brooks of water, and wheat, and barley, and figs, and oil, and honey in the promised land, before he said anything about the iron and brass. He put those last."

Pleasant's stealthy step and the dog's patter were now heard approaching the door into the dining-room from the kitchen, and Mrs. Sidney abruptly changed the conversation.

"Here, Kitty! Come here. Grandma's got something for you," she said, drawing some candy hearts out of her pocket. As Kitty came up to her Mr. Mabie entered the room.

"Please don't give them candy," he said, lifting his hand with a deprecating gesture. "I don't think it's good for them."

"Nonsense! Sweets are healthy for children. Baby want one, too?" She changed her voice with the last word, and added with a beaming smile as she made eyes at the little ones, "Yes, grandma will give her babies goodies."

Mr. Mabie smiled painfully, but he did not say anything. He went into his bed-room and came out presently with his shaving materials. He then began to shave himself before the mahogany-framed looking-glass on the wall. During this operation, there was comparative quiet in the room. Helen talked to him a little from time to time, receiving meaning grunts in answer. Mrs. Sidney rocked back and forth, knitting and occasionally darting glances at her son-in-law.

When Pleasant gathered up his paraphernalia, returned to the bed-room, and closed the door, Mrs. Sidney looked up sternly at Helen. "Are those Blondin sisters in town yet?" she asked.

"I don't know."

"You may depend upon it, Helen, a man who gets himself up as sleek as Pleasant does, when it isn't a habit with him, has got something in the wind. It's wonderful the way a man can run down when he gets away from civilization, and there's no end in the downward career of a man who's only worked upon by outside influences. The world can't hold him up. Nothing but the Holy Ghost in his heart can do it. What is Pleasant going into town for, anyway? Jenkins did your marketing for you this week."

"There are a number of little things he wants to do. He wants to get some chloroform to kill the kittens."

"Why doesn't he gird up his loins like a man and drown the kittens?" returned Mrs. Sidney scornfully.

"These are the kittens of that favorite Maltese cat of his. We all feel tenderly about killing the offspring of those we love," said Helen, and she thought of her husband's visionary schemes, which she always was chloroforming as gently as possible.

"Is that all he's going for?"

"No. He told Hetty he'd buy her a new hat. She likes his taste."

Hetty was the maid of all work of the Jenkins family, the nearest neighbors, whom they had shared with Helen since the baby came.

"So it's a hat that Hetty and he have been getting their heads together over? I wondered what important undertaking Pleasant had got hold of now. Well, if that isn't ridiculous!"

"It's a little thing to give him pleasure, mother," said Helen simply. "If it gives him variety and cheers him up, why should I take the gratification away from him? He doesn't get much pleasure. A farmer's life is a hard one."

"Let him get along with your associates," responded the older woman uncompromisingly.

"I haven't any," answered Helen, unsuspiciously falling into the trap.

"Yes, that's just it. You rather get along without."

Both women looked toward the bed-room door, at which Mr. Mabie had unexpectedly appeared. He had on a clean shirt and a starched collar, but he had not yet put on his coat. He held out a letter to Mrs. Sidney, saying rather sheepishly, "I just found this in my coat pocket. I got it last week when I went to town. Guess I must have forgot to give it to you."

"It's from Stephen," said Mrs. Sidney, catching the envelope from his hand and tearing it open. "Here! There's something for you, Helen. Some poetry, I guess. Keep still, Kitty. I want to read a letter. Pleasant, send that dog out into the kitchen." She looked resentfully after the cur, continuing, "I can't stand it to hear that dog's toe-nails on the bare floor." Then she adjusted her spectacles and began to read. Presently she got up unsteadily and left the room.

She returned when the baby wakened, with a shining face.

"I was reading over your father's letters when I was in my room, Helen," she said as she laid the cloth on the table. "There's been so much going on these last six weeks, I haven't had a chance to call my breath my own. It seems to me I see new things in his letters every time I read them."

She passed into the kitchen, and came back soon with the plates.

"Oh, what a wealth of love his heart contains!" she said.

Again the large figure disappeared. Back it came laden with a tray of dishes.

"There was one passage which quite struck me in the last letter. I read it while I was dressing the baby, and I was so flurried, I didn't take it all in."

The voice died away in the kitchen. Then came the rattle of knives and forks.

"He said he'd been looking over his old college mementoes and letters in the hair-trunk up in the attic," said Mrs. Sidney, returning, "and he came across a picture of his first sweetheart—a girl he loved when he first went to Williams."

"How can mother tell of it?" thought Helen during the pause.

"And he told how pretty and bright she was, and he said that when he saw the little daguerreotype it brought it all back again."

Another disappearance.

"And he went on to say that it made him feel young again, and he asked me to forgive him for remembering, but it fairly made him smell the little wild things, and see the poplar trees sway, and the way the dragon-flies darted over the trout stream."

Mrs. Sidney halted by the kitchen door, her hands upon her hips.

"And he said that the little picture was so sweet to him that he was going to get a little frame for it, and hang it up in his office, and— and—"

"Don't cry, mother. Don't!" exclaimed Helen, half rising. "I believe it was all a joke. Father never loved anybody but you. Anyhow, that was thirty-five or forty years ago. If you could see the fat old thing now, you wouldn't care."

Mrs. Sidney's weeping changed into hysterical laughter. She sat down and held her hands to her sides.

"Do control yourself, mother," said Helen in distress. "Father says you'll break a blood vessel laughing someday."

"But he said, Helen—he said he wanted to—to get it in a little frame because—because—because—"

"Because what?"

"Because he wanted his children to know—how their mother looked when she was young!"

Helen did not laugh. She hardly realized the incongruity of her effort to console her mother. Her eyes were fixed on a horse far down the road coming toward the house at great speed. She had been longing for some advent in that long white road. It had come, and it struck a chill to her heart.

"It is John Cummings," she said. "He is coming here."

Mrs. Sidney hurried to the window.

"He is!" she cried after a moment. "He's got a telegram. Your father's sick. Oh, I never ought to have come away and left him."

Mr. Mabie came out of his room upon hearing their excited voices. He held a set of papers containing statistics in regard to the adulteration of sugar, which he was preparing for publication in the town paper. He started leisurely toward the door, but by the time he reached it Mrs. Sidney was back with the telegram in her hands.

Her own eyes took in the message before the sheet was fairly opened, and she read it aloud:

Father very ill. Come immediately. Bring Helen if possible.
AGNES.

"What time is it?" asked Mrs. Sidney, looking at the clock.

"Helen can't go," said Pleasant, disregarding the time.

"The cow money has got to go on the mortgage. She's too weak, anyway."

A strange expression flitted across Helen's face, but there was no reproof in it. She knew too well the bitterness of poverty that shuts in the sentiments of the heart, and then gnaws their life away. Pleasant's reference to the money necessary for her journey fell upon ears that were listening to a remote voice which, in the light of this news, was tinged with indefinable melancholy.

"I have had an enclosure from father's letter," she said. "It is a draft for fifty dollars which he says came to him unexpectedly. He told me to keep it for an emergency. It seemed to me just now that I could hear him telling me to come. I'll take the cow money, and Pleasant can cash this."

"Oh!" said Mr. Mabie, and he appeared relieved about his wife's weakness.

"It's half-past eleven," said Mrs. Sidney, who had been listening with a pang, wondering if her husband had anticipated this emergency. "That train goes at two."

"Can't make it," volunteered Mr. Mabie. "It would take an hour and a half to drive to town with a good horse. Betsey is lame and I was calculating to drive her in slow and get the veterinary to look at her. All the others are at the mill."

"We have got to make it!" exclaimed Mrs. Sidney instantly. "Jenkins' horses aren't at the mill."

"Mebbe Jenkins might let me take Spitfire if I explained. I'll run over and ask if it'll be convenient."

"You tell him we've got to have her whether it'll be convenient or not!" cried Mrs. Sidney from the kitchen door-way, where she had rushed to see to her dinner. "And don't you stop to explain, either!"

"Mebbe I'd better bring Hetty back," said Pleasant, sticking his head in the door again, but not waiting for an answer.

"Do you think Pleasant and Hetty can take care of the other three?" asked Helen. "I'll have to take the baby, of course." She looked anxiously at her mother, who was hurriedly putting food on the table.

"I guess they can. We can generally do what we've got to do. Sit right down here and eat. I'm going upstairs to pack. When you get through, you can dress the baby. Then I'll come down and help you. Pleasant can eat after he gets back from the station."

She left the room, but was back again within half an hour, dragging a handbag.

"I packed your things and mine in my trunk," she said, "and the baby's things in this bag. Here's your dress!" She sat down with a groan.

"Eat something, mother," said Helen, taking the garment.

"Yes, yes, I will. Never mind the dishes. Pleasant can clear them up afterwards."

When everything was ready, the clock-hand pointed to half-past twelve, and Pleasant had not returned.

"I wish—I do wish I could be in two places at once," said Mrs. Sidney. "I'd have had that horse here half an hour ago. There he is now. Way down by the frog-pond. Helen, we've got time enough to pray. Kneel down here by me. You kneel down, too, Kitty. Nellie, put that fork down. Put it down, I say! Now, Helen. Just tell the Lord to keep Stephen alive till we get home. Later on, we can ask Him to let him get well."

"Mother," said Helen, with eyes full of agony, "we mustn't tell the Lord what to do."

Mrs. Sidney fell on her knees with a sob.

"O God! I'm a miserable sinner. O God! make me humble! Thy will, Lord, Thy will! But, oh, let him live! Let him live! O God, have pity on Thy servant, Thy miserable, miserable servant! But let Thy countenance shine upon me. Oh, pity us! Let him live! Amen. Amen. For Christ's sake."

She caught hold of the chair in front of her, pulled up her heavy body, and took the baby, while the tear-drops and beads of perspiration ran in streams down her face.

Pleasant was still some distance away, driving Spitfire before Jenkins' democrat wagon. Hetty and a strange woman were riding with him, and the loyal dog was under the wagon.

"If you can walk by yourself, Helen," said Mrs. Sidney, "I'll carry that satchel. Pleasant won't be able to leave the mare. Kiss grandma good-by, Kitty. Be a good girl and God will bless you. Good-by, Dannie! Good-by, Nellie!"

Helen's knees trembled, but she kept pace with her mother, and was the first to get into the wagon.

"I'm Jenkins' sister," said the strange woman. "I'm up for a visit, but I'll take turns with Hetty staying here."

"I knew the Lord would provide," said Mrs. Sidney in a shaken voice, smiling through her tears, and she nodded reassuringly at the friend. "Cast thy bread upon the waters, madam, and it shall return to thee after many days. Look out, Pleasant! You'll trip on that cat."

The Maltese cat knew Pleasant would not step on her. She brushed affectionately against his legs and purred contentedly.

"Now, take the baby, Helen, and I'll help Pleasant bring out the trunk. Thank you, ma'am!" as Jenkins' sister stepped up to hold the mare. She turned and followed Pleasant to the house.

"Does that dog belong to Mr. Mabie?" asked the stranger, wishing to make conversation with Helen.

"Pleasant found it when it was a pup," replied Helen, "It was sick, and he nursed it and took care of it. He's always kind to sick animals."

Pleasant's kindness to sick animals was well-known throughout the neighborhood. The farmers laughed at the crop of weaklings on his stock farm, and were wont to say that strong animals didn't stand much of a show with him till they were run down. Some men grow bitter under defeat; some grow stolid. Pleasant developed an abnormal sympathy with everything else that was under par. It is a hard thing for a man to behave admirably who realizes that he has made a failure of his life, and that he has lost the esteem, once proudly possessed, of a woman for whom he was going to conquer the whole world. Pleasant might have done worse. Where many men crave drink, he craved only affection. His little daughter Kitty looked down upon him, and since Mrs. Sidney had come to live with them there was a similar tendency on the part of Dan. Pleasant suffered under the attitude toward him which he saw developing in his children, and he sometimes blamed Mrs. Sidney's talkativeness for it, and sometimes blamed Helen's silence. It never occurred to him that the one woman only pushed the hand of fate, while the other labored to retard it, and that his only hope of escape was that he himself could unclasp those iron fingers.

They rounded the curve by the station an hour later, and as soon as the mare stopped Mrs. Sidney sprang out of the wagon. "Give me the baby!" she cried. "Here, quick! Pleasant can bring the satchel and help you. Never mind the trunk. He can send it on."

She ran across the weed-grown road and reached the train as the whistle blew.

"Hold on!" she panted to the conductor who had pulled her up on the car. "That lady over there has to get on yet."

"Can't wait," said the man gruffly.

"You've got to wait. It's a matter of life and death. Take your hand off that rope!"

The man, startled by the dominant voice, involuntarily obeyed, and Helen reached the steps almost fainting.

"There, my poor child, there!" said Mrs. Sidney. "Good-by, Pleasant."

Then, as the train pulled out, she turned to the conductor with a long sigh. "I'm much obliged to you, sir," she said, with a wholesome smile. "Perhaps you'd better give the lady an arm. Now we've got to make connections at Chicago."

The suddenness of the departure stamped it all with unreality, and as the afternoon wore away they seemed plunging deeper and deeper into strangeness. Mrs. Sidney soon fell asleep in her seat. Heroic action and profound rest divided her time. There were no moments left for nerves and dreams. Helen stayed awake with her head pressed against the window sash, hearing now the mysterious whispers of the great cotton-woods as they approached and passed them, now the sound of peepers from some pool, following on the night wind. She thought of the forlorn home she was leaving; of her husband, crestfallen, worried in business, and diffident in heart. Gradually the light grew paler, mists crept along the shallows, spirits beckoned and saluted and waved farewells. They seemed to call messages to her, and she sent many in return to the lonely ones left behind. Who knows but that that night the phantom couriers passed into the bare chamber of a little farm-house and kissed the occupants while they slept, and strewed their pillows with amaranth and asphodel, the flowers that are ever blooming side by side in the melancholy paradise of human love?

CHAPTER VII

THE day after Agnes' last long conversation with her father, Dr. Sidney had come home late in the afternoon and had gone at once to his room. Agnes left him unwillingly in the evening to go out with Fred and Beatrice. Her uneasiness grew upon her until she excused herself in the midst of the entertainment and came home alone. To her alarm she found her father's horse standing still hitched to the buggy where the patient animal had been left hours before by its usually careful master. After caring for the neglected beast, Agnes looked into her father's room. He was still sleeping heavily but restlessly, as he had been when she left earlier in the evening. Four days later, she sent the telegram to her mother and sister to come.

Fred Sidney met his aunt and cousin at the station and drove them to the house. Mrs. Sidney had taken off her wraps on the way to the house, and, as the horse stopped at the office door, she took an apron from the satchel and tied it about her waist. Then she walked into the office, equipped for nursing.

As Agnes saw the familiar figure coming quickly through the door toward the bed-room where she waited by her father's side, she seemed to awaken from a nightmare; but it came back upon her, as she looked down on her father's face, which the grim sculptor was chiseling closer each hour to the death's head we all carry about with us concealed.

"Mamma is here," she said, kissing his forehead before she went to meet her mother.

She said but the one word, "Meningitis," as she kissed Mrs. Sidney, and then stole out of the room to help Helen with the baby.

When the two sisters returned, Mrs. Sidney was giving her husband cracked ice. He had settled back more easily upon his pillows, and there was a shade of contentment beneath the ever-recurring expressions of suffering.

"You—will—see—to—things—now, Kate," he said presently, seeking to turn his head toward his wife, but failing in the attempt. "I can't—I can't—anymore." He closed his eyes, then opened them toward Agnes, and added: "And—my—poor—little—girl—"

He did not finish, but she knew that he wished to speak in her favor, and his effort to do so broke the girl's heart.

Sooner or later, the time comes when fate brands us. Like dumb, driven cattle, Agnes shrank with mortal agony and terror, felt herself held under the iron that burns with the fire which is not quenched, quivered forth marked with the stamp time cannot wear away, and passed on into the in numerable herd.

Very soon after the arrival of Mrs. Sidney and Helen, the terrible spasms of meningitis began, but it was not until a week later that a physician said quietly, when leaving, "He will not live out this night."

Agnes slept through the early part of the night. Mrs. Sidney had promised to call her in case of a change. Toward midnight she heard her sister's voice summoning her. Agnes responded at once.

Helen was standing at the foot of the stairs, a candle in her hand. As she lifted it to light the way, Agnes observed the dignity and quiet of the waiting figure. The tenderness and transfiguration in the dark face looking up at the unhappy girl irresistibly recalled Dr. Sidney himself.

"Is it over?" Agnes asked.

"No," replied Helen gently. "I have had a wonderful hour with him. I am sorry that you must see him as he is now, not as he has been until now." She paused and said earnestly, "It is but a struggle of the poor body now. His spirit is at rest."

They went into the chamber and Agnes approached the bedside. One of her father's hands was near her own. Helen Mabie had inserted a handkerchief, before it clenched, that the nails might not cut the flesh.

"How merciful it is," said Agnes, "that he is not conscious under this. Dr. Crocker said he was not."

She sat down near the others, and the three women waited.

"Don't you think you should have let Dr. Quinn stay all night, mother?" asked Helen. "He was ready to do so."

"There are others who need him more tonight."

They heard the timepiece as it ticked steadily on.

"I believe your father's aunt—Aunt—Uncle Samuel's wife—died with spinal meningitis," said Mrs. Sidney. "What was her first name, Helen?"

"I am thinking. Was it Edna?"

"No, it wasn't Edna, but I think it began with E."

"There is a man outside the window," said Agnes, suddenly. "I saw his head through the blinds."

"It is only that young reporter from *The Times*," answered Helen. She rose as she spoke and went out of the room.

As she left it, Dr. Sidney's face relaxed. He moved his arms a little, and seemed trying to speak.

Agnes sprang to his side, and leaned over close to his lips. He was whispering.

"Her—name—was—Eunice."

"Mamma!" said Agnes, in a voice of anguish, "Dr. Crocker was wrong. He is conscious."

Mrs. Sidney was already at her husband's side.

"Can you understand me, Stephen?" she asked, bending down.

His eyes answered her.

"I have been thinking of the smell of the little wild things, and of the way the poplars swayed in the wind, and how the dragon-flies darted over the trout stream, and—and how happy we were."

The brilliant eyes were fixed upon her.

"And I've been thinking of the little home as it was at first with just three rooms, and how we loved it. We loved it. There are many mansions—a house of many mansions—and a place is prepared for us, Stephen. But oh, *we loved it!*"

He tried to move his hand toward her.

"And then the little baby came, and—"

Agnes crept away and joined Helen in the kitchen. Time had gone back now. A quarter of a century had slipped away from her parents' minds. She had no place in that love which, with all her life-long knowledge of her parents' devotion to each other, had just come upon her as an apocalypse.

When the sisters returned to the bed-room, Dr. Sidney appeared to be sleeping, but his breath sounded loud and labored. Mrs. Sidney was sitting in a chair by the bed side. They had hold of each other's hands, but she, too, was sleeping. As the girls entered, she sat up with a start. "Where have you been?" she asked.

Helen answered in a low voice. "In the kitchen with the window open. I wanted to get a breath of fresh air."

"You wanted to get what?"

Helen spoke with a dry throat: "I said I wanted to get a breash of freth air."

Mrs. Sidney laughed.

"Mother," said Helen painfully, "how can you?"

"You said 'breash of freth air.' You left the 'sh' off of fresh' and put it on 'breath.' Oh, how can I? How can I?"

Helen sat down with a heartsick look in her face.

"Helen," said Mrs. Sidney, after a minute, "I'm made that way. It's terrible. I can't help it. When my own mother was dying, she asked me for a glass of water, and when I brought it to her, she couldn't see very well. I believe it was the blindness of death. She put up her hand in a queer way, and said, 'What is it?' And I laughed! I laughed!"

There was a long silence, until at last Agnes said, "I think he is moving."

The three women drew near the bed.

Dr. Sidney opened his eyes as if with a violent effort. He moved one finger upward as he spoke, and he said in a thick voice, "I say—live!—not die—live!" Again, the finger pointed.

In a moment the heavy breathing was resumed, ever slower. They stood motionless, listening and waiting for the beating of the heart to stop. Slower and slower came the labored breaths—there was a pause—another breath— and the wait the wait—until the end of time, the wait.

As Mrs. Sidney raised her face, her daughters turned away.

"He has gone to his long home," said the widow; she placed one hand over the sightless eyes, closing them tenderly, while she placed the other hand beneath the chin.

"Helen!"

"Yes, mother."

"Bring me a towel. Agnes?"

"I am here, mother."

"Go into the kitchen and get the ironing-board. Your father's clean clothes are laid out in the closet. Bring me also his best broadcloth suit. Now, Helen, carefully."

Agnes turned away from the room with a sickening heart. She did her duties, and waited to be told of more. Mrs. Sidney went to the mantel-piece and poured something into a glass.

"Helen and I will not need you any longer," she said. "You had better get in bed with your Aunt Mattie, but first drink this."

Agnes took the glass and drank what her mother had prepared.

Mrs. Sidney took the girl's head between her hands and kissed her. "Try to sleep," she said. "He shall not come back to us, but we shall go to him."

Agnes went out of the room and closed the door behind her. As she was going through the dining-room she heard the office-bell ring. She went to the door and asked who was there. A voice said, "I am from *The Times*." The office clock struck three as she answered, "Dr. Sidney is dead."

Then she walked back slowly through the dimly-lighted offices. The gray afghan was thrown back from the back-office lounge, as though her father had just left it. There on the table lay the volume of Cowper. She took the book up in her hand, and it fell open. Her father's pencil marks drew her attention to the lines,

"One sheltered hare
Has never heard the sanguinary yell
Of cruel man, exulting in her woe."

She closed the book and put it back again, and went upstairs to her aunt's room. Aunt Mattie was sitting up in bed, hushing to sleep Helen's baby, who was lying in a cradle close to the bed. "Who is it?" she asked as she heard the steps coming.

"It is I—Agnes. Papa died just before the clock struck three."

"Can I do anything?"

"I think not. Isn't there something to do here? Shall I keep the baby?" She went in, stood by the cradle and looked down at the flower-like sleep of Helen's child.

"The baby is all right now. It was very kind of you to think of taking him. I'm sorry for you, Agnes." She put out her hand and the girl pressed it.

Agnes did not get into bed with her aunt. She went into her own room and looked at herself in the glass. She was startled that her face had not changed.

Then, for the first time since she had heard her father's words, "You must see to things now, Kate. I can't," she forced herself to face the judge who would never pardon—her own soul.

"He wanted mother. He needed her. She spoke the truth. I thought I loved him best, but she was necessary here to take care of him, and to take care of me. I wanted to get rid of her. It was not to make him happy—it was to get my own way. I didn't take care of him the way she did. *It is I who have killed him.*"

She walked to the window and opened it. The ground was covered with snow—the first, light, unexpected fall of the season. Far out in the still morning she heard the whistle and rumble of a train. There came to her the words from Lear:

"I might have saved her; now she's gone forever.
She's dead—dead as earth."

She sat still looking out into the morning until Helen came up, went to her boy, and after a time approached her door.

"It is all done," she said, entering. "He looks very beautiful," and she sat down by her sister.

"Where is mother?"

"She is down with him."

After a long time Agnes said, watching her sister, "What are you thinking about, Helen?"

Helen raised her head. "I was thinking of the wild flowers he used to bring me, and of how I never thanked him. He spelled my name in forget-me-nots, one summer, and I didn't pay any attention to it. I used to keep him waiting in the cold when he called to get me with his buggy. I never knew how to put myself in sympathy with him as well as you did, Agnes. I think it was because he was away in the war when I was little, and I was a little afraid of him when he came back."

Agnes was silent. She looked at her sister and analyzed her grief. "She feels remorse," she thought, "but she is innocent. She can talk of it. There is no human soul whom I can tell."

Presently she crept into bed and lay there cold and calm. It was the first night since she could remember that she had lain down to sleep without saying a prayer which she had learned in childhood. The Garden of Eden was shut behind her, and the angel with the flaming sword guarded the gate.

PART II

CHAPTER I

IF one had walked into the Sidney house the day following Dr. Sidney's burial he would have found everything going on in much the same way as usual. Mrs. Sidney had opened the windows, and fresh air and sunshine surrounded her while she worked. Agnes again had filled the house with flowers—shaggy autumnal flowers, whose pungent and woody smells were fast conquering the faint hot-house odors lingering from the day before; and her pupils were back again reciting to her, as they had done regularly till her father took to his bed. Aunt Mattie's quiet was as impregnable as ever. Only the presence of Helen and the baby was out of the common. That Dr. Sidney himself was absent would scarcely have attracted notice. He was often away from home at meal-time and in the night, and though he never would come again Mrs. Sidney had no intention of permitting life to succumb to death.

One who knew the family intimately would, in the course of some weeks, have begun to notice changes in Agnes and her mother. They were hardly discernible to the ordinary eye. Mrs. Sidney was more active even than she had been before! She read her Bible still more, catching a moment now and then to pick up a new verse or incident, which she would meditate upon while working. And her Biblical quotations had undergone the same tempering process that had softened almost imperceptibly her uncompromising nature. She spent less time with Elijah beneath the juniper tree, and with Jeremiah in the pit. She rarely marched to battle with Joshua. But she walked often with Moses up and down the mountains of the wilderness, she mused with David in the valleys and pastures. Every evening Mrs. Sidney led the family prayers, as her husband used to do, and her daughters wondered that she could keep her face serene and her voice steady. After they had said good-night, and she was left alone downstairs in her bed-room, she would take up her Bible again for her solitary devotions. It always opened of itself, at a page in Ezekiel, and she always cried as she read,

Son of man, behold, I take away from thee the desire of thine eyes with a stroke! yet neither shalt thou mourn nor weep, neither shall thy tears run down. Forbear to cry, make no mourning for the dead. So I spake unto the people in the morning, and at even my wife died; and I did in the morning as I was commanded.

Agnes was beginning to find herself less in sympathy with many of her acquaintances, but she was coming into touch with a widening circle of friends toward whom she but recently had been unsympathetic. She was generally cheerful, but she no longer had the insolent cheerfulness which has not known grief.

One day about a fortnight after the doctor's death Mrs. Sidney and her daughters were sitting at the table eating the midday meal. There had been a long silence and Mrs. Sidney's face had relapsed into its occasional expression of grief. But she knew she must not allow herself to think too much, and she roused herself abruptly and looked toward Agnes. "Haven't you a letter there, Agnes? Who's it from?"

"From Miriam Cass."

"Why don't you read it? Is she the girl who's going on a sailing vessel?"

"She's gone." Agnes rebelled at this catechism, not realizing, as her mother did, that a counter-irritant is a good remedy for grief.

"Who's she gone with?" persisted Mrs. Sidney, trying to keep her mind on the subject.

"She's gone with her father," replied Agnes shortly. Then she added hastily, anticipating the next question, "Her mother died when she was little."

"It's a great misfortune for a girl to be left without a mother." Mrs. Sidney heaved a weary sigh and took up a glass of water.

Agnes watched her mother with rising impatience. Presently she said irritably,

"Mamma, I do wish you wouldn't gulp that way when you drink. It seems as if I should go crazy. I've tried my best to keep still, but I just can't do it."

Mrs. Sidney's face involuntarily hardened into reproof, then voluntarily softened. Agnes was surprised and mortified when her mother finally spoke, saying with an unexpected smile, "Well, I'll try and not do it, and I hope you'll never know what it is to be as thirsty as I am. Sometimes it seems as if I could lap up the water like Gideon's men."

There was a little pause. Then Agnes said, "That was nice in you, mother. Excuse me for speaking the way I did," and she left the room and went upstairs.

There, amidst the mementos of her old Winston life, she opened Miriam's letter. Her friend had passed through Winston during Dr. Sidney's illness, and was now on the water. The letter had been mailed from New York. It was a plain note, written in the self-unconsciousness of Miriam's deeper moods. It told about her mother's death and burial at sea and the impression it had made upon her as a child. When she came to speak of Agnes' grief there was a quiet in her words which recalled the hand of death itself. It was the only one of all the letters Agnes had received which attempted no word of consolation, and it was the one which brought it most, because everything she wrote was simple and full of love.

When Agnes came down into the kitchen later to help her mother with the work, Mrs. Sidney was washing dishes. The wiping of them was left for Agnes. The girl often had been touched of late by her mother's efforts to divide the labor so that the daughter's hands might be spared the rougher work.

As soon as the dishes were put away, Mrs. Sidney brought out the remains of a roast of mutton. We had better out this up for a meat-pie tomorrow," she said. "Then we can put on the bone for a soup tonight."

"Do let's have a change tomorrow!" Agnes exclaimed impulsively. "I can't eat mutton another day, really. Let's kill a chicken."

"A live chicken keeps better than a dead sheep," answered Mrs. Sidney sententiously. "Those chickens are all we've got to depend upon for fresh meat now, till they kill another calf at the farm. I shan't run in debt one cent from now on. We've got to pay as we go, and if we can't pay, we'll eat beans—that's all."

Agnes caught at the opportunity to suggest something she had had in mind for some days back. "It seems to me that we are trying to carry too much, mamma. We have this place and the farm to keep going. Why can't we sell the farm, and invest the money more profitably? The farm just runs itself and doesn't bring us in anything but worry."

Mrs. Sidney stopped working and turned toward her daughter. "I'd worry a good deal more if we didn't have a farm running itself," she returned. "If it comes to selling any place, it will be this house. There's nothing like having a piece of land in a good farming country to fall back on. Banks fail, buildings burn up or rot down, and nobody knows how long a business will be profitable; but a few acres of land will always raise potatoes and beans enough to feed us, and keep hens and cows and sheep enough to clothe us. You can spin and I can weave if we have to."

Agnes smiled unwillingly. "I'd rather earn my clothes singing or tutoring, mother. I think we'd have more than if we sheared the sheep and spun and wove our garments."

"Don't grow up with the idea of depending entirely on other people, Agnes," Mrs. Sidney replied decidedly. "Much as we love this home, it doesn't support us. We support it, and please God we can keep it. But your father always said the old farm where his father and grandfather lived was the place to rely on! and my mother used to tell me, as long ago as I remember, 'Don't you ever marry a man unless he has got land, Kate. It's the only thing to be sure of in this world; and don't you ever let him mortgage it!' She was a wise woman. When you have mortgaged anything, you're improving other people's property at your own expense. If you can't keep things going, sell 'em outright before they run down, but a person with brains and self-denial can always live on a farm and keep it thrifty. So we will keep the farm, I guess."

She beamed upon Agnes for a moment, and then turned back to her work. "Don't repine at the farm mutton, either. You may be thankful enough to have your meat provided. I'm going to poach an egg for Helen tonight, but the rest of us will have a good soup."

"Don't cook anything extra for me—please," begged Helen with desperate earnestness "I don't know what's going to become of us all. Papa has helped us so much lately. I don't see how we can do without him, and oh, we ought to be in a position to help you!" She broke down and began to cry.

"You'll rile your baby's milk," said her mother, not pausing in her work. "It isn't necessary he should be troubled about his food. I guess the Lord will provide for His own."

Helen still continued to cry silently.

"Control yourself, Helen," her mother said again more brusquely. "Haven't you got any grit?"

"I used to have some, mother, but it's gone. I'm tired out. Hope long deferred maketh the heart sick."

Mrs. Sidney faced about toward her daughter and eyed her watchfully while she wiped her hands on a hanging towel. Then she glanced about the clean and tidy kitchen, felt of some ears of corn which hung in golden rows above the mantel-piece and sat down.

"You run in the sitting-room, Agnes, and bring me my sewing," she said to her younger daughter, and then as Agnes disappeared through the door she turned to Helen. "You may think you are done for, Nellie," she said not ungently, "but you're just at the end of your first wind. You won't be able to "keep up at the pace you've been going—kindergartens and Italian concerts—but you can keep up a moderate gait."

She looked up as Agnes came back with her work, and took it from her, continuing her talk in a different manner. "Before the doctor died, you were all used up because things were so bad then. Now you look back on that time and think you were pretty well off. Just let that teach you a lesson. The time may come when you'll look back to this day and think you were a queen."

"Don't, mother!" cried Helen. "Things are bad enough now. I didn't tell you the worst of Pleasant's letter, but he says the pigs aren't doing well. They've got the scurvy and he's afraid he'll lose them all."

"He won't if he does as I say," replied Mrs. Sidney, impatience struggling in her face, "Why didn't you tell me that before? You write a letter this very minute. Tell him to wash the young ones off in kerosene in the morning, and with soap and water at night. Or else he can put the kerosene on at night and wash them off with soap and water in the morning. It won't do the old ones any harm either. But mind you tell him to be sure and not get the oil in their ears. Don't you forget that. If he does, they'll hang their heads around for a while and then die. I've seen them. Dear me, how I do wish I was there and could see to it myself!"

Helen arose and went into the sitting-room. During the cool days following Dr. Sidney's death, they had formed the habit of sitting in the kitchen and thus economizing fuel. There was a return of summer now, but the habit remained.

"She's weak, poor child, and can't help herself," said Mrs. Sidney to Agnes. "This has all been terrible for her so soon after the baby came, but there's no excuse for you. Don't you let me see you get down in the mouth."

"I'm not down in the mouth, mamma."

"Why did you send Babbie Monks away in the middle of her lesson, yesterday?"

"I got to thinking about papa, and I just couldn't give it to her." Agnes spoke in a trembling voice and turned toward the window.

"Why weren't you thinking about cube-root? That's what you're being paid for."

The girl's quivering lips parted in a slight smile as she looked back toward her mother. An intuition of the policy behind these sallies came to her. "Mamma, I haven't words to praise you," she said almost tenderly.

Then, with a certain embarrassment at her unwonted attitude toward her mother, she added quickly, pinching a leaf of the rose geranium which stood with some other newly potted plants near the window, "I was all right while I was teaching her. But this was when she took a long time working out an example by herself, and I had to wait and think."

"The next time think that a cheerful heart doeth good, but a broken spirit drieth the bones," returned Mrs. Sidney sagely. "How much do you think you can make a week now, with the offer they've made you for singing?"

"About ten dollars, if I take the church money. You know papa never wanted me to."

"Neither do I," commented Mrs. Sidney, "but the Lord has put it upon us. Forty dollars a month. Many families live on less than that. It won't buy us a stalled ox, but I guess we can get a dinner of herbs on it." She interrupted herself to remind Agnes that the sweet marjoram should be picked and dried, and then went on: "We'll have to eke out something for Helen. I never knew how things were till I got out there. They've got a mortgage on the farm. I had to worm it out of them. I don't know what I shall do about it yet."

Agnes made no reply. The change in her situation, which she now suddenly realized when her mother referred to her as the main support of the family, stunned her. Yet she felt exhilaration in the shock. She was to take care of her mother and sister and aunt and all the helpless children. The faintness of the struggle was to come later.

"It's a good thing your father didn't leave any debts," said Mrs. Sidney again. "I've got enough on hand now to clear up what few things there are. We won't collect a quarter of what's on his books. Fred paid for the funeral expenses out of his savings. That's got to be made up. He'll need it to get married on. He was in here while you were upstairs. He's just got a letter from Beatrice Mott, and they're hurrying up with the wedding at the lake. They have given up having a large one out of respect to your father."

There was a pause.

Then Mrs. Sidney went on. "Dr. Quinn is going to buy your father's practice, and he'll take Peggy, too."

"Oh, don't sell Peggy!" cried Agnes. "What would old Peggy think? After she went through the war with papa, and then to sell her only child!"

"I know it cuts to the quick," answered Mrs. Sidney, wiping her eyes with the corner of her apron. "I'm glad it's going to be Quinn. You can trust Quinn. He's a little slow of speech, but so was Moses. He'll have a room here, too, and I'll board him."

"Oh, that's good!" Agnes felt her load lightening now that she saw some addition to her own earnings in their income.

"He offered to buy the library, but I shan't sell that. He can use it, but we'll keep the books. Maybe you'll marry a doctor."

"I won't marry Quinn, if that's what you mean."

"I guess Quinn don't want you. He didn't say anything about you—just the mare. I guess we'll get along. We aren't foundered yet."

She put her hand in the work-basket and handed Agnes her thimble, which suggestion the girl accepted and went into the sitting-room for her share of the sewing. During the conversation with her mother the thought of Donald Ballington had come repeatedly to her mind, and she appreciated the fact that now that a marriage with him might be an ignoble temptation, her mother had not mentioned him. Helen had finished her note, and was nursing her baby when her sister came into the room. Agnes sat down on the sofa near her, and took up a black skirt which her mother had cut out for her from one of her own.

"Agnes," said Helen presently, "there's something I want to say to you before I go. I want to caution you to be very kind and considerate to mother. She's a wonderful woman in keeping up, but we don't either of us realize what this has been to her. I know you don't see it, but at heart, she's very sensitive. Won't you try to be more affectionate to her?"

"I do try, Helen. I don't know why it is. I can't be affectionate to mamma. I just can't make myself. I said before I came downstairs this morning that I'd go and kiss her when I came into the room, and I stood in the kitchen door two or three minutes trying to make myself go up to her. She turned around and asked me why I was waiting, and, oh, Helen, she didn't ask it crossly. She was just surprised and kind. When she turned away again, I felt as if she knew what I was trying to do, and I couldn't do it. It was just the same at the dinner-table. When she was so nice to me about my miserable fault-finding over her drinking, I wanted to throw my arms around her neck, or go down on my knees, and so, of course, walked upstairs. What on earth is the matter with me?"

Helen Mabie sighed.

After a little while, Agnes took the initiative with her. "Helen," she said, reddening, "do you think respect is enough to marry on?"

"It depends. I wouldn't have said so once."

"Do you think a woman could be just as happy as though she fell in love?"

"Happier, if she'd only know it. But she wouldn't know it. So I think she'd be cheated out of something. Girls always think there's some romance coming, and they've a right to their castles in the air."

Agnes sewed on for some time without speaking.

Then she said, "If a man is a good man, is that enough? Do you think it makes any difference if he isn't her equal mentally?"

Helen laid down her baby tenderly, arranged her dress, and stood looking away from Agnes as she answered, "It makes all the difference in the world. Don't ever do that. It isn't possible for a woman to be married to a man beneath her intellectually without henpecking him. No amount of self-discipline can prevent it."

She took up a bit of crocheting, some soft work with a baby sweetness in its color and form, and the room was quiet again.

Agnes was the first to remember that Mrs. Sidney had been left alone in the kitchen, and she suggested to Helen that they take their work and join their mother.

As Helen collected her zephyrs, she said hesitatingly, "When mother came to us, she told me something about Mr. Ballington. Do you—are you—"

"No," said Agnes, rising and turning away. "I think I never shall marry, Helen. Anyway, a woman can't depend upon marriage to form her life for her. She must do it herself. I am going to try to be good to mother and take care of her." She waited, then added in a broken voice, "There's nothing I long for so much as to be good to mother. My future can look after itself."

CHAPTER II

THE second week in November Helen Mabie went back to the plains. A young man with spectacles and sandy hair sat in the doctor's office, used his horse and buggy, and ate his meals with the doctor's family. Agnes taught daily and sang in the church on Sundays. The family managed to get along upon her earnings, the little income which came from Dr. Quinn, and the produce of the farm. There was also a deposit in the bank which grew slowly as Mrs. Sidney took in hand the collecting of the doctor's outstanding bills.

Agnes now had given up all hope of returning to college, but since she had tasted the salt of adversity her thirst for knowledge had become unquenchable. She gratified the craving in her scant leisure by solitary study, as her father had done. She, too, began to rise early, read or write in quiet and loneliness, walk about meditatively in the back garden among the stripped vines and bushes. She found her father's books and papers marked, as if definitely for her. And there began to grow up during that winter, which to outsiders appeared to be so barren and forlorn, a mental and moral companionship with her father.

Another mind too, was exerting an increasing influence upon Agnes. Miriam's letters had grown frequent, and Agnes turned more and more earnestly to the stimulating mental outlook which her friend kept persistently before her. The correspondence put a sustained glow of eagerness into her otherwise hard-working and introspective existence.

A few days before Christmas, in answering a ring of the door-bell, Agnes found herself face to face with Donald Ballington. It was the first time she had met him since June. He had answered her dismissal with a kind note, and had sent her some lilies with a card of sympathy shortly after Dr. Sidney's death. What had touched the girl more was the memory of Donald among a group of Kent men who stood on the walk with bared heads as her father's casket was carried from the house.

As they met each other, now, each recognized at once the difference in their relation. The intense sympathy which he felt for Agnes relieved his manner from bashfulness, and she, now out in a world where all are striving, achieving, failing, was less conscious of herself and her effect upon him.

After they had talked on impersonal matters, he said with a recurrence of timidity, "Like all men who want something very much, I have kept a little hope that I might get it after all. I have no reason to speak of love to you again. It might be possible, however, that among the other changes grief has brought you, you might have come to feel differently about me."

Agnes was moved. Yet, at his words, the kindliness in her heart for him froze upon her lips. She felt herself hardening once more into the willful, capricious, but honorable girl who had repulsed him the summer before.

"I wish I could love you," she said. "I am afraid there is something wrong with me that I don't; but in order to marry you I ought to feel something for you which I do not."

"I won't urge you," he replied gravely, "I did not come here to do that. But there is a saying, you know, that man loves before marriage, and woman after. I sometimes have thought that with a woman of your spirit there might be some truth in the latter part of the statement."

"Still, I could not take the step feeling as I do," she answered. "I must do with myself what I can, and make the most of my life here." She looked up with a smile that meant to be brave, but was only pitiful.

His heart ached for her, but how could he help her? He looked down at the floor and waited for her to speak again.

Presently she resumed, with a frankness that relieved the situation and placed them at once upon a basis of friendship. "During the last week an opportunity has presented itself which my mother and I are considering. We have not yet spoken of it to anyone else. Would you care to hear?"

"I should—thank you!"

"Mr. Stoddard, from the Schubert Conservatory of Music in New York, has been visiting in Kent. He heard me sing in church two summers ago and remembered my voice. He was interested in it at that time, but knew that my parents preferred a quiet life for me. Now that I am obliged to earn my living, he felt at liberty to come to see me. I liked his straightforwardness. He said he had heard better voices, but never so good a voice in combination with so good a mind. He compared me not unfavorably with Caroline Holt, whom he brought out in oratorio two years ago. He has made me a generous offer. It is to teach me for three years, and then to bring me out in oratorio. He offers to take me into his own family, and to get me a church position in New York at once with a salary of eight hundred dollars a year; and he will ask me nothing for my lessons until I appear in oratorio."

Agnes paused. Donald said nothing.

"Of course," Agnes continued, "if it were anything but oratorio my mother never would consent, or if I were to go among strangers. Although I am anxious for the Opportunity, both for the money and because I love to sing, I should not go without her approval. I shall not leave any way until the new term of the Conservatory opens in February. My mother is to decide before that time."

The solemnity which hangs about decisions that are to turn the course of lives was upon them both as she finished. For a little time he did not speak, but only looked at her, loving the erect, strong pose he knew so well, but which now was suffused with something he never had seen in it before—humility which softened without weakening its vigor.

"I hope that whatever you decide will be for the best," he said at last as he rose and stood looking unhappily toward her.

Agnes, too, rose. She was oppressed with a feeling that this parting meant the severing of another link that held her to her girlhood. Real grief and affection were in the face she lifted. She drew a short breath and then stood quiet, her hands loosely clasped before her as she waited for his good-by.

"You will not be at your cousin's wedding, I suppose?" he asked.

"No, we are not going."

"I hear from Miss Mott, that, when they return here, there is to be a supper party to open their new home. Possibly you will be present?"

"Possibly."

"I shall hope to see you there, then."

His hand was on the door. Then, turning, he said with a dignity which she never had seen in him before. "This is my good-by to you as a lover. But I am your friend—now, and always. If I ever can help you, command me. I want to say to you, also, that I feel deeply your kindness to me today. I thought as I saw you sitting there that I never saw before so womanly a grace and dignity. God bless you!"

CHAPTER III

FRED and Beatrice were married soon after New Year's. Agnes heard repeatedly from Beatrice meantime. She wrote gaily of her trousseau, of the house General Mott was furnishing in Kent for their country home, of her quarrel with Fred over his refusal to leave work long enough at this time for a European trip, of her concession for the nonce in order to bring him to terms when once his wife. There were occasional flighty references to Tom, to Donald's admiration for Agnes, and now and then some innuendos respecting Ferdinand Ballington. On Christmas Day the letter which came contained a twenty-dollar bill with the words pinned to it: "Buy yourself some knickknack and think of Bee." But with all the good-will and unrestraint of the letters there was never a repetition of the intimate confidence which Agnes on one occasion had known from Beatrice. Indeed, since the day Beatrice had cried and looked her love for Fred against her will, Agnes never had seen her off guard, and she wondered at the reserve underneath Beatrice's apparent candor and carelessness.

Fred and Beatrice went to New York after their wedding, and an unusual quiet settled down in Kent. Agnes did not notice it, for she was absorbed in her work and study. She wrote twice a week to Miriam Cass, narrating her life and thoughts and hopes with that simplicity and honesty which she had shown to Miriam alone of all the world.

One evening early in February Agnes was attending choir rehearsal at the church. She was standing in the loft with the other singers, waiting for the organist to strike into the last anthem, when she noticed the vestibule door open and a man's dark figure enter and quietly take a seat in the rear of the church. Although the auditorium was so dimly lighted by the few gas jets in the choir that the man's face was in shadow, she felt an instant shock of recognition. She sang through her recitative in a voice that seemed to her to be telling the curious dread and happiness which she felt, and it was a relief to her when other voices swelled and covered her own. It was not unusual for escorts to call for the singers, and no one in the loft gave more than a passing glance at the man near the door.

When the rehearsal broke up he rose and came forward to meet Agnes. As her eyes rested upon the advancing figure there swept across her memory the odor of linden blossoms. She saw a man standing by the pillars of the Ballington house, looking after her and Donald as they followed Miriam and Tom down the path to the gate.

"Why, Mr. Ballington!" said Agnes as they met in the aisle, and she could not control a shake in her voice, "is it possible that you have remembered me?"

Ferdinand Ballington did not answer her immediately. Instead he took the plaid which she carried on her arm, opened it and folded it to a cape, and then wrapped it around her fall jacket. Their eyes met as he drew it across her shoulders, and she noticed that he was looking at her with a deeper intensity than that which she had observed in his eyes the summer before.

Then he said, "Yes. I have remembered you." And he added, with a smile which subtly challenged her perversity, "You are to come home with me. Your mother said I might call here for you. Are you ready to go?"

Agnes had a whim to stay where she was, at least long enough to say, "Perhaps I won't go with you even if my mother did say so," but both her humor and her shyness were only playing over a flattered acquiescence which was immediate and instinctive.

They left the church. She took his arm and they walked some distance in silence.

"When did you come to Kent?" she asked, speaking first.

"An hour ago."

She waited some seconds for him to take the initiative in conversation, and then asked again, "It is unusual for you to come here, isn't it?"

"Somewhat."

Again there was a long wait, during which Agnes listened to the crunch of the snow under their feet, held up her face to the drifting flakes, and promised herself that she would walk the remaining blocks in silence rather than speak first again. Ferdinand's content, however, over what he had already accomplished, and ardent determinations for the future which were going on in his mind were so satisfying that he was unaware of the girl's uneasiness. He came suddenly to the realization of it when he felt her withdraw her hand from his arm, and, looking at her in inquiry, was answered by a glance half roguish and half petulant, which said as plainly as words, "I can *walk* alone, too."

Put it back again," said Ferdinand, standing still in the street.

Agnes laughed and replaced her hand. "Why don't you talk to me?" she asked.

"That isn't necessary," he replied.

"Then I will give in and talk to you. There are many things I want to ask you. I hope Mrs. Ballington and her sons are well."

"I believe they are. I haven't been in Winston for a week."

He was returning to his home then. That accounted for his passing through Kent.

While she was thinking of something else to say, a reminiscent smile came to Ferdinand Ballington's lips, and presently he looked down upon her in amusement. "Your anthem," he said, "made me think of the time my mother made me commit the twenty-third Psalm to memory. I was six years old, and the only thing that aroused any interest in me was the phrase, Thou anointest my head with oil.'"

Agnes looked up and caught his expression. She was conscious of a disagreeable sensation, but she answered naturally, "I learned it too, when I was little. It's a lovely psalm. I like to sing it."

"What do you find lovely in it?" pursued Ferdinand, still regarding her.

Agnes hesitated, then tried to tell him what he had asked. "I think it is the quiet. Then there is a lovely landscape. But, most of all, it's the something underneath the quiet—the rapture of gratitude. Every time I read it I can feel the same thing welling up in me, as clear and full as the still waters." She lifted her face with an eagerness of look which Ferdinand had early noticed in her, and exclaimed, "How surprised the shepherd David would have been if he could have looked on all the peoples who should sing his song! It's a wonderful thing for a song to fill the whole earth."

Ferdinand watched her, enjoying the effect which the Sidney's eyes and the naiveté of mind which he felt in Agnes made upon him. "She has the eyes of a strange woman and the heart of a child," he reflected, pleased at his Biblical phraseology.

Her enthusiasm for David, however, was a little trying, and he could not help replying, although indulgently, "David had all the attributes of a good musician, so it is only right that his song should fill the earth! but it's rather hard on the Deity that such a man should be spoken of as after the Lord's own heart—a man who committed every crime in the calendar."

"The times were different then," explained Agnes earnestly, "and he sincerely repented." She was surprised and hurt at her companion's levity in speaking of the sweet singer of Israel.

The gentle dignity which came over her with the words and the open look she gave him as she raised her cold-flushed face to his stirred the young man's longings. She drew her plaid closer about her throat, and the movement called his attention to the fact that it was the only bit of color she wore. He was not ordinarily intuitive, but he could not fail to see the poverty which strove thus to supplement the mourning garments which were insufficient against the winter cold. He drew her arm more firmly within his own, and saw visions of sealskins which he hoped one day to bestow upon her.

The silence between them became so grave that Ferdinand aroused himself and asked her if she still kept up her interest in Winston College.

The girl's expression changed instantly. "Yes, indeed," she replied; "my class graduates this year."

"You lose little by not being among them," Ferdinand returned considerately. "The college is too old-fashioned and Puritanical. Those Puritan ancestors of ours are a nuisance."

Agnes looked up again disturbed. Why should he speak like this? "How can you say that of men who did what they have done?" she demanded with quick rebuke. "Think of living your whole life for duty and principle."

"But supposing there were no such thing as principle, only custom?" he queried.

"No such thing as principle!" exclaimed Agnes in astonishment. Unconsciously she stopped walking, and her next words were accompanied by a gesture that implied finality, "You don't know my mother!"

Then she resolved to bring the conversation up out of deep water. "Does Tom Ballington play the flute now?" she asked determinedly.

Ferdinand preferred the Puritans to Tom as a subject of conversation, but he answered with patient courtesy, "I believe he has given it up. Metal work is his fad, now."

"I think you said you are not a musician," Agnes continued in a business-like tone.

"No, I never have been able to afford that luxury."

"You are fond of music, though, aren't you?"

"I like to watch you sing."

"Thanks," she said with some hauteur. "But I didn't mean that. I meant really good music."

"Don't you consider your own music good?"

He thought of her abandon in singing at Winston as he spoke, and immediately afterwards of the quiet with which she then had met his compliment. The fire and vitality of the girl stimulated him, but those moods of dignity and control which unexpectedly crossed her spirits checked and baffled him.

She spoke in one of these now as she answered him. "No. I used to, but I've learned better. I know I have an uncommon voice, but it needs much work upon it."

There was a purpose in her words which moved him to say, "You speak as though you were ambitious to become a singer?" There was a certain hardness in his tone, and involuntarily he checked their pace in order to gain time for argument, for they were approaching Agnes' home.

"I am. It is my talent. I don't want to wrap it in a napkin."

They reached the gate as she replied, but he delayed to open while he still held her hand within his arm. "The walk has been too short," he said, with unmistakable regret. "I wish it had been long enough for me to convince you that the career of a professional singer is too hard and too thankless a one for you. Perhaps we may continue the conversation some other time."

Agnes made no reply, and Ferdinand opened the gate and allowed her to precede him up the steps.

As she turned at the top to speak to him, he carefully removed her shawl from her shoulders and was folding it up, when the front door opened and a party of callers just leaving blocked the doorway. As Agnes stepped past them into the hall, she was embarrassed to recognize in the callers John Talbot, his wife Molly, and their three-year-old boy. Talbot was a brakeman, and had been a member of her father's Sunday-school class. Before ninety-nine people out of a hundred Agnes was rather proud than otherwise to greet the humbler of her acquaintance. Unfortunately, she had with her to night the hundredth man, and she was mortified by the inevitable introduction. Mrs. Sidney, however, was untroubled by incongruities, and took the occasion to tell Mr. Ballington that if he were as good a man as Talbot by the time he reached the brakeman's age he might be satisfied with himself.

"Get a lump of sugar for Sidney, Agnes, said Mrs. Sidney as the child was ready for the evening ride home. "I always let my children have sweets, Mr. Ballington. Children need sweet things, and it does them good."

"I believe Herbert Spencer says the same thing," responded Mr. Ballington.

"Does he? Well, he is right. Good-by, John. Good-by, Molly. We'll be out to dinner on Wednesday. Agnes, John and Molly have asked us out to a boiled dinner next Wednesday. Kiss Auntie Sidney good-by, Sidney!"

Agnes closed the door behind the visitors with a feeling of relief, and returned to the parlor in time to hear her mother saying to the hundredth man, "Yes, I like a boiled dinner, and so does Agnes. A little pork cooked with the corned beef improves it."

Agnes did like a boiled dinner with a little pork cooked with the corned-beef, but now she blushed at her tastes. She was desperate to change the topic under discussion.

Ferdinand observed her embarrassment, and with a conversational inspiration came to her relief. He felt it desirable to get on friendly terms with Agnes' mother as soon as possible, and he combined chivalry with business by remarking, "Your old-fashioned church building has a dignity which the new churches nowadays can't get. I am surprised that your congregation had the wisdom to keep it as it is."

Mrs. Sidney's face kindled. "How glad I am to hear you say that!" she exclaimed. "It was Stephen and I who saved the old church. Most people like the new ones best. Did you notice the walnut wood-work?"

Ferdinand replied mendaciously in the affirmative, and then described his mother's fruitless struggle to save the old church building in Winston.

Agnes felt a fascination in the gravity and directness of this controlled man. She knew that there were strong emotions underneath, and something told her that these were for her. She sat a little back of her mother and watched their caller as he talked to Mrs. Sidney.

When he rose to leave, Agnes went with him into the hall.

He put on his ulster with its heavy cape, and then said, as he stood hat in hand, "I shall remember this evening. Have I your permission to come again?"

"Come whenever you are in town," she answered, and as she said the words she felt them to acknowledge even then a bond.

"I shall make it a point to be in town," he returned without smiling. Then he said good-night and opened the door.

Agnes stepped forward to close it, and as she did so, he turned upon the veranda and looked at her. Then he put on his hat, and she heard his footsteps, with a very slight drag of the left foot, going down the path.

"Come here, Agnes," called her mother from the sitting room. "I want you to read the letter I have written to Mr. Stoddard. I've told him you can come to New York."

For weeks Agnes hardly had dared to hope for this news. Now she hesitated, then excused herself from her mother, and went at once upstairs. She retired in the dark, re-living his last look. She felt a fire flare through her veins, and with it stole a strange faintness—the fever and languor as old as human love.

CHAPTER IV

A WEEK passed, and Ferdinand came again. Agnes soon began to look for him every Thursday. She put off going to New York until the following fall, and meantime life in Kent had taken on splendor. Ferdinand was accustomed to call for her at the church at the close of the early choir rehearsal, and they would walk home together. There they would find the shades drawn, the lamps lighted, a back-log blazing in the old-fashioned brick fire-place, where they toasted bread and cheese and roasted chestnuts in the ashes. They could hear the wind and snow and hail outside, and sometimes Winter would come in to stand before the open fire in the square person of Dr. Quinn, covered with icicles from a long country ride.

Sometimes they would talk and read until late, but commonly they gave up part or all of the time to another entertainment. Mrs. Sidney long ago had sat in judgment upon popular games. "We'll have to keep a close rein on Agnes. She's hankering after gambling games," she once had warned her husband, whereupon the doctor exhibited a characteristic method of his in dealing with dangerous allurements, namely,—the substitution for them of something more attractive which was at the same time innocuous. The result was that he introduced into their circle in Kent the Rajah of amusements, which stands with a smile of oriental subtlety equally aloof from vulgar chance or stupid mathematics, the only game worthy of great men—chess.

Agnes was a brilliant chess-player. Singularly enough, chess happened to be the one indoor recreation which Ferdinand professed to enjoy, and he proposed the game himself. Agnes brought out with pride the unique set of antique ivories, which had been given to her father along with other curios, by a Chinaman whose family he had attended for years. Evening after evening Ferdinand and she sat opposite each other, silent as idols, while between them a mimic war was waged by warriors yellow with age. Powers advanced and laid down their lives in defense of their sovereign and his courtiers; knights challenged each other haughtily; perilous intrigues were carried on between bishops and queens! castles were stormed; even kings now and then made an independent strut under cover of their retinue; and through it all the idols sat huge and impassive, watching each set of puppets play out their desperate game, and then sweeping them from the board to watch another campaign on the same field between the same warriors in another generation, with other plots covering the same passions.

At first Agnes held her own, but soon she began to be afraid of that firm hand encircled with the stiff cuff-rim, as it moved slowly back and forth over the board, and before long she acknowledged to herself her inability to cope with its owner. One thing consoled her pride: that although Ferdinand now usually won, he never showed a disposition to give her points, or to offer her any other advantage, and she interpreted this as courtesy.

Perhaps owing to her realization of his superior mental discipline, Agnes cherished the more her power over him. She knew that if she wished she could with a glance disconcert him for the moment, and cause hesitation in his speech. But he never showed confusion. His pauses were at times conspicuous, but when that indomitable voice began again, it always was under command, the train of thought never suffered, the man's mental vision never blurred.

One evening in May when they had been standing by the open window to smell the budding grape-vines, Agnes said to him, "My cousin Fred and his wife returned yesterday. They are to have a supper party Monday at their home on West Hill. Beatrice told me to tell you that she would be happy to have you come. Your cousins are coming over from Winston." She waited a moment and added one sentence more, "I hope you can come," and she colored vividly.

Ferdinand hesitated. She thought that he was about to decline. Her suspicion of antagonism between him and Beatrice recurred to her, nor was this suspicion entirely dispelled when a moment later he asked, "I may accompany you?"

"Yes, thank you. That will be pleasant."

All day Monday a storm threatened. Light thunder rumbled fitfully from time to time, and lightning flashed, but the rain waited for the ominous afternoon to pass.

Ferdinand came for her with a carriage, and although the drops were not yet falling, he held his umbrella over her as she hurried down the path. As he opened the gate a gust of wind tore the honeysuckle vine from the veranda.

The horses were pawing and tossing their heads. Ferdinand helped her into the coupé and entered it after her.

She shivered as the door of the carriage shut with its clean click, and drew her cape close. "I like this," she said with tingling nerves. "You are early, though. We shall be the first guests," and her tawny eyes darkened as she looked at him.

"I did so purposely," he answered.

The driver touched up his horses, and they rode straight into the storm. A black pall rose higher up the sky as they advanced. Now and then, a flash of lightning pierced the gloom. To the south along the horizon, a bank of clouds rolled up like flame. They and the drifting rain above them looked like a prairie on fire. Suddenly the first gust whipped the windows; there was a dash of water, a salute of thunder, a hiss of rain driving against them, and then they seemed plunged into a wild tumult. A pair of crows passed, driven on heavy wings before the wind. As they approached the base of the hill a drove of horses in a meadow were rushing panic-stricken hither and thither, and night was closing in.

Now they had reached the fork of the road. Off to the left Fred and Beatrice were waiting for their guests. The horses veered to the right and raced along the road that skirted the foot-hill.

For a delirious second Agnes did not correct the driver's mistake. She let herself give up to an ecstatic fancy that she was being kidnapped and carried away in mad flight to the fortresses of the mountains. The next second she exclaimed, "Stop him! He is going the wrong way."

She was struck with the strange sound of her voice, and recollected that neither of them had spoken during the ride.

"Are you afraid?" asked Ferdinand, in a low tone.

"No," she said after a moment.

It was the only time they had been alone together except during the walks from choir rehearsal. Mrs. Sidney's indefatigable presence when her daughter received callers had been turned into a maxim by Fred, who once said that for a man to make a success of business he must stick to it as Aunt Kate did to the parlor when Agnes had company.

"The driver is following directions," said Ferdinand. "He will take us to your cousin's in time. I have something to say to you—and I wanted you alone."

"Yes?" said Agnes, quivering.

There was a very long pause. By a sudden flare of lightning, she saw that his face was drawn hard with emotion.

"I cannot live without you! You are like light and air!" he said, and he put out his arms and drew her to him passionately.

She did not resist. The carriage, the hills, the whole world reeled, as she felt the violence of his embrace. When she heard his voice again, there was a new tone in it, a vibration which thrilled her from head to foot.

"When will you marry me?" he asked.

"I don't know. My mother must say."

"Let it be soon."

"Yes." He sat now with one arm about her, the other tense hand holding hers. Her cape became disarranged, and one by one, the petals of the orchids he had given her, and which she wore at her breast, fell upon their clasped hands.

After a time the driver turned and started back the way they had come. The rain fell in a steady downpour around them.

"What are you thinking?" Agnes whispered.

"That I should like to kiss you. Will you let me?"

He felt her face lifting to his, and presently he said, "That is the first love-kiss I have ever given a woman, and no other than you shall ever know one from me."

"When did you first care for me?"

"When I was born."

At last they heard the splash of another carriage passing them; they felt the tug of the horses as they ascended the incline of the driveway; there were sounds from the porte-cochére; the carriage stopped, and the door was opened from the outside.

Agnes stepped out, and went through the hall and up the stairs ahead of her escort. She let the maid remove her wraps as in a dream, and did not speak to some acquaintances who were leaving the dressing-room. Ferdinand waited for her impatiently in the upper hall. They passed along the heavily-paneled corridor between the rows of palms. The orchids were gone; nothing relieved the black of her attire.

Beatrice, with arms and neck heavy with topazes, came forward affectionately. "Agnes!" she cried eagerly.

Her expression changed as she saw the look on the girl's face. Her manner was more subdued as she kissed Agnes and her eyes rested upon her questioningly as she released her.

Then she turned to Ferdinand with a frank stare. "To think you actually came! Of course I am delighted to see you."

Immediately upon the last words she took Ferdinand by the elbow with one hand, made a large gesture with the other, announced with intolerable effusiveness, "An old family friend, Ferdinand Ballington," and then suddenly turned away, leaving Ferdinand in the midst of a stiff bow to a semi-circle of ducking people in front of him.

One man in the semi-circle grew into prominence from the fact that he did not bow. Agnes recognized him, caught the glance which passed between him and Beatrice, a glance which spoke unmistakable dislike of Ferdinand, and a consternation which she instinctively felt was for herself. The man was Tom Ballington.

CHAPTER V

LATER that evening, after her guests had said good-night, Beatrice drew a breath of relief and strolled into the conservatory off the drawing-room. Fred was outside seeing the last carriage away from the house. The conservatory faced the village in the valley and from its window Beatrice could see the lights of the town. The storm was over and the moon showed dark clumps of wet foliage upon the hillside. A syringa bush moved its dripping branches just outside and brushed against the lattice. Above her hung a tropical creeper over-trailing its moss cage, and its florid, yellow flowers just touched her hair.

She stood in relaxed content waiting for her husband. The evening had gone successfully. Fred's looks had satisfied her pride and it had given her pleasure to present him to his townsfolk as the master of her luxurious establishment. Fred had behaved irreproachably in acceding to every suggestion she had expressed so far as to the arrangement of their domestic affairs. The time was ripe at last, she felt, for her to broach the subject of his leaving the bank. She was congratulating herself on her patience and self-control in having let that matter rest until she was sure of conducting it to a happy issue, when she heard her husband's voice calling her.

"Here I am in the conservatory!" she returned buoyantly.

A moment later Fred entered. His face lighted with pleasure as he caught sight of her before the window. The tropical glow of color in the creeper and the topazes, the shining folds of her satin gown, the drift of laces that fell from arms and bosom, the rich tints of hair, face and shoulders, the grace and latent strength of the young figure, filled him with the triumph of possession. Tonight it was accompanied by an anxiety which he tried to disguise from himself. He approached her, and stood looking at her thoughtfully.

Beatrice did not seem to notice his silence, however, and presently she put a hand on his arm.

"Come over here, Fred. I want to talk to you," she said, drawing him over to the bench under the window.

The window-sill was banked with violets, whose damp odor in after years always brought with it a fleeting memory of a moon-lit conservatory with palms and tropic creepers and a dark woman in amber jewels.

Beatrice slipped down to a stool at Fred's feet and threw an arm over his knees.

"How wonderful Agnes looked tonight," she said reminiscently. "That was a made-over dress she had on, too. How she carries those plain things." Beatrice looked down at her own jewels.

Then she took down her arm and leaned her head against his knee. Both were preoccupied, and for some moments, they waited in quiet. She was thinking how she would suggest that they travel for a time, when he had left the bank, then perhaps go into diplomatic life. For Beatrice loved the world: its excitement, brilliance, intrigues and display. She was not morally sensitive, although she had shrewdly pitched her affections upon a husband who would not have to be watched. That would leave time and energy for other things. She felt sure that no amount of freedom or even extravagance would corrupt Fred. The question was how to launch him.

Fred was thinking that he had missed getting hold of that serious-mindedness in his wife which he had divined in his betrothed. A turmoil attendant upon the building and furnishing of the great house had swept them apart in the weeks preceding and following the wedding. Their attention had been focused on material things. His longing for a closer intimacy in the noblest sense had been disappointed. There was no time for it. He saw a hereditary impulse in Beatrice to indulge herself and those whom she loved without stint in the good things of this world. In time, it would become all of life to her, as it was to her father. She never had had the discipline of self-denial as a preliminary to attainment. The trend of her life had been toward enjoyment of easily-gotten luxuries, an enjoyment which in weak natures easily degenerates into monstrous riot! but Beatrice was not weak, and Fred saw that in her the tendency was not toward intemperance of the senses, but rather in the line of craving for emotional excitement. Restlessness was growing upon her. He must touch in her the dormant longing for the real things of life and awaken her from the phantasmagoria which she had hitherto regarded. He thought of a way to lead up to the subject, and he was unconscious that the way he chose was a peace-offering to his own hurt pride. He leaned over and tried to put into her hand a roll of bills.

"What is that for, Fred?" she asked, drawing her hand away sharply. She was on the alert at once and looked up keenly to meet his answering look of determination.

In a flash, the benevolent schemes of both for the future were lost sight of in the clash of will over something nearby. The trifle which Fred had intended to introduce a spiritual union all at once became ultimate.

"For my tuxedo," he replied briefly.

Beatrice made a gesture of dissent. "That's all right," she said nonchalantly; "I gave it to you. You didn't really need it, as you said. I wanted you to have it."

Fred's expression was gentle. He, as well as Beatrice, was endeavoring to conciliate. "It is natural for you to be generous, Beatrice, and I know you mean it kindly. But we must understand each other before it gets any harder. I didn't say anything at first. Buy what you like for yourself besides what little I can give you. Nobody knows how glad I would be if I could have given all this to you." His gesture took in their surroundings. "As it is, the only thing that can give me any self-respect is to stop being a pensioner and live within my salary."

"Salary!" Beatrice spoke with unrestrained but not irritable feeling. "Oh, Fred, why do you talk about salary? This is all yours as much as it is mine. Look at the money we have, dearest, my General and you and I! What is the use of your spending your youth in Bucher's penny-bank? You belong to our family now."

Fred's color rose. "I never should have asked you to marry me, Beatrice," he replied still gently, "if I had not promised myself a different relation. I felt that I had something to give, as well as you; but so far I have been only a receiver."

"Nonsense, Fred!" said Beatrice heartily. "You have given me everything you had. In spirit you have given me the whole world, and that is the whole thing. Don't let's haggle over details. What does it matter whether a few thousands of dollars come from the Mott side or the Sidney side? It's all in the family."

There was reserve in Fred's tone as he rejoined, "I can't consider myself as having any right to your father's money, Beatrice. That is all in your family, not ours."

Beatrice sat up and wheeled round to face him. "I am my father's only child," she said crisply.

She caught a curious flicker on Fred's face, and her own darkened instantly.

"Don't you ever dare to put that thought in words!" she said with suppressed fury. "I'll not listen to one word against my father from you, of all men in the world." She sprang to her feet and stood over him threateningly.

After a moment Fred spoke in a deprecating tone. "Surely you don't think me capable of that, Beatrice." But his look had probed to the sore place under Beatrice's loyalty.

"To think a thing is as bad as to say it!" she flared out. "You have lived all your life here and you are as narrow-minded as a woman. My father has his faults, but he is a prince among men as you find them out in the world. I'm proud to be known as his daughter anywhere—even in this saintly town," she said scornfully.

Fred's face grew stern but his voice was quiet as he replied, "It is quite true I look at some things the way women do, and I was thankful that, although with no credit to myself, I could offer you something I prize more than anything else in the world. That is a name that for many years, at least, has been stainless. It was all I had to give you, and I am sorry if you think I overrate it."

For a moment the vehemence of Beatrice's feelings prevented her from speaking. Fred was shocked at the look she gave him. A bewildered warning of danger ahead cooled his resentment. A feeling of compunction at having unintentionally hurt her feelings softened his mood.

"Your father is a generous and straightforward man, Beatrice," he hastened to add. "I respect his good qualities and I am very grateful for his treatment of me. I hope we may never recur to this painful conversation. You and I are concerned alone with our own family life. The dearest ambition I have is to live in perfect harmony with you in a family life in which each shall keep self-respect while loving and respecting the other."

At last Beatrice's conflicting impulses struggled into words. "Just what kind of a life do you propose?" she demanded.

Fred hesitated, desiring to make it as attractive as possible.

"Much the kind of life that we are now living," he replied at length, "you to have the exclusive possession of your own property, allowing me, if you see fit, to look after it as some small contribution to the support of my family; allowing me, in addition, to do what I can for you out of my own salary."

He looked at her wistfully. He had not said one word of that which had filled his mind when he started out. The conversation had all come back to money. The best he had offered was to take charge of her property and live a life much like their present one.

Beatrice returned his regard for some moments in silence. Then she burst forth with mingled rage, disappointment, and tenderness. "Fred, you're an ass! You'll have to learn to manage me better than this. You'd better take lessons of my father."

"Do you wish you had married a man like your father?" Fred asked with his heart in his throat, for fear of a second explosion.

But his wife's mood had changed. "No," she said listlessly; "I took you because you were different from all the men I ever knew. I didn't care whether your family was good or bad. We mustn't quarrel any more. It doesn't lead to anything."

Fred's heart fell as the meaning of the words grew upon him. How futile had been his effort to arrive at a better understanding! He had succeeded only in making the future look less attractive to them both than it had looked before.

A moment later Beatrice sank down on his knee and put a hand on each shoulder. "Fred," she said with an entire change of manner, "Agnes and Ferdinand Ballington are engaged."

Fred started. "Who told you that?" he exclaimed in astonishment.

"My own eyes," she replied bitterly. "To think she would pass over Donald and take him! Why, if she didn't like Donald, why couldn't it have been Tom?"

A look of disappointment followed her last words. "What a lovely situation that would have been!" she exclaimed regretfully.

"What would have been?" queried Fred.

"Oh, Agnes refusing Ferdinand and marrying Tom."

"Beatrice, I have wanted to know for a long time what you and Tom Ballington have against Ferdinand," Fred said earnestly; "I have always heard him very highly spoken of. If he isn't the right kind of man, Agnes mustn't be allowed to marry him."

"Well, he isn't the right kind of man," exclaimed Beatrice impetuously, rising to her feet. "You can put up your bottom dollar on that. I have hated him ever since I was a child. He is a mean, hard man."

"If you know anything definite, I think you ought to tell me," Fred objected. "You must have some reason for hating him."

"Definite! Reason! I knew you wouldn't understand an antipathy. Well, here is something you can understand, but it is really nothing to my constitutional hatred. When Tom and I were going together, he gave Tom a long lecture one day warning him that he would be a fool to marry me. And after I became engaged to you, he said that I did it out of pique because Tom had followed his advice and thrown me over."

A black look passed across Fred's face. "Did he say that?"

Beatrice's face lightened as she saw her husband's anger. "Don't let it worry you to that extent," she said with returning good humor. "I am not the only one he has tried to injure. He tried to get the best of Father on a railroad deal, and he would have done it only one of his tools at the last minute couldn't bring himself to ruin my father. So he went back on Ferdinand and told the whole scheme in time for us to get out without losing very much."

"Who was the tool?"

"The banker, Balch. We lent him some money a couple of years before when he couldn't give security."

"Balch a tool in an underhand deal!" exclaimed Fred incredulously; "Balch is an honorable man!"

"Of course. I don't suppose there ever was a word exchanged between him and Ferdinand on the subject. But you may be sure there was a silent pressure brought to bear on Balch that he didn't dare resist."

Beatrice dwelt upon this part of Ferdinand's career with satisfaction, but Fred's brow did not clear. "I am going to tell Aunt Kate. I wish we had known this was going on."

"So do I," assented Beatrice, "but it is too late to change Agnes' opinion now. She is the important one."

"No, she isn't," said Fred with conviction; "Aunt Kate is the one."

"Well," said Beatrice impatiently, "you won't find out anything against Ferdinand. He is too smart. He has an excellent business reputation. When he does anything a bit risky he does it through other people. His workmen get the highest wages and every municipal improvement counts on him for a moderate subscription. You might as well save your breath. What good will it do to tell Aunt Kate I don't like him?"

She turned away from him petulantly. "I am going to bed. I wish you would see if Saunders has locked up the silver. Good-night."

"Good-night," replied Fred, looking after her with preoccupied eyes.

Saunders was turning off the lights.

For a moment, Beatrice gleamed down the alley of over-arching palms. Then the lights went out. Fred thought she had left the conservatory, when her voice came to him once more.

"Fred!"

"Yes. What is it?"

"You'll let me give you that tuxedo, won't you?" The voice was pleading under its pride.

Fred was reluctant to answer, but he told himself that he must be firm. Concession now would place him in a worse position than his old one had been.

"Let's not open that discussion again, Beatrice," he said kindly. He thought she had gone again, when her voice came out of the darkness a second time.

"I was going to ask a greater favor of you, Fred. I'll ask nothing now but the tuxedo. It means a good deal to me. Don't be stubborn."

Fred's discomfort was passing into irritation. "See here, Bee," he said, rising and groping his way toward her. He tried to make his tone cheery, half-jesting. "I'd like to have an impartial witness as to which of us two is more stubborn."

"You make a big mistake tonight," her voice came back to him instantly. "You'll be sorry some day you didn't compromise."

There was a soft rustle of satin trailing away. A feeling of loneliness gathered upon him as he felt his way into the great drawing-room. Huge pieces of carved furniture blocked his way. Rugs impeded his feet. When he reached the doorway into the hall, his fingers touched a curtain of Gobelin tapestry. The newel-post of the staircase had been plundered from a moldering Venetian palace. Fred groaned as he touched its traceries. What wealth was this in which he lived! He could give her nothing that she needed. What a mockery his position was! He had no authority. He was a guest in his own home. Would he always be a welcome one? Ferdinand Ballington had said she married him only for pique! His heart was heavy with grief and foreboding. The deep gong of the hall clock struck one. The solemn tone vibrated off into the dark, and he slowly began to mount the stairs.

CHAPTER VI

WHEN Agnes, accompanied by Ferdinand, reached home again after Beatrice's supper-party, Ferdinand left her at the door.

Agnes found her mother sitting up for her, as was her custom. Mrs. Sidney was nodding as she sat beside the sitting-room table, and woke with a start when her daughter came into the room.

Agnes went up and kissed her. "Mother," she said, "Ferdinand has asked me to marry him, and I have said I will. He didn't come in because it was so late, but he is going to see you."

The news had come sooner than Mrs. Sidney expected, but she took it quietly. She put out her hand and drew up to the table beside her a chair which had been turned toward the wall. Aunt Mattie's shoes were still on the floor in front of it, where Mrs. Sidney had removed them.

"Sit down, Agnes," said her mother. "I want to talk to you."

Agnes took the seat with foreboding. The solemnity in her mother's face drove away the afterglow of Ferdinand's presence.

"Agnes," said the elder woman, looking at the girl with anxious care in her steady gaze, "I saw when Ferdinand first came here to see you that he loved you, and I asked God to direct him and to direct us. If God had meant me to root out this love-making I think He would have made it clear to me. The Ballingtons are good people. Your father knew them and respected them. Ferdinand is known to be an upright and moral man. It might have been a man we didn't know about and a stranger to your father. On the other hand, Agnes, Ferdinand isn't a Christian man. 'He who is not for Me is against Me.' Have you thought of all these things?"

"We have talked of them before, mamma," said Agnes in a low voice, knowing as she said the words that though she had talked of these things with her mother, she never had felt them fully till tonight. Even now, it was not anxiety about Ferdinand's religious views that turned her faint with apprehension, but fear lest her mother should ask her to give him up.

In the wait before her mother spoke again the irrevocableness of what had happened came over the girl. She felt herself hardening against renunciation, but along with this she recognized the selfishness of her instinct, and there was a shock in the sight of herself as she now knew herself, absolutely fixed on holding to Ferdinand Ballington. She put her hand on the table to support herself. For some moments she could not command her voice to speak. She remembered that six months before she had groveled in anguish of soul, beseeching God to vouchsafe her some way to expiate her sin—any way He would. Then this thing had come, not slowly so that she could reason about it, but, as it seemed, suddenly, full-grown. And now—was this the way to expiate? to give up—this?

Agnes recognized her situation. She knew, too, that for her there was but one outcome to that struggle, that she had been bound over by generations of stern and righteous forefathers to the more than Spartan law, "If thy right hand offend thee, cut it off. It is better to enter into life maimed than having two hands to be cast into hell."

"Mother," she said, and her face was ashen, "there is something I must say to you, in spite of feeling that I do not mean a word of it. I am hooting myself in derision for saying it. Yet I will hold to what I say. Tell me to give up Ferdinand if it seems right to you, and I—I promise you, on the memory of my father, I never will marry him. I never voluntarily will see him again. I will—give him—up."

She dropped into her chair again, her head sank upon her clasped arms on the table, and shook with the convulsion that followed the agony of soul.

Mrs. Sidney sat still and waited until the spasm had spent itself, but to herself she kept repeating fervently, "O God! I thank Thee."

Then she leaned over and laid her hand, which still had a thimble upon one finger, on her daughter's arm. "No, Agnes, I don't ask that of you. If I had been going to ask that I should have stopped Ferdinand's coming here before this. I have been sore troubled all these weeks. If it had been Donald, the way would have been clear. But God's ways are not our ways. I have talked to Ferdinand when we have been alone. It may be that God is using this way to touch Ferdinand's heart. Have you ever asked him to come out and make a stand for Christ?"

"No."

It had, indeed, often occurred to Agnes to speak to Ferdinand upon this subject, but every time she had come near to doing so an uncontrollable reluctance had taken possession of her. She never had doubted that in time he would take this all-important step. All the good people she had known sooner or later professed religion, and she had consoled herself for her hesitation by thinking that after marriage conversations which now seemed difficult would shape themselves naturally and easily. She would have marveled, indeed, had anyone told her that men and women often live their lives together in the closest of relationships, and find it easier to confess an ideal, a yearning of the soul, to a passing stranger than to that other who has learned intimately the humdrum current of every-day companionship. During all these weeks wherein she was thrilling with the exquisite reticence that surrounds young love, it would have been hard for her to believe that there comes a time between wife and husband when a second tragic reticence exists concerning the early confessions of heart and soul they once exchanged; a reticence which covers on the part of each in finer natures the pitiful acknowledgment of unattained ideas of self-reproach, and of mortification, which shields itself in silence; while ignoble natures expose themselves in jest and mutual raillery concerning their dreams of youth.

"Will you ask him?" continued Mrs. Sidney.

Agnes' hands clasped each other. She drew a painful breath. "Yes."

"Then, I will leave it to you. You can do, Agnes, what God requires of you. You have shown tonight that you can pluck out your right eye and cast it from you. I am not afraid to trust Stephen Sidney's daughter anywhere the Lord may send her."

Agnes felt a soul-cheer that went out from her mother's gaze. It was as if a veteran in a sublime warfare had fallen upon the unexpected heroism of a recruit, and had called out, "Hail! brother."

A joy so great that it was pain rushed over the girl. "You mean, mother—?" and the color surged back to her face.

She stopped. She was shocked once more with the selfishness at the bottom of her impulse. It was consent to the marriage which she craved, not, Ferdinand's soul. She looked at her mother helplessly, saying nothing, alarmed at what she thought her own hardness of heart.

"We must leave that in God's hands," said Mrs. Sidney. "'In all thy ways acknowledge Him, and He will direct thy paths.' Good-night, Agnes. God bless you, dear child. I trust you."

The tears flowed down both faces as mother and daughter kissed each other. Agnes took her candle and went to her own room. Her load was immeasurably lightened by her mother's conditional approbation of the engagement. She again saw divine approval in the joy that was hers. Yet in spite of her returning faith that the happiness in store for her was a promised land, her direct heritage from God, the signal in the distance was no longer a pillar of fire illuminating a quiet night with supernatural glory, but it was changing to a pillar of cloud brooding over a day-weary earth. There it hung ahead of her, an ominous guide waiting on the outskirts of the wilderness whither we all must go for our temptation or our years of wandering.

When Agnes reached her own room she set the candle down on the floor by a chintz-covered chest in one corner. In this chest were the papers she found in her father's desk, of which he had spoken to her. One, a sealed envelope, had borne the direction, "For my daughter Agnes to read when she is thinking of marrying." This package had consumed her with interest for months, but she never had felt justified in opening it until now.

She found the envelope and had untied the string which her father's fingers had fastened, when she heard her mother speaking to her from the foot of the stairs. She arose and went into the hall to answer.

"Don't sit up reading tonight," said Mrs. Sidney. "We shall both have a hard day's work tomorrow. Go right to bed, and try to go to sleep."

Agnes acquiesced. There was a kind of peace in obeying her mother in the smallest detail. She put aside the letter which now seemed of such absorbing interest to her, and went to bed.

But not to sleep! Ferdinand had come and gone. His presence haunted the room, his voice was in her ears, his face met her in the dark wherever she looked. No more renunciation tonight! Let it come in the future—years long—but now let her give up her thoughts to all that could make absence and heart-hunger endurable! She had lived much since that morning. It was sweet to think of him. He was thinking, too, of her, and this thought was so lovely that she was almost in tears at the certainty of it. After it all she was not satisfied, no, not tonight. What she wanted was no brief moment stolen from a jostling crowd, but a long communion in quiet like the night about her. Then, perhaps, she might tell him all that consumed her; then perhaps he might read her soul, and she might feel that he opened the secret chamber of his and took her in. The foundations of the great deep had been broken up. She was tossed from billow to billow, and she longed for the heart that could understand as the storm-beaten sailor longs for the quiet harbor. She thought of their union as no longer if—if, but where—when! Hour by hour she lay unvisited by sleep, her wide eyes gazing on the visions that allure in the delirium of that fierce, sweet fever.

As she sank at last into slumber that shadowy world that had wavered before her waking eyes came nearer in vaguely remembered harmonies. The last thing she realized before passing into dreamlessness was a chorus of women's voices singing through the night out of distance. To her it was only an echo from the buoyant college years that formed so large a part of her memories. Tannhäuser was but a name to her; the Venus-music was a girl's part-song led by a German music teacher. Yet tonight as it eddied around her it filled her darkening senses with uncontrollable longing, and she was borne out to oblivion on its tumultuous tide.

Naht euch dem Lande
Naht euch dem Strande,
Wo in den Armen
Glühender Liebe,
Selig erwarmen,
Still eure Triebe.

CHAPTER VII

WHEN Agnes asked Ferdinand full-heartedly, upon their return to her house, to come in with her and tell her mother of their love, he had with some difficulty resisted. It was a new and sweet indulgence to him to give up his will, for the time being, in response to a woman's influence, and only his long and habitual regard to policy saved him from presenting himself to Mrs. Sidney in his relaxed condition.

Upon leaving Agnes he did not go to the hotel immediately, but dismissed his carriage and walked for an hour or two through the still, wet streets of Kent, allowing himself to feel to the full the poignancy of the emotions which possessed him. He did not think, he only felt, abandoning himself to passion in order to get all there was out of it. Again and again he called up to his mind two pictures of Agnes: the first, as she came down the steps of her mother's house to the carriage, her hair wind-blown across her eyes as she met his look; the second, as she met him again with her orchids gone, in the upper corridor at Fred Sidney's. His cheeks burned as he persistently held this view of her in his memory—pale, beautiful, a star-like luminousness in her eyes, an unearthly grace in her motion. He knew that she was consumed with the memory of what they had experienced during their ride together and that the experience had transformed her. He remembered how she had stood a moment breathing deep, her beautiful neck and arms defined by the lines of her black dress, her face and manner suffused with unconscious feeling. He knew, and the knowledge thrilled him, that the flood-gates of her nature had opened, and that all the fullness of her vitality was pouring out toward him. It angered him to recall the memory of Beatrice which followed hard upon this, but he was unable to banish Fred's wife completely from his mind.

After a time Ferdinand checked himself and began to notice the houses he was passing, now and then one standing out from the rest with some show of town importance, others thriftily struggling to hold themselves, their yards, and their barns to the standards of local dignity. Ferdinand smiled as he looked at them and quickened his steps toward Agnes' home, which he thought he should like to pass on his way to the hotel. He felt a sense of satisfaction that he had been discerning enough to overlook much in Agnes' circumstances which would have deterred the ordinary man of his position from making her his choice, and he relished the anticipation of eventually displaying his discovery when he had relieved her of her prejudices, cultivated her mind, and given her person its proper setting. She was full of health and life, of richness and roundness. Her very lack of development attracted him, for it meant that she had but few false notions to be rid of, and then he could freely train her into the perfect woman for a man. She would be an ornament and a comfort to his house, would stimulate and reward his efforts, and, more than that, she could thrill him, at least for a time, and a longer time than most husbands enjoyed.

Ferdinand's cup of contentment continued to fill as he walked and thought, until at last he paused before the Sidney house. It was a nice little house, he told himself, as he looked at it, rather pretty with its vine-draped porch, old-fashioned blinds, and little tucked-up office in one wing. He felt a certain kinship with the poets who have sung of simple houses and loves and hopes. They were not so far astray, after all; they only did not understand themselves so well as he understood. Ferdinand did not deceive himself in the least; of that he felt quite sure.

When at last he was once more indoors at the hotel he put aside emotional and poetic, and therefore childish, things, and set himself seriously to the manly business in hand, that of surmounting the final and critical obstacle between him and the accomplishment of his purpose. Before he fell asleep that night, he had resolved how he should approach Mrs. Sidney.

Ferdinand called upon Mrs. Sidney the next morning. As he went up the steps of her home he drew out his watch, and seeing that it lacked but a few minutes of noon, he appeared satisfied. As he expected, he found Mrs. Sidney alone and busy. Agnes was at the Buchers', giving a lesson to little Alfred.

"Sit right down in the parlor and wait," said Mrs. Sidney cordially. "Agnes will be home to dinner in half an hour now. I'll just put on another plate for you. We're going to have a roe shad. Old Peter Osgood brought it in this morning."

"Thank you," answered Ferdinand, "but I am in haste. I have only a few minutes in town. It is you whom I wished to see."

Mrs. Sidney had stood waiting for his answer, and so Ferdinand had not accepted her invitation to be seated. Now, however, they both sat down, and each of the two strong faces settled at once into seriousness. To his straightforward request for Agnes' hand Mrs. Sidney frankly stated the one objection she had to an engagement.

"It would be hard for me to attend to my duties while in a state of uncertainty as to my relations with Agnes," Ferdinand said after a pause, and she read in his face that what he said was true. "I am not sure that we are so far apart as you think in regard to religion. In fact, I have often thought, Mrs. Sidney, that had our education been similar, we should have been in entire accord. Am I to understand that the only hesitation you have in accepting me, is in regard to my religious views?"

"Yes, Ferdinand, that's all," said Mrs. Sidney, meeting the young man's gaze with friendly eyes.

Ferdinand regarded her not unkindly and said respectfully, "When we last spoke of these matters, Mrs. Sidney, you asked me to make an effort to bring myself into sympathy with the Christian religion. I may say I have since done so."

Mrs. Sidney looked up quickly, and surprise gave way to gratitude and joy in her expression. "God will bless you, Ferdinand!" she said at length fervently. "Knock and it shall be opened unto you, seek and ye shall find.' God's promises are true."

"I cannot say that I am prepared to make a profession of faith," continued Ferdinand carefully, "but I can say this: if you will consent to this marriage, I promise you now that it shall be the conscientious effort of my life to come into sympathy with Agnes in all views, and most especially in those pertaining to religion. I have for some years owned a pew in the Presbyterian Church of Winston, but I have rarely attended church. I will, however, do so from now on with her. Until she and I are entirely in sympathy—and I may say that I have no doubt eventually we shall be—I will not permit myself to put the matter out of mind, or to relax my efforts in seeking this unison of feeling."

Mrs. Sidney's eyes were now overflowing. Surely God had answered her prayers. "I can ask no more than that, Ferdinand," she said, holding out her hand. "I would not want you to join the church till your heart is dedicated to the service of the Lord, but if you seek Him, you will find Him. He has said so, and His words are true."

"I have your consent, then, to the marriage?"

She thought a moment, and then said, "You have my consent, Ferdinand, and my prayers. She is a good girl. She was always like Stephen. He used to wake her up in the night and take her out in the dining-room to play with her when she was a little baby. When Helen was a baby he was away in the war. Agnes hasn't got any money, Ferdinand, but she's worthy of any man. She's been very good to me since Stephen died."

During the pause which followed Mrs. Sidney's reminiscences Ferdinand's quiet bearing suggested deference to them.

Then he said, "I should like to marry her in a month."

Mrs. Sidney awoke to the present. "In a month!" she exclaimed involuntarily.

He waited again for her to adjust herself to his wishes, then added, "I should like to take her to Europe, and my business will let me off in the summer better than in the winter."

"You want to marry her in a month. Four weeks!"

Ferdinand went on with soothing impassivity. "I have traveled considerably myself, but a trip of this sort would be of inestimable advantage to Agnes. I shall, of course, be able to provide for her abundantly. It will not be necessary for you to give yourself any trouble about preparations."

"Agnes shall have everything a girl needs," answered Mrs. Sidney briefly. "I wasn't thinking of that. A month seems pretty soon, but Stephen never believed in long engagements."

She waited. It cost a struggle to say the word.

"I should like to engage our passage without delay," continued Ferdinand, a slight urgency coloring his voice, and he rose and took up his hat from the floor. "We shall cross on the English line. It is the safest."

He stood waiting. Still Mrs. Sidney said nothing. Ferdinand saw that her mind was occupied. She was praying, although her eyes were open. At last the answer came.

"Be good to her, Ferdinand," she said, and she looked up to him with something of beseeching that indescribably saddened her face. "She was the apple of Stephen's eye."

"I shall make it an object of my life to do well by her," he replied earnestly.

He went to the door alone, for she remained where she was still silently praying.

Ferdinand waited an instant outside the gate. He felt a strong pull toward Mr. Bucher's house. "Self-denial for the present is the key of future success," he said grimly, and he turned and walked to the station.

CHAPTER VIII

MRS. SILAS BALLINGTON sat by her library table fingering a blue-covered book with lettered edges. Her hair rose in stately rolls from her forehead, and her face was judicial. Tom Ballington was sitting at the other side of the table. He looked straight before him at the floor; his legs were stretched stiffly in front of him and his hands were shoved into the pockets of his short morning-coat. Donald stood in front of the empty grate, one foot nervously pressing and re-pressing the crumpled corner of a handsome rug. His face showed his distress, and he looked uneasily from his mother to his brother.

"Here it is, Donald," said Mrs. Ballington, referring to a page near the front and another near the middle of the volume. "Here, in the front, it says—the letters 'a-b-c,' n-m-p,' 'x-y-z,' all mean 'slow payment.' Now, over here in the B's I read this: 'Ballington—Thomas F., Clerk in Ballington & Ballington—Mnfrs.—Car Springs—x-y-z.' Now, Donald, doesn't that mean what I said, that your brother has been advertised as a dishonest man?"

"Well, hardly that, mother," Donald answered slowly. "You take this a little too seriously. These trust-books are issued every six months. I've never seen Tom advertised in one before. You haven't been, have you, Tom?"

"Damned if I know!"

Donald spoke again instantly.

"This doesn't necessarily mean any disgrace, mother. I'm sure I don't know who could have reported Tom, but we'll see that—"

"I tell you!" exclaimed Tom, drawing up his knees suddenly, "I know who did it! It was—"

"Sh!" said Donald, frowning. "You've no right to say that. Whoever he was, he shall be paid, mother. I'm sorry you should have found the book."

"I'm very glad I found it," answered Mrs. Ballington significantly. "I mean to see this matter cleared up. What is the distinction in these letters—'a-b-c,' 'n-m-p,' x-y-z' all mean 'slow payment'? Why is the 'x-y-z' by Tom's name?"

Tom jumped up, and thrust his fists deeper into his pockets, curling in the edges of his jacket. "Oh, a-b-c means 'slow payment,' he said looking full at his mother, "and 'n-m-p' means 'slower yet,' and 'x-y-z' means 'really, too damned slow, you know!'"

"Donald," said Mrs. Ballington, rising, "do you think it's proper to allow your brother to use such language? You are just as irresponsible as your father was."

Donald left the grate to open the door for his mother, but as she was passing through he remarked with a worried expression, "I don't like Tom's swearing any better than you do, mother."

When the door closed after Mrs. Ballington, he added to Tom, "Since swearing is so inexpensive, I should think you might drop it, Tom."

Tom made no reply. His gorge was rising, as it always did on the periodical occasions when he had to ask Donald's help.

Donald waited a moment, then inquired shortly, "How much do you owe him?"

Tom turned on his heel instantly. "Owe whom?"

"You know."

"So you do think he did it?" exclaimed Tom with exasperated triumph.

"I don't know who did it," Donald answered cloudily, "but I think he'd better be paid."

"Well," said Tom airily, "there's just one thing hinders me from paying my debts, Donald."

"How much do you owe him?" repeated Donald, unmoved by his brother's attempt to introduce a little cheerful ease into the conversation.

Tom's dogged manner came back upon him. "Somewhere in the neighborhood of five hundred dollars."

"In the neighborhood of? Well, what does that mean?" persisted Donald.

"It's eight hundred and fifteen without interest."

"And interest for how long?"

"About two years."

"Give it to me in months." Donald had taken his notebook and pencil from his pocket.

"Oh—two years and nine months," exclaimed Tom vindictively.

The elder brother jotted down the figures. Then he went up to the table, and made out a check to his brother's name.

"Now, Tom," he said earnestly, handing it to him, "you let me see the receipt for this to-night. Don't buy any more old jewelry until you have the money to pay for it, and let this be the last time you go out of the family to borrow. Not that I want to keep lending you money," he added on second and wiser thought as he left his brother.

"You're a brick, Don," said Tom with the unction of relief, and he folded and pocketed the check. Then the spirit of the repentant moralist came upon him and he added, "You're the wisest of us after all, Don. You always keep out of trouble."

"God knows I have troubles enough," answered Donald as he went out into the hall.

Tom stood by the table for some moments following his mother's example in examining the trust-book. He let his eyes run through the two names above his own.

"Ballington, Donald S.—firm of Ballington & Ballington—Mnfrs.—Car Springs. H. G."

"Ballington, Ferdinand—firm Ballington & Ballington—Mnfrs.—Car Springs. G."

"H. G." muttered Tom, referring to the front page. "H. Here it is— prompt payment. G. G pays cash. Yes, I might have known it. The old spider would pay cash, of course." He shut the book together spitefully, and carried it to his own room.

When he again emerged he was dressed for the street. In the lower hall, he passed Donald, who was brushing his hat.

"Is Ferd to be at the office this morning?" Tom asked in a virtuously business-like tone, pausing near his brother.

Donald continued to brush. "I think not," he replied with a preoccupied air. After a pause he added, "You'll probably find him at the farm."

"Well, Don," said Tom benevolently, "if you brush that hat any longer, you'll have a hole to hang it up by," and he went out the front door whistling.

Donald flushed slightly and hung up the brush. He had been turning over in his mind a thought that had troubled him for some time and which was forced home upon him in a new light by Tom's suspicion that it was their cousin Ferdinand who had been the anonymous informer against a member of his own firm. He was startled to see how instinctively he had felt the necessity of Tom's paying Ferdinand first of all his creditors. From Tom's relations with Ferdinand, his mind leaped with growing anxiety to a trouble that had lain in the background of his mind for several weeks. He had observed the regularity of Ferdinand's trips to Kent. Ferdinand always had shown so little attention to women that this new development was all the more noticeable. Donald knew, too, that there was no doubt about Ferdinand's business promptitude in whatever he did. This particular business was peculiarly harassing to Donald; for, aside from his disappointment in the loss of Agnes, he found himself looking forward with a foreboding to the consequences to her of a closer than business relation with his partner.

Ferdinand and he had been boys together, and he had watched the growing apart of his own ideals and methods from those of his cousin. They now had arrived at the point where they were opposed along lines of religious thought and in matters of sentiment. Even on questions of business policy, the partners were not rarely uncomfortably at variance, and Donald realized that nothing except his own control of a large part of the firm's money enabled him to compete with Ferdinand's iron will. He dreaded a situation for a woman where Ferdinand's will would meet with no financial check. Ferdinand's agnosticism, too, assumed even graver proportions than was its wont. So did his utilitarian attitude on questions of sentiment. These things always had worried him, but now he found himself speculating upon other things which he never had allowed himself before to think about. In short, Ferdinand's character had been assuming in Donald's mind a vital significance as it approached Agnes Sidney. This anxiety was now overshadowing his brotherly worry about Tom.

Meantime Tom went whistling on his way to the farm, but as he neared it, his whistling dwindled and died away. His relief at being able to pay his cousin began to be counteracted by several chronic grudges. Added to these, he naturally thought of a new one. He, too, had noticed Ferdinand's trips to Kent, he remembered the advent of Ferdinand and Agnes together at Beatrice's supper party, and he now worked himself up to quite a state of disinterested indignation. Donald's late generosity added fuel to his wrath at Ferdinand's success where Donald had failed.

As he drew near the old Ballington homestead where Ferdinand lived, his feelings reached an inflammable state. The place had been originally a farm, and, although it had lost most of the signs of its rural origin, it was still outside the city limits. Tom remembered it as it had been when Ferdinand's father was living. The brick wall that shut it out from the road had been overgrown with a tangled luxuriance of woodbine, wild grape-vine, wild buckwheat, wild clematis, wild morning-glory. Climbing honeysuckle and bitter-sweet had also dropped down and rooted in the interstices. Wasps' nests gave a pleasing excitement to certain parts of the wall. Humming-birds whirred and drummed around it in the summer. Tom remembered the rapture with which he had watched their green and bronze wings and the fruitless searches he had made for their tiny nests. He remembered the big, poppy-colored wings of the butterflies that used to flutter aimlessly over the blossoms and the blundering humble-bees stumbling around the stamens and pistils, so loaded with pollen that they could hardly walk, but working with an intensity that put the sweating plowman to shame. In the angle of the wall some sumachs had started, and Tom remembered how his Uncle Tom had watched them spread with the meditative remark that he supposed he ought to cut them out before they took in the whole door-yard, but that it was written that the wicked should flourish and that he thought such wickedness was rather ornamental. The unkempt walls, the sumach thicket and all the wealth of insect and bird life that they harbored were like a fairyland in the background of Tom's memory. Now as he approached the familiar spot and saw the bare bricks with a row of iron spikes along the top, a straight stone walk between the avenue of cedars leading to the house where once an old dirt path had straggled, carpeted by cedar needles which muffled the tread, and a symmetrical, artificial seat where the old broken willow had swayed with the breeze, his anger burned within him to think of all that sweetness and grace banished by the hand of law and order.

One sole apple-tree remained to welcome him of all the original fruit-trees which formerly had occupied the yard. This was a concession to the tears and entreaties of Miss Margaret Ballington, Ferdinand's aunt and foster-mother. The tree had been planted when she was born, and she, like it, was now the only survivor of her generation. The little old lady felt real kinship with the gnarled but stately and spreading branches which brushed the eaves of the house, sending an odorous breath through the south-side windows—the fragrance of flowers in springtime, and the more than Arabian Spitzenberg perfume in autumn.

As Tom lifted the latch of the freshly-painted iron gate which now interposed a barrier where formerly ingress and egress had been hospitably free to all, he caught sight through the bars of his cousin Ferdinand superintending the clipping of his cone-like cedar trees, which were being retrimmed into symmetrical smoothness. The ground was covered with the newly-cropped twigs and the aromatic odor of resin filled the air. Tom stopped, picked a long grass, mechanically placed it between his teeth, passed inside, and closed the gate with a vicious click behind him. As he approached Ferdinand the latter looked up, but they evidently felt no necessity of saluting each other. Tom paused by Ferdinand's side and the two looked on in silence at the gardener.

At length Tom made an indignant gesture toward the trees. "Do you like that?" he asked shortly.

"Do you mean the trimming?" inquired Ferdinand impassively.

"That's what I mean."

Ferdinand eyed his companion gravely a moment, noting his ill-humor. Then he said quietly, "Evidently."

"Well, I don't!"

Ferdinand walked away a little and pointed out to the gardener a sprig which projected beyond the others. Then, returning to Tom's side, he asked without seeming interest, "What is your objection to it?"

"It's like slitting a dog's ears and docking a horse's tail and tattooing the human body. It's a mark of barbarism. This used to be the finest row of double trees in the Atlantic States, and you have made them look like a lot of funeral dunce-caps."

Ferdinand did not answer.

Presently Tom said again, "Seen Field's Trust-Book this month?"

"No," said the other, a flash crossing his steady eyes.

After a moment Tom continued with rising color, "You ought to look at it. You'd find something there that would interest you, although it's about only me."

"How so?" inquired Ferdinand.

"I guess you know as well as I do."

The other made no reply.

"Nobody would ever take you to be the son of a Ballington," Tom declared, his face still hotter as his eyes traveled again from the cedars to the row of spikes along the wall. In his mind these objects were irrelevantly connected with the trust-book. "No Ballington would ever do such a dirt mean trick as you've done me. You lured me into borrowing that money in the first place. It gave you a handle on me. Well, it didn't work, did it! So you took it out of me. If you didn't have my Uncle Tom's blood in you, I'd punch the head off of you!"

The subject of these belligerent remarks remained in his place a few seconds, surveying his cousin coolly. Then he turned and walked toward the house.

"Hold on there!" cried Tom, overtaking him. "Here's your money. I'll go inside and take a receipt!"

It was the first time for years that Tom had allowed himself the luxury of using the kind of language to Ferdinand he always wanted to use. The check in his pocket gave him the feeling of financial independence necessary to proper self-expression.

Ferdinand hesitated. "Very well," he answered, resuming his walk at the same gait.

As they went up the steps to the old-fashioned front door Tom remarked with sardonic surprise, "I see you've left on grandfather's old brass knocker! What did you do that for? Nobody uses it, since you've got the electric button."

"It's a valuable piece of brass," said Ferdinand indifferently. "You know as well as I do that they're putting knockers on all the new houses."

Ferdinand opened the door as he spoke and went in. They passed down the wide hall and turned into the library. The heavy furniture was arranged symmetrically along the walls, as Tom always had remembered it. It was the arrangement that Ferdinand's mother had inaugurated, and it had stayed the same during the easy-going years following her death, when Ferdinand's father had been in control, only because it couldn't grow into change as the yard had done.

Tom stood looking on darkly while Ferdinand sat down and made out a receipt.

He took the paper when it was completed and read it ostentatiously before folding it up and putting it in his pocket book. "I wanted to be sure the date was right," he said. "I see you neglected to put down the hour of the day."

Ferdinand said nothing as he passed around the table on his way to the door.

"They've reported me in Field's this month. You're at the bottom of that!" Tom exploded.

Ferdinand paused, turned around.

"You're mistaken about that," he returned coldly.

"No, I'm not mistaken, either, and you know it!" said Tom, chafing under the futility of words to express his feelings.

Ferdinand's face grew a shade paler. "I'm glad you are reported," he said, keeping his unwinking gaze on the young man's flushed face. "But I had nothing to do with it."

He turned away as he spoke, went into the hall and up the stairs. Tom was left alone with the receipt in his pocket. Ferdinand had the better of him again in manner, and he also had his money. Tom felt the loss of the money more keenly than he did the loss of his temper. A new exasperation rushed in upon him. Why had he not asked Donald to give him a little more, while he was about it? The sting of poverty followed too closely upon his late affluence. He ejaculated something under his breath, jammed his hat down over his eyes, and went out doors, taking care, however, to close the front door gently behind him. He knew Ferdinand was expecting it to slam.

CHAPTER IX

THE next day after Tom's interview with Ferdinand Donald was sitting in the neat office of Ballington & Ballington trying to work. At last he gave it up with a sigh and leaned back in his chair. What was the use of working when he had something else to do and it was only a few minutes now before it must be done? Over night he had come to the decision that it was his duty to talk to Ferdinand upon a subject from which he shrank with inexpressible reluctance. It was upon the vital question of the relations which might exist between his partner and Agnes Sidney. To the natural delicacy he would have felt toward such an interference under ordinary circumstances there was added the objection that his motives would probably be misconstrued, thus vitiating any success he might hope to have. He feared that it never had dawned upon Ferdinand that a girl brought up as Agnes had been would suffer intensely in endeavoring to relate her own standard of conduct to different ones of her husband. Donald had appreciated a deepening and developing in Agnes following upon her father's death. He remembered her manner and the look she gave him when she refused him finally. If he had not seen that look his duty would by no means have been clear to him, but now there seemed laid upon him the moral responsibility of pointing out to Ferdinand what it was which he was about to take into charge; of suggesting to him that the inevitable adjustment which must be made between two persons who are to live together must be a mutual one.

Donald almost had worked himself up during his night's vigil to the point of going to Kent and expounding his cousin's character to Mrs. Sidney, but with the first rays of the rising sun he realized the impracticability of such an act. Moreover, a sincere concern for Ferdinand himself had warned him from interfering in a series of events which might lead to his cousin's religious awakening. To Donald's knowledge, Ferdinand never had come under the influence of love, and Donald often had used this to explain in the other what he did not admire.

He was nervously turning over in his mind the best way of opening the subject when he heard Ferdinand's characteristic step approaching the door.

With the feeling that a crisis was upon them he turned in his chair as his cousin entered the room.

As he lifted his troubled but resolute face to greet Ferdinand he met in the other an expression of justified self-satisfaction, the look of one who knows himself to be a true prophet. This look of Ferdinand's checked the words which were already on Donald's lips.

Ferdinand walked over to his desk, seated himself, and said, tilting his head, backwards to look at Donald, "Well, the bank's shut down!"

"Is that so?" Donald exclaimed with reaction of mood.

"Yes. It came a little earlier than I thought it would. I thought Balch would hold out another month. Well, we got out just in time, didn't we? My prophecy wasn't far off."

Donald looked at the floor thoughtfully. It was true Ferdinand had prophesied this, and he himself had yielded unwillingly to Ferdinand's insistence that they should withdraw all the firm's funds from the bank. He was about to acknowledge frankly his cousin's superior judgment when a second thought stopped him.

Presently he spoke, "Balch will say that it was our withdrawal that broke him."

"I suppose so."

"He expected to tide over his difficulty. Our move probably caused the run."

There was a pause.

Then Donald continued with feeling, "I do think we might have helped him. The use of a moderate sum very likely would have pulled him through, and it wouldn't have hurt us any. I'm sorry for Balch. I didn't think this really was going to happen. He's an honorable man, and I've always thought he was a good manager. You thought so, too, two years ago, when you put our money into Balch's hands."

An unpleasant expression crossed Ferdinand's face. "I saw he had a chance to add twenty-five percent to his capital without the slightest risk. He failed to do it with his eyes open. I saw he was no business man and made up my mind then."

Donald did not reply. He was thinking that the announcement of Balch's failure was especially ill-timed as a prelude to the conversation he intended to have with Ferdinand, because it had apparently demonstrated Ferdinand's good sense. His own dissatisfaction with the methods employed by this good sense would count for nothing in face of their practical results.

"Is that Ferguson's new brand of cigars over there?" Ferdinand asked after a moment.

Donald glanced at the box absent-mindedly, "I believe it is."

There was another pause.

"They say Balch has been running his affairs on borrowed capital at the rate of nine thousand a year for four years. I suppose Mott has been behind him." Again, Ferdinand's voice prevented Donald's beginning on the subject uppermost in his mind.

"That's bad!" Donald said with real distress in his voice. "It doesn't seem like Balch." He added after a moment, "What is the talk in town?"

"Sympathy for the college mostly. Isn't that just like a sectarian institution, to put all its eggs in one basket?"

"Doesn't Balch expect to meet his creditors after a little?" asked Donald with growing hopelessness.

"There's no telling," replied Ferdinand indifferently.

He did not turn to his work, and presently he remarked, "I believe I'll try one of those cigars."

Donald passed him the box and his cousin selected a cigar carefully and lighted it.

"Ferguson knows a good cigar," he said, after puffing for some moments. "Curious what poison most people will draw into their circulation, isn't it?"

Donald sat looking at Ferdinand without saying anything.

Ferdinand observed it, and, leaning forward to knock the cigar ash into a silver tray, said with a slight hardening of tone, "There is something else I wanted to speak to you about."

An intuition that he had lost his opportunity flashed across Donald's mind. "What is it?" he asked briefly.

"I suppose you know why I have been going to Kent lately," said Ferdinand, still needlessly tapping his cigar on the edge of the tray.

"Yes."

"Agnes wanted you to know it at once. We are engaged."

A wave of bitter rebellion surged up in Donald's breast. His emotions checked his utterance; the primeval instinct of jealousy, the protective instinct toward Agnes, and a feeling of helplessness in the hands of fate. It took him some time to master himself.

Ferdinand watched him not unkindly, and as soon as he thought that he could finish, he added, "I am going to marry her in about a month."

Donald felt that his mouth was closed.

Ferdinand, out of consideration, continued to bear the burden of conversation. "Yes. I want to get her away from there. She has to work hard, and in addition her mother is very exacting."

As Donald's expression did not change, Ferdinand ended more slowly, "I think you ought not to feel that I have taken any advantage of you. I did not approach her until your attentions to her had ceased."

"I have nothing to complain of in that respect," said Donald with dignity; "she never would have married me."

After a pause Ferdinand began speaking again. "I am expecting to take her to Europe for three or four months," he said. "I think I can be absent just now without causing much inconvenience."

"Yes," said Donald slowly, "business is dull this time of year."

"I wouldn't care to go again myself," Ferdinand went on. "I saw all I wanted to see when I went over two years ago, but it will mean a good deal for Agnes. It will broaden her out amazingly. She needs culture."

Donald was stung at this unequivocal language concerning the girl they both loved. "It's rather strange you should have been attracted by so crude a girl," he said bitterly.

Ferdinand regarded him seriously, and answered after a pause, "No. Agnes is a wholesome girl and she has charm. You can see from her mother that her health is likely to last. These cultured town girls won't be able to compete with Agnes in a few years." After a moment, he added with a shrewd smile, "A man ought not to pick out his wife for five years when the chances are he'll live with her forty. Agnes may start handicapped, but she'll win out in the long run. She's sound." His satisfaction deepened upon reflection. Mrs. Sidney is a hale old lady still, a good deal better preserved than most women fifteen years her junior. Agnes comes of good sturdy stock. This little New York girl Stafford has married will be about as animated as a piece of chalk by the time she's thirty. By that time Stafford will be bankrupt. Why can't people use some business sense in getting married?"

There was a moment's silence.

Then Donald turned to his companion with a gravity which at once caught the other's attention. "I believe you never met Agnes' father, Dr. Sidney?"

Both of them were conscious that Donald's voice had a tenseness unusual to it.

Ferdinand fell on guard. "No, I never did. He treated my father at one time. I never happened to meet him."

Donald leaned forward. He realized that he had let slip the chance of influencing events before they had come to pass. He had tried to speak several times, but circumstances always had thwarted him. It would have been worse than useless to open the subject when Ferdinand was in certain moods, and on two occasions, when his cousin seemed especially open to appeal, vexatious interruptions had come between them. Donald had tormented himself, too, with self-accusations of procrastination and cowardice. He had rebuked himself for not making opportunity, for his ineptitude in dealing with hindrances as they arose. The burden of Agnes' future had come to rest heavier and heavier upon him until he almost morbidly regarded himself as responsible for her happiness. His decision to speak now was the result of a reckless impulse to ease his conscience at any cost. It took this form toward Ferdinand. It was to take a more deliberate form toward Agnes.

"There's something I want to say to you, Ferdinand, about Agnes' relations with her father. As you never met him, it's impossible that you should know how much he stands for in Agnes' life, how largely he has formed her character. Her ideas of conscience and duty are bound up with her memory of him, and there is therefore something peculiarly sacred and sensitive about them. Of course you have found out that the way she and her mother look at things is opposite to your own in many respects." Donald paused and grew a shade paler as he nerved himself for the next sentence. "I have always known you, Ferdinand, and, much as I admire you in many ways, I think you have it in you to make a woman like Agnes as miserable as it is possible for her to be, unless you treat her with more sympathy than I ever have observed in you."

Ferdinand sat still, looking through the window.

Donald continued deliberately, "You are in love with Agnes now, and I believe that that has led you to disguise from her and her mother some of your most cherished theories. Otherwise I don't believe that Mrs. Sidney or even Agnes herself would consent to this betrothal. It would make me very happy," Donald continued in a gentler tone, "to believe that they see deeper into you and know you better than I do; and that is, of course, quite possible."

He paused, but Ferdinand still looked through the window.

Presently Donald drew a long breath as he resumed, "Well, Ferdinand, I've just one excuse for saying this today. It ought to have been said before. God knows I've tried enough times. I dread the effect upon Agnes of awaking from an illusion. If you have allowed one to arise," he said slowly and significantly, "let it continue." Then, shocked at his own cynicism, he added hurriedly, "Live up always to what you feel now."

Ferdinand turned his face long enough to give Donald a glance.

Donald's heart beat heavily.

Ferdinand made as though he were going to reply, then he turned resolutely to the window again. Had he spoken, what he would have said is this: "In other words—that is, in plain words—you are a jealous man using Christian terms."

The sound of a carriage driving up outside arrested Ferdinand's attention. He walked over to the window, then turned back to Donald. "Here comes your mother," he said, and he tossed his cigar into the ash-tray.

The door was opened by Mrs. Ballington in great excitement. Her state of mind was further evidenced by her attire, of which she was ordinarily scrupulous. She had thrown on hurriedly an amorphous cape over an elaborate morning dress.

"Did you know the bank has failed?" she asked in a flurry of her son.

"Ferdinand has just told me so," answered Donald.

"What about the firm?" she continued breathlessly.

"We withdrew our funds Friday."

"So that's true!" She sank into a chair with an expression of relief. Then she sat up again, demanding, "Why was this kept from me?"

"It wasn't kept from you, mother," said Donald with an unhappy gesture. "I intended to tell you, but I've had a good many things on my mind. Besides, we had no idea this would come so soon."

"It looks very much as though you did know it. They are saying all over town that Balch made the firm a preferred creditor. There's a crowd around the bank now. When I drove by some of the men called out at me."

Donald flushed and reached hesitatingly for his hat. "I never would allow the firm to benefit at the expense of the savings of workingmen."

"I wouldn't go over to the bank now," Ferdinand remarked with a slight smile. "Some bright person in the crowd will be sure to recollect, if he is given time, that a bank can't make preferred creditors."

Donald still hesitated.

"It's always rash to face a mob," Ferdinand continued. He flicked some cigar ashes from his light trousers.

Donald sat down again.

"Of course disagreeable things will be said about the firm," finished Ferdinand. "I don't see that that need worry us."

"How did you know Balch was going under?" asked Donald.

Ferdinand met his cousin's gaze easily. "By having eyes to see, and seeing. I believe I keep Scripture better than you, Donald."

"He didn't mention anything of the kind to you, did he?" Donald persisted.

"No."

"I was intending to call at the bank to draw some money on McMaster's check," said Mrs. Ballington. "Can you cash it, Donald?"

"For how much?"

"Two hundred."

"I can," volunteered Ferdinand, as Donald hesitated. He went into an inner room where the safe was kept and soon returned with the money.

During his short absence Donald had striven to force himself into communicating the other piece of news to his mother. It was not till his cousin's return, however, that he succeeded. "Ferdinand has just told me, mother," he said stiffly, that Agnes Sidney and he are engaged."

"Indeed!" said Mrs. Ballington with a cool stare at her nephew. He returned her gaze civilly. Unwilling as she had been that Donald should marry Agnes, she was nettled at its being prevented by this means.

Just as she was leaving the office she turned back. "Does Margaret know?" she asked significantly.

"Donald is the first one I have told," returned Ferdinand, and he stepped forward to open the door for her.

After Ferdinand closed the door behind her the two men without any further conversation seated themselves at their desks and began to write. The minds of both, however, were busy with other thoughts than business. Ferdinand, with the triumphant satisfaction of the successful lover, was again dwelling upon that first look of passion and self-surrender with which Agnes had met him in the corridor at Fred Sidney's house. Donald, on the other hand, continued to brood upon the look of awakened conscience and self-abnegation he had caught in her face the first time he had seen her after her father's death. As the two wrote on with automaton-like regularity, nothing was heard in the office but the ticking of the clock and the scratching of pens.

Meantime Mrs. Ballington went out to the carriage, where she found Tom talking familiarly with the coachman. He included her genially in the discussion as he stepped forward to help her into the carriage.

"Well, mother, John tells me the bank is bust!"

Mrs. Ballington made room upon the seat and beckoned him into the carriage. After an instant's hesitation Tom entered and his mother directed the coachman to drive around the block.

After they had started, she said in a low but impressive voice, "Tom, Ferdinand and Agnes Sidney are engaged."

Tom sat silent while his face turned a dark crimson.

"Well, I wish her more joy than she's likely to get," he said at length. "A girl that will turn down Donald for Ferdinand—deserves Ferdinand." The last words came out with a vindictive click. A moment later he added more calmly, "My sympathies go to Aunt Margaret. You mark my word, she'll be put out somewhere to board."

Mrs. Ballington considered. This was a new idea. The position of Ferdinand's aunt and foster-mother had seemed a natural and permanent one in the family.

"Tom," she said finally, "Ferdinand never would dare to turn Margaret out of doors. Why, she was born in that house!"

"What if she was born there?" replied her son moodily. "Ferdinand owns the house. The idea of his owning that house! It might as well be a car-barn for all the sentiment he has toward it. Here are Aunt Margaret and I, who really love it, and we have to see the vines dug up and the trees dug out and the walk weeded and stoned and the fence spiked as though it were a prison court-yard. I declare it just drives me to the devil to think of that! And he knows it! He knows it! He only keeps the house because Donald tried to buy it, and so he can clip those evergreens. When I went there yesterday and walked up the avenue to the front door, it was exactly as though I were going through the graveyard up to the family vault. I wonder if I ever shall have the privilege of attending Ferd's funeral there?" he ended, in a kind of black reverie.

They finished the circuit of the block in silence, and drew up again in front of the office door.

"Well," said Tom philosophically, as he left the carriage, "it must be a relief to you, mother, to get Agnes Sidney married. Don's safe now, at last."

Then he turned to the driver and added, "Drive home by Linton Avenue, John. Don't go past the bank."

Mrs. Ballington settled back on her cushions, raised her lorgnette to her near-sighted eyes, and passed in state up Linton Avenue. But the state was only outward. Within she was upset. It was even more humiliating to have Donald refused by a country doctor's daughter than to have him marry one; it was especially bitter to her to reflect that Agnes had achieved a double victory. She not only had refused Donald, but by marrying Ferdinand she would still attain a social prominence equaling that of Mrs. Ballington herself.

As they reached a wide curve of the road which led toward the eastern suburbs, a thought came to her. "John," she said, "you may drive me out to the farm."

The man turned obediently and presently drew up in front of the old Ballington residence.

"I should think, with all the other improvements," Mrs. Ballington muttered as she descended from the carriage, "that Ferdinand would have a drive-way put in here."

She went up the walk to the front door, noticing with unwilling approval the alterations in the place which had so infuriated Tom. She mounted the front steps clumsily, impeded by her morning-gown. The door stood ajar. She stood a moment to breathe after her hasty walk from the carriage, then pushed open the door and entered unceremoniously.

"Margaret!" she called in the voice of one who bringeth tidings.

An inner door was opened hastily in answer to the summons and Miss Margaret Ballington, with a startled look on her face, stepped out into the hall. "Is that you, Sarah? Why, what's the matter?"

Of the two women a stranger easily would have taken Miss Margaret to be the mother of Donald Ballington, had it not been for an unmistakable air of withered maidenhood about her. Her face had the same fair symmetry and her eyes and hair were like his grown old. She was a fragile creature, as transparent as a frosted flower, and withal she had something of the flower's unconscious innocence.

"Is there anybody around here?" asked Mrs. Ballington.

"No. Why? What is it?" said Miss Ballington in a flutter of nervous surprise.

"Margaret Ballington, will you promise not to let anyone know I've told you, if I tell you something now?"

The widow spoke with such solemnity that Miss Margaret's nervousness became trepidation. "Yes. I won't speak of it. What is it? Sit down somewhere. Let's go in here."

She turned and led the way into the green parlor. It was the room in which she had been born.

"What is it?" she repeated breathlessly, sitting down on a green lounge with a rustle of her lawn skirts.

Simultaneously her visitor seated herself upon the edge of a large rep chair, and punctuated the ensuing conversation with dabs and fluent waves of her lorgnette.

"You'll probably hear it from Ferdinand tonight. You know that girl I've been afraid Donald was going to marry? Well, Ferdinand is going to marry her."

Miss Margaret leaned forward with a horror-stricken face and began to tremble. "Ferdinand? Ferdinand?" she said confusedly. "Is Ferdinand going to marry? How do you know he is? He'd never marry a variety singer such as you said she was. No, Ferdinand wouldn't. He doesn't like music."

The satisfaction which Mrs. Ballington felt in the success of her communication acted as a healing balm. She settled herself back more comfortably in her chair to enjoy Miss Margaret's dismay. Her lorgnette made an almost benevolent circuit through the air as she replied, "Yes, he is,

Margaret. He is. He's told me so himself. I thought of course he had told you first. I came out at once to find out what you are going to do about it."

Little Miss Ballington sat as one stunned. She had looked forward vaguely to something of this kind, but it had come without warning. She was more hurt by the fact that Ferdinand had not given her his confidence than she was by the engagement, dreadful as that seemed to her.

After a moment she spoke with trembling lips, with a pathetic effort at dignity. "There is but one thing for me to do, Sarah. That is to receive Ferdinand's wife." Then she broke off with a look of indecision and entreaty. "What should you think I ought to do, Sarah? Perhaps the girl isn't all bad. I've always said that when it came to it, I should greet Ferdinand's wife kindly. It shouldn't make any difference with my staying here—here where I was born. Should you think it ought?"

The lorgnette was folded portentously. "What *I* think, unfortunately for you, Margaret, isn't going to regulate this matter. I think you are in a very painful position."

Miss Margaret's distress approached a tearful state. "Ferdinand has always been very considerate to me, very. You know that everyone has said that we get along together wonderfully. I've always thought no one else quite under stood Ferdinand. You know I love him as though he were my own child. I've learned how to take him, too. Can you smell that chicken cooking in here?"

The last sentence was spoken with an abrupt change of voice. The fussiness of the housekeeper for the moment put to flight less immediate troubles.

"I don't think I can perceive it," answered Mrs. Ballington, sniffing, and then she started on a new tack suggested by the last remark.

"When the household gets a new mistress, things won't be as they are now. The piano will be all littered up with music and she will be—" Mrs. Ballington hesitated for an effective word. "Carousing," she said at length, "with her mother and that deformed aunt, all over the house—in here, in the sitting-room, in the spare bed-room." The lorgnette located the scenes of future dissipation.

Miss Ballington winced. Presently she rallied bravely. "I have considerable hope for the young girl," she volunteered. "General Mott spoke very highly of her father. He called him a most estimable man—a most estimable man—a man of very great skill in his profession, though a little impractical in a business way. But many of us are impractical, Sarah. I should not look down on Dr. Sidney for that. It was his nephew whom Beatrice married, you know."

"Yes, I know it was. These Sidneys seem to have a faculty for wriggling into rich families."

"You don't think the girl is going to marry Ferdinand *for his money*, do you?" cried Miss Ballington in alarm.

Her sister-in-law laughed unpleasantly. "What else would she marry him for?"

A look of shocked bewilderment greeted this last remark. "What else would she marry him for?" Miss Margaret repeated vaguely; "why, love, of course. If I were a girl, I can understand how—" She stopped in painful embarrassment.

Miss Margaret had taken care of her nephew from the time of his mother's death, when he was but six years old. He never had been a dependent child, and upon his father's death, when he was but halfway through his teens, he quite naturally had succeeded him as the head of the house, Miss Margaret becoming a mere figurehead. Miss Margaret, quite as naturally, gave him all she had to give, and loved him the more for it. She lavished upon him all the wealth of maternal sentiment of which her starved heart was capable, and, in addition, idealized him with the unfulfilled longings of her girlhood.

A moment later she was struck by another thought, and exclaimed, "You don't think Miss Sidney is in love with Donald still?"

"I judge not. Tom says it's probable she never was in love with him. It might have been just his money. But I'm inclined to think there was a passing infatuation."

"How happy you must feel for Donald!" Miss Margaret said sadly.

There was no reply.

"Do you know how soon—how soon Ferdinand will be married?" she asked with difficulty.

"No. But I presume it will be soon." Mrs. Ballington spoke with the cool impartiality of a judge sentencing a criminal to hang by the neck till he is dead.

"Do you think that he is—that he is happy?" persisted the wretched woman.

"I presume he feels a satisfaction in being the successful rival for Agnes Sidney. Difficulty adds a good deal of zest to courtship."

Miss Ballington half rose. "You misjudge him, Sarah. He wouldn't enjoy hurting Donald. You never understood Ferdinand."

"He's just like *her*," replied Mrs. Silas, with a wave of her lorgnette at an old-fashioned portrait hanging over the lounge upon which Miss Margaret sat.

Miss Margaret always spoke of Ferdinand's dead mother as "Estelle." Mrs. Ballington rarely mentioned the name, but everyone in the family knew of whom she was speaking, when, with a peculiar intonation always employed in this connection, she said "she" and "her."

"Estelle was misjudged, too," Miss Ballington said in a low voice with a twinge of memory.

"You know you never liked her," insisted Mrs. Ballington acrimoniously. "You were always complaining of her."

"I did not mean to complain of her."

"Oh, well, it's what would have been called complaining from any of the rest of us. Of course you never complain."

"Perhaps I do. I have long thought that I misjudged her, too. She wasn't like other women. The Landseers are all different from other people. But Estelle was a very brilliant woman. Thomas, you know, said his wife had more brains than all the Ballington family put together. Perhaps he was right, Sarah. Perhaps he was right. We were not qualified to appreciate her. Just the invention of the car-spring, now—"

Mrs. Ballington rose. "I never did believe that story," said she grimly, backing toward the hall door. "Thomas, no doubt, talked to her about his inventions. It was childish the way he always courted her opinion. Well, good-by, Margaret," she said, pausing a moment in the doorway, "I will send the carriage for you whenever you want it, you know. I suppose Ferdinand will get one now he's going to be married." A moment later, she was sweeping down the walk toward the carriage.

Miss Margaret remained where she was on the green lounge, helpless despair hanging like a pall over her gentle inconsequent spirit, and here Ferdinand found her an hour later with slow tears coursing down her withered cheeks, in a very different grief from the impulsive hysterical kind to which he was accustomed.

CHAPTER X

A MONTH later Margaret Ballington lay in a reclining chair, a light rug wrapped about her little form, and a moist cloth tied about her head. She had been ill for some days, and now was sitting up for the first time. Now and then she closed her eyes, as an expression of sickening pain passed over her white face. Sometimes she raised herself to a sitting posture and listened intently. In the next room Ferdinand was dressing to leave for Kent, where he was to be married that evening to Agnes Sidney. As Miss Ballington heard his slow footsteps going back and forth in his preparations she passed the most agonizing hour of her life.

After some time Ferdinand's door opened, and he stepped into the hall. Miss Margaret heard him approaching. She fell back in her chair and closed her eyes, while a gray pallor crept over her face. He rapped gently, and, hearing a low summons to enter, came in. He was dressed for traveling, and he held his hat and gloves in his hand. She had heard him set down his portmanteau in the hall.

"I am just leaving," he said, coming up to her and standing quietly near her chair.

Her eyelids fluttered, lifted, and she looked at him with misery in her gaze.

He felt that it would be easier for both his aunt and himself if he could get away without exciting her; and, with this in his mind, he laid down his hat and took out his pocketbook in a matter-of-fact but not inconsiderate manner.

"I have made a list here of certain things which will need attention during the next three months," he said, turning to lay a slip of paper on her desk. "I have given Sam his directions about the yard. He will need watching. I have told Eliza that she is not to leave you alone evenings. Is there anything else you would like to have me mention?"

She shut her eyes again and answered in a faint voice, "No—Ferdinand. Thank you."

He regarded her a moment in silence and then took out another paper.

"Here is my check for next month's expenses," he said gently, "and here is the dime you paid the messenger boy. You may hold the accounts till my return. We probably shall be back in three months. I have arranged with

Donald that he is to have an eye to you from time to time, and I will send you my check so that you will receive it by the first of each month. I am leaving a card here which contains the address of my bankers. I should like to hear how affairs are during my absence."

She made no reply at first. He waited, uncertain whether or not to repeat what he had said, when the same voice answered, "Yes—dear."

"I think that is all, then," he said, the restraint of his words covering an uncomfortable realization of her sufferings. "Is there anything else?" he continued, trying his best to be kind, although his voice did not relax.

"No, nothing else."

"Then I will say good-by. I am sorry to leave you in this condition. I have left word for the doctor to call regularly."

He was waiting for her to open her eyes before offering to kiss her good-by. But she answered again with them closed, "It doesn't matter, dear."

Then he stooped down and kissed her worn face lightly. Before he could rise again the thin arms went up and clasped his neck, while the sick woman burst into hysterical crying, every other instant giving a high wail in her struggle to speak.

He extricated himself gently, and said, looking uneasily down at the palpitating little heap on the chair, "This crying will make you ill, Aunt Margaret. I wish you wouldn't do it. There isn't any occasion for grief. Why can't you take my word for it? Agnes will be a companion for you."

She heard his words, but they were stones for bread to her. She wanted no companion but him, and the thought that she was losing him convulsed her body now as it had been convulsing her mind for days past.

He looked down at her in distress, took out his watch, glanced at it, and then spoke to her again. "You will soon adjust yourself to the new conditions, Aunt Margaret. You are ill now. Things will look brighter to you in a day or two. I must go, but I will send Eliza to you."

He laid his hand for an instant on her forehead, but furtively, so that she could not catch hold of him again. Then he took his hat and gloves and walked to the door.

"You will hear from me before I sail," he said from the doorway, "and I will write regularly afterwards."

Then he went out of the room, and she heard him go down the stairs and speak to someone in the hall below.

Donald was down there waiting for him. Donald had wished to spare himself the anguish of being present at Agnes' wedding. He soon saw, however, that in case he declined the invitation Ferdinand would have no representative from his own family. Mrs. Ballington had refused to go. Tom had gone off on a fishing excursion on purpose to be absent, and Miss Margaret's nerves could not carry her through such an ordeal. Therefore, in spite of his own torture and his mother's ridicule, Donald had resolved to go.

"The carriage is at the door," he said, as Ferdinand appeared. "We have just twenty minutes."

They passed down the walk together, each busy with his own thoughts, and entered the conveyance. Neither spoke during the ride to the station, and when they boarded the train they occupied different seats.

Each one of the little group of guests who met in Mrs. Sidney's parlor to witness Agnes' wedding felt less of the joy and more of the solemnity than is usual on such occasion. Even Beatrice, when she arrived, was subdued into the prevailing mood. Helen Mabie could not afford to come, and the only guests were Fred and Beatrice, Aunt Mattie, Donald, and Dr. Quinn. Agnes moved among them, greeting each with a grave fullness of sympathy which removed her indefinably from the girl of yesterday.

As Donald watched her, meeting from time to time the friendly earnestness of her eyes, he felt his distress and misgiving slipping away from him, while in its place sprang up a trust in the future, out of which he did not wish to reason himself. He let her pass him several times, therefore, before he brought himself to do what he had determined upon several days before.

When he could no longer postpone his intention, he went up to her almost regretting his pertinacity. "I wish you would take me to see your presents, Agnes. I have brought my own little gift, and I should like to give it to you in person."

Agnes willingly preceded him into her father's back-office, and they stood together looking at the gifts which had pleased and flattered her mother's appreciative heart.

"Mother has given me papa's cherry desk, and see, it is filled with things which his friends have sent in," she said. "There are the Ballington gifts!" and she pointed to a table nearby loaded with silver and cut-glass.

She turned back to the desk, opened one of the little drawers, and took out an inlaid box which she unlocked and opened. Inside, reposing on a satin lining yellow with age, was a long gold chain with carved links of Renaissance fretwork, joined hands forming the clasp. "Miriam gave me this," she said, and took another box from the same drawer. "This is Ferdinand's." The latter was a little casket of ivory, and inside was a set of diamonds.

Donald looked at them, too preoccupied to speculate on the suggestiveness in the two gifts, and as Agnes replaced them in the drawer, he drew a package from his pocket and balanced it in his hand as he said gravely, "Here is mine. It is something I have thought over ever since I heard you were engaged. I want you to promise me not to look at it for three months, and I want you to promise up to that time to keep it a secret."

Agnes drew back slightly with clouding eyes.

Donald went on. "And, after three months, you are at liberty to speak about it or even to return it to me. I want you to consider that I am giving it to you with your father perhaps more than you in my mind."

The gentleness and kindly affection in his face and manner, with the quiet and assured reference to her father, overcame Agnes' reluctance to receive a gift so mysteriously given. Besides, nothing seemed strange to her on such a day. She took the package Donald held out to her and acknowledged it simply, "I will take it, Donald," and, with a look of trust and confidence, turned away from him to return to her mother.

The childlikeness of her reply moved Donald profoundly. He turned away to the door opening out of the office into the back garden. It seemed to him as if he could not return to the others and go through with the ceremony. Grief and apprehension choked him and blinded his eyes. As he stood in the doorway the memory of Dr. Sidney pervaded the little office and the garden, not accusing, but gently warning and entreating him. The same gentle presence seemed to pervade the little sitting-room when he returned for the marriage ceremony.

Mr. Carter married them with a bare, Puritan brevity against which his soul impotently rebelled. It seemed to him heathenish in Mrs. Sidney to hold out against the wedding ring. When he began to speak, however, memories of the Spartan weddings at which he had been present in boyhood came back upon him, and there was a simplicity and dignity in his tones which he vaguely realized were more impressive than any he ever had been able consciously to achieve.

After the little collation, which had been prepared by Mrs. Sidney's hands, Agnes dressed for traveling.

She said good-by to the little group, and then followed her mother into the office.

"Good-by, mother," she said, feeling faint.

Mrs. Sidney's voice shook as she replied, "Good-by, Agnes. God bless you, my child."

Agnes put out her hands instinctively. "Don't, mother! We shan't be separated long."

"No. No. But all the evening I've been seeing you as you looked in your little white dress with the tears in your eyes, when your father went off to the war, and he said to me, 'Take good care of the little baby, Kate.'"

"But I wasn't born then, mother. That was Helen."

"So it was! So it was!" and a smile broke over Mrs. Sidney's face.

"I'll write you from New York, mother," Agnes continued unsteadily, "and you can depend on me to send you something, too. I know that Ferdinand expects to help you."

"I'll get along alone," said Mrs. Sidney, mastering her emotion. "When you're abroad, Agnes, remember to have proper respect for your father's family. You are leaving as good a family as you are marrying into," the old lady added with dignity.

As Agnes looked at the older face she appreciated as she never had before the fine pride and power apparent there. She threw her arms around her mother's neck with a thrill of gratitude and devotion. "I'm not leaving this family," she said, "and I want you to know that I honor you more than I do anybody else in the world."

The two remained for a moment in each other's arms.

Then Mrs. Sidney released her daughter. Agnes picked up her little handbag and joined her husband at the door.

As they opened it, a straggling crowd waiting outside broke into a hearty cheer. There were old and young faces, mostly from the common walks of life, care-worn women, sturdy laborers, hard little newsboys, half-grown girls; and their good wishes followed Agnes as she went down to the carriage. A little rice was timidly thrown, but more flowers.

As Ferdinand held open the carriage door for her, Agnes turned suddenly, with bursting heart, untied the ribbon from her bride bouquet, and flung the great sheaf of roses broadcast over the motley crowd. She knew that their feeling toward her was because she was her father's daughter, and she tried to thank them in her father's name, but her voice broke, and she turned and entered the carriage weeping.

Mrs. Sidney, standing in the door, the tears streaming down her face, called out in a ringing tone as the carriage drove away:

"Agnes appreciates this and so do I."

At the station a similar but smaller group greeted Agnes' arrival.

As she reached the car steps John Talbot came running up to them. "God bless you, Agnes!" he cried, shaking her hand in his two hard ones. "God bless you, too, Mr. Ballington!"

His loud tones caused a smile on the faces of some standers by who watched the little group of three sympathetically.

"Oh, I'm so glad to see you, John!" said Agnes eagerly. "I wrote a note thanking Molly for your lovely present, but I feel better to tell you yourself how much Ferdinand and I will enjoy it. Won't we, Ferdinand?" and she turned confidingly to the tall figure beside her.

Ferdinand bowed to John, and assisted Agnes up the steps and into the car.

As they sat down in their stateroom. Agnes remarked his silence, and, looking up into his face, caught an expression of discontent.

"What has annoyed you, Ferdinand?" she asked, sensitive to his coldness, and with a sinking of the heart.

Ferdinand did not reply at once. When he did, it was with an effort to be light in manner, "Oh, perhaps I don't like to have the brakemen on our wedding trip call you by your first name. You are Mrs. Ferdinand Ballington now."

"Why, that was John Talbot," returned Agnes in surprise. "He meant it kindly, and he was my father's friend."

"He can be kind without being familiar," rejoined Ferdinand briefly.

Her look, which had not left him, became bewildered, then indescribably hurt. She turned and glanced through the window. The familiar sights of her childhood were passing rapidly. There was the tannery, there the mills, there was John Talbot's house, and—yes! Molly was waving a handkerchief from the door. Over beyond was the plank road where she had loved to ride with her father. Now came the car shops—then fields, fields, fields. She looked back till the last outskirt of the town trailed away in the distance.

With sudden forgetfulness of all save her longing for sympathy, she turned spontaneously, with tears on her lashes and a smile on her lips, to Ferdinand, who was sitting opposite her.

He had been watching her intently, but had not disturbed her good-by to the home of her girlhood. The wait was becoming intolerable to him. As she looked toward him he leaned over and caught her hands in sudden passion. "My love!" he said in a very low voice, "My wife!" and he bent his head down and rested his throbbing forehead on their clasped hands.

PART III

CHAPTER I

THE months in Europe marked a great change in Agnes Ballington and in the relations between Ferdinand and her.

The first change in her was an external one, for soon after reaching London Ferdinand had disregarded carelessly a good share of the hand-made trousseau which Mrs. Sidney had toiled over day and night to make for Agnes, and had supplied in its place costly and conventional garments of his own selection. Agnes tried to thank him for his presents, but there was a lasting hurt in her heart. She remembered her own dissatisfaction with her trousseau. Now such clothes as she had craved might be hers, but when she looked at them she saw only a tired woman stitching by lamp-light. When Ferdinand criticised laughingly her country dresses, her heart went out to her mother in an agony of love such as she never had felt for her before. She would have given all this new world of art and beauty for that old cheaply-held privilege of bringing a smile to her mother's weary eyes.

The change was not alone in soft drapery and Rembrandt plumes. A subtle metamorphosis was noticeable in the young wife's eyes. They held no longer the clear, light-hearted gaze of a girl. There was an awakening of something less assured, more poignant. Ferdinand did all the planning for the trip, and he conscientiously got down to the business of pleasure-seeking. They went the rounds of the sights in the different cities they visited, Agnes often weary, but struggling on to fall in with her husband's desires. She soon felt the difference between the old companionship with her father, with its ever-patient courtesy and deference to her taste, its ignoring of conventional and artificial standards, its lingering over rare and modest beauties ordinarily passed by, and this new companionship, insisting upon promptness, order, thorough-going putting-through of a stereotyped schedule. At first she rebelled a little, once even refused to carry out Ferdinand's programme for an afternoon, insisted instead on loitering away the time in a park, but before the afternoon was over, she had repented of her petulance and apologized for it. She did not indulge again a recalcitrant spirit, but there came over her now

131

and then a vague dread of a time coming when two alien natures might challenge each other and when she might be strong enough to walk along the way her own nature impelled, not in willfulness but in resolve.

An uneasiness, too, about her financial position grew upon her as the weeks passed. She had left home with the last dollars of her earnings in her purse. They soon were spent in petty requirements of which she felt shy about telling her husband, and Ferdinand offered her no more. She worried about her mother's needs, was hurt that her husband never referred to them or to his promise to see that her mother was cared for, and presently began to worry about herself. Once or twice she gathered courage to ask Ferdinand for little sums of money, but he usually replied by inquiring what she wished, and then buying it for her himself. In London, she suggested laying in a stock of gloves, saying that she would like to send some to Helen and her mother, but Ferdinand had answered that it never was economy to buy more than one needs, and he made no reference at all to her proposed gifts. Agnes' shame in thinking of her mother increased as she learned from Beatrice's newsy letters that she was taking embroidery lessons from Mrs. Sidney and paying her for them. Once Agnes came to hot words with Ferdinand over a wedding present she had wished to send an old Kent friend. The girl was poor, and when Agnes was married had made her a gift commensurate with her means. Ferdinand had required, not discourteously, that the gift they returned should be no more expensive than the one which they had received. To Agnes' insistence that great love had come to her with her friend's gift, he had replied good-humoredly, "Pay it back in love. No good ever comes from mixing coin."

These incidents brought Agnes to a first attempt to reach a financial arrangement with her husband which would be satisfactory to both of them. Up to this time, she had adopted Beatrice's motto, "Carpe diem." She had tried to drug her increasing anxiety with the sophistry natural to brides that her first duty was to please Ferdinand, but she was becoming so exhausted and low-spirited, and Ferdinand so sated with attentions, that there was desirability of a change if they expected to pass their lives together.

Agnes' latent common sense awoke one morning. Maxims of her mother passed through her mind—homely but wise precepts about the necessity of keeping the mind off one's self, about the mistake of pampering healthy natures into querulousness, "A foolish woman can spoil the best man that ever lived, inside of one year," Agnes remembered her mother saying on several occasions when Mrs. Sidney had vetoed some of the doctor's cherished plans. Her father had yielded after mild expostulation. Agnes had been indignant at seeing him yield, and her mother's proverb had seemed to her a self-satisfied and ostentatious proclaiming of victory. But with better understanding of her mother, she realized now that Mrs. Sidney had disguised not the joy, but the pain, of victory by arraying the latter on the side of age-old wisdom. "Mother was a sensible woman to face disagreeable situations as they arose," Agnes reflected. "That is what Ferdinand and I must do. I have been putting off this money discussion long enough." She finished dressing her hair and stuck a shell-pin into it aggressively. "It looks like the feather on the head of a Pawnee chief setting out on the warpath," she said, pausing to survey herself before she left the mirror.

They had completed their tour of Germany, and were to start that morning for Lucerne.

During breakfast Agnes' resolve filled her with unusual vivacity. When they were halfway through, Ferdinand put down his newspaper to look at her curiously.

She caught his puzzled expression and touched the ornament in her hair. "That is the white plume of Navarre, Ferdinand."

"Indeed?" her husband replied seriously, and returned to his reading.

Agnes' spirits were dampened. She fell into a thoughtful mood, which lasted until they were aboard their train and well started on their southward journey.

At last, with an effort of will, she turned to her husband, opened her empty pocketbook, and held it out to him, looking him full in the eyes as she did so.

He made no effort to take it, but returned her gaze, apparently oblivious of the entreaty in her eyes and of the embarrassed flush on her cheeks.

"Ferdinand, I want some money," she said at length. A subtle impulse of anger in her heart helped out the words.

"Do you wish to buy something? Tell me what you need and I will get it for you."

His tone was considerate, but Agnes' eyes flashed as she answered, "Perhaps I don't need anything, Ferdinand. When I do, I like to get it myself.

I don't want to ask you for everything. I have to ask you to post my letters, and then I have to explain why I'm writing so often to the same people."

Ferdinand ignored her last sentence as he replied courteously, "You will always find stamps in the portfolio. I don't see why you should feel as you apparently do, since I do not recall that I ever have refused to get you anything within reason which you desired, and I have endeavored to anticipate your wishes."

Agnes was ashamed of her exclamation, and when she next spoke, it was in a different mood. "That was a small thing for me to say, Ferdinand. I'm ashamed of myself. The fact is, for some time back I've never been dependent upon other people for money. I used to earn money from my father and by giving lessons, and I've been accustomed to an independent purse. I'm convinced that you should allow me this privilege. It will be a source of endless friction and humiliation, if you do not."

Ferdinand reflected, then took out his pocketbook. As he did so he looked up at his wife. "I have a system of accounts which I have kept ever since I was twelve years old. I had intended to explain it to you when you should assume the housekeeping. I wished to make this time as free as possible for you, and I knew how difficult it is for women to be orderly in money matters. It may, however, be a good plan for you to begin accounts on a small scale now." He opened his pocketbook, took out a gold louis, and handed it to her.

The red in Agnes' cheeks rushed over her whole face. "I don't want alms, Ferdinand. Keep your louis!" she said vehemently, and turned to the window to hide her face from him.

"Agnes," Ferdinand said gently.

She made no answer.

He crossed over to her, put out his arm, and tried to draw her to him. She drew herself away from him decidedly, but turned her burning face, with tears running down it, toward him. "Take away your arm!" she said.

He sat still a moment, then rose, took his own seat again, and picked up his guide-book.

Presently he laid down the book, glanced through the window, and remarked civilly, "We are passing through a remarkable country. You may never see it again."

"I am looking at it," she answered, a mist obscuring everything before her eyes.

They reached their destination late in the afternoon. Agnes went at once to her room, where Ferdinand left her, saying he would go for a stroll and get their mail. His last words advised her to take a nap before dinner.

Agnes closed the door behind him without replying, and instead of sleeping sat down to think over the situation in which she found herself.

It was the first time she had realized unmistakably what the consequences might be of relinquishing independence. As a child, and later on as a girl, she had taken naturally to a general supervision by her mother of her expenditures, but she always had earned a little, and of late had been the principal wage-earner of the family. To pass from the position of supporting a household to being childishly dependent was galling. "I have nothing of my own except the clothes I brought from home and my wedding presents," she thought. The sense of distance from her home and friends deepened the helplessness she felt.

As her mind reviewed the little property she possessed in her own right, Donald's unopened gift occurred to her, and she remembered that she had been married a little over three months.

She rose at once to get it, grateful to have her thoughts diverted. She took the packet from her trunk, removed the outer wrapping, and saw a second envelope with these words:

These packages are to be opened one a month and used by Mrs. Ballington as she likes.

She opened the first packet, and, with a feeling of bewilderment as though a miracle
had happened, found five American twenty-dollar bills inside.

The color slowly rose in her face as she looked at them. Astonishment, humiliation, an impulse to return the packet to Donald, struggled within her. She began to tie it up again with trembling fingers, but her thought outstripped her hands. Presently she paused and the packet sank unheeded in her lap.

It had come when she most needed it. The impulse to return the money vanished before an irresistible longing for it. It was hers, had been given to her in her father's name. This thought forced the explanation of the gift home to her. "Ferdinand does not intend to give me money to do as I like with. Donald knew this and wanted me to have some. He didn't want me to open it for three months because he wanted me to be familiar with Ferdinand's ways and so use the money well; and he didn't want me to use it all at once."

She turned the matter over in her mind, realizing that the first crisis had come in her married life, and that her decision now might have serious consequences. She already felt from stray remarks of Ferdinand's that there was a latent irritation in her husband's heart toward his partner. If she went to her husband now and laid the matter before him she felt that trouble would ensue between Ferdinand and Donald which might result in permanent estrangement. A wave of bitterness at being forced to this pass surged up in her. Again, she felt rebellion against her husband, but it presently spent itself, and her mind went on dispassionately. "If I tell Ferdinand, I'll either have to return the money to Donald or there will be a serious quarrel between us. In either case the relations between all three of us will be awkward indefinitely. Moreover, I need this amount and more, and Ferdinand never would give it to me. He has refused to allow me to send gifts to my mother and sister. Donald knows some things about him better than I did."

As her mind went back to the time Donald had given her the package, she remembered his open and friendly expression. Her thought passed from that memory to all that she ever had known of him, and a look of decision grew into her face. "I am going to trust Donald's judgment," she concluded.

A letter already written to her mother was lying unsealed in her portfolio. With a thrill of relief and happiness, she picked it up, enclosed three of the bills in it, and sealed it. A few moments later she had written a short letter to Helen, inclosing the fourth bill to her. Then she rang for a servant, sent the letters to the post, that there might be no possibility of recall, and put the fifth bill in her own pocketbook. The four remaining packets she returned to the bottom of her trunk.

CHAPTER II

THE same maid who had taken Agnes' letters to be posted returned a little later, tapped at the door, and brought in a small parcel which Monsieur had wished delivered to Madame.

Agnes took it with a feeling of apprehension. It was a velvet case containing a ring; a triple loop of diamonds, rubies, and pearls.

Agnes looked at the jewels with mixed feelings. It was undoubtedly Ferdinand's peace-offering. If she declined the gift, as was her first impulse, she would hurt him. If she accepted it grudgingly, he would think she was not satisfied with its value. If she showed much pleasure, he would be inclined to think that it was greed which had made her ask for money.

She finally submitted to the latter embarrassment, dressed hurriedly for dinner, put the ring on her finger, and sat down to wait till he should come for her. She put aside an uneasy regret at having used Donald's gift beyond recall.

Some minutes, a half hour, passed.

She looked at her watch and saw that dinner was already in progress. She had heard Ferdinand enter his room, but for some little time no sound had come from him. She got up and went to the door opening into his apartment and knocked.

There was an instant response, and in a moment he had reached the door and opened it.

She noticed that he was dressed for dinner, that he was slightly pale, and that he looked at her intently with eyes which seemed a deeper blue than usual. She tried to smile. "Are you ready, Ferdinand?" she asked. "I have been waiting for you."

She hesitated, then raised her hand with the ring upon it. "It is very, very beautiful," she said sadly.

"You are pleased with it?" he asked.

"Yes—it is exquisite—and most so because you gave it to me." There was a ring of sincerity in her voice.

Ferdinand appreciated the tone, and kissed the fingers and palm of the hand raised to him.

They went together to the dining-room, conscious of a reconciliation.

As they walked together down the long hall he noticed her heightened color, and a momentary return of his first keen zest in the possession of her gave to his eyes and voice that early devotion for which she had been hungering for days. "You are very beautiful tonight," he said.

She smiled an answer, fearing to speak lest she should break the spell, but in her heart she was thinking, "To him that hath, it shall be given."

During dinner Ferdinand's concentration upon her died a natural death. She knew that she was losing his attention, and the disappointment fired her into effort. He responded to her conversation perfunctorily, and at last said, when she paused, "I came across an acquaintance of mine while I was out—Frank Rousseau. He belongs to the Jean-Jacques family. It was rather agreeable to see someone I knew. Would you like to meet him?"

"Yes, if you wish," she answered. "Is he staying here?"

"I believe he is. We made a partial engagement to meet this evening at a pavilion near the hotel. An operetta is going on there. It is a cheap affair, but somewhat popular."

Agnes acquiesced in the arrangement, and after they had finished dining they walked across the hotel lawn to the summer pavilion, where they found two men waiting for them, Rousseau and a friend of his, Mr. Partlow.

As Ferdinand presented her to his friends she felt a natural desire to do him honor. With something of an effort she entered into conversation with young Rousseau, but with her mind upon Ferdinand. She saw that she was succeeding in interesting the strangers and she felt an impulse to arouse the same interest in her husband. It was with fear and distress at the realization that she had lost the power to do this last that she turned instinctively to the weapons with which nature armed the female sex. She simulated an interest which she was far from feeling, in Rousseau's anecdotes. Ferdinand entered occasionally into the conversation, but more often sat silent, watching his wife.

Presently the conversation turned upon religion, and as it was introduced, Agnes' artificial zest died out. This was an even more tender point with her than finances. Ferdinand and she had circled about it in an ever-narrowing spiral for three months, but of late an instinct of self-preservation had warned her to keep away from it. What she had dreaded to approach while she and Ferdinand were alone was doubly painful now that it was touched in public.

Mr. Rousseau, however, did not lose his zest. As Agnes withdrew from the conversation his evident desire to retain her in it increased. His manner was colored by indirect gallantry which was no longer acceptable. Nor was the strength of Mr. Rousseau's argument helped thereby, as was evidenced by a sardonic gleam in Ferdinand's eyes at his friend's hope less mixture of compliment and Calvanism.

"Are you a rationalist also, Mrs. Ballington?" asked the young man finally.

"I don't know what you mean," Agnes answered reddening.

"My wife is 'wobbling,'" commented Ferdinand dryly. His observation of his wife had led him to the explanation which Agnes had foreseen. He concluded that the ring had restored her good-humor and that the admiration of the strangers had completed her feminine satisfaction. Vanity and the love of admiration were fundamental in women, as was also hysterical religious emotion, which now logically followed.

"No, I'm not wobbling!" exclaimed Agnes decidedly. "I'm a Christian! I'm a Presbyterian!"

Rousseau cast upon her a look of blandishment. "Thy God shall be my God," he said with invincible complaisance. "In deference to you I shall become a follower of Calvin."

A satirical smile from Ferdinand rewarded his covert witticism.

Agnes stood up and looked down upon the speaker with a quivering face. Without knowing it she was making him a scapegoat for her own and her husband's short-comings. "You are a blasphemer," she said distinctly. " Ferdinand, I wish to go to the hotel."

Ferdinand arose, but made no movement forward. He was irritated. Feminine traits were becoming too pronounced, and he was beginning to regret his gift.

"This walk along the lake is very beautiful by moonlight," he said, without noticing his wife's exclamation. "Suppose we take a stroll." He turned away with Mr. Partlow, leaving Agnes to the attentions of Rousseau.

Rousseau sprang to assist her. She received his aid trembling with humiliation, and walked some distance across the pavilion deaf to his nervous efforts at apology. Her weakness in thus yielding galled her pride indescribably, and as they neared the steps to the lawn she was debating a decisive move.

Mr. Partlow and Ferdinand were a little in advance. Agnes quickened her pace and spoke to her husband as they descended the stairs. "I don't care to walk, Ferdinand. You misunderstood me. I wish you to take me to the hotel."

Her eyes were fixed intently upon her husband, and, not heeding the last stair, she stepped too heavily to the ground, turned her ankle as she did so, and uttered a cry of pain.

She noticed Ferdinand's face change. He was beside her at once, pushing Rousseau aside as he took the support of his wife, and said to her with concern in his voice, "Are you hurt?"

"No, it's nothing." She tested the foot carefully. "It hurts a little."

"Let me carry you across the lawn," he insisted.

"It's all right," she replied hurriedly. "Let us move away from these men."

When they had gone a little way: she broke down and began to cry from mortification over the scene they had passed through.

Ferdinand felt her tears, thought they proceeded from physical pain, stooped and picked her up in his arms. "You are suffering," he said. "Why did you try to walk?"

He carried her as though she were a child through the almost deserted yard to the side door of the hotel. "It isn't my ankle," she kept repeating hysterically. "Do put me down." His only answer was to hold her more determinedly in his arms. She resigned herself to the situation.

When they reached the elevator he put her gently upon her feet. "Is Madame ill?" asked the man running the elevator, to whom Agnes always had given a friendly smile. Ferdinand met the man's eyes and made no reply. The man turned immediately to his rope.

In the upper hall Ferdinand supported his wife to her room, where he laid her down upon her bed, and unlaced the shoe from the injured foot. Agnes lay quite still while he went through her trunk in a man's vague search for something out of which to make a bandage. She felt an inclination to laugh at his air of professional complacence as he at last unearthed and tore up a home-made undergarment to which he always had had an aversion. She continued to watch him while he bound up the supposedly injured member tightly, pointing out where it would begin to swell, and explaining just how a bandage should be put on in order to stay on. The humor of the situation grew upon her as she remembered how many times she had assisted her father in the same operation, but she refrained from telling Ferdinand that he was doing it wrong, and they said good-night amicably on both sides.

After Ferdinand left her, Agnes lay in the quiescence that follows the cessation of nervous tension. She realized that she had entered a new phase of her relations with her husband, that she no longer expected complete understanding or sympathy from him. It was not only Donald's present that forced this fact upon her. It had been growing upon her ever since she left home with Ferdinand. She had thought she understood him before they were married, and she had put off the discussion of certain topics until after they were married, thinking that the intimacy of the complete union would make it easy to talk over vital subjects. It had seemed enough to her that they had confessed a mutual love. She had believed that such a confession involved a life-long effort to attain a spiritual union for which only the marriage bond offered opportunity. She had waited with unimaginable eagerness for that sacred unveiling of the inmost thoughts and aspirations with which she had peopled Ferdinand's reticent soul. She had felt that this revelation of him would help her to understand herself spiritually. She had waited the three months in vain. At first she had expected him to take the initiative, and when that hope was disappointed she tried timidly herself to talk upon subjects her father conversed upon as freely as upon family affairs. It puzzled her that Ferdinand responded to her advances in a way which showed that he had misunderstood her desires, and when she endeavored to explain herself met her with a humorous indulgence. Then Agnes instinctively ceased seeking more than he wished to give. Something warned her that she was happier than she would be after a complete understanding with him. Where she formerly spent hours in day-dreams wondering what he was like, she now found herself shutting those speculations out of her mind. Ferdinand's change of manner this evening, from the cold insult of his disregard when she wished to be relieved of Rousseau's society to his solicitude when she strained her ankle, had occasioned one of those rare periods in which she allowed herself to think of this old mirage of their higher union. Why was it, she asked herself passionately, that they had been disappointed, so far, of what she had yearned for as the highest good? It could not be that Ferdinand did not love her. She remembered expressions that were unmistakable, moments when he had forgotten himself and seemed to think only of her. She had tried to use those moments to lead to something less transient, and then she always had lost them. She confessed to herself at last that these moments of forgetfulness on Ferdinand's part were growing rarer and briefer. She had been eager for one tonight, and she reflected upon the means she instinctively had employed to bring it about. She had failed ignominiously to evoke sympathy in her mental suffering, but a chance accident had enabled her to use a turned ankle with instantaneous success. Was it true that Ferdinand was dead to everything except physical suffering? material appeals? palpable success? Would she have to live alone that inner life for which she felt so weak and helpless, whose long road she was so unfit to travel without a guide?

CHAPTER III

DURING the night after the last conversation and the day following it Agnes' state of mind changed. Second and cooler thoughts came to her. She felt that she must not let this critical financial and religious discussion pass without its bettering the relations between Ferdinand and herself. She had thought over Ferdinand's offer of the Louis, and of his immediate attempt at reconciliation after her refusal.

She assured her husband in the morning that her ankle was quite strong, and they spent the day as he had planned, taking a long ride on horseback along the mountain roads to spend the night at a chalet. The precipitous grandeur of the Alps and the blue peace of the lake below affected her as nature always affects the non-egoist.

The long day's ramble wearied them both, and after dinner they went early to their room.

As they stood on the balcony, looking in silence at the purity of the mountain peaks, on which the flush of twilight and the white glory of the moon were shining, Agnes was conscious of a gentleness and serenity surrounding both her and her husband. She felt for the first time that it would be easy to speak to him on vital things, and she said to him naturally and unaffectedly, "Ferdinand, when you offered me money in the car yesterday I was wrong to refuse it as I did. I have thought it over, and I am willing to accommodate myself to your domestic arrangements. What I said was impulsive, and I am sorry for it."

Ferdinand's face showed relief and appreciation. He was glad to have the subject re-opened. "Thank you," he said. "I am glad you have spoken of it again. Let me make my position clear to you. I have a pretty fair income, but I am obliged to meet many demands upon it. My affairs would not be in their present condition if I had not always shown self-denial and system. The largest income in the world might slip through the fingers of a careless person without his knowing where it had gone."

"Yes, I know," Agnes commented sympathetically.

"The Ballingtons as a family have a constitutional weakness in this way. My grandfather died a pauper, having wasted a fine inheritance from his mother.

He left his children no unencumbered property. It was the invention of the car spring which pulled things together."

"You must be very proud of your father," Agnes returned.

"He didn't invent it. My mother did. She was the one who held things together. My father wasn't worth much more than Tom. He was shiftless and a drunkard."

Agnes started. "How can you speak so of your father?" she asked drawing back a little.

"Why should I hesitate to tell the truth about him? From the time of my father's death, until I came into the business matters were slovenly enough. Uncle Silas did better than my father, but he was no manager. Much of my property—all from the Landseer side—is invested otherwise than in the shops, but I have quite an interest there."

Agnes was quiet for some time. A new and exquisite hope was dawning within her. At last, a real understanding was arising between them and it was because she had acted like a rational being. Money suddenly seemed a very small consideration.

It was with an effort that she brought herself back to respond to Ferdinand's last remark. "Donald must be a great help to you in managing the business, Ferdinand."

"He is a good enough office man."

Again Agnes felt the shock of Ferdinand's downrightness.

"How about Tom? Is he no help?"

"No." There was no mistaking the contemptuous dislike in the word. "He might have done better to make his gold salt-cellars."

Agnes glanced up uneasily at her husband's face. She was reassured by the care and responsibility which were apparent there.

"Well, I will try to be a help, beloved," she said earnestly, putting her hand over his on the railing. "I know very little about business, but I will learn."

He responded to her touch with a look which brought the color to her face. Neither of them spoke. The thin notes of a zither and the distant barking of a sheep-dog baying the moon filled the pauses. Laughter and snatches of song floated up vaguely from a little tavern down in the village. The glimmering lights in the low, flat-roofed houses and the sounds aforesaid were the only things in all the world of blue heavens, mountain peaks, glaciers, precipices, and pine-girdled abysses, down which the wild music of mountain cataracts plunged and was lost, which related it to the infinitesimal day of man's life and endeavor.

"Ferdinand," she said gently, "there's something I've wanted to speak to you about ever since we have been married."

"Why have you waited so long?" he replied in a low voice.

"I don't know. I think I've been afraid. It's always been hard for me to talk about religion. I wish you would talk to me about it. What is your religion?"

Ferdinand did not reply at once. He had known that this conversation must come some time, but he had been putting it off, feeling that the time was not yet ripe. Agnes' reasonableness in coming around after their financial difference decided him, however, to meet her inquiry without evasion.

"I am an agnostic," he said quietly.

Agnes looked at him steadily. "Do you mean, Ferdinand, that you don't believe the Bible is what it is claimed to be? And that you don't know whether there's a God or not? Do you really mean that, Ferdinand?"

Ferdinand was more disturbed by the anguish in her voice than he would have believed possible. "I can't help believing what my reason tells me, Agnes. You wouldn't have me do otherwise, would you?"

Agnes took her hand away from his. "Ferdinand," she said in an unnatural voice, "why did you tell my mother that you were confident that you soon would think as I did on religion?"

"I didn't tell her so," her husband replied. He knew it was coming now.

"You did not?"

"No. I said I was confident that we eventually would think alike; and I am still. When you have seen enough of the world, you will broaden out. I can wait. You have good mental qualities, and I shall give you every means of education."

Ferdinand weighed his words. He was prepared for an outburst. It would be a shock to Agnes to realize that he had misled her mother and herself.

The indignation did not come, however, as he had expected. On the contrary Agnes turned white, and when she spoke her voice was low and there was a note in it which alarmed him. "You deceived my mother, then. You deliberately let her think you meant one thing when you meant something which would have broken her heart."

Ferdinand, too, grew pale. "Yes, I let her believe one thing while I meant another," he answered, "and I would do so again. I can't accept Christianity. It would be equally impossible for your mother at her time of life to modify her views. Neither of us is accountable to the other, and my course of action saved us all three much unpleasantness."

"But do you think there will be less unpleasantness when she finds out that you deceived her?"

"I shall not undeceive her. You may do as you think best."

As she did not speak, he said again, "I foresaw that the struggle would come upon you. You would either be obliged to go against your mother, or to give me up, and I wished to prevent a family rupture."

He wondered from her continued silence if she understood just what he had been saying and all that he had spared her. And he repeated, "You see you would have had to choose between your mother and me, and it would have resulted in your never having easy relations with your mother afterwards."

He need not have reiterated the words. She was realizing with a kind of moral shock that the whole question in Ferdinand's mind had been how to conciliate her mother; that he had contemplated no difficulty or struggle with her own conscience! nay, he had ignored her conscience as if she had none; and he never once had considered it remotely possible that she would have given up him if the choice had rested upon her.

At length she looked up and spoke. "Perhaps you were right about me. I find that I am glad you did not put the choice upon me."

This was the sentiment upon which Ferdinand had counted, but there was a sub-meaning along with it which made him uneasy.

When he would have drawn nearer to caress her, she still held off. "Yes, I'm *glad*," she repeated, leaving an emphasis of scorn on the final word which she spoke so low that he caught the scorn more clearly than the significance of the word itself, "and yet I did have some conscience. I faced that very question, and I found that I could make the sacrifice. More than that, Ferdinand, I surely would have made it. My mother will remember."

She stopped speaking, but he could see that she was following out some line of thought.

After a few moments he resumed, "Besides, Agnes, I knew that your views were bound to change, and if you regard yourself closely you will see that you have changed considerably already. I have watched your progress with great interest and satisfaction. When we were first married you never would have taken this ride with me on Sunday. Now you—"

His wife turned suddenly and went into her room.

When he followed her he found her sobbing on the bed. He stood looking down at her, utterly at a loss what to do. "Why do you cry, Agnes?" he asked uncomfortably.

She did not answer, and he sat down by her and put out his hand to stroke her hair.

Gradually her shame and wretchedness came under control. Her regret at having taken the ride began to fade before the memory of the Sabbath stillness of the mountains and the influence that had brooded over their own spirits all day. Then, too, she was Ferdinand's wife now. Past deceit could not be helped. What concerned them was to see that there should be no more. She felt the need of spiritual help for the future.

"Ferdinand," she asked, with a last effort, "do you ever pray?"

There was a moment's hesitation. Then he replied, "No."

"Won't you—with me?"

Ferdinand's voice was uncertain as he answered, "It would be hypocrisy for me to do so."

"Won't you try? If you love me, do."

Ferdinand was thoroughly unhappy. She seemed like a child imploring him to search with her for a pot of gold in a rainbow. It was contrary to his nature to allow misunderstanding under such circumstances. When Agnes was yet to be won she was to be approached cautiously, but once his wife the sooner she accommodated herself to the situation the better. Yet he was almost disheartened as he took his hand from her hair and answered briefly, "I cannot."

She was so lovely as she looked up at him with hurt eyes and with the baffled pleading in her face that he could not leave her so. "Agnes, be content with my love," he said with feeling. "You will understand me better in time."

As he left her and went into his room his last words, with their assurance of present love and of future understanding, fell upon her tortured spirit like a benediction. "Better to know it all. Better so," she thought in mingled grief and devotion. Then the solemnity of what was laid upon her deepened as the night hours passed. She faced the conviction that she must live her spiritual life alone, and live it so that he who now was part of her must be brought into sympathy with it. How easily she had accepted nominal Christianity from her parents as a girl! How dependently she had looked to her husband to support her in her higher life! It was made plain to her at last that every man liveth to himself. Her inner experience must be an individual one. What did it mean to be a Christian? She must find that out for herself. The horror of her husband's repudiating Christianity was clearer than her understanding of just what he had repudiated. It was not riding on Sunday, or drinking wine, or going to the theater, or any of the gradually accepted customs which at first she had reproved. In these, she had changed. Could it be possible that she would keep on changing, as he said? Agnes' anxiety gradually lessened as she recollected his words. "I can wait. Be content with my love. You will understand me better in time." He, too, had been waiting for sympathy and comprehension as she had been, but he had waited patiently and silently. She was as unfit to meet his demands as he had been to meet hers. He, too, had much to offer which always had been outside her ken—business discernment, scientific discipline, organized and focused energies. If she could prove to him that her great heritage was worthy his consideration while she accepted his, what unity and power and happiness they might attain! This, perhaps, was what God had meant in bringing them together.

Occasional conversations like this stood out in Agnes' memory as marking successive shocks of mutual readjustment, after which they would go on for a time without friction. It was when they reached England some weeks later that she saw the extent of the change in their attitude toward each other. She found herself looking with different and older eyes upon the scenes she had witnessed five months before. Then everything had been a background for Ferdinand. It was so no longer. A hunger for wider vision, for clearer understanding of the world about her, had awakened within her. The mind had thrown off the shackles of passion, and she realized she was leaving Europe just at the point when she could appreciate her advantages. She had learned to discriminate and enjoy.

A foreboding weighed upon her spirit as she saw England sink below the horizon into the Atlantic. Would it always be so? Would she learn to value the greatest things in her life only as she parted from them? So her college life had

slipped away from her, her father, her mother's encircling devotion, this last
Renaissance with its rich opportunities. What would be next?

CHAPTER IV.

"DO you think the table looks all right, Sarah?"

Miss Margaret Ballington daintily drew back from the antique epergne which she had been adorning with sprays from her fuchsia plants and looked up hopefully.

"Elegant," said Mrs. Ballington approvingly.

Miss Margaret drew a breath of relief. The next moment she glanced back at the table, this time at the candelabra, and asked with increasing uneasiness in each phrase, "Is that shade a little crooked? Will you please straighten it, Tom? Be careful that your cuff doesn't catch in the flowers, dear. Is that a carriage I hear? Shall I serve the salad with the oysters or in a course by itself? Which would you, Tom?"

"Both," said Tom promptly, narrowly escaping a decanter with his elbow.

A momentary color passed like a shadow of youth over his aunt's face. "Don't joke me, dear. They'll be here before I can decide. Which would you do, Sarah?"

As Mrs. Ballington was arranging herself to reply, for the sequence of salad and oysters was not a thing to be disposed of flippantly, the dining-room door was opened and a large woman of forty or upwards, with red hair and little despotic gray eyes, appeared on the threshold and stood with her hands on her hips, nodding at the long table, "Shall I put on that loaf of mate, Miss Margaret? It'll want cooking the long half of an hour."

"Not just yet. Not right away, Eliza," her mistress fluttered. "Isn't that Ferdinand's step I hear on the walk?" Miss Ballington rustled to the hall door, opened it and listened.

"You sit down, Aunt Maggie. I'll watch for the carriage," said Tom. He moved a chair where Miss Ballington was standing, lifted the little woman up as he spoke and, after having smoothed down her skirts as though she were infant in long clothes, seated her in it.

"Tom! Be careful, Tom!"

Tom gave her an affectionate pat, released her and turned to the servant. "Get back to your den, Eliza. How do you know what that meat's doing?"

"And oh, Eliza!" Miss Margaret sprang to her feet again. "Hadn't you better—will you please put a clean apron on?"

The Irishwoman glanced carelessly down. "This apron is clean," she said aggressively.

"But I'd a little rather—you know Mr. Ferdinand likes everything neat. You can have my little apron with the clover blossoms on it. You'll find it in the second drawer of my bureau in the pile on the left-hand side, a little back. Be careful not to—" Eliza disappeared and closed the door before the sentence was finished.

Mrs. Ballington looked after her with indignation righteously thrilling every nerve in her body. "Margaret!" she proclaimed, "you ruin your servants. Sam is utterly spoiled. He won't mow our grass since Ferdinand went away without an extra fee."

"I know I do, Sarah," said Miss Margaret miserably. "I wouldn't have given that—but there!" She listened breathlessly, like a startled deer. "Do you hear anything, Tom?"

"I think I do," said Tom resignedly.

Mrs. Ballington walked before the long mirror at the end of the room, where she turned slowly, eyeing herself. Miss Margaret sat down suddenly in her chair. Tom was about to open the hall door, when the kitchen door flew open and Eliza, with face aflame, strode through the room and into the hall before him. She threw the front door open wide, and was the first to greet Agnes Ballington as she walked up the steps between Ferdinand and Donald.

"Welcome home to yez, Mr. Ballington!" cried Eliza, her face beaming, "an' welcome to your swate young wife!" She opened her big arms, gave Agnes a hug, then stepped back and nodded critically at the bride.

Agnes smiled and straightened her drooping hat as she returned the old servant's welcome. After greetings from Tom, the party entered the house.

Ferdinand set the luggage down in the hall and opened the door into the green parlor. "Come in here, Agnes," he said. "Aunt Margaret will be here presently."

"She wants to see you alone first. She's in the dining room," whispered Tom. "I'll go in with your wife. Mother is here in the parlor."

Agnes already had seen Mrs. Silas Ballington, and she was so occupied with that lady's somewhat distant greeting that she did not notice her husband's annoyed expression and subsequent disappearance. She glanced eagerly around the room, noting for the first time the interior of her new home. There was something attractive and something repellent in the formal arrangement of pictures and green mahogany furniture. It was a handsome apartment, but cold and austere. Agnes felt like an alien sitting on the edge of one of the big pieces and looking up to meet the still gray eyes of Estelle Landseer, Ferdinand's mother, looking down from the gold frame on the wall over the green lounge. She returned Mrs. Ballington's greeting mechanically. "It was very kind in you to welcome us home, Mrs. Ballington," she said, her eyes still resting on the portrait. She traced Ferdinand's features in the grave face. There was something ascetic, something despotic, in the expression, and, along with these, something inscrutable. Agnes found herself trying to interpret it by Ferdinand's face, and failing. It seemed to her as though her husband's mother were passing her in review, challenging her strength, questioning her wisdom, warning her of the stubborn and masterful spirit whose home she had entered. "He is my son," Agnes almost heard her say. "Are you equal to it?"

"I'm sure I'm delighted," said the once-admired society voice of Mrs. Silas Ballington.

Agnes started, trying to remember what Mrs. Ballington was delighted about. Her interest in the picture, however, overtopped everything else. She pointed to it. "What a remarkable face! And she actually invented the car spring!"

If Agnes had cast about her for a long time she could not have searched out a more infuriating remark. Mrs. Silas drew herself up and darted a poisonous glance at the new and unwelcome addition to the family.

Agnes interpreted it as a reproach for failing to understand her new aunt's last remark, and she hastened to atone. "It was so nice to see Donald at the station," she said. "We hardly expected such a home-coming."

The moment it was out she realized that she had made matters worse.

At that instant Tom came in from the hall, saw that something was wrong, as usual, with his mother, and promptly went up to Agnes and kissed her.

"Tom!" exclaimed his mother; then grandiloquently to Agnes, "You must excuse my son, Mrs. Ballington."

"I wish you would call me 'Agnes,'" said the bride, trying to smile, but feeling like crying.

"With pleasure," Tom answered immediately, and he looked around at the chairs. "Which one do you advise me to sit in, mother?" he asked, with interest.

The dowager was casting a withering glance at her son, when the dining-room door was opened, and Ferdinand, still in his ulster, entered with his aunt. She wore a flowered silk of mild shades, with tiny pink bows sprinkled over it, and she looked to Agnes like a little Dresden figure come to life.

"This is my wife, Aunt Margaret," said Ferdinand.

Agnes rose and came forward, smiling with genuine pleasure.

Miss Margaret gave a little gasp, then held out both hands, and lifted her face to be kissed. She kept hold of one hand as she said, "Come, dear, I will take you upstairs. Your room is all ready, Ferdinand. There's a little fire in the grate."

She fluttered into the hall and up the stairs, still leading Agnes, who felt clumsy and stiff beside her.

They went into a roomy apartment which was dressed sedately in old-fashioned watered silk. A gilt mirror hung against the wall, and this was draped with fresh muslin. There were flowers on the table, a tray containing a glass of cracked ice, and a small champagne bottle.

Miss Ballington closed the door, went up to Agnes, looked at her with a timid smile, kissed her, said, "Will you love me a little, dear? and kissed her again.

"Yes, I love you already," answered Agnes, laughing in some embarrassment, yet altogether charmed with her husband's aunt.

"You dear child. I shall try to make you happy, dear. You will love me, won't you? You know there's nobody I love quite as I do Ferdinand. He's all I have. You wouldn't want him not to love me, would you?"

"No, indeed," replied Agnes, still smiling.

"I knew you wouldn't. I knew you would add your sweet love to his. I won't find him changed, do you think?" The last sentence caught Agnes' attention with its child-like pathos.

"No, I think not," she said gently.

"And I shall call you 'Agnes' right away. You want me to, don't you? And you will call me 'Aunt Margaret,' just as Ferdinand does?" continued the little lady. She always spoke rapidly, and excitement now made her almost unintelligible.

"Of course I will," said Agnes heartily.

"Call me so now, dear. Will you, dear?" and Miss Margaret looked up tenderly at her new niece.

"Why, yes—Aunt Margaret," answered Agnes, wishing her aunt would give her some natural excuse for saying 'Aunt Margaret.'

Something in her manner may have conveyed Agnes' awkwardness to Miss Ballington, for the latter turned away from her guest and tripped across the room to look into the water pitcher. Then she went out into the hall and closed the door behind her softly.

"Oh, Agnes dear," she called through the keyhole.

"Yes?" asked Agnes, opening the door again.

"I didn't mean to disturb you, dear. You needn't have opened the door. I just wanted to ask if I could do anything else for you."

"No, I thank you," said Agnes in a daze.

"And shall I have dinner served soon?"

"I shall be ready in ten minutes." And Agnes recovered her senses briskly.

"Very well, dear. Don't hurry," and light little steps went down the stairs.

Agnes hastened to change her traveling dress for a coral colored silk which her mother had made. It had been the best dress of her trousseau, and she still preferred it to the more elaborate gowns her husband had given her since. She was just finishing when Ferdinand knocked and entered the room.

They went down together and met the others in the drawing-room, from which they all passed on to the dining room, Ferdinand still keeping by his wife's side.

Miss Ballington previously had considered whether she should offer Agnes the head of the table at once, and had concluded it would be better to make the change later in private. Now, however, she looked from one to the other in embarrassment.

Tom, perceiving the emergency, slipped into Ferdinand's place and said to the latter with a flourish of his hand, "Above the salt, Mr. Ballington. Take your seat there. Tomorrow Mrs. Ballington and you may take possession, but tonight you are the distinguished guests of Miss Margaret and Mr. Thomas

Ballington." Tom's annoyance with the situation gave place to good-humored mischief as he took his place at the head of Ferdinand's table.

Ferdinand's ghost-smile hovered around his lips as he seated himself beside Agnes.

The burden of conversation fell upon Tom. He addressed himself especially to Agnes, whom everyone was watching. She had changed somewhat during the short absence, was a little fuller in figure, had grown into a quieter manner, a greater reserve in speech, and a noticeable courtesy in listening. In repose there was a luminousness in her dark eyes which marked a growing likeness to Dr. Sidney; and when she became animated a radiance of expression flushed her face with delicate color. Altogether, she was a richer and quieter figure than the girl Tom remembered.

Miss Margaret Ballington's surprise and delight in her nephew's wife became more and more evident. Happiness transformed her. She seemed years younger than when she had listened for the carriage wheels, while the nervousness of elation had driven out and replaced in her always apprehensive little body the nervousness of foreboding.

"I presume you fully appreciate the fact that you successfully passed Minos in the hall, Agnes," said Tom when conversation lulled a moment.

Agnes turned to him with a tinge of diffidence in her manner.

"He means Eliza," explained Ferdinand.

"The proprietress of the establishment," continued Tom impressively. "The Proserpine of the kitchen. Let me give you a word of advice, Agnes. Eliza has all the rest of us under her thumb. Unless you start out by putting her down, the Ballington family is doomed."

As if the reference to Eliza had summoned that person, she appeared at this instant, displaying a blur of tomato juice on Miss Margaret's apron, and nodding approvingly at Agnes across the room.

"Yez hev struck luck, Mrs. Ballington," she said, tilting her horse-like head to one side as she included Ferdinand in the next nod. "Mr. Ferdinand is the prime pet of fortune, sure."

"We think Mrs. Ballington is a pet of fortune, too, Eliza," put in Donald.

"Thin two pets have met," rejoined the red-haired woman promptly. "Did ye see Ireland on the other side, Mr. Ferdinand?"

"We are waiting for the salad, Eliza," suggested Miss Margaret.

The cook shrugged her shoulders with a side look at Agnes in reply, and went back to the kitchen.

"You're on the right side of Eliza," Tom exclaimed when the door closed. "Now let time and tide work their will."

When they went back to the drawing-room Miss Margaret drew Agnes to her side on the lounge and pressed the girl's hand impulsively. "You dear, dear child," she whispered.

Agnes blushed and tried to return the pressure, but Miss Margaret's demonstration embarrassed her. She diverted herself by talking a little to Mrs. Ballington and wondering that she no longer was impressed by that lady's lofty bearing.

"Won't you favor us with a song? asked Mrs. Ballington, at length.

"Agnes is too tired to sing," interrupted Ferdinand.

"We ought to be going, Tom," said Donald, rising. "We mustn't stay too late the first night. John will be here for you shortly, mother."

The brothers said good-night, shook hands with Agnes and left the house together.

Soon afterwards, the carriage came for Mrs. Ballington. As she was departing, she drew Miss Margaret outside and whispered something in her ear which brought a startled exclamation to Miss Margaret's lips. When the latter re turned to the parlor, there were signs of confusion in her face and manner.

"You must be very tired, dear," she said effusively to Agnes. "Is there anything you would like?"

"No, thank you, Aunt Margaret. I have just told Ferdinand I think I will go to my room. Thank you so much for your kind reception." Agnes turned to the door as she spoke.

"Thank you, dear child. Will you kiss me good-night? Good-night. Sleep well, dear."

After Agnes had left them, Ferdinand turned to his aunt. "I noticed the lawn has not been cut back of the house," he said questioningly.

"No, Ferdinand, said Miss Ballington, at once on the defensive and voluble with excuses, "Sam has been very unreasonable—very. I've had to raise his wages, too." She sighed. "He was going to leave, dear. Don't you think I did right to raise his wages? Are you offended with me, Ferdinand?"

"No. I knew when I left you, you couldn't manage the place," returned her nephew philosophically.

"I'm so sorry," she replied at once, on the verge of tears. "I really tried, dear."

Ferdinand hastened to change the subject. "Are the accounts at hand?" he inquired, not noticing her half tearful lament.

"Yes, dearest. Right here. I have them all ready."

She hurried across the room, opened a tiny drawer in the inlaid cabinet, and returned with a small leather book.

"I have told Agnes you had better continue the management of the house for the remainder of the year," said Ferdinand before opening the notebook. "Then she can begin the first of January."

"Yes, dearest. Very well," responded Miss Ballington with a gleam of hope.

She stood behind his chair, and caressed his hair, occasionally leaning down to bestow a kiss upon it. Presently he stirred, moved his head restlessly. The patting ceased a moment, then began again.

"You'll tire yourself," he said, pausing at length in his reading and moving his chair to one side. "Sit down, Aunt Margaret."

"No, you sweet dear. I love to stand here." She laid her faded hair alongside his dark head. "It's so good to have you here, dear! I've missed you so!"

Ferdinand arose, walked to the center of the room and stood under the hanging lamp. His aunt's caresses worried him, as they had done ever since he was old enough to run away from her.

"This isn't added correctly," he said.

"Isn't it, dear? Are you sure it isn't?" asked Miss Ballington, her attention instantly diverted to her perennial source of worry, the balancing of accounts. "I went over it eight times. You see there's nine cents unaccounted for. I don't know. I'm not sure but that cabbage that's down in August somewhere—I've got it underlined—there it is that cabbage may have been four cents instead of two. I'm not just sure. That would account for two cents."

"The fault is in the adding," Ferdinand said, returning the book. "The expenditure adds to nine cents more than you make it. You have about thirty dollars on hand, I see."

"Yes, dear," said Miss Margaret with pride in her thrift.

"You have done very well. It's remarkable what method the most unsystematic women may acquire under training. You may have the balance."

"Have the thirty dollars! Do you mean without keeping an account of it, Ferdinand?" gasped his aunt.

"Yes."

Oh, thank you, dear. There are some—" She hastily checked her inopportune disclosures. Thank you *very* much."

"Good-night. We have breakfast at the usual time?" Ferdinand asked as a matter of form.

"Yes, yes. You wouldn't like it changed, would you, dearest?" said Miss Margaret, on the look-out for new afflictions with Eliza.

"No," said Ferdinand indifferently.

"Ferdinand!" she exclaimed, suddenly forgetting breakfast and Eliza.

He had reached the door, but he turned at her ejaculation.

"You aren't angry with me, are you, dear?" she interrupted herself to ask anxiously.

"Certainly not."

"Won't you kiss me good-night?" she persisted, approaching him hesitatingly.

He stooped and kissed her forehead.

"This doesn't make any difference, does it, Ferdinand? She won't come between us, will she, dear? You were such a dear little baby, Ferdinand. You'll always be my baby, you know. I think she's lovely, *lovely*. And she says she loves me, loves me already. She doesn't brush her hair quite up in the neck. But that doesn't matter. I love her dearly."

She clung to him as the disjointed sentences came out. He indulgently disengaged her arms, turned, and went up the stairs.

Five minutes later she tapped at his door.

"I don't mean to disturb you, dearest. I just wanted to ask if everything is all right. There's a fresh cake of soap in the dish, isn't there?"

"I have my own." The voice came through the closed door patiently.

"Ferdinand!"

After an instant's hesitation, the door was open and he stood once more looking down at her.

She flushed consciously, looked down at her hands and smiled a very little, then looked up wistfully.

"Yes?" inquired Ferdinand, waiting.

"There isn't anything you'd like to tell me, is there, dearest?"

Ferdinand was puzzled. "Tell you? I think not," he said.

"I mean any little confidence. I'm like your mother, you know, dear."

She looked up at him half expectantly.

"There is nothing," he replied briefly.

She took alarm at once. "Oh! Good-night. You aren't angry with me for asking, are you? I only asked from interest, dearest, the most loving interest. Good-night."

His door closed. Miss Margaret walked down the hall a little, hesitated, turned back and approached his door, then paused again and turned resolutely to her own room.

Just then she heard Eliza's heavy step going up the back stairs. She leaned over the banisters. "Eliza didn't turn out the lights or lock up, again," she said to herself, putting her hand up to her head. "Oh, dear! Oh, dear! I must go down."

Then the tired little feet went down the stairs, and through the long halls. She locked the doors, stood up on the chairs to fasten the windows, paused in the green room to kiss a baby miniature of Ferdinand, and turned out the lights. Then she climbed the staircase in the dark and felt her way to her own room, where she undressed and cried herself to sleep.

CHAPTER V

AFTER Donald and Tom left Ferdinand's home on the night of their cousin's return, they started on their homeward way in silence. It was not until they passed the border-line of their cousin's property that Tom thrust his hands into his pockets and spoke abruptly, "Oh, hell!"

"You did splendidly tonight, Tom," answered Donald, ignoring the ejaculation; "the evening would have been very trying without you."

"Yes, I saw that. Now, you don't get me to go near his house again. Down in the office I don't care a damn."

"Agnes looked very beautiful," continued Donald thoughtfully, still without heeding his brother's ill-temper.

"You're right, she did," Tom agreed. "The green parlor made me think of the sea, and she of that spray of coral in the cabinet that Uncle Tom gave me when I was a baby and that Aunt Stella took away from me. By gad!"—Tom's voice became suddenly louder—"I'll smash into that cabinet some day!"

Donald smiled. He remembered his brother's boyish passion for the coral.

"Aunt Maggie seems quite taken with Agnes," Tom went on presently.

"Yes," said Donald dubiously, "I hope it lasts."

"Did you see Aunt Maggie get me out into the hall for a confidential chat before we left? She thought she'd hurt my feelings by saying something about my mussing her dress."

He finished with an impatient sigh which told of other matters on his mind.

Donald looked at him. "What is it, Tom?" he asked. "Oh, nothing, nothing. If I could get together fifty or seventy-five cents, I'd go off on a trip. I need a few cents for clothes, too. I'd be thankful to have the wardrobe of a Zulu. I don't ask to be arrayed like Solomon."

After a pause Donald asked in an apologetic voice, "You haven't been playing the stocks again, have you?"

"Now look here, Don," said Tom irritably, "there's reason in stocks just as there is in everything else. It's unscientific in you to object to something you know nothing about."

Donald raised his hand imploringly. Tom muttered something in his throat. The brothers walked on a little distance without speaking.

Donald was reviewing Tom's new fever for speculation, and one result which seemed to him particularly unfortunate. This was a renewed and growing companionship with Beatrice Sidney.

"Tom," Donald said thoughtfully, at last, "do you see much of General Mott?"

"See much of Mott? Why, no, why should I?"

"Well—you go out to the lake house often enough."

"Well, I don't go to see him," said Tom crustily.

"You seem to be going there a good deal," persisted Donald. "I don't think it looks altogether well. It seems to be a good deal more convenient for you to get out there than it is for Sidney. Of course I know it's all right, but I think you ought to be a little careful."

"Well, I'll be 'a little careful'! I know what you mean. Now Ferdinand is back, we're in the world of gossip once more. If he could do Beatrice a mean turn and get a slap at me at the same time, one of the main objects of his life would be accomplished." Tom's tone was full of venom.

Donald tried to turn the conversation back into its original channel.

"Why is it, Tom, that Beatrice spends so much of her time away from her husband? She no sooner got that great place built than she leaves it. I thought she was staying with her father out at the lake."

"How long is it since you've begun to gossip, Don?" exclaimed Tom angrily. "Old Mott's down in New York speculating in stocks, with a long-distance telephone put in at the lake house. Bee has her ticker and she has made a tidy little sum herself."

A look of alarm came into Donald's face. "I hope you're not interested in the Mott speculations," he said earnestly. His worries with regard to Tom took on a change of front. The General's going to get caught some day."

Tom gave a disdainful laugh. "That's what Ferd thinks. But his hope has been deferred a long time. The Motts are a cool-headed lot. Father and daughter have got enough put away to buy our car-barns at the price Ferdinand puts on them, and they won't touch it either, even if they lose every cent of their floating capital. Old Mott never goes in over his depths, and when he's drunk he doesn't go in at all."

"What started Beatrice at this?" said Donald after having turned over in his mind Tom's disclosures.

"Oh, she went into it this last summer. It was awfully dull in Kent, and she couldn't get Fred to go anywhere else. Sidney made such a row about her having a ticker in Kent that she put it in at the lake house to keep peace in the family."

"Do you mean to say, Tom, that you are countenancing Beatrice in a position of antagonism to her husband's wishes? I don't see how your sense of honor can allow you to take such a step."

"See here, Don," replied Tom with a ring of determination in his voice, "my family have had a good deal to say about my course of life, hitherto. I haven't had character enough to cut loose and do what I was made to do. I am a good natured, shuffling leaner like Uncle Tom. Here I am, on a clerk's salary in Ferdinand's office. I won't have a cent of capital till I'm thirty years old, while mother and you, the executors of my father's estate, dole out to me enough to buy shoestrings and neckties. Mother would like to buy them for me if she could. Looking forward to that thirtieth year has been the ruin of me. I'm not going to look any more. I'm going to get some money now, anyway that's feasible, do you understand?"

"I have never refused you money within reason," said Donald in a hurt voice. "I have offered you a European trip twice—told you to take a few months off. I make you the same offer now."

"I don't want a few months off. I want the privilege of being of age before I'm in my second childhood. When I go abroad it will be on my own money, to stay as long as I like."

The bitterness in Tom's heart astonished Donald. For the first time he saw that he might be the author of more dangerous developments in Tom's character than would have taken place had his brother been left to his own harmless, if meaningless, ambitions. Perhaps his mother and he had made a great mistake. Perhaps Tom should have been allowed at eighteen to follow out his queer passion to be a goldsmith. He wavered, was almost at the point of proposing to Tom the long-wished--for study of goldsmithry abroad. Then the thought of Ferdinand's and his mother's indignation at his weakness in seconding Tom's madness steadied his judgment.

He laid his hand regretfully on Tom's shoulder. "Tom, we all have to give up things. I know you are worried and exasperated."

Tom interrupted him savagely, "For heaven's sake, spare me that, Don. I'm not worried about anything. I'm as peaceful as a boiled egg. You and mother needn't sit on me any longer. There's no hope of my hatching."

They walked on in the darkness until they reached the outskirts of the town.

Then Donald spoke again, "I've been thinking about something for some time, Tom. If you have any inclination to marry, I want you to feel perfectly free to do so. An arrangement can be made to give you a suitable income in anticipation of your share in our father's estate."

"I don't want to get married," replied Tom moodily.

Then a memory came back to him. There was a new tone in his voice as he continued, "There's one woman who might have made something of me."

"Who is that, Tom?" Donald asked with an impulse of hope.

"That young woman Agnes brought to our house the time she came to dinner. She talked to me about Benvenuto Cellini when I took her home. She said if a man had it in him to be anything, he'd be it. If a man had that kind of woman around, he might," Tom finished gloomily.

"Agnes was telling me about her this evening," replied Donald, forgetting his own memories of that night in his surprise at Tom's reminiscence. "I did not know you took an interest in her. You never have spoken of her. Isn't she older than you?"

"Oh, Lord, Don, you make me sick!"

Tom turned away from his brother abruptly, and started across the street.

Donald put out his hand and caught him. "Hold on, Tom! Come along, home. I didn't mean anything by that."

"No, you haven't enough brains to mean anything when you try." Tom's voice shook with passion and his face looked white under the gas-lamp.

Donald was arrested by a look of desperation in his brother which he never had seen before. "See here, Tom," he said decidedly, "I believe you are right. I don't mean about the brains, but about Miriam Cass."

He stopped and the two looked at each other. Tom was strangely quiet.

Donald continued. "I think she is a remarkable woman, a woman worth loving, and why shouldn't she love you? The age doesn't make any difference. Why have you never spoken about her before?"

The color slowly rose into Tom's face. "Why haven't I?" he groaned.

A pang of sympathy pierced to Donald's heart. He turned away and began to walk along slowly.

In a few moments, Tom caught up with him. "Don!" he exclaimed.

There was a tone in his voice that made Donald's heart leap. The next moment he felt Tom's arm thrown over his shoulder and around his neck. "Let's talk about her!"

The world as it is vanished from Tom as he spoke. The world as a boy dreams it came in its place. A sudden adoration that rises none knows whence nor whither possessed him, the innocent passion that longs to give and not to get, the idolatry of youth with all its rainbow glory.

Donald did not dare glance at him. He knew the ethereal fragility of that mood, but he knew that if Tom could keep it, it would be his salvation. With his heart in his mouth, he began to talk of Miriam Cass, and when they reached the house and separated for the night the tears were wet on his cheeks and Tom's mood was unbroken.

CHAPTER VI

SEVERAL days after her arrival Agnes was busy arranging her own and her husband's rooms when she heard Miss Margaret's delicate tap at the half-open door. Miss Ballington entered without waiting for an invitation, holding a large pasteboard box in her arms.

Agnes hurried to help her. "Let me take the box, Aunt Margaret. You'll drop it," she said, holding out her hands.

"You dear child," ejaculated Miss Margaret ecstatically. "How happy I am since you've come here. I've never found anybody—except Ferdinand, of course, and those who have left us—with whom I've felt quite so much in sympathy. I don't mean anything against Sarah or Donald or dear Tom. You don't think that, do you?"

"No, indeed," said Agnes; "what have you there? It looks wonderfully interesting."

"I knew you would love to look at these things with me," said the elder woman delightedly.

She fluttered around to Agnes' side of the box, and gave her several butterfly kisses. Agnes took off the cover and sat down on the floor by the box.

"Why! They're baby clothes," she said, lifting an exquisite, old-fashioned garment without sleeves.

"They're what dear little Ferdinand used to wear," said Miss Margaret, patting the dress. Estelle made them herself. "She was an expert needle-woman. She had had lessons from the nuns."

"They are beautiful," said Agnes, turning over some of the garments and thinking of her own mother's equally beautiful but self-taught work. "Think of Ferdinand's ever getting into this shirt!"

"He was the sweetest baby," said Miss Margaret. "Sometimes Estelle would let me give him his bath. See this little brush. It's the very one I used to brush his hair with." She laid down the brush and took up a package of letters, tied with a faded ribbon. "I'm going to leave these for you to read, dearest. They're my most precious letters. They're from Tom—that's Ferdinand's father, you know—and Estelle, and some from Ferdinand, too. My brother Tom was a very attractive man, so good-hearted. I don't believe he ever said an unkind word to anybody in all his life. I wish you could have heard him sing. He used to sing at all the church sociables."

Here Miss Margaret's reminiscences became too vivid for mere narration and she began singing softly in a sweet, thin voice:

"Kathleen Mavourneen, the gray dawn is breaking,
The horn of the hunter is heard on the hill."

As Agnes watched her she felt the ghost of the first Tom Ballington behind his sister as she knelt on the floor, a gentler and sweeter spirit than his son had sketched him.

She shook off the eerie feeling and resolutely took up the letters. "I have wondered what Ferdinand's mother was like," she said; "I can't tell how glad I shall be to read her letters."

Her evident interest filled Miss Margaret's cup of satisfaction to overflowing and she became girlishly confidential. "And here is some of Ferdinand's hair when he was two years old," she said in a half whisper. "Isn't it soft? I used to rock him to sleep in my arms sometimes in that little white chair in my room. Some time, perhaps, I'll give the chair to you, dear."

"Oh, I wouldn't take it away from you, Aunt Margaret. I'd like a little wisp of this hair, though, to put in one of my lockets, if you don't mind."

"You shall have half. You don't think I ought to give it all to you, do you?" Miss Margaret paused apprehensively.

"No, indeed," exclaimed Agnes.

"Thank you, dear. I thought these things ought to belong to you now. But you'll let me keep one little set, won't you? I'd like to have one set for my very own."

Agnes was touched, Miss Margaret was so evidently giving away her dearest treasures, and yet they must not be refused. "Certainly, dear Aunt Margaret. It's very good in you to give any of them to me."

As she spoke Agnes replaced the little pieces in the box, with the exception of the one set, and with a look of friendly gratitude, picked up the box and carried it into her closet.

When she returned Miss Ballington was sitting in a rocking-chair picking nervously at a bow on her dress.

"Agnes, dear," she said.

At the sound of her voice Agnes' mood instinctively clouded over. "Yes?" she asked guardedly.

"We love each other, don't we?"

"Why—yes. Certainly."

"There ought to be perfect confidence between us. Don't you think so?"

Agnes made no reply.

"Don't you think so, precious?" repeated Miss Margaret, and she went over and put her thin arms over the back of Agnes' chair.

"Wasn't that picture of Ferdinand too pretty for anything?" Agnes exclaimed evasively, rising and going to the closet again. "I'm going to have it out here till he comes home. There! Doesn't he look dignified?"

She did not sit down again, but stood looking at a picture which she had placed on the high mahogany bureau. She was trying to bring back the easy relations which had characterized the opening of the interview.

Miss Margaret rose and slipped her arm around Agnes' waist. "Isn't there a soulful look in his eyes?" she asked. "He used to look at me that way sometimes when he was a little boy. Dear little fellow. I've thought he must look at you that way, doesn't he, dear?"

Agnes was divided between a desire to laugh at the soulful glances of the baby Ferdinand, and resentment at the starved sentimentality which was timidly trying to claim kinship with her young and full experience, but the pathos of the ridiculous situation gagged her exasperation into a futile reply. "Why—I don't know."

"Wouldn't you—you wouldn't be angry if I ask you something, will you, dear?" Miss Margaret hesitated at her own temerity. Then she took courage. She had at last found someone who was kind and who might give her a glimpse into that world from which fate had shut her out. "I'd so like to know what he says to you sometimes. Won't you tell me some of the pet names he calls you, dear? I'm going to let you read my letters," she added tremulously, frightened by the sudden flush on Agnes' cheeks and brow.

Agnes' sense of humor came to the rescue. "He generally calls me 'Agnes'."

"Don't be angry with me, dearest. Please don't."

Miss Margaret moved hesitatingly toward Agnes and stood trembling in front of her. As the young wife glanced down and saw the sterile hopes and blasted instincts in the withered face her heart smote her.

"I'll tell you what he called you the other day," she said smiling, a sudden thought coming to her. "He called you a carnation pink."

Miss Margaret's face took on an illumination. "Did he?" she said softly. "How sweet in you to tell me, dear."

Agnes was glad of the diversion, but her conscience pricked her a little at the construction she had put upon some words of Ferdinand's.

Miss Margaret did not go, however.

"I never thought I could be so happy with Ferdinand's wife here," she said presently, sitting down and drawing a crochet pattern from her pocket. "It's so nice to have someone to chat with mornings. Sarah comes sometimes. "But Sarah is rather unapproachable, don't you think so, dear?"

Agnes smiled shrewdly. "I shouldn't think she would attract confidence," she said.

"I never can forget how unjust she was to you, dear. You are the very last person in the world to call bold. I'm sure nobody could think that of you. Ferdinand was angry, when he heard it. Oh!"

Agnes' smile suddenly vanished. Indignation at Mrs. Ballington was aggravated by impatience at herself for having given Aunt Margaret a loophole for gossip.

Miss Margaret stammered on confusedly. "I oughtn't to have told you that. I promised Donald—no, it was Ferdinand I promised. He said just wait a year and see what you would be. He said he was going to give you every advantage. Every advantage that money could buy. Wasn't it sweet in him?"

Miss Margaret paused with a hopeful expression.

"Very," responded Agnes icily.

"I'm sure you are lovely already, dear," exclaimed Miss Margaret, ill at ease. "You look pale, dear child. You aren't ill, are you?"

"No, not at all."

"I want you just to rest and take your ease here. You had to work so hard at home." If Miss Margaret had had Machiavelian designs of enjoying herself at another's self-invited discomfiture, she might now have congratulated herself upon her success, but she went on, innocent of any such motives: "I know all about what a hard home life you had, and how exacting your mother was."

A flood of color swept into Agnes' face. "My mother was—a saint—a martyr!" she said abruptly. "I was a miserable, shiftless, good-for-nothing girl."

Miss Margaret laughed delightedly, dropped her work, and reached up to give Agnes a little hug.

Agnes turned away to the bureau and looked at her watch. The conversation was growing intolerable.

"Are you faint, dear?" asked Miss Margaret solicitously.

"No," came the laconic reply.

But Miss Margaret's evil genius was in full control of her. "You aren't very strong, are you, now?" she continued.

"Now?" Agnes turned and met Miss Margaret's look full.

The dark gaze and the somberness of the one word would have warned off anybody but a little brow-beaten creature expanding for the first time under the genial influence of sympathetic kindness. So she added the finishing touch to her unintentional but none the less artistic inquisitional torture.

"I mean, dear—it's all interest. I thought perhaps Ferdinand or you would have told me before this. I've tried to show that I love you. I'm just like Ferdinand's mother. Won't you tell me, dear?"

Agnes was smarting under the realization that she herself had been the source and Ferdinand the channel of Miss Margaret's knowledge, such as it was, of the Sidney family. Her heart bled at the thought of her mother's pride and loyalty in the family, and her own foolish garrulity.

"You remember I have not seen my mother since my return," she said haughtily, and, as she finished speaking, she walked across the room toward Ferdinand's door, her heart on fire with love and longing for the woman who had borne her, nursed her, and then given her away just when she had arrived at a point where she could do something in return. What a thankless office motherhood is! She went into the adjoining room and closed the door after her.

Miss Margaret sprang up, letting her crochet work drop to the floor, and flew to the door. "Agnes! Dear, dear Agnes!" she called excitedly. Then she bent down to the keyhole and modified her voice. "Won't you let me come in just a minute? Just a little minute? I do want to tell you—"

She turned the knob gently and had slightly opened the door, when it was pushed back from the other side and the key turned in the lock.

Miss Margaret stood still, trembling. "She's turned the key on me. She's locked me out," she said with a bewildered expression. Then her face quivered. She turned and ran out into the hall and to her own room, where she shut herself in and stayed until night.

Agnes lay upon the bed in Ferdinand's room until the summons to luncheon. She was faint in mind and body, and torn with rebellion as she realized the physical and mental impotence so relentlessly gaining upon her. She realized that she was abnormally sensitive and she shrank as she thought of the future.

She ate her luncheon alone, making no inquiries for Miss Ballington, and answering Eliza in monosyllables when the latter attempted a conversation. In the afternoon, she wrote a long letter to Miriam Cass, who was in New York studying art. When the letter was done, Agnes dressed for dinner. The habit of fastidious care as to her personal appearance was growing upon her as insidiously as was the instinct of timidity and caution in her physical exercise. Once she had been fearless in her movements, careless in her looks, but the diffidence which had attacked her mental life was spreading to the physical.

The time of Ferdinand's return at night was the happiest part of the day. Tonight Agnes looked for him as for the shadow of a rock in a weary land. She heard his ring of the bell, heard Eliza pass through the hall to admit him, and went to the stairs to meet him.

Miss Ballington was already greeting him in the lower hall. Agnes heard her words, "Will you come into the library, Ferdinand? I wish to speak to you." She saw her husband follow the drooping little figure, and then she went back to her room and waited.

Downstairs, Ferdinand remained standing in the library. And Miss Margaret, after having seated herself, got up again.

"Ferdinand, something exceedingly painful has happened," she said, with difficulty.

"What is it?"

"Your wife has locked me out of her room—turned the key against me."

There was no reply.

"She turned the key in my face, Ferdinand," Miss Margaret went on more earnestly.

"Evidently she wished to be alone."

Ferdinand was displeased at this beginning of domestic discord.

"I have nothing to do with this," he added.

"No, of course not. I wanted you to ask her if I could come up to see her. I want to tell her I'm sorry. I did not mean to force myself upon her." Miss Margaret's misery was acute and patent.

"I will give her your message," her nephew responded briefly.

He was turning toward the door when his aunt spoke again. She was struggling to keep her self-control and to conciliate him. A brave attempt to smile resulted only in a look of desperate beseeching.

"And, dear, before you go, I want to tell you how very, very happy you've made me."

He stood waiting.

"Agnes told me the sweet name you gave me. You don't mind her telling me, do you? I shall always love the flower more after this. Carnation pink!"

He looked at her uncomprehending. Suddenly a recollection darted into his mind. Several days previous, when commenting upon his aunt to Agnes he had remarked, "She has about as much logic as that carnation pink."

"If there is nothing else, I will go upstairs," he said, turning away.

He had been chafing under the delay which kept him from his wife until the pink was mentioned. Now, however, he went directly into his own room without speaking to Agnes.

When they were called to dinner, he opened the door into her room and entered. Then, with only a cold salutation, he remarked as he opened the hall door for her, "Aunt Margaret wished me to tell you that she was sorry she intruded upon you, and to ask if you would let her explain."

He was already softening toward her as he looked at her, but Agnes was now sore from his leaving her alone. "I will apologize to her tonight," she said, feeling his words a rebuke and too proud to explain the episode.

Ferdinand never asked for explanations, so he put his own interpretation upon her silence, and changed the subject.

Miss Ballington was in the dining-room when they entered. Agnes spoke to her at once.

"I was very rude to you today, Aunt Margaret. Forgive me."

"Don't speak of it," exclaimed Miss Ballington in a new distress of remorse and pain. "It was all my fault."

In spite of the mutual apologies, the dinner hour was not comfortable. Agnes was on the verge of crying. She excused herself at the dessert and returned to her own room. "She hasn't forgiven me," said Miss Margaret plaintively, as Agnes' footsteps died away. "How cold and straight she sat there. Do you think she is hard-hearted, Ferdinand? She isn't hard-hearted, is she?"

Ferdinand rose in cold disgust and went into the library, where he spent the first part of the evening reading. It was part of his system of self-control to allow no external annoyance perceptibly to disturb his comfort. He believed in leaving people to their humors. With Agnes, however, he found this rather difficult. At last, he got up, put down his paper, selected a book from the case and went upstairs to his wife's room.

He found her sitting idly by the window in the dark. "Come, Agnes. This is foolish," he said, and he lighted the lamp.

"Let me be the judge of my own actions," said a low, quivering voice, and Agnes turned her eyes with their enlarged pupils toward her husband and the light. She was thinking of his promise to exhibit her in a year.

Ferdinand looked at her in surprise; then he said, "You remember a conversation we had in Paris on the subject of religion?"

Her face softened instantly. "Yes—yes," she said, half rising, and sitting again.

"I didn't wish to unsettle you while we were traveling," continued Ferdinand. "But now I should like you to begin a course of reading which will bring us into understanding. This is a good book to begin with." He came toward her and held out the volume.

She looked at the title, saw, "Controversial Essays. T. Huxley," and said, turning to the window again, "I shall not read it."

Ferdinand had hit upon a most unfortunate time for introducing Agnes to Huxley. It gave her a chance to retrieve what she considered past disloyalty to her mother. Her afternoon of lonely brooding over Miss Margaret's unlucky disclosures had resulted in a series of self-accusations and resolves.

He still held out the book.

"Do I understand that you refuse to read this book?" he asked.

"I refuse. I will have nothing to do with heretical works. Mother wouldn't allow them in our house. I shall not read one of your series."

The words ended in a sob.

He waited a moment longer, turned slowly, laid the book on the table, and walked toward the door. Then, before leaving the room, he said, looking toward her, "the last time we spoke of this you were reasonable, although ignorant. I have left the book on your table. When you become reasonable again, we will discuss it further. There is one quotation I will leave for you to consider before you take up the reading: 'He who dare not reason is a coward; he who will not reason is a bigot; he who cannot reason is a fool.'"

Then he went into the hall and closed the door after him. As soon as Ferdinand left her Agnes broke down entirely. When she was somewhat relieved, she picked up the volume of Huxley's Essays, carried it into Ferdinand's room and left it in the middle of his bed. "If he brings it back," she said, to herself with flashing eyes, "I shall throw it into the fire."

She was partly undressed, when, happening to catch sight of the letter she had written to Miriam, she put on a wrapper, got out her writing materials, and added another sheet to the letter, then sealed it up and went to bed.

Her sleep was troubled. Toward morning she began to rest. Suddenly she woke up feeling someone near her. She was frightened and sat up instantly. A little figure in white was standing at the foot of the bed, just visible in the pale dawn. "Aunt Margaret," exclaimed Agnes, "is that you?"

"Yes, dear. I couldn't endure it. I've hardly slept all night. I never ought to have asked your confidence. And I ought not to have spoken to Ferdinand afterwards. Oh, I'm very miserable, Agnes dear; do say you forgive me."

"Yes, Aunt Margaret," Agnes answered sadly. "If there's anything to forgive, I do. You mustn't stay here. You'll catch cold."

"No, I won't. I won't, dear. I'm going to try to make you happy after this." And Miss Margaret turned and hurried away.

Ferdinand made no further reference to the Huxley. It stayed in his room on the table where Eliza put it when she found it on the foot of his bed. Agnes tried to put the circumstance from her mind, but with pretty poor success. She was unrelenting in her refusal of Ferdinand's request, and might long have remained so but for Miriam's next letter, one portion of which read as follows:

I can understand what you write to me about religion. I have been through it, and came to the conclusion that we need not trouble ourselves about "dangerous doctrines." No danger is quite so great as that of mental timidity. Why should one be afraid to find out that certain things one has believed are foolish? If you like we can read some together.

The same day this letter was received came two books from Miriam. Agnes began them with a will, finished them in a few days in a thirsty state of mind, and took the book of Huxley's from Ferdinand's room into her own.

He noticed it, and congratulated himself upon his coup d'état. Ordinarily women were to be left to the illusions of faith. They were not formed for stronger vision. He had chosen his mate, however, for intellectual as well as material companionship, and he watched with satisfaction her progress along the path which he had marked out for her.

CHAPTER VII

FOR two months Agnes found herself the center of Winston attention. She received many calls, returned them with Miss Margaret or Mrs. Silas Ballington, attended a large reception which the latter gave for her, more to prove that there was no ground for the rumor of Donald's and Ferdinand's rivalry than for anything else, and was present at the various other festivities. She felt considerable interest in meeting socially the influential townspeople whom she used to usher to their seats at the college musicales and lectures. College itself was entering upon a struggle with poverty under new and cold management, but it was still a familiar and memory-haunted spot which she sought from time to time when she felt lonely.

During these first weeks in Winston Agnes was also getting an insight into the family which she had entered. Ferdinand's differentiation from the rest of the Ballingtons grew upon her, and the more Miss Margaret talked of her dead brother Tom the clearer became Agnes' conviction that Ferdinand must be a Landseer with little or nothing of his father in him. She fell into the way of questioning Miss Margaret about the mother, Estelle Landseer, about the grandfather, rich old Ferdinand Landseer, and his eccentric wife, Estelle's mother, whose hermit life prevented anyone from knowing her. Miss Margaret was not at ease, Agnes soon discovered, under this catechism, and the painfully conscientious replies confirmed Agnes in her preconceived notions of the uncompromising and silent nature of her husband's mother. She often looked at the baby-clothes, wondering that the woman who had invented the car-spring should be so exquisite a needle-woman and so painstaking a housekeeper as her letters showed her to be. These simple and formal letters, written for the most part about ordinary domestic occurrences, brought Agnes into closer touch with the woman whom she dimly felt to be the key to much she could not understand. Here and there on the neatly-written pages sentences stood out in startling contrast to the rest, like flashes of fire struck out by the collision of her will with her environment.

One of the letters was a curious, proud apology for having taken with her, against the doctor's orders, the three-year-old baby Ferdinand when she was ordered from home for rest and change. "I know you and Thomas would do everything for the baby, dear Margaret, but he is a greater care than most children, owing, I believe, to his having inherited my stubborn will, and I could not feel right about leaving him. I often tell myself, when tired, that we must not spoil the man in humoring the child. I hope and pray that he has been born to glorify God. Whether we enjoy or not is relatively unimportant."

Agnes pondered over this letter. There was the same note of dominant character here that there was in her own mother's letters, but along with it was a reserve to which Mrs. Sidney was a stranger. Agnes suspected that Ferdinand's mother had planned the trip away not to get rest and change for herself, but to get the child away from its jovial, easy-going father and its weakly-indulgent aunt.

After reading the letters it did not surprise Agnes to learn of her mother-in-law's stern adherence to the Calvinistic faith in which she herself had been born and bred, but she appreciated a vast difference between the Calvinism of Dr. Sidney and the Calvinism of the old letters and the markings of the religious books which once had belonged to Ferdinand's mother. With Estelle, the unflinching theology, grimly accepted, seemed ever-present and was even apparent in that period of her correspondence when, owing to her mother's peculiarities, old Ferdinand Landseer had put her in a convent school to learn French, music and sewing.

Once when Agnes commented to her husband upon his mother's rigid orthodoxy he answered her with a reminiscent smile, "One of the few things I remember her saying is a sentence she quoted once to my father, 'For whom He did foreknow He also did predestinate.' It was shortly before she died, and the reason I remember it is that she was stopped in the middle by a fit of coughing, but it didn't prevent her finishing the sentence a word at a time. My father began to laugh, but when he picked her up to carry her to the lounge he was crying. As soon as she had breath enough to get up she walked back to her chair." Ferdinand's smile had vanished, and he added with that respect and satisfaction which he always showed in speaking of his mother. "My mother was a logical woman." It was a long time before Agnes understood what connection there was in Ferdinand's mind between logic and this incident, but that was one of the things she came to know.

Agnes now had been married seven months and yet had not visited her mother. Although she had made the trip alone repeatedly as a girl going to and from college, it seemed to be a matter of pride with Ferdinand to accompany her on her first visit home, so she was obliged to control her impatience until he could leave his business. Finally, at Christmas time, he proposed that they go to see her mother. Agnes would not confess to herself that she would rather have gone alone.

Dr. Quinn met them at the station with Peggy, and Agnes' heart went out to the doctor when she saw his placid spectacled face through the car window. The town seemed oddly still, and as they drove up to her mother's home it looked low and broad and isolated from the wide world she had known since she left its doors. But the woman on the porch, stretching out hospitable arms to her, held the knowledge of that world in the clear eyes which met her daughter's with understanding.

"You'll find your room all ready," Agnes, said Mrs. Sidney, picking up some of the luggage before Ferdinand was able to grasp it. "The train was late, and dinner's been waiting. Hurry up and get ready. God be praised, you're safe at home again."

Agnes went upstairs with a youthful heart. "Mother will take care of everything now," she thought.

She looked in upon her aunt, greeted her affectionately, then hurriedly took off her furs and wraps. The bedroom looked low-ceilinged, but she never had loved it so well before. She thrilled with pleasure when Ferdinand said, "It is very homelike, more so than our house."

"Isn't it lovely!" Agnes answered in delight, running through the upstairs rooms in a fervor of joy. "And smell the turkey!" she cried as her husband met her and they descended the stairs. "This is just too good. I have my little blue teacup, and we'll have our tea with the dinner. How lovely everything is. How your face shines, mother. It makes me think of Moses when he came down from the mount."

They all sat down at the table, Dr. Quinn at the head.

"You shouldn't speak flippantly about Moses, Agnes, said Mrs. Sidney after the doctor had asked the blessing, but there was a happy smile on her face. "If my face shines, it is with soap and water."

"At all events, then," remarked Dr. Quinn, looking at Mrs. Sidney with friendly eyes, "it shines with the next thing to godliness."

As soon as the dinner was over Agnes rose and said, "Give me an apron, mother. I'm going to help with the dishes."

Ferdinand, Dr. Quinn, and Aunt Mattie were energetically ushered into the parlor by Mrs. Sidney, who seated them around nuts and apples, furnished them a topic of conversation by telling Ferdinand that his two companions had been arguing for a week past over Cleopatra's mummy, about which he now would be able to tell them all there was to know. Thereupon she went back to the kitchen and closed the door behind her.

It was with a deep sigh of content that she took her daughter's face between her hard hands and kissed her soundly. "They're settled in there, and now we can have a good, long talk," she said.

Agnes began at the beginning, and gave the history of their travels abroad. Mrs. Sidney listened with a pleasure that was almost keener, Agnes thought, than she herself had experienced in making the trip. Indeed the mother's satisfaction was unbounded in the fact that Providence had given Agnes such opportunities.

When Mrs. Sidney had been satisfied about the wedding trip, she questioned her daughter about her new relations in her husband's home, and she listened with a half-wise, half-humorous expression to Agnes' confidences. It did not take the older woman long to get a better idea than Agnes herself had of the state of things at the farm. She shook with laughter when Agnes finished a heated description of Miss Margaret's well-meant intrusions into her personal matters. "If you two had more work to do, you wouldn't bother yourselves or each other. You ought to take example by me, Agnes. Since you've gone away and I've had less to do, I've taken up giving Beatrice lessons in housekeeping. She needs it as bad as anybody I ever knew, and she pays me generously."

As Mrs. Sidney wiped the tears of laughter from her eyes, her face underwent one of those sudden changes from mirth to sternness which Agnes remembered so well. "I don't know that I would go out to give lessons at my time of life," Mrs. Sidney continued, "if it wasn't that I thought Beatrice needs something even more than housekeeping lessons. The way she is going on with Thomas Ballington again has been a great care to me, Agnes."

The thought of her mother's being assisted by Beatrice while she herself was doing so little for her caused Agnes keen suffering. To disguise her emotions, she answered hastily, "Don't worry about that, mamma. It's only nonsense. Social forms aren't as rigid as they used to be." As she spoke, Agnes remembered impatiently how Ferdinand continually had thrown out innuendoes about various people, conspicuously Tom and Beatrice.

"Don't say 'nonsense,' Agnes," her mother returned gravely. "Whatever social forms may be, results follow causes nowadays just as much as they ever did. Beatrice and Tom can't walk on hot coals without getting burned."

Here Mrs. Sidney wrung out the dishcloth, cleaned up the sink, hung up the towels, and, after casting a glance around the neat little kitchen, turned to her daughter, with her hands on her hips: "It seems to me Ferdinand looks a little thin, Agnes."

Agnes smiled. "Yes," she replied, "he's been worried about some business—a matter that's all right now, and, at the same time, he took it into his head that he was getting too fat and began to diet."

Mrs. Sidney shook her head disparagingly. "I never did believe in dieting," she said, looking down at her own substantial form. "Vanity is at the bottom of it. I think, too, that Ferdinand had better begin to lay up treasure in heaven. Has he said anything about uniting with the Church yet?"

"No, not yet," replied Agnes in a low voice.

Mrs. Sidney cast a keen look over at her daughter. She was struck with an expression of helplessness in Agnes' face which she never had noticed before and also a look of embarrassment which she did not understand. It never occurred to her simple faith that her daughter's attitude toward religion could change. She had been pleased from the first with her son-in-law's sobriety, and thought it but a question of time, under the right influences, until he would, as she expressed it, come into the fold. Mrs. Sidney's pointed question, however, suddenly revealed to Agnes how great a change had been effected in her by a few weeks' critical reading and correspondence with Miriam Cass. She was embarrassed to find that her old eagerness for Ferdinand's formal profession had fallen into the background of her thought.

Mrs. Sidney, however, answered Agnes' expression as she interpreted it. "Deal courageously, Agnes, and the God of your father will be with you. Get Miss Margaret to help. When two or three are joined together, you know. And I'll be here. You can depend upon the Lord's word being true, Agnes."

Agnes laid her hand affectionately on her mother's shoulder. "I know that, mamma," she said earnestly, "and I'm trying to know what that word is more than I ever did before. Since I've gone away from you, I've wished every day that I had been a better girl while I was here, and I have thanked God continually that I was born and brought up in a Christian home."

Mrs. Sidney's apron went up to her eyes, and she sat down in a chair with a sob. "It was the Lord who put it into your heart to say that, Agnes," she said indistinctly. "I'm glad you don't forget your father. Sometimes I think I never shall be good enough to get where he is, to see him again. I don't doubt the Lord's word," and she looked up over her apron, "but it's hard for me to be humble. Still," and here the apron went down altogether, "if Stephen Sidney had had a humble wife, the whole world would have imposed upon him."

At this moment Aunt Mattie appeared in the doorway. "Quinn had to go on his rounds," she said, "and Ferdinand decided to ride with him as far as the Buchers'."

Agnes was pleased. The visit had started in well, she thought.

The days went swiftly by. Agnes was conscious of a lack of interest in her old friends and spent most of her time at home, but there was one memorable evening at the home of the Kent rabbi, where, to her surprise, she discovered a new sympathy with the seedy old gentleman who had read Dante with her father; while his son-in-law, who always had seemed silent and awkward, suddenly discovered a wide and brilliant acquaintance with the topics most interesting to Ferdinand. She sat back with the rabbi and his daughter and listened while the two younger men talked. Unconsciously she contrasted the thin subtle-faced German whose ancestors two thousand years before had kept sheep on the hills of Palestine, and who had learned by the experiences of his persecuted race to regard impartially many hypotheses, with the successful young business man who spoke for agnosticism as a partisan. To the latter it was the one method. The rabbi was listening, too. From time to time, the old man's eyes lit up with a fire that might have meant anything from anger to amusement, but when his eyes met those of Agnes this inscrutable expression changed instantly to one of kindly penetration.

Agnes was heavy-hearted when the last day of the visit came around. They were to have a quiet evening at home and return to Winston on the late train. Mrs. Sidney had made an effort to please her daughter's taste in preparing the supper. She came to the table herself with beads of perspiration standing upon her forehead. Agnes looked gratefully at her mother. The fair skin and open pores pleased her eyes. But the food almost choked her. She wondered at the comparative ease with which she had left home upon her marriage.

After supper Mrs. Sidney covered the table with a cloth, saying she would leave the dishes till after her children had gone, and they all went together into the parlor.

"Well, Ferdinand," said Mrs. Sidney cheerfully, "I've been hearing a good deal about your trip from Agnes. I'm very thankful she had such an opportunity. I'm surprised at all the things she's remembered. The doctor used to have just such a good memory. I tell Agnes that the trip will be capital for her whole life. I'm very glad she had it, and had it now. Stephen always wanted to travel. I used to think the time would come when he could, but now his days on this earth are done with."

Ferdinand listened courteously, but made no reply. The relaxation of the short vacation was over, and he was already considering how he should best start in the new year with his wife.

"Didn't you find Agnes a very creditable traveling companion?" continued Mrs. Sidney, as she looked with pride and happiness upon her daughter.

"In some ways." Ferdinand had no intention of being unkind. He was merely saying aloud what he had been going over mentally in considering their future relations.

Agnes moved a little. She had been congratulating herself that the visit had passed without anything disagreeable between her mother and Ferdinand. She was alive to the subtle change in her husband's mood, and pained at the surprised look in her mother's face. She hastened to speak herself.

"You know, mother, Ferdinand had been all over the ground before and it was rather tiresome to him. I suppose I tried his patience many times."

"Tiresome!" exclaimed Mrs. Sidney, looking at Agnes disapprovingly.

"I shouldn't have cared to cover the ground a second time for myself," said Ferdinand, crossing his knee. "Few people benefit by a first trip, however, because they are not fitted for traveling when they undertake it. They are ignorant of the history of the countries they visit, and they are not able either to observe or to reason. Most people drift."

"Well, Agnes didn't drift," responded Mrs. Sidney proudly, "and her father always said if there was one thing she should have, it was an education. Stephen always said a well-educated family was the best legacy a man could leave."

Agnes grew gradually paler during her mother's speech. Her eyes were fixed upon her husband with a beseeching expression.

"It was unfortunate Agnes couldn't have attended some high-grade school for a short time," returned Ferdinand, oblivious of the mute appeal.

"High-grade school!" exclaimed Mrs. Sidney, sitting up straight in her chair. "Agnes had three years at college. She would have been a graduate with a diploma if her father had lived."

"She's just as well off without a diploma from Winston," Ferdinand remarked, still preoccupied.

"I've always told Ferdinand that my ignorance was caused by my own lack of thoroughness," interposed Agnes, trying to avert an unpleasant collision on a tender point of her mother's. "It is not the fault of the school. Neither is it too late for me to learn now. I want to learn, and Miriam and I have begun reading together."

She felt sore toward her husband for having made this avowal necessary before her mother. Her color came back into her cheeks and there was an intensity in the dark eyes.

"School-girl friendships are very picturesque," volunteered Ferdinand, looking at his wife indulgently. He was thinking how well she looked in the girlish pose, and he was wondering whether or not he should cross over and sit beside her on the sofa. "This wonderful Miss Cass and Agnes are going to become great scholars," he added amiably.

"No," said Agnes, "I never shall become a scholar, but I shall become less ignorant."

"Don't you call yourself ignorant, Agnes!" cried Mrs. Sidney, a grim determination beginning to assert itself through her hurt feelings. "It's just as wicked to slander yourself as to slander anyone else. 'Who hath given understanding unto the mind?' Be careful how you charge the Lord, Agnes. Agnes is a very unusual woman, Ferdinand. She's the peer of anyone. She's the peer of a statesman."

"That's a pretty broad statement," replied Ferdinand smiling, and analyzing the excitement in Mrs. Sidney's face. "It would be a dangerous experiment to trust our country to statesmen of whom Agnes is a peer. It always has seemed curious to me that a woman of Agnes' native ability should be as ignorant as she is. I marvel at it continually."

"Ferdinand! Don't let me hear you say that word again!" said Mrs. Sidney, raising her voice authoritatively.

Ferdinand would not confess to himself that he was glad of a chance to speak with perhaps unnecessary plainness to his mother-in-law. He always had been secretly nettled at the misunderstanding which he had necessarily allowed Mrs. Sidney to have about himself and his motives at the outset of their acquaintance. Moreover, her absurd complacence in her daughter's accomplishments ought to be corrected.

"What word—ignorant?" he said imperturbably. "Agnes is—a very ignorant woman. She isn't the peer of various other women I have met, to say nothing of the average man. She is very inferior to what my mother was at her age. Agnes has fair native ability, but it is just as she says—she has not cultivated thorough mental habits. Her mind is—yes, I regard it as in a more undisciplined condition than that of any woman of equal advantages I know—excepting your nephew's wife, Mrs. Fred Sidney."

Mrs. Sidney stood up.

"Don't stop me, Agnes!" she said as her daughter approached her. "As the Lord liveth, I shall tell Ferdinand what I think of him. Who is he to come among us clapping his hands and multiplying his words—"

She turned at a slight noise. Aunt Mattie had arisen and was helping herself out of the room by means of chairs.

"Never mind, mamma," broke in Agnes, taking advantage of the interruption and pushing her mother gently toward a chair, "Ferdinand doesn't mean to make you feel bad. Men state facts without regard to feelings. When we aren't used to it, it hurts! but it isn't so hard when one gets used to it. It is true I am ignorant, just as he says, but I don't intend—"

Mrs. Sidney sat down. They saw the tears start to her eyes when Agnes corroborated her husband's words.

"I'm glad Stephen Sidney didn't live to hear his daughter say this," she said, the look of a mortal wound in her eyes. "After all Stephen did—and my scrimping and going without a new bonnet and a sewing-machine—"

"Don't! Don't, mother!" Agnes broke in desperately.

There was a short silence after the cry. Then she turned back to her mother, and continued rapidly, "I never forget it night or day, what papa and you did for me. Sometimes it seems as if it would kill me."

No one spoke.

She broke the silence again. "I didn't use it when I had the chance—"

She did not finish, but was turning to leave the room, when Ferdinand spoke from the window where he had retreated. At his voice she paused.

"Agnes has taken the right attitude," he said, with a desire to conciliate, "and I shall give her every means of educating herself."

"I ask for no other means than those I have," returned Agnes instantly. "My mother is not the only one who has made rash statements about me tonight. There are other women besides Beatrice as lacking in mental discipline as I am. Aunt Sarah and Aunt Margaret are two. I don't know the Landseers, but there are some perhaps who disgrace the family as much as I do."

"You don't disgrace the family, Agnes," said Ferdinand uncomfortably. "Ignorance is no disgrace when one wants to learn. On the contrary, in your remarks tonight, all but the last, you have been a pride to the family."

He turned again to the window, and she stood still in silence, bitterly appreciating that he had criticised justly her last remark.

"Someone is coming in at the gate," said Ferdinand changing his voice. "I think it is Fred Sidney and his wife." He added more hurriedly, "I did not say I knew no other women as untrained as you, but I knew no others of equal advantages."

He was cut short by the sound of the front door thrown noisily open. A moment later Beatrice, after a resounding rap, blew into the room, shaking the snow from her fur cap and coat, her gypsy hair and scarlet cheeks wet with the melting flakes. Fred Sidney followed quietly. Panting and laughing, Beatrice nodded familiarly to Mrs. Sidney, caught Agnes in her arms and kissed her on each cheek.

"We walked all the way from West Hill," she announced breathlessly, as she released Agnes and made for Ferdinand with the evident intention of including him in her salute. "How d'ye do, Cousin Ferdinand! First we endure, then pity, then—"She raised her arms and pursed her short upper lip dangerously near Ferdinand's coat-collar. Then, laughing at his expression, with a supple combination of a shrug and the graceful curve of the ballet-dancer, she turned unexpectedly and melted in real affection upon Mrs. Sidney's straight but unhappy figure.

Her face was still against Mrs. Sidney's cheek as she demanded briskly, "Well, what have you all been doing? You look as if Ferdinand had been telling the story of his life."

Then, dropping her voice to a whisper, she said in Mrs. Sidney's ear, with an accompanying glance at Ferdinand, "I have two new customers for your butter. Thirty cents the year round."

Giving the substantial shoulders a gentle shake as she released them, she gave a sliding step in the direction of Agnes, and, with another venomous glance at Ferdinand, whispered in her ear, "Go over and talk to Fred and your mother. I have some business with Ferdinand. It's about real estate." The glib lie occurred to her as likely to allay any discomfort that might arise in Agnes' mind.

Fred Sidney's quiet but hearty greeting did much to dispel the awkwardness of the situation, and Agnes allowed herself to be drawn over to the corner, where she sat down between him and her mother.

Beatrice, meantime, took Ferdinand by the arm, gently pushed him into a chair and drew up another one facing him. Before they were fairly seated she began a voluble conversation, asking his advice upon bits of property which she invented upon the spot and described with a flow of words from which Ferdinand could not escape without pointed discourtesy. He was making, too, an effort at courtesy because of the events that had taken place earlier in the evening.

He endured the torrent for about fifteen minutes, then he rose deliberately and stepped around her. She chose this particular moment to make a dive for her muff directly under his feet, which nearly threw him headlong. With an unnaturally long step he partially regained his equilibrium and proceeded unsteadily in the direction of his wife. Beatrice buried her face in the muff a moment before she turned with dancing eyes to follow him. "I wanted to ask you about the advisability of that artesian well," she continued in an uncertain voice.

Ferdinand paid no attention to her, but took out his watch. "I think I will go out and engage a sleigh, Agnes," he said. "It is snowing hard."

"Quinn left the big satchel at the station for us," Agnes replied at once. "I'd rather like to walk. Perhaps Fred and Bee will go up with us."

"We'll go," said Beatrice.

"It will be better for you to ride," replied Ferdinand with an air of finality. "I shall be back in half an hour." And without waiting for a reply, he left the room.

As soon as Ferdinand was out of the house Beatrice, with ready good-nature, picked up Fred's hat, and, with a shrewd glance at Agnes and her mother, exclaimed, "We must be going. It is a long way home and we must walk." After a hasty farewell, she propelled her husband out through the front door by means of a vigorous and supple hand between his shoulders.

Ferdinand did not return at the end of half an hour, and Agnes and her mother had the evening together.

Near the end of it Agnes said shyly, "Here is a little New Year's gift for you, mother. Get yourself something," and she laid one of Donald's packets in her mother's hand.

Mrs. Sidney hesitated as to how to decline. "I don't like to take Ferdinand's money from you," she said, handing back the roll of bills, but comforted by the thought that her son-in-law was at least generous with money.

"This is not Ferdinand's. It's mine to do as I like with."

Mrs. Sidney persisted, but kindly, "I can get along without it. If the time comes when I can't, I'll let you help me."

"Take it for Aunt Mattie, mother!" Agnes cried in a suppressed voice. "Do that for me! I have a right to help her, too."

Mrs. Sidney caught the anguish in the tone, and, after a moment's struggle, conquered her pride.

"Very well," she said briefly. "It will be a godsend for Mattie."

Unable to control herself any longer Agnes hastily left the room, ostensibly to say good-by to her aunt.

When she returned her mother clasped her in her arms.

"Don't get down in the mouth, Agnes," she said. "The Lord won't let you be brought under if you hold fast your integrity. Don't think He doesn't know what's going on. The eyes of the Lord run to and fro through the whole earth. Keep your heart perfect in His sight and never mind Ferdinand."

Agnes met her mother's smile, but she said at once, "Don't think about that conversation, mother. I'm beginning to comprehend Ferdinand now, and I'm going to be better and broader for having married him. Here he comes. Good-bye! Good-bye! It's been heaven here."

She kissed her mother and went down to the sleigh, where Ferdinand had preceded her after a civil but somewhat distant farewell to his mother-in-law.

Ferdinand tucked his wife in carefully with the furs, and she knew that his light sigh as he sat up again meant that he considered that he had done a duty and that he was relieved that the visit was over. There was a jingle of sleigh bells, a crunch of crisp snow. As they passed the church Agnes heard the choir practicing a familiar New Year's anthem, and there passed before her vision the picture of her father in his pew with his hand behind his ear, listening as she sang from the choir loft. The sleigh turned the corner, and she looked back at the old home. For an instant, she saw the light in the kitchen-window; then the elms shut off the view.

Agnes turned her face resolutely toward the north.

CHAPTER VIII

ACCORDING to Ferdinand's programme the months intervening between his marriage and the beginning of the new year were a season of preparation. The first ardor of the honeymoon was to pass by a gradual and natural transition into that permanent condition of orderly conjugal responsibilities and comforts which were to ballast and cushion his life henceforth. The heart-burnings, the rebellious starts, the spasmodic agonies which Agnes could only half conceal from him he took philosophically, smiling, like Milton's Adam, "with superior love."

At the beginning of the new year he brought a daybook to Agnes, and with some ceremony invested her with full control of the household expenses. Agnes had been looking forward to this time, hoping that some settlement of a personal income upon her might restore to her that financial self-respect so necessary to every normal mind. She was indescribably disappointed, therefore, even dismayed, to find that the monthly allowance was for household expenses and that she must keep a rigid account of every penny spent and subject this account to Ferdinand's approval; that for her personal expenses she must, as heretofore, consult him and be allowed or refused as he saw fit. She submitted to the inevitable, modeled her bookkeeping upon Ferdinand's system, and as she was naturally quick at figures the work did not tax her as it had taxed Miss Margaret.

Ever since his third call at Kent Agnes had known from Ferdinand that he was assisting two families besides his own; his step-grandmother on the Landseer side, and a great-aunt upon the Ballington side who received equal contributions from Ferdinand and Mrs. Silas' household. These dependents were discussed freely and impersonally by Ferdinand. "If I had not been prudent and self-denying, I should not now be able to support three families," was one of his frequent remarks to relatives and acquaintances. In listening to him, his wife always shrank from the thought that any of her kin might sometimes be obliged to accept his aid, and by so doing become subject to his comments.

The little gifts which, during her betrothal, Agnes had fondly planned to send her mother and sister were not sent; but they lingered as sore spots in her memory. The privilege of her girlhood, to deny herself in order to give a present to a friend, was no longer hers. Ferdinand was proud to indulge his wife in such ways as seemed suitable to himself, and he insisted upon luxuries Agnes cared nothing for, which he deemed imposed by his position, but the habits of hospitality, personal benevolence, and loving gift-making, to which Agnes had been brought up, were regarded by him as faults, and he held his wife closely restricted in such ways. At the end of each month he carefully examined Agnes' accounts, together with his own, and those from the grandmother Landseer and the great-aunt Ballington.

Agnes now had remaining the last two hundred dollars of Donald's wedding gift. Knowing that she had nowhere to look for any more money for her private disposal, she laid the balance away for an emergency, and with almost a miser's instinct began to cast about for means to increase the hoard.

It was at the close of March, shortly before the birth of her first child, that she attempted an experiment with her accounts. She watched Ferdinand furtively as he ran his eye up and down the columns, and she knew what was coming when he paused and looked up at her.

"I notice," he said, with a queer scrutiny, "you have an item here marked 'nine dollars—personal.' I don't like to have you form the habit of generalizing in this way. It is slovenly. Always be able to tell where every penny has gone. If you put down each item, you will grow more judicious as to what these items are."

He noticed her color rise, and he added kindly, "I have learned this by my own experience."

Agnes' long-rankling sense of injustice quivered in her voice as she replied, "Ferdinand, suppose I demanded that you submit your accounts to me each month, and that I did not approve of about half of them." Here she checked herself and went on more gently: "The money which was yours is ours now, you see. You have with all your worldly goods me endowed."

He looked at her flushed face, and flushed a trifle himself. There was a disagreeable familiarity in his smile as he said, "You misunderstand the word 'endow.' According to law 'endow' means to give a wife her widow's dower. My worldly goods are mine while I live. However," Ferdinand went on, giving her time to realize that his concession was voluntary and not necessary on his part, "you are welcome to look at my accounts. The business accounts are kept at the office. My personal ones are on file in the second drawer of the library desk. Here is the key." He took a ring of keys from his pocket, detached one, and handed it to her.

There was a pause, during which Agnes went through a shock of sickening revelation. Then she glanced at him and turned away without replying.

He still held out the key to her. "I have no matters private from you," he said, without taking his eyes from her face.

"You misunderstand me," she replied simply, and, without looking at him again, quietly left the room.

He replaced the key on the ring and returned it to his pocket, satisfied to have passed through an inevitable episode with his usual success in averting domestic friction.

That night Agnes added nine dollars to her savings. She handled the little pile jealously, feeling that it had reached its limit.

About the middle of April Estelle Ballington was born. Ferdinand had expressed a wish that if a daughter were born to them she might hear his mother's name. It was the first sentiment of its kind that Agnes had known in her husband, and she gladly complied with his request. She was very happy with the baby, and in being the recipient of Ferdinand's renewed devotion. She used often to recall the look in his eyes when the child was first put into his arms and his gaze passed over the infant held close to his heart and rested upon her.

"He is like an old Roman father," she told herself with a smile half dependent and half rebellious. "The baby is one thing more to be taken care of, brought up in the way it should go."

Every day Agnes longed for Ferdinand's return at night, and this anticipation helped her to bear patiently her slavery to her nurse, her helplessness under Miss Margaret's incessant attentions, her exasperation at the treacle-like manners of her fashionable doctor, and Mrs. Silas Ballington's tri-weekly calls. Agnes had been brought up in a doctor's family and had imbibed unconsciously her mother's sensible ideas about nursing. It seemed to her that she was being scientifically starved to death and kept in bed like a paralytic when she was perfectly able and frantic to get outdoors in the sun.

At length, in desperation, she poured forth her wrongs and the wrongs of their firstborn into Ferdinand's attentive ears, and was promptly championed.

In a few brief and biting remarks the obsequious doctor and the insultingly-bland nurse were prescribed limitations which they did not venture to overstep. The head of the house stood by directing the nurse how to dress Agnes, and then he took his wife in his arms, "as though I were one of the Sabine women," Agnes thought with a grim humor, and carried her downstairs into the garden, while the nurse followed ignominiously with the child in her arms, and Miss Margaret came pitter-pattering along in the rear, a meek mound of cushions and blankets.

This triumphal progress was repeated for several days, the masculine protective instinct in Ferdinand's soul being mightily gratified at Agnes' appeal and at his own athletic ability to respond to it. He felt a glow of satisfaction in the creaking of his joints as he went up and down the stairs, casting back deep-breathed exhortations to the nurse not to drop the baby, and to Aunt Margaret not to get entangled in the blankets and so precipitate herself upon those descending before her.

The convalescence soon came to an end, however, and life became vitally complex for Agnes during the following months. She found herself living both a superficial and a profound life; the first with the bustle and worry and sweet cares of a young mother's busy round of duties; the second remote from this, in the quiet of an elemental change. This deeper existence was generally submerged beneath the eddies of the superficial life, unexpected swirls produced by conflicting currents setting in from unforeseen sources and intermingling perplexingly. Yet, in the midst of these obvious perplexities, Agnes was conscious of a slow and steady movement of the unseen deep. Whither was that slow tide tending? Was it to unite with a kindred deep in her husband's soul, as in her hopeful moods she told herself, or was it drifting away into inevitable solitude? Upon the latter alternative Agnes did not permit herself to speculate. She felt that nothing she could do could arrest now the course of fate once set in motion, and so she held herself cheerfully and pertinaciously to her obvious duties, trusting that, if she did not fail in these, she need not fear the unknown toward which her nature moved.

To Ferdinand the year was passing, on the whole, satisfactorily. Except in one respect, he believed that Agnes had adjusted herself to his views, and his domestic life seemed to be proceeding in serene accord with his control. He thought with complacence that in one year he practically had transmuted

Agnes' religious and financial traditions. Her bigotries had fallen away from her, her accounts were methodically kept, disturbing exhibitions of temper and rebellion were matters of the past.

Agnes, too, sometimes persuaded herself that she had grown into contact with her husband's point of view, but this state of mind came only in answer to an effort of the will. At other times she was dimly aware of "abysmal griefs hidden under the current of daily life and seemingly forgotten, till now and then they came up to the surface—a flash of agony-like the fish that jumps in the calm pool." When she held herself to the letter of their original differences she confessed that Ferdinand had been right in forecasting her development.

Her realization of the expanding and modifying process her views had undergone since her marriage again and again checked hasty judgment of her husband now when their opinions clashed. When she went deeper and began to brood upon the spirit of their differences she invariably became uneasy. All the religious, educational, and financial questions at issue between them looked at in themselves seemed trivial enough; but when she regarded them as successive phases illustrating a divergence that went far deeper than any one of them, they seemed grave and terrible manifestations of an organic, atomic repellence. She became afraid to look at things this way and evaded it by keeping her attention to the letter of their discussions. She almost never now referred to the spiritual contents of the gospels with her husband, but spoke more of dates, of disputed authorship, spurious passages, verbal renderings. Nor did she any longer argue over gifts she could not make or purchases that were discountenanced. She accepted her husband's strictures in silence, and discussed with him prices, grade of goods, and preferred shops for the merchandise he favored. In the latter case, too, realizing her inferior judgment, she submitted usually to his experience, waiting quietly for the time when responsibility would naturally devolve upon her trained and capable judgment. At the best her peace of mind was never sanguine as was Ferdinand's. She knew that, so far, she had kept things pleasant by avoiding the disagreeable, and that, at any time now, something not to be avoided might arise. Hitherto she had put away the thought of this crisis, hoping that, before it arrived, they might both of them have gained wisdom and forbearance enough to meet it wisely.

Before Estelle was many weeks old, however, Agnes began to realize that something which it was impossible to avoid or to isolate and so deal with objectively had come into their mutual relations. This new element also furnished the one exception to Ferdinand's conjugal satisfaction. The exception bade fair to be an obstinately unpleasant one, too. Here he found himself in contention with an instinct rather than a tradition in Agnes, and the regulation of her maternal love presented difficulties of unreasonable magnitude. The differences which arose between them about the habits of the baby at present, and the vague foreshadowings of later and graver differences in training a developing child, were not only more obdurate now, but seemed likely to be longer-lived and to multiply far beyond any previous ones.

From the day when Agnes had appealed to Ferdinand against the nurse and doctor, his instinct for over-seeing things extended itself to the sick-room and the nursery. He had enjoyed the pride of defending his wife, and his care and vigilance were really tender and were acceptable to her, but as she regained her strength and he felt no longer any physical demand for sympathy, the tenderness went out of his vigilance, while officialism took its place. Agnes soon saw, to her sorrow, that by once having exposed the doctor and nurse to her husband's scorn she had given him a precedent for disregarding their advice and regulations when she gladly would have observed them. "You and I will manage this child ourselves," he said decidedly, and presently the young wife realized that she was expected to be as silent a partner here as in their other mutual responsibilities. The nurse left as soon as possible, and they were together without interference to settle Estelle's little way of life between them. Almost at once, their minds and wills grappled. On this one subject all through the summer, they remained under full strain, quite quiet, as wrestlers who are evenly matched.

Meantime, the outer life of reading and driving and smiling went on, while the unconscious baby, somehow or other, survived experiences which angered Ferdinand and tortured Agnes, and managed, for all the trouble it was causing, and the vicissitudes through which it was passing, to bring a wondrous amount of joy and love into the Ballington household.

CHAPTER IX

ONE morning in early autumn Agnes sat at her desk before the open window writing to Ferdinand's dictation. A bough of the old apple tree outside now and then brushed softly against the window-sill, while a ray of hazy September sunlight glanced fitfully through the leafy screen and played over the half-written page. As Agnes wrote on mechanically to her husband's monotonous voice, she half smiled to see the ethereal lances strike and shatter themselves against the sooty and troll-like words she was setting down.

"This constitutes virtually a ball-and-socket joint, uniting great strength with freedom of motion."

A warm gust of wind outside shot a whole arsenal of golden arrows quivering and gleaming to impale the "ball-and-socket joint," in airy mockery of its grimy and laborious strength and freedom.

Agnes' smile deepened, and, as Ferdinand paused to consider his next sentence, her eyes strayed out into the green shadow of the apple tree, and rested there. She had recovered full strength and animation, and there was a fullness and gentleness of sympathy in her expression that lent a new charm and dignity to the brilliance and vigor of her girlhood.

She was so lost in her musing that she did not hear Ferdinand when he resumed, and he looked up, half impatiently, to see why the pen had ceased. Instead of recalling her to her task, however, he sat still, watching her with analytical admiration. The richness and delicacy, the unconscious grace of her figure, reminded him vaguely of old Italian pictures, and when a light wind lifted the waving hair a moment on the temples and a sunbeam passed waveringly across her dark eyes, the breeze seemed to bring with it out of the past a fleeting memory of a ford across a country stream with the wind lifting the forest foliage overhead and the sunlight losing itself in the brown water underneath.

The charm held him for a moment only, however. Then he rose and stretched his arms, breathing deep with the relief of a change of position.

With a start Agnes came back to herself. "I'm afraid I'm absent-minded," she said apologetically. "You're not through, are you?"

Without answering, Ferdinand came and stood behind her chair.

"Isn't that a new picture?" he asked, pointing at a small etching on top of her desk. As he spoke, his eye compared it with another one of the same size in a similar frame which stood beside it.

Agnes reached up, took down the etching, and looked at it with pride. "Yes, it is new," she said, "and isn't it beautiful?"

Ferdinand bent over to look at it with her. It was an etching of the portrait of Huxley with the skull in his hand. As Ferdinand scrutinized the strong, nervous face, the determination and grace of the pose, his eye went back again curiously to the companion picture on the desk— Booth as *Hamlet*, with the skull in his hand.

"When did you set up in the undertaking business?" he said at last, straightening up and looking down at her. "Haven't you a new frame on that *Hamlet*?"

Agnes put the Huxley back on the desk, then turned to her husband. "Miriam sent me the Huxley last week. It's an artist's proof. You remember Tom gave me the *Hamlet* my last birthday. When I showed him the Huxley, he asked me to let him take the two and get them framed alike, for an equinoctial present. They just came today. Tom has good instincts," she added reflectively, turning back to the etching.

"He saw at once the poetic affinity of those two pictures."

Ferdinand thrust his hands in his pockets and turned away. "All the relation I see between *Hamlet* and Huxley is that their names begin with 'H.'"

As he spoke he paused beside a bowl of white roses on the table. After a moment he took one of his hands out of his pocket and touched the roses delicately as he counted them.

"Donald sent you these?" he asked, looking at his wife over his shoulder.

The almost imperceptible emphasis on the word "Donald" arrested Agnes' attention. She looked up instantly and met his gaze. "You saw him give them to me yesterday at the shop," she said. "He bought them of the cripple at the door."

As she returned her husband's look something in his expression embarrassed her, and to her annoyance she felt herself blushing. Donald had been in the habit of sending flowers to the house not infrequently, and Ferdinand had accepted it naturally enough at first, until a slight circumstance in the spring had irritated him. As it happened, Donald was the first to send

Agnes flowers after Estelle's birth, and Agnes noticed at the time that Ferdinand resented deeply the fact that Donald's roses came before it had occurred to himself to get any. He had occasionally commented upon the episode since, and they both instinctively thought of it now. As he turned his eyes away, she dropped hers to the desk, and began to sort and arrange the papers scattered over it.

"The baby is six months old now, Ferdinand, and, much as I regret it, she will have to be weaned. Mother wrote me that she would help me if I could come down to Kent for a week."

Ferdinand walked the length of the room before he replied. "I believe I'll take you down," he said reflectively. "I rather want to see that young doctor again."

"Who? Quinn?" said Agnes in surprise. She was wondering at her husband's unusual friendship for her father's silent young assistant.

"I don't know when I've met a physician with so good mechanical ideas," continued Ferdinand. "He has a little surgical contrivance that I might as well get patented and put on the market at the same time I'm putting through my own invention. I think he has a good thing and I'm inclined to take an interest in it."

"My father suggested it," said Agnes eagerly. "Quinn is only completing it."

"Indeed?" said Ferdinand, pausing in his walk.

"Papa invented a number of things, but he gave them all to the profession. He didn't think it was right to patent them."

Ferdinand resumed his walk, vouchsafing no reply to this weak-minded sentiment.

Presently the summons came for luncheon, and they went down, meeting Miss Margaret at the foot of the stairs. She was just coming in from outdoors in a state of secret elation. As soon as they were seated at the table, Ferdinand turned to his aunt.

"Wasn't that Flynn's wife I saw you talking with a few moments ago out in front?" he asked quietly.

"Yes—yes, dear, she was here," answered Miss Ballington with visible embarrassment. "You don't object to her coming here, do you, Ferdinand?"

"What did she want?" he returned immovably.

Miss Margaret hesitated. "She was begging. They are having a terrible time since her husband has been out of work; a terrible time, Ferdinand. Some of the time, the children have only dry bread to eat, dry bread."

Ferdinand disregarded his aunt's appeal. "I don't wish you to have anything to do with the family. Tell her so, if she comes again."

Miss Margaret's face fell, but she persisted faintly, "Yes, dear, if you really mean it. The baby has no milk."

"I mean it."

"The baby has no milk, dear." It was a last frightened expostulation.

"Flynn knows how he can get it," answered Ferdinand grimly.

"Ferdinand is going to take me out riding this afternoon, Aunt Margaret," interposed Agnes. "Wouldn't you like to go? We can take the drag and call for someone else—Miss Sewell, if you like. You could have a nice visit with her in the back seat, while Ferdinand tells me about Professor Dimmock's lecture in front!" She looked at her husband in the hope that he would second the invitation.

"You dear child!" exclaimed Miss Margaret, beaming, "how sweet in you to want me! But you shall have the phaeton all to yourselves, dear. Sarah is going to bring over her work this afternoon. She is coming early. There's the bell now."

A moment later Mrs. Silas Ballington entered and was greeted effusively by Miss Margaret, who tripped around the table to meet her.

"Ferdinand and Agnes are going to drive, Sarah," she said at once to her sister-in-law. And then, turning to her nephew, she asked, "Would you just as soon go by the stores, Ferdinand, and get me a bottle of witch-hazel?"

"Certainly," replied Ferdinand with civility. "Is there anything else?"

"Yes," said Miss Margaret, taking advantage of the unexpected opportunity, "I'd like a box of blue notepaper, and—and—" Her courage suddenly evaporated. "That's all," she finished weakly.

"What else do you want, Aunt Margaret?" asked Agnes when Ferdinand had left the room. "Tell me. I'll see that Ferdinand gets it."

"You dear child. Isn't she sweet to me, Sarah? I do want a spool of that little baby-ribbon, pink, or bird's-egg blue, or corn-color. It doesn't make any difference which."

"Margaret," said Mrs. Ballington, looking at the little woman with a patronizing pity, "it's absurd the way you have to tell Ferdinand every time you want a spool of thread. You ought to make him give you some pin-money. I shouldn't tolerate such a system."

"But I like it, Sarah," Miss Margaret said with loyal mendacity. "It saves me so much trouble. I never cared for shopping anyway."

Agnes' heart ached as she looked at her aunt. She knew that the little woman was never so happy as when fussing about the fancy stores.

"Well! I shouldn't like it," rejoined Mrs. Ballington, waving her lorgnette. "I feel free to say that I should not enjoy it in the least. It's fortunate that you—and Agnes—do."

Her prominent eyes swept by Miss Ballington and challenged the younger woman. Agnes returned her look steadily, and the prominent eyes wavered and turned away.

"There's Ferdinand at the gate," broke in Miss Margaret nervously, looking through the window.

Mrs. Ballington turned to her. "Since you have no nurse I suppose we are to take care of Estelle," she said pointedly.

"Oh, I love the baby," exclaimed Miss Margaret instantly. "I'd love to have her with us, but she's asleep now. When Eliza has the dishes washed, she's going to wheel her out in the park."

"Eliza has her hands full," remarked Mrs. Ballington when Agnes had left them. "You look out, Margaret. She'll strike for more wages." Her voice dropped its society tone when the door closed.

"It's because no other girl can get along with Eliza, Sarah, that we don't have a second girl," replied Miss Margaret earnestly. "The little time Agnes had a nurse Eliza and she had a hand-to-hand fight—"

"Well, wasn't it Eliza's fault?" broke in Mrs. Ballington aggressively.

"I don't doubt it was. But Ferdinand thought—I presume he was right. I didn't witness the fight myself. Shall we sew upstairs?" Miss Margaret suddenly broke off and changed the painful subject.

They went up to Miss Ballington's room and settled themselves for the afternoon. As they sewed Mrs. Ballington catechised Miss Ballington as to the past, present, and future of the family plans. She regretted to see that Estelle had no teeth. Tom had one at four months, but he was a very remarkable child, and she should not expect the same of Estelle perhaps. It was time, however, that Estelle showed an inclination to creep. It was time, too, that Agnes should call again upon Mrs. Mortimer Tompkins, and Miss Margaret ought to see to it that Agnes kept her social engagements better than she had been doing. People were beginning to talk about her eccentricities as well as Ferdinand's. "I am pleased to see, however," she finished approvingly, "that Agnes has given up her music. It shows some attention to the baby."

Before she had been there an hour Mrs. Silas had reduced Miss Margaret to the state of mental disintegration and indiscriminate apology for herself and everybody else which usually followed upon her sister-in-law's visits. She now proceeded to fill up the bewildered little woman's brain with gossip. She informed her of the return of Fred and Beatrice from their summer's trip to Europe, adding that the young couple were seriously divided on the question of Fred's return to the bank. Tom had been appealed to by Beatrice to talk to Fred on the subject, but had promptly packed his grip and left the city on a vacation. Her son had dropped the remark before he left that Fred could clerk it in the infernal regions for all he cared. The dowager sighed regretfully because Donald had not more of his younger brother's spirit. "Donald is very wearing to live with; he is like his father in many ways. Here he might marry Geraldine Tompkins, and he prefers to go around with the face of a grave-digger, saying he doesn't care to marry."

Mrs. Silas then referred to the approaching visit of Agnes' mother. Miss Margaret had not heard anything of it, and expressed her surprise, whereupon the dowager smiled meaningly. Probably Agnes was ashamed of her mother and was keeping her visit a secret as long as possible. Everybody knew Mrs. Sidney was an ignorant and undesirable connection. As for Mrs. Silas herself, she intended to be out of the city while Mrs. Sidney was in it, and she advised Miss Margaret to accompany her.

The little lady was overcome on the spot by a vision of Agnes' mother descending like a bird of prey on her peaceful home, but she bravely replied to her sister-in-law's invitation by stating her intention to stay and entertain Ferdinand's mother–in–law "as though she were the first lady in the land, Sarah. We can never forget that, whatever else she may be, she is little Estelle's grandmother."

Meantime, Ferdinand and Agnes were driving through one of the beautiful suburbs of the city. They had conversed fitfully on indifferent subjects, but Ferdinand had been brooding over Donald's flowers to Agnes and her blush when he had referred to them. His irritation had extended to Tom's frames, which Donald, of course, would have to pay for. The insulting spendthriftiness which could not find enough legal holidays to celebrate with presents, but must needs compliment the movement of the seasons, was insufferable. Then there was Flynn's wife flaunting Flynn's impudence in the very bosom of his family! While Ferdinand was brooding over these things, a letter which he had received that morning occurred to him as suggesting a new grievance.

"You remember Frank Rousseau?" he asked, watching Agnes narrowly as he spoke.

The color crept slowly into Agnes' face. "Mr. Rousseau whom we met in Switzerland?" she asked. "Yes. I remember him well."

"He is coming to Winston on business soon. I am thinking of asking him to the house for a few days."

Agnes said nothing.

"You would like me to ask him to stay with us?" persisted Ferdinand.

"No, I should not like it," Agnes returned in a low voice.

"What is your objection?"

"Mr. Rousseau's manner at the close of that evening was not gentlemanly," she forced herself to reply.

Ferdinand leaned back in the phaeton. "It is curious," he said slowly, "that men always are considered the aggressors in such affairs. He never would have looked at you as he did if you had not led him on by flirting with him."

Agnes looked at her husband in astonishment. "Flirting with him! I have never flirted with men."

"It was quite decorous, of course," her husband replied in the same tone.

The remainder of the drive was almost without conversation. Agnes listened to the sharp, clean foot-falls of Dan on the earth road, and lived over again the evening at Lucerne. She remembered her exhilaration consequent upon her husband's early demonstrations of emotion, her desire to call his feeling into play that night, her conversation with Mr. Rousseau, and what followed. She recalled Ferdinand's quiet pose and control.

When they were nearly home, she spoke again. "Ferdinand," she said reluctantly, "I think it is true that I did coquette with Mr. Rousseau. I am ashamed of it."

She saw Ferdinand's face change as soon as she had spoken. When he spoke, however, his voice was under control. "I admire your honesty," he said.

"It is the only time that I ever was guilty of that, and I am sorry."

An expression she was familiar with, but which she had never understood, came across his face.

"The fault, perhaps, is mine in having introduced such a man as Rousseau to you. The best thing men and women can do is to be honest, and now that you have become so, I will endeavor to keep you out of temptation."

"Ferdinand!" cried Agnes in alarm. "You don't think—" She drew away from him into the comer of the carriage.

When she had mastered her indignation enough to think, she finally spoke. There was a strong reminiscence of Mrs. Sidney in the manner, and of Dr. Sidney in the matter, of her remarks. "Ferdinand, you have been telling me for some time about my faults. Now I have been noticing that there is a streak of coarseness in much that you say and think. I have observed it in your remarks about other people, but it is especially brought home to me now that you are beginning to apply it to me. You seem to like to degrade human nature and to think it is a mark of your superiority. It isn't, though. It is a sign of moral degeneration, and if you don't rid yourself of it speedily your evil imagination will contaminate your actions."

Ferdinand had the confused sensation of a commander-in-chief who has been halted suddenly on the picket-line by a private whom he has himself placed on duty.

He rallied himself, however, and replied, "Far from being a mark of moral degeneration, it is a mark of honesty. You sugar-coat every unpalatable truth. Now, I see life as it is, no matter whether I like it or not. You call that being coarse."

"You see life as it is not," she replied stolidly. "You misrepresent me in such a way that you insult us both. I must insist upon one thing. I sometimes sought the admiration of men before my marriage, and that once afterwards, but I never should have been in danger of anything more."

He made no reply, but assisted her from the carriage, and drove to the barn.

Agnes went directly to her room, where she remained with her baby until dinner.

Mr. Rousseau came to Winston and went away, but he did not come to the Ballingtons', whether because he had received no invitation or had declined one Agnes never knew.

CHAPTER X

AUTUMN was almost over; the ground was covered with crimson leaves, and the sky crossed by sailing lines of birds. A bacchanalian frieze of scarlet woodbine and yellowing wildgrape, ripe with purple berries just ready to drop from their stems, framed Mrs. Sidney's veranda. It was tangled here and there with bronzed honeysuckle sprays still bearing one or two late clusters of flowers. The autumn wind, which was lifting the leaves from off the old maples and elms and floating them down like the spirits of carbuncles and topazes through the smoke-veiled air, touched Agnes' cheeks with color and blew her hair about her face as she sat on her mother's porch, surrounded by some leather-bound volumes. Ferdinand sat near her, smoking.

"I still can follow the Latin, I see," she said, looking up at her husband, "but I'll never be able to read any of these," and she held up a volume of Sophocles bound in rich but faded green leather.

Ferdinand took his cigar from his mouth to answer her. "You will have that much less lumber in your mind. It's curious how people go on loading their minds with exploded ideas two thousand years old."

Agnes went on with her work without replying. She had been aware vaguely when Ferdinand first came out from Dr. Quinn's office a few minutes before that his apparent serenity was masking some annoyance, and his tone, affable though it was, confirmed her suspicion. As she turned over her father's despised classics in silence, her mind wandered from the Greek and Latin and Italian pages to speculations upon what had taken place between her husband and Dr. Quinn. By the time Ferdinand had finished his cigar she had satisfied herself that Quinn had refused Ferdinand's offer to push the surgical invention and take an interest in it.

As Ferdinand rose at last and picked up his hat, Agnes spoke to him involuntarily, "Doesn't Quinn want to go in with you?"

"No," said Ferdinand, pausing before he turned to the steps. "He says he's in no hurry to patent and that he'd rather go slower and be independent." He did not look at his wife as he started to descend to the yard.

Admiration and trust in Quinn flashed into Agnes' mind, but the next instant apprehension possessed her. Ferdinand would not forget the doctor's self-sufficiency, and this outcome to the purpose which had been chief in bringing her husband to Kent might cloud over the home visit.

She hastened to detain him with words meant to conciliate.

"Don't go!" she said eagerly. "Come in and see mother give Estelle her dinner. She has learned to drink out of a glass."

Ferdinand hesitated, then turned back more readily than his wife had hoped, and they found Mrs. Sidney and the baby in the dining-room.

"Don't let her see you, Agnes," Mrs. Sidney warned the young mother. She held a glass of milk in her hand as she spoke.

Agnes approached softly behind the child, and Ferdinand and she stood watching. The baby made a little hitching motion with her body and leaned forward toward the milk, drinking a little daintily as her grandmother held the glass. Ferdinand looked on gravely.

When the meal was finished he remarked, "I notice you do not use the nursing-bottles I bought. I didn't wish to disturb you this time, but I prefer to have Estelle suck her milk. It causes a flow of saliva and is better for her digestion."

"She is old enough to drink now, said Mrs. Sidney complacently, proud of the baby as well as of her own success.

Ferdinand eyed her a moment before replying, "I prefer to have her use a bottle."

"How do you suppose I got along before you were born, Ferdinand?" asked Mrs. Sidney, looking up with a twinkle in her eye. "I've taken care of more babies than you've years to your life. It won't do the child one bit of harm to drink her milk, and it's a good deal easier for the mother. Nursing bottles are hard to keep clean."

"I should not think it very difficult to wash a bottle," remarked Ferdinand, and Agnes noticed sensitively that the hint of a sneer was creeping into his voice.

She stood, her back to the table, both hands resting upon it, her head slightly lowered, as she rapidly thought over how she could ward off a quarrel between Ferdinand and her mother.

"You might not think so, but it is," returned Mrs. Sidney, looking at her son-in-law openly. "It's a nice little thing to do, especially when there are a million other things to see to at the same time, and it isn't just one bottle; it's eight!"

"What will be the expense of hiring these washed per day?" inquired Ferdinand, feeling for his purse.

Mrs. Sidney's offended surprise leaped into indignation.

"Ferdinand Ballington, you ought to be ashamed of yourself. I'm an old woman and I know how to take care of babies. Estelle is my grandchild, and I'm not going to teach her to suck a bottle now. It doesn't look well to see a child sucking a bottle. Come with grandma, Estelle."

"I don't care to discuss the matter, Mrs. Sidney," insisted Ferdinand evenly, but with an edge in his voice.

Mrs. Sidney picked up the baby and crossed the room with her.

As they disappeared within the bedroom Ferdinand finished, "You understand my wish. I want nursing-bottles used."

Mrs. Sidney answered him from across the threshold, "I don't care to discuss it either, Ferdinand. This child is in my house and she's going to *drink*!" and the bedroom door closed.

"Have you any plans for the afternoon?" asked Ferdinand, turning to Agnes.

She lifted her face for the first time, and looked at him with eyes whose pain added to their luminousness.

As she was silent, he repeated his question.

Then she released her hold on the table and turned away from him, saying mechanically, "Nothing definite. Beatrice spoke of taking us to drive."

Ferdinand looked at his watch, considered a moment, and then said enigmatically:

"It is now half-past two. I am going out on some errands."

She let him pass without replying, and watched him thoughtfully through the window as he disappeared down the street. When he was out of sight, she returned with slow steps to her mother.

"Well," said Mrs. Sidney, looking up buoyantly when her daughter entered the room, "I hope I taught Ferdinand a lesson." She was hard at work on short clothes for the baby, and as Agnes sat down by her she held up a fluffy hemstitched ruffle. "He needs discipline. It's perfectly ridiculous, his setting himself up as an authority on babies. I've humored him long enough. It's something new each day. The child can't suck its thumb, can't be rocked, can't suck a sugar lump or a crust of bread. 'Farinaceous food isn't digestible.' I've seen it digest. You mark my words, Agnes, Ferdinand needs a good talking to once in a while. He's my son and I love him, but he'd better be careful. 'Pride goeth before a fall.'"

"Never mind, mother," Agnes answered tenderly. "It's a little thing. I'd just as soon wash the bottles." And she smiled with sudden warmth.

But Mrs. Sidney, with instant keenness, rebuked her daughter's concession. "The Lord helps those who help themselves, Agnes," she said, her face sobering. "How dare you ask the Lord to bless you when you shirk your duty to your husband? I tell you it's high time you took Ferdinand Ballington in hand to correct his faults if you ever expect him to amount to anything."

Agnes laid her hand on her mother's knee as she said quietly:

"Ferdinand isn't like papa, mamma."

"I shouldn't be talking to you like this, if he were," returned the older woman undaunted. "You know what the Bible says about a man wise in his own conceit. There is more hope of a fool than of him. I wish I'd told Ferdinand that."

Agnes stood up without answering. She was turning over in her mind the Bible words of her mother's which had caught her ear, "There is more hope of a fool than of him."

"Now, when your new baby comes," went on Mrs. Sidney earnestly, "don't you begin by holding it off for three hours when it wants to nurse. Their little stomachs are only as big as a thimble. Look at my thimble here and see how little it is. Does a calf have to wait three hours before the cow takes it? I guess God's own little image has as good instincts when it comes into the world as a calf has."

Agnes came to herself as her mother talked, and when Mrs. Sidney had finished, she bent down and kissed her mother on the forehead. "I shall have you there to manage this time, mother," she said. She lingered a little, speaking of other things. Then with a change of voice she said, "I think I will go and dress for the ride with Bee." She passed her hand lightly over Mrs. Sidney's forehead. "Do take a rest, mother. You'll spoil your eyes."

Mrs. Sidney pushed back her spectacles and pressed her own hand hard on her eyes.

"Estelle and grandma will blow soap bubbles!" she suggested the moment after, beaming upon the baby on the floor, who was looking uneasily after her mother.

As Agnes passed through the hall she saw a messenger boy coming up the steps. Her heart sank as she took the note he brought, for she recognized her husband's handwriting, and knew that what she had been dreading was upon her.

"The gentleman said there was no answer," the boy called back as he ran down the steps.

Agnes tore open the envelope and hastily read the following note:

DEAR AGNES:

Make your arrangements to leave for Winston on the evening train. I shall not be back for dinner, but shall call for you with a carriage in time to reach the station.

Yours,

F. B.

Agnes stood quite still with the open message in her hand. Grief, bitterness, and anger raged in her heart as she recalled her long wait for this little visit home, the short happy two days she had had with her mother, and the weary winter ahead in the companionship of Miss Margaret and Eliza. Then a torrent of tears rushed to her eyes and she went up the stairs quivering.

When she came down she was dressed for driving. She found her cousin Fred in the parlor talking to her mother.

"Why, Fred! How do you happen to be out so early?" she asked. Then she recollected that it was Saturday and the bank closed at noon.

"I thought I should find Bee here," answered Fred. "She had left the house with the double carriage and should have been here by this time."

Agnes forgot even Ferdinand's note in her eagerness at finding herself at last free to talk with Fred. Except for a hasty hand-shake in the bank, it was the first time that she had seen him for many months. He had spent the summer in Europe with Beatrice. It was his first trip and he had taken it as a hard concession to his wife's insistence. Agnes remembered what her own travel had done for her, the changes it had made in her views of life. Surely the journey had meant this, too, for Fred, had broadened him, freed him from his provincial aims and brought him into a more sympathetic understanding of his wife's nature. On the other hand, the variety and activity of many weeks of traveling, together with the success in getting Fred out into the world, must have quieted Beatrice's restlessness and discontent. How much the summer might have done for both of them in closing up what threatened to be a dangerous breach in their relations!

As she drew up a chair and sat down by her cousin Agnes searched his face with anxiety and hope for signs of new interests. The glimpse of him at the bank had told her nothing, while Beatrice's manner during the one visit she had had with her had been jovial but inscrutable. All that Agnes knew about her cousin and his wife since their return was what Donald had told her, and that was that soon after the Sidneys' return to Kent Tom had gone out to the lake house to see Beatrice, and upon his return had asked urgently for a vacation. He had earned it by months of steady work and, accordingly, it was willingly granted. Had Beatrice herself put a period to their bohemian comradeship, or was Tom's trip an escape from her? Which conjecture was true neither Donald nor Agnes could tell.

To Agnes' disappointment she did not see in Fred's face the expression for which she had hoped. He looked sadder, quieter, more ascetic. It was not the face of a man who had grown into closer sympathy with such a woman as Beatrice. Rather it was the face of one who had been settled more firmly in his convictions. Agnes was alarmed at the gentle and refined fixedness that was becoming the habitual expression of her cousin's face.

"Fred," she said impulsively, "I'm sorry you came back to this country so soon. It was your first trip. You ought to have stayed over there longer."

"I didn't wish to over-stay my leave of absence."

"I don't believe it would have made much difference," she persisted. "Kent is an easy-going town. The bank wasn't suffering."

"I was away a good while for me," Fred returned with a faint smile. "Beatrice wanted to stay longer."

"I think you might have consented; wives like to have their husbands amenable on an outing. And then, too," she said, with a nervous laugh, "when you come right down to it, Fred, what are you in the bank at all for?"

Fred flushed. "It is the only self-respecting course for me to follow," he said doggedly.

"Indeed it is," interrupted Mrs. Sidney. "Fred must fill a husband's position. He must be a bread-winner."

"But, mother, where is the use of winning bread for a table that can afford fruits out of season?" queried Agnes. "If Fred wants to win bread, he could win a good deal more by letting Beatrice set him up in business."

Fred's brows contracted irritably. "A man ought not to be dependent on his wife for everything," he said sententiously.

"A man ought to do more than be financially independent of his wife," said Mrs. Sidney authoritatively. "He ought to rule his house. Beatrice makes her money in ways of which her husband does not approve. She gambles in stocks. She uses that as an excuse for some other things."

"Not now, mother!" interrupted Agnes, lifting her hand.

"How long is it since Thomas Ballington was at the lake house?" asked Mrs. Sidney sternly of her nephew.

Agnes interposed. "Tom has been away for some time, mother, in the Maine woods."

"Aunt Kate, I think we had better not talk about this," said Fred in a controlled voice. "It can do no possible good and I decline to hear it."

"Fred, I brought you up," his aunt replied instantly. "I'm going to talk to you as I would to Agnes, and you needn't get up on your dignity. You sit where you are!"

Fred hesitated, then leaned back stolidly.

Mrs. Sidney went on with rising energy. "It is the mark of a man and a husband who expects to be the father of children someday, to be the head of his own household. You ought to make Beatrice understand this. She needs a controlling hand. She is good-hearted and generous. She would have done a good deal for me if I had let her. But she has had no bringing up. Her own willful desires are her only law. Instead of wisely controlling her, you think your duty stops with going down to that bank all day every day, while she is out at the lake with Tom Ballington, gambling by telegraph."

"I tell you, mother,—" interrupted Agnes.

"You keep still, Agnes! Gambling by telegraph! When your hours are up at the bank, you should go where your wife is. Thomas Ballington's hunting-trips don't last very long. When he comes back, you should forbid him the house. I don't think he would come again if you did this."

A pause followed Mrs. Sidney's last words.

Then Fred said in an impersonal voice, "The house is hers, Aunt Kate."

"Beatrice is yours," returned Mrs. Sidney instantly. "If you don't make her feel that pretty soon, she won't stay yours."

There was another stillness.

Then Fred spoke again in the impersonal tone. "My wife belongs to herself. If I should take the course you suggest, she would retaliate by a reckless defiance which could have but one end, the severing of our relations."

Agnes sat up and began to speak eagerly. "Fred, if you allowed Beatrice her way in financial matters, I believe she would recognize your right as a husband to exclude unwelcome guests from your home. Does it not seem that there is a needless irritation between you on that point?"

"Good God!" exclaimed Fred, springing to his feet and looking down upon the two women with burning eyes. "Do you want to take away my last shred of independence—to take away my only shadow of authority?"

"I don't know what Agnes wants," said Mrs. Sidney promptly. "If you have got any authority, I'd counsel you to use it, and try to extend it beyond that bank. Be the head of your family, not a bank-clerk."

Fred's face grew white. "Since you are so full of advice," he said rapidly, "tell me this. How is a man to control a self-willed and passionate woman who has grown tired of him, and for whom, therefore, a legal release, his only weapon, has no terrors! I tell you I can do nothing with her!"

He looked down into the startled faces a moment, then turned, went out of the room abruptly, and a moment later had left the house.

Agnes and her mother sat where he left them, but upon Mrs. Sidney's face a righteous displeasure was growing. She was about to speak when Agnes drew a quick breath and anticipated her.

"I have had a note from Ferdinand, mother. He is suddenly called home on business and says that we must return tonight."

Mrs. Sidney looked steadily at her daughter. "Agnes, don't tell me a falsehood. Ferdinand isn't going away for business. He is going to take you home because I gave Estelle her dinner out of a glass. He can't control his ungodly temper."

Agnes did not reply, but Mrs. Sidney had a logical mind, and presently she resumed. "Well, I guess you will have to go. It's a pity that Ferdinand didn't marry Beatrice. He might have done some good there."

She waited a moment, and when she spoke again there was a quaver in her voice. "So he is going to take my daughter away from me, is he, after two days?"

"Mother," cried Agnes passionately, "I won't go."

All that she had striven to keep from her mother's knowledge flamed in her face, and Mrs. Sidney read it clearly. There was a moment's struggle in the mother's heart. Then conscience triumphed over instinct.

"Agnes," she said, "a husband has the right to say where his wife and child shall be. Ferdinand is well within his rights."

"He has not the right over the child till it is seven years old," interrupted Agnes, in a tense voice. "The custody is the mother's until then, if she is a good woman. Think of it! She bears it, and cares for it, and suffers with it, and has a right to it only for the period of infancy, and then it belongs to the father. Oh, the cruelty of it! A man mustn't touch his wife with his little finger, but he can torture her mind and crush the soul out of her, and she must bear it."

Mrs. Sidney watched Agnes closely as she was speaking. When she had finished, the older woman asked, "Where did you find out all these things?"

"In a play."

"The theater!" There was both grief and reproof in the mother's voice.

Presently she spoke again with unusual gravity. "Agnes, you have been thinking of leaving your husband. My daughter, you can't leave Ferdinand. The Lord has put a work upon you. You've got to sanctify him."

"Mother, I have been beside myself because he wouldn't let me do for the baby what I thought I ought to do. He said I was training her to cry because I took her up when she did cry, and he made me leave her to scream all by herself until she would stop from exhaustion. Sometimes she cried because she was hungry, and sometimes she was sick."

"How did he keep you away from her?"

Agnes did not answer.

"Did he tie you up in a chair?" demanded Mrs. Sidney, pressing her.

"No, he said I mustn't go," said Agnes, scarcely above a whisper.

Mrs. Sidney pressed her further. "And that kept you! And you would like to make laws to let women go away from their husbands—women who sit still and let their babies scream because a man tells them to?"

"Mother," said Agnes, looking down at her clasped hands, "he would take Estelle into his room and lock her in. I couldn't get to her."

There was a considerable pause after this confession.

Then Mrs. Sidney asked, "Why didn't you lock her up in your room first?"

"I would when I could get her first," said Agnes, the clasped hands trembling. "He said that he did not want to do what he did, but that I needed discipline as much as the child."

Mrs. Sidney's indignation at her daughter's revelation was counteracted by her alarm at the consequences which threatened to follow Ferdinand's conduct. She ran over rapidly in her mind various ways of dealing with him.

When she resumed, there was decision in her voice. "Now, Agnes, listen to me. It isn't the law that makes a home. It is character. Once you let the law step in and it isn't a home any longer. Ferdinand is your husband and you've got to love him—"

"I do love him," interposed Agnes with dignity.

"So much the better," went on Mrs. Sidney. "Now you see to it, that, along with your loving him, you make him understand that you mean what you say just as much as he does. You've got to take your own stand. The law can't take it for you."

"Mother, isn't this a little inconsistent with the way you were talking to Fred a moment ago?"

"No," responded Mrs. Sidney stoutly; "the cases are different."

"They are indeed," replied her daughter. "If I had money—" She broke off. "It does no good to oppose Ferdinand. You see how much good it did when you held out against him."

"I am not his wife." Mrs. Sidney rose. "I've got to submit to a mother-in-law's position." Her face passed through bitter struggle to grim control as she spoke.

Then an obtrusive sense of humor manifested itself. "Do you think it would do me any good to want to make laws upholding mothers-in-law?" She looked at her daughter with a real smile as the words came out.

The smile faded, however, as she continued, "I didn't mean to say to Fred that a wife is the husband's property. She is his companion, and Ferdinand's wife above all must not be a moral coward."

As she finished she left the room and went into her bedroom. Once inside it she gave way to a spasm of weeping, which she interrupted every now and then to utter some words of prayer.

In accordance with Ferdinand's demand, Agnes packed their trunk, and was ready to go when her husband came with the carriage.

"Good-by, Ferdinand. God bless you!" called Mrs. Sidney from the veranda. But she did not trust herself to go down to the carriage with Agnes. Nor did Ferdinand come to the house.

He was considerate toward Agnes during the home trip, silenced Miss Margaret's questions on their arrival and kissed his wife when he said good-night. She accepted his caress silently.

Agnes continued to feed Estelle from a glass the following day, but she took pains to do so when her husband was out of sight. It must come to a contest between them, but in weariness, she longed to postpone it.

In the afternoon a letter came from her mother. She noticed that her mother had written a letter also to Ferdinand. He read it, and handed it over to her without comment, a grim satisfaction in his face. Agnes read it with mingled torture and admiration. She knew how much effort the apology had cost her mother.

MY DEAR SON FERDINAND: I thought the Lord was going to let me teach you a lesson. But I guess He saw fit to let you teach me one. It won't do your baby any harm to drink out of a glass, but I'm not the one to say what shall be done to your and Agnes' child. I oughtn't to have interfered, and I hope you'll forgive me and bring Agnes and the baby back to see me. I've got a lonely heart, and I love you all. I pray God to bless you all.

Your mother,
KATE SIDNEY.

The tears streamed down Agnes' face as she handed the letter back to her husband. "My poor mother!" she said brokenly. "You'll answer it, Ferdinand?"

"I see no reason why I should do so," said Ferdinand, pocketing the letter. "It is no more than she ought to have done, and it has been a good thing for her. You have told me yourself that she always has been tyrannical."

Agnes remembered only too well. In the first flush of her love for Ferdinand, she thoughtlessly had made him the confident of her girlish impatience with her mother, as well as of her father's unworldly ideals of life. Once more, she felt the regret which follows impulsive self-revelation.

"I do not regard Mrs. Sidney as wholly to blame," Ferdinand continued. "The fault is more with your father. He ought to have controlled her till she was able to control herself. Personally, I admire your mother's character the more of the two. Her faults are the faults of strength, whereas his faults—"

"Don't say anything against papa!" cried Agnes abruptly.

She walked across the room and back before she continued.

"Please write to her. Tell her you will take me back," she said, stopping in front of him. Then she added deliberately, "Won't you do it for me? Won't you write her an affectionate letter?"

There was the desperation of a forlorn hope in her face, but Ferdinand ignored it. "I have no affection for her," he said.

He started to pass her as he spoke. There was a sudden motion forbidding him, and then Agnes drew back trembling.

"Ferdinand," she cried in a vibrating voice, "mother is inclined to be tyrannical, but she is not a deliberate tyrant, as you are. More than that, my mother has risen above her feelings and has made you an apology which has cost her a struggle of which you have no conception. A poor old woman at her time of life! She conquered herself. And you, a young man, a young, strong man, who has won his point and disciplined an old woman who has worked her eyes out for his child, you can't conquer yourself. You can't even respond to her apology. She does love you. She means every word of it, and you don't feel a spark of pity or affection for her."

Suddenly in the midst of her agony a memory flashed across Agnes' mind. It was Donald's voice saying, "You should do for your parents whatever you might wish. I can understand the desire, and it would be my happiness and my honor to gratify it." There was despair in her heart as she cried bitterly to the man she had chosen, "Oh, you can't know how you make me feel toward you! I wish to God I had married Donald!"

A sudden stillness fell over them as they looked at each other. A comb that Agnes wore dropped to the floor. Both started as though it were a pistol shot. The soft and shining waves of Agnes' hair gently uncoiled and shadowed her eyes as they still held Ferdinand's.

A new expression flashed into Ferdinand's face, called up by the fierceness of her beauty. In an instant he was straining her to him so violently that a low cry of pain was forced from her.

"Ferdinand, I have never wished that what I said," she said indistinctly.

After he was gone Agnes sank back upon the lounge. She began to doubt her power to control her moods, and she knew that what influence she had over her husband would fade with her self-control and endurance. On his part, Ferdinand never forgot Agnes' outcry. Before this there had been more or less of oscillation in their hopes and desires in each other, but from this day, although the oscillation continued, it began to be accompanied with a graduated fall.

PART IV

CHAPTER I

FERDINAND never answered Mrs. Sidney's letter, but twice during the winter he took his wife for a brief visit to her mother's. Moreover, although he never yielded openly to his mother-in-law's methods of bringing up children, he tacitly gave way to them more and more. He had decided, as have many others before him, that it is generally best to allow the world's efficient people to have their own way.

In May the long-expected visit of her mother to Winston, to which Agnes had been looking forward with longing, came about. Miss Margaret had anticipated it with trepidation owing to Mrs. Silas' persistent innuendoes. The latter lady had carefully suppressed in Miss Margaret every budding impulse of hospitable pleasure as fast as it appeared, and had repeated her original assertion that she would leave as soon as Mrs. Sidney should arrive. She did not leave, however, which confused Miss Margaret's ideas well-nigh hopelessly during the first week of Mrs. Sidney's visit.

Mrs. Silas herself regarded Mrs. Sidney with unstable emotions. She had intended to stay in town just long enough to impress the doctor's widow, and then to leave without having cast over her the mantle of her own social prestige. Her stupefaction which followed upon the speedy discovery that it was quite hopeless to impress Agnes' mother, and that, furthermore, she herself unwillingly was impressed with the newcomer, passed by a natural transition into a desire to make Mrs. Sidney the engine of social retribution upon the distinguished Mrs. Mortimer Tompkins. For a generation now Mrs. Mortimer Tompkins had been a rival too wealthy, too small-minded and infinitesimal-hearted for Mrs. Silas to get the better of her. There was a kind of fascination in the thought of watching the rival affronted, enraged, and finally routed by this obscure but indomitable person from Kent. Accordingly she gave a luncheon for Mrs. Sidney, and her unconscious guest carried herself so well and irritated Mrs. Tompkins to such an extent that Mrs. Silas then and there conceived as small a dislike of Agnes' mother as it was possible for her to extend to any of her fellow-beings. Mrs. Silas' relations with her acquaintances were measured by varying degrees of disapproval. These took the place in her of what in less highly organized people were friendships.

Mrs. Sidney took an early occasion to give Mrs. Ballington a warning on the subject of her son Tom's relations with Beatrice. Mrs. Silas received the communication haughtily, but, finding that her loftiness had no effect whatever, a certain hard common sense which she had at bottom, and which Mrs. Sidney addressed, made her think better of it, and she agreed to use her influence in keeping Tom occupied away from Kent.

Miss Margaret and Mrs. Sidney became friends, and, except for the guest's condemnation of Miss Margaret's recent conversion to Christian Science, they had no altercation worth mention. Miss Margaret was meek and deferential toward Mrs. Sidney, having a bewildered idea that Mrs. Sidney must be a great social power indeed. Mrs. Silas' consideration could flow from no other source, and Miss Margaret's naturally ornate phraseology took on an added stateliness as though she were addressing a member of the royal family.

The same naturalness which characterized Mrs. Sidney's entrance into Winston society characterized her entrance into Ferdinand's home. Ferdinand did not interfere with his mother-in-law and was away much of the time, and Eliza met her Waterloo in her first encounter with the guest.

As for Agnes herself, the month was one of the easiest during her married life, and she always felt an added tenderness toward her little son, because it was her mother who first laid the baby in her arms, saying in a tone of fervent thanksgiving, "He's a fine, healthy boy, Agnes, and he shall be called Stephen Sidney Ballington."

Only one thing happened to cloud Agnes' month with her mother, and this took place just before Mrs. Sidney left. Agnes knew that her mother was worried over something, and she guessed what it was, for she had seen Pleasant Mabie's handwriting on a letter that had come from the West. As soon as an opportunity offered, she questioned her mother as to her news from Helen. Mrs. Sidney hesitated, then decided to tell the truth. The mortgage on her son-in-law's farm was about to be foreclosed. Pleasant had written to her, imploring help, but she was unable to give it.

"I don't believe it would be wise to send Pleasant money, if I had it to send," she concluded. "He would manage to get rid of it someway without paying off the mortgage. The Ethiopian can't change his skin. I'd have told him so, only I was afraid Helen would see the letter."

Agnes sat still and looked at her mother in extreme distress. She was thinking of her sister's condition, with the lassitude and discomfort of which she could, in her own weakness, so keenly sympathize.

"I can just barely make both ends meet," Mrs. Sidney went on. "Mattie's sickness just about played me out."

"You can't stand it, mother! You can't work so hard!" cried Agnes, her anxiety shifting. There was an instant's hesitation, during which her heart was wrung by her own impotence to help in this crisis. Then she said abruptly, "Why don't you let Beatrice help you?"

Mrs. Sidney turned and looked at her daughter. "My strength will be as my day, if I trust the Lord," she said with a different tone; and she added more gravely, "If I accepted Beatrice's money I should be countenancing her way of life."

"What will Pleasant and Helen do?" Agnes asked presently.

"I don't know. I have written to him that they can come on and go on your father's farm. It would be the best thing they could do. The house is pretty old, but I have had some new sills put in to support it. Pleasant doesn't want to do it. He says people won't respect him for coming back to live on his mother-in-law. Pleasant's very particular about his self-respect. He's got some fine pigs, too, and he wants to stick to pork-raising. If he hadn't paid out so much for pigs, he'd have kept the farm."

Agnes did not press the matter further. She did not tell her mother that she too had received a letter from her brother-in-law soliciting her aid. The letter had been written without her sister's knowledge, but it narrated in some detail Helen's feebleness and discouragement over their impending misfortune. Agnes had a slender opinion of Pleasant's financial ability, but she shrank from exposing him, and her sympathy for her sister had become a passion since her own marriage. Her recollections of the farm did not encourage her to believe in the feasibility of her mother's solution. It would be impossible for them to be comfortable there.

She thought over the situation during the day, and that night she called Ferdinand in to her before he went to bed. It was hard for her to do it, but she put down her pride, told her husband the situation, and begged him to give her money enough to save her sister's home. As soon as he began to speak she was sorry she had made her request. He asked her many questions about the Mabies, pinned her down to confessions she never had wished to make, and at last, after eliciting the exposure of Pleasant's and Helen's condition, he said that he was willing to buy the place himself and hire the Mabies as his tenants. This Agnes declined instinctively. She was learning to dread a mood that came over her from time to time which made life seem to her a web where she and those dear to her were caught flies and Ferdinand the spider.

After he left her she could not sleep. All this misery for want of a few hundred dollars and her husband worth hundreds of thousands! She rose and went to her desk at last to count over the money she still had left of her own. Then she took out the account book and added in what she had saved from housekeeping money and which she was holding subject to Ferdinand's order. Even though she could use it all there would still be about fifty dollars lacking. She went back to bed worried and restless.

In the night an idea came to her. She had recently bought and paid for some table-linen at one of the stores. The entry had been made in her account book and had been approved by Ferdinand. But the goods had not been used. In the morning she drove to the store and asked the privilege of returning the linen. The request was granted and the money refunded. Agnes put it with all she had on hand and sent it on to Pleasant.

One anxiety for the present was silenced, but another of a different nature replaced it, for the entry of the linen purchased remained unchanged in her account book. She had yielded to a great temptation.

During the following months this secret, her growing worry for her mother and sister, her at last certain knowledge of the hopelessness of any real sympathy from Ferdinand, the increasing difficulty in tactfully managing her husband, the loss of respect and confidence in herself, the strain which she was under to dissemble her unhappiness and depression, all these, along with physical weakness and weariness, began to tell noticeably upon her.

Ferdinand was the first to feel the lack in her of physical elasticity and mental buoyancy. After waiting what he considered a more than reasonable time for her to recuperate from her son's birth, he began to make significant remarks about the advisability of other members of the family besides Aunt Margaret interesting themselves in Christian Science. He began to take Agnes quite methodically to all the lighter theatrical entertainments that wandered their way. When Agnes expressed a dislike for vaudeville, he replied that she needed it; while Agnes observed that under the pretext of benefiting her he was developing a taste for a species of entertainment that was unutterably wearisome to her. It seemed to her, too, that her lack of vitality hastened in her husband the development of certain sinister characteristics and tendencies which until now had been held in abeyance. It was no longer possible for her to remain blind to the fact that his will was the ultimate factor to which all their differences must be resolved.

At last, he began to express openly his impatience at her continued depression, and when he found that she no longer responded to his stimulants, the home life bored him more than it ever had done before. He looked on with scarcely concealed irritation at her devotion to their children. He told her that she was getting morbid, allowing them to absorb her duty to him. It seemed to her that he ceased looking for the mental understanding and companionship between them which he formerly had expressed himself as expecting. It was, therefore, no shock to her when he told her one day, what she felt he had told himself already, namely, that she was a weakling, unable to adjust herself mentally or physically to her surroundings.

Having reached this point, with an inward sense of rankling injury Ferdinand made up his mind that the only course consistent with his dignity was to make the best of what threatened to be an unsatisfactory bargain. He would not confess to himself that he had made a mistake of judgment in selecting her. The fault lay in her willfully refusing to develop along the lines he had expected. She had shown her ability to do this at first, and he suspected that the flagging of her energy was a symptom of waning devotion to himself. Her involuntary cry contrasting him with Donald, recalled instantly though it had been, rose oftener in his memory, and he found himself watching her for other indications of fickleness and discontent.

No one but Donald suspected how far Agnes' depression was drifting. He saw that it was accompanied by a corresponding coolness and indifference in Ferdinand. After watching Agnes closely for some time and thinking anxiously over her matters and Tom's, Donald made a business trip to New York the spring following Stephen's birth, and while in that city he made a point of calling upon Miriam Cass.

Early in June it came about, quite naturally, that Miriam came up to Winston for her first visit to Agnes since they left college five years before. Their regular correspondence had developed an unexpected strength and depth in their friendship. Their mental companionship had become a confirmed and eager necessity for both.

When they met, Miriam held her friend a long time, a hand on each shoulder, looking at her intently; then releasing her, she said with a smile that was half-sweet, half-ironic: "It has been better that we weren't together these five years. We have kept all the idealism, and separation has made our intercourse a refuge and a luxury, but it is lovely to meet again," she added, the old smile which Agnes knew so well vanishing in a splendor of emotion which was a new and rich enchantment to the young wife.

The old boldness and power Agnes from the first had recognized in Miriam were still there, but there was a new ardor and a deepening sympathy. A kind of impatient fullness of humanity took the place of the old caustic spirit. On the other hand Miriam noticed the steady luminousness into which her friend's old flighty enthusiasm had concentrated. She felt respect for the judgment and the controlled will which were even more apparent in Agnes herself than they had been in her letters.

The richness, wise understanding, and healthful exhilaration which came to Agnes' life with Miriam's visit told at once upon her physical and mental well-being. The spring and buoyancy came back into her mind. Miriam's bitter and loving drollery whipped her into answering sallies. Transfigured nonsense flashed again, here and there, like will-o'-the-wisp through her conversation. Fits of laughter, ending breathless and speechless, again overtook her. She fell to walking straight again, giving the old piquant twist to her hair; the flush of sunrise crept back to her neck and arms, and quick, vital gestures punctuated remarks which again came out frankly.

Donald's sore and self-accusing conscience felt unwonted ease as he watched the success of his venture. Before long a second hope began to grow within him. Miriam seemed to touch and bring to life what was most manly and ambitious in Tom. Beatrice was forgotten, and Tom gave up without a struggle to an adoration of Agnes' friend that was pathetic to witness. She was Tom's superior, Donald knew, and older than he, but their tastes were similar, and Tom was lovable. His Aunt Stella had married Ferdinand's father. Might not Miriam marry Tom?

Ferdinand's feelings for his wife's friend were not easy to decipher. Miriam treated him with a mixture of suavity and inscrutable deference which the simple Donald misread as unaffected courtesy; which Tom interpreted, much to his own discomfort, as an indication that Miriam was humiliatingly taken in; which Miss Margaret thought was appreciation; and which Agnes alone realized was the perfection of tact.

CHAPTER II

"ICH hatte einst ein schönes—"

"Tom!"

Tom scowled at the words on the music-rack in front of him and said rapidly on the key he had just reached in singing, "Fire away, mater! What is it?" then touched the third note above sonorously with the first syllable of "Vaterland."

"What is that song you are singing? It is a very dull song. All the songs you sing now are dull. Where did you get them?"

As Mrs. Ballington put her question Donald glanced up from the paper he was reading and asked encouragingly, "They are the songs Miss Cass suggested, aren't they, Tom?" and without waiting for Tom to commit himself, Donald continued to his mother, "It's better music than Tom has been singing. After a little while you'll like them, mother."

Behind Tom's back Donald and his mother exchanged a swift look, accompanied on the part of each with a gesture. Donald's pantomime said, "Fall in with the music. It's a good thing," while the dowager answered with an expression which came easily to her face and hand, implying, "Oh, well, I suppose I must make the best of it."

Donald had been watching his mother with uneasiness during Miriam's visit, her manner recalling painfully to him the period of his own courtship of Agnes Sidney. It was even harder for her to give in to Tom's devotion to Miriam, because her common sense argued the extreme advisability of it, and Mrs. Ballington grudged concessions to common sense as well as to any other common thing. She refrained from criticism when with Tom, however, making up for it to Donald when they were alone together, and this Donald accepted cordially, knowing it to be a safety-valve for his mother.

As soon as Tom finished the song he gave a supple wheel around on the piano-bench and jumped up briskly. "Time to go, Don! The guests are assembled. The bridegroom stays late.'"

The brothers said their adieus to their mother, took their hats, and went together into the afternoon sunshine. A spirit of perverse silence descended upon Tom, which Donald did not venture to disturb. They went down the walk to the gate, down the street to the car-line, boarded a cross-town car, and rode for a couple of miles.

When they left the car they were in the neighborhood of the Ballington farm. There still remained several vacant lots, however, between them and Ferdinand's home, and they struck across these, following a time-worn little path along which a generation ago the Ballington cows had come at night. It still meandered in its leisurely way under the butternut trees across the newly laid-out city lots with their rectangular corners, ignoring the upstart iron hydrants and the street lamps—that mark of blasé city life where night never comes with sweet silence and rest. Here and there a clump of bushes strove gallantly to repel city limits and bring back the genius of the wood. As they followed the path the two brothers instinctively fell into their boyish custom—Donald walking ahead, Tom strolling behind.

As they reached the largest butternut tree the Ballington homestead came into full view, its trim brick wall and avenue of symmetrical cedars standing out uncompromisingly in the bright sunshine. Tom thrust his hands into his pockets and stood looking resentfully at Ferdinand's domain. "The look of that place just turns my stomach!" he exclaimed.

Donald looked back inquiringly. "What's the matter with the place?" he asked obtusely.

"Oh, don't make me talk about it," Tom responded furiously. "This poor old cowpath and Uncle Tom's butternut trees are a bad prologue to Ferdinand's necrological improvements. The little love for my kind I have left will turn sour when brandy-soaked old Tompkins planks down his tons of pressed brick on this lot and that vox et praeterea nihil, his spouse, desecrates the ground once trodden by grandfather's crumple-horned white bull. I feel like the ghost of that bull. I wish I were!" he blurted a moment later; "I'd clean out the upper circles of this town. I'd toss 'em into the lower part of eternity!"

A slow smile on Donald's face answered this tirade. The elder brother felt at last at liberty to speak. "It's no use worrying about things you can't help, Tom," he said placidly as they resumed their walk. "If you haven't anything worse than Tompkin's new house to worry you, you're a lucky man."

Tom's brows contracted slightly and he began to whistle softly a strain from the song he had been practicing before they started out.

After a moment, Donald continued hesitatingly, "I think Miriam Cass' visit has been a providential thing all around, Tom."

Tom flushed darkly, but said nothing.

Donald went on earnestly: "She's an extraordinary woman, and there's just one thing for you to do. Make yourself worthy of her respect and love. She certainly likes you, and I think you have it in you to win more from her."

Tom met his brother's eyes frankly. "I know you wish me well, Don," he said affectionately, "but you and I both know I am not worthy of her; still, notwithstanding Fred's insinuations about me, I haven't committed any unpardonable sin yet."

"I don't think you ever could get your own consent to commit an unpardonable sin, Tom," responded Donald gravely.

"Well," Tom began more briskly, "you might—" He broke off with an embarrassed laugh, then finished irrelevantly, "Well, I guess we'll let it go at that."

"Do you want something, Tom?" asked Donald encouragingly. "I'll do anything for you I can. Do you want money again?"

"Well—yes, thanks. That wasn't just uppermost in my mind, however. I was thinking that you take so much stock in—in praying, you know—why, damn it! here's a case of need at your own door. If the throne of grace doesn't help me out in this deal, I guess I'm out of the race."

There was a huskiness in Tom's voice that made Donald's eyes blur. "Tom!" he exclaimed. "My dear brother!"

"Oh, don't rub it in!" Tom interrupted quickly, as he hastened his pace. "You needn't order the funeral flowers just yet. Here we are at the family vault," he resumed a moment later as they approached Ferdinand's gate. "We're in the right mood to march down the avenue abreast."

They entered Ferdinand's yard and Tom walked solemnly down the path between the cedars.

When they had nearly reached the house there was a collapse of his stiff carriage which preluded an exclamation from him. "There she is in the side yard under the apple-tree!"

They hurried over the smooth-shaven lawn and approached the apple tree under which Miriam Cass was sitting reading. She rose when she saw them coming and walked slowly forward to meet them.

A thrill of fear and exaltation swept all Tom's nerves. He felt with a passion of despair and adoration an irradiation of genius over the deep bronze hair, the stern set of the black brows, the scarcely perceptible line—it might be of sadness, it might be of cynicism—drawn from the sensitive nostrils down to the corners of her mouth. It flashed from her hawk like gray eyes and magnetized her old unobtrusive manner.

She shook hands cordially with the brothers and returned with them to the rugs spread out beneath the apple trees. Agnes' thirteen-months-old baby was asleep near by in a hammock.

Tom took his place a little behind Miriam where he could watch the sun on her burnished hair and the bold yet finely cut outline of her features.

"I'm afraid we interrupted your reading, Miss Cass," Donald began. "Go on and finish your chapter. Here comes Agnes. We can talk to her." Donald rose as he spoke and Miriam looked toward the house. Agnes was coming toward them across the lawn leading little Estelle by the hand.

"Ferdinand sent up word he'd be fifteen minutes late," Tom said to her at once.

Miriam moved slightly and made a gesture inviting Agnes to sit down beside her.

Agnes, however, smiled a refusal, went over to the hammock, lifted the baby, and smiled again at the others as she started toward the house. The baby moved its head about on her shoulder, now exhibiting a head worn bare of hair at the back, and now a face ludicrously like Ferdinand's.

Little Estelle started forward, too, both arms out, in a hurry, and tumbled down. "Never mind, Estelle. I'll carry you," said Donald, and he picked her up and overtook Agnes.

Tom pulled a pillow toward him, cushioned the trunk of a tree, and leaned back against it, clasping his hands behind his head. As soon as the others were out of hearing he began, "I've been wanting to ask you ever since you came what your conclusions are about Ferdinand. Do you like him?"

Miriam's eyes smiled. "You don't," she said.

"Right, there!" replied Tom promptly. "Agnes would have done a long sight better to take Don."

Miriam looked quizzical. "Mr. Ballington has some admirable traits," she commented quietly.

"So have I!" blurted out Tom, "but you'd never think of marrying me, would you?"

He had not realized the full import of what he was saying until after it was out. Then he turned pale with a sense of the irrevocableness of his blunder. To be suddenly launched all unprepared into a proposal of which he scarcely had dared dream in the utmost flight of his imagination filled him with dismay.

Miriam' s impulse was to laugh, when something in his look checked her.

Tom leaned forward with decision. "The Lord knows, I didn't think what I was saying," he began incoherently. "A man doesn't propose to a woman like you quite so rapidly. But what's the use? You might as well know it. I'm not fit to black your shoes. If I thought I were, I would ask you if I could do it. If I thought the time ever would come when you'd take me for your shoeblack, I'd wait and be happy. What a fertile ass I am to be talking to you like this. For God's sake, tell me you forgive me, or excuse me, or ignore me. You've done Agnes a world of good since you came. She needed a change and stimulus very badly." Tom's manner underwent a change in the last two sentences. He instinctively tried to ward off his catastrophe.

Miriam, however, disregarded his attempt. "I appreciate the fact that you blundered into saying something that you did not intend," she responded slowly, and I'm going to answer by saying something I did not intend to say. You have the making of a fine man in you and you ought to live so that you wouldn't feel you had insulted a woman by asking her to marry you."

Tom's face turned a deep crimson. "You're right," he replied with an effort after a moment, "and if you cared about it ever so little, I'd try to get within gunshot of being such a man."

"It doesn't make any difference whether I care or not," Miriam replied steadily; "we have to be our best selves independently, or we aren't our best selves at all."

Tom's lip trembled, but he answered bravely, "I know it. Of course I had no right to ask you to care. I'm going to make a try of it anyway, just for having known you. You won't grudge me that."

A gentleness came over Miriam's manner which was dangerous to Tom's self-control. "I do care. I'm a lonely creature myself. I never shall have anything but friendships in my life, and, if you will, you can make one of these."

A look of gratitude and humility passed like a refining fire over Tom's face. "Thank you," he said. He was thinking of Miriam's inner life into which he had seen. For the first time he realized something of the sacrifice she had made for her profession. It abashed him, but at the same time it made him rebellious. What was art to stand between such a woman and happiness? She would be the greater sculptor for marrying.

As he looked at her his eyes were drawn beyond her by a figure turning in at the gate and coming up the walk. It was Ferdinand, and Tom's quick mind leaped to a kindred situation. Agnes had had a future in her voice, and she had given it up for marriage. The logic of the wise saying, "No man can serve two masters," was borne in upon him, as matrimony, in the person of Ferdinand, advanced relentlessly up the walk.

"Here he comes!" he said in a dead-and-alive tone.

Miriam looked up and saw Ferdinand coming across the grass toward them. From her first sight of him this summer until today, her last day in Winston, Miriam always had experienced a curious sensation whenever she and Ferdinand met. It was the instinctive bracing of her nerves for the defensive. Like Ferdinand, however, she never was visibly confused, and she gave him a smile as slight as his own as he approached, and waited for him to speak.

He removed his hat and said, looking from one to the other, "I am a little late. I think we had better go right in to dinner." He held out his hand to assist Miriam to her feet, and walked slowly beside her while Tom sauntered along on the other side.

"Were you reading?" asked Ferdinand.

"No, I was talking with your cousin."

"I saw you were carrying a novel. Occasionally I find time to read fiction myself. Agnes has gone into it rather too freely, it seems to me; and while we are on the subject, I would like to suggest to you that you use your influence with Agnes to read more judiciously. I've been surprised to see that she has taken to reading Fielding lately."

"You have read him, haven't you?" asked Miriam seriously. "I have myself."

"You are ready for it, Miss Cass, while Agnes is hardly prepared to use the same liberty of choice."

Miriam walked on in silence between her two companions, looking at the ground. Tom's collar began to choke him. When they reached the walk leading up to the front steps he broke the silence.

"Agnes is just as ready for it as Miss Cass," he exclaimed indignantly, looking first at Ferdinand and then at the woman he loved. "I can tell you exactly why she is reading Fielding. It's because you're always quoting him." He abruptly checked himself as he saw the corners of Miriam's mouth twitch.

They entered the house without further conversation.

As they reached the dining-room Miriam paused in the doorway to look at Agnes. The eye of the artist took in the beauty of the picture. Agnes stood in front of the golden cherry buffet putting a huge bunch of Maréchal Neil roses into a Russian glass bowl. A thin ray of afternoon sunlight fell across her, throwing into relief the beautiful head, and lighting up the subdued colors of her Roman silk blouse, belted in at the waist. Her back was toward them and she looked straight and young, the raised arms supple and muscular.

At the sound of their approach she turned her head over her shoulder, then, with a vivid smile, clasped the bowl of roses with both arms and turned toward the newcomers, looking through and over the flowers at Miriam. "For you and me," she exclaimed, "from Donald and Tom! We are in the vale of Kashmir in the month of roses."

"Well, Agnes," returned Tom, "you just stand there the rest of the evening and hold them. You ought to be preserved as you are. If I had a wand I'd wave it over you!"

Agnes stooped a moment over the roses, drew a long breath, turned and replaced them on the buffet.

As she came forward to the table Tom noticed that she was wearing cameos at throat, waist, and cuffs. As soon as they were seated, he leaned forward and examined them.

"Where did you resurrect those?" he asked delightedly. "You can't fool me. Those are two hundred years old if they're a day. And the setting belongs to the same period. If you ever want to pawn them, I'm your man."

Ferdinand's brow contracted.

Agnes laughed. "Miriam brought me these," she said. "She gave me the waist, too. Don't they go well together?"

"Well, they're not like the rest of your things," Tom commented with satisfaction. "There's a kind of old-aristocracy air about you in those. You always look fine, but somehow I can't get away from the thought that most of your other things are the same material that Mrs. Mortimer Tompkins might buy,—or any other rich person," he finished, without glancing at Ferdinand. "Now I might have bought these myself."

Ferdinand smiled.

"If you mean that they're within reach of your purse," he commented, "I guess Mrs. Tompkins would have the best of it. Those cameos are very expensive."

"Of course they are," returned Tom affably. "That's another reason why I would have bought them, while Mrs. Tompkins would think twice about it."

Ferdinand disdained to respond, and Miriam, feeling the awkwardness of the conversation, turned to Tom, holding out her hands for inspection. "Royal compliments are in the air. The visiting monarch has received his parting gift."

Tom wondered if it were satire or pleasure in her tone as his eye was caught by a ring on the first finger of Miriam's hand. It was a pear-shaped jade lozenge in a massive setting, the jade outlined by a continuous row of small but brilliant emeralds.

"Did Agnes give you that?" he asked incredulously.

"That's pretty good for America!" He pretended to be still looking at the ring, but in reality he was studying with passionate renunciation the compact and flexible hand held out without a tremor disturbing its statuesque repose.

"Ferdinand picked it out," said Agnes. "I think he showed excellent taste."

"Agnes and Mr. Ballington gave it to me this morning. It is truly a beautiful remembrance," Miriam added.

Tom withdrew his eyes. It was with difficulty that he refrained from remarking, "I wonder which one of Tiffany's clerks he got to select it for him," but he contented himself with asking querulously, "Why do you wear it on the first finger?"

"It's true I ought to wear it on the thumb?" said Miriam reflectively. "It's a weak concession to public opinion. Sennacherib and Alexander Borgia wore theirs on the thumb."

Ferdinand looked up inquiringly. Aunt Margaret was hopelessly mystified. Meantime Tom's fury of rebellion was reaching the danger point. Ferdinand, by a deliberate subterfuge, under cover of his wife, had given Miriam a ring! Tom had wild thoughts of combining with Aunt Margaret and Eliza in the purchase of an Assyrian thumb ring which should eclipse the jealous emeralds which Tiffany's clerk had induced Ferdinand to buy.

There was a gleam of amusement in Miriam's eye as she glanced side-long at her dinner-companion. She divined what was going on behind his grim face. A moment later she put her hand up to her throat and drew from beneath the embroidered collar a little string of old coral which Tom recognized as one Agnes had worn the evening of her arrival in her new home. It had been given to Agnes' father by an old sea captain, who got it in the South Sea. "One more gift," she said. "This is my amulet." As she slipped it back again she resumed her previous manner. "I shall will the ring to Estelle, who, I hope, will have the courage to wear it on her thumb."

Miriam's eyes were so full of kindness and humor as she looked at Tom that his resentment was suddenly assuaged. "She's seen through him all along," he thought with a leap of ecstasy. "She's willing I should know it while he hasn't a suspicion of it." Meantime the dinner progressed rapidly as an early start was to be made for the lake. Miriam spoke appreciatively of the old glass and silver which were used tonight in greater display than hitherto. Agnes replied with a look of pleasure, "Aunt Margaret and I set the table ourselves in honor of your last evening."

After supper they went to the lake. They took their seats in a rowboat, Ferdinand at the oars, and the boat slipped out upon the water, with Tom silent in one end, and Agnes trailing her fingers through the water at the other, both of them heavy-hearted over Miriam's approaching departure. For some moments there was no sound but the dipping of the oars.

Presently, with a sigh, Tom began to play his guitar softly. A moment later in a tenor voice he sang, "Ich hatte einst ein schönes Vaterland." He looked up at the stars as he sang the three short stanzas. Miriam's eyes were fixed on the water. When he had finished he laid his guitar across his knees and leaned upon it looking at her.

After a little silence Miriam roused herself. "Sing 'Gelb rollt mir zu Füssen,' Agnes," she demanded, and Tom slowly brought his guitar into position again.

Ferdinand stopped rowing and the boat drifted while Agnes' voice floated out over the water with its old daring and a fullness of tragic meaning that was new. The barbaric pride and swing of the beginning sinking into the half-articulate sob at the end of the song made the party feel as though some disembodied spirit were crying after the life that had slipped away from it. Tom shivered and turned up his coat collar. "I feel as if the angel of death had just flown over us," he exclaimed in an unsteady voice.

Miriam leaned forward with a determined look in her gray eyes. "Agnes," she said, "you have a great future in that voice. I want you to remember what I say. From now on I want you to practice an hour every day. Such a gift as that is the greatest thing a human being can be endowed with, and it's blasphemy to let it rust unused."

Agnes' fingers trailed in the water and she did not look up. "I know it is," she said, "and I am going to practice henceforth."

A moment later she found Miriam's eyes still gazing intently at her. A quiet seemed to settle over the party upon their return trip. Even when they drew near town and saw the pavilion gleaming like a jeweled order upon the breast of the lake, and passed the other rowboats, gay with music and bright colors, it did not affect the mood of the five who were together for the last time.

When they landed, Donald again walked with Agnes and her husband, leaving his brother alone with Miriam. As they reached the farm he hesitated and looked toward Tom, but Tom was already saying good-by, and the brothers walked away together.

"Are you willing to tell me what passed between Miss Cass and yourself, Tom?" Donald asked as soon as they were out of hearing.

"She refused me," replied Tom briefly. "But it's the best thing that ever happened to me. She'd been a fool if she hadn't. Says she isn't going to marry anybody. I guess she's the only woman that ever meant it. Anyway, I would rather be her friend than the husband of anybody else in the world. Now, you see, this time I mean business!"

Donald started to reply, when Tom cut him short. "Shut up, Don! I know all you've got to say. We're both in the same boat with the women. I don't say that celibacy is an attractive state, but if we've got to enter it, we've got to ornament it." A moment later he added with emotion in his tone, "I never realized before all you've had to stand. If I had to sit around in the same office with Miriam Cass' husband I'd shoot him inside of half an hour."

"No, you wouldn't, Tom," said Donald gloomily.

"No, I'd strangle him! I'd kill him very slowly and painfully."

Donald made no reply to this primeval remark, and they made the rest of their way home in silence. A feeling of depression was weighing upon the elder brother. He had little faith that Tom would remain in his present renunciatory state of mind, nor was he in sympathy with Miriam's notions about platonic friendships. They were unnatural and had wrought endless mischief in the world. She should have refused Tom for an adequate reason—because she did not love him, or thought herself too old. Love, not art, is the arbiter of marriage. He was dissatisfied with Miriam's coldness. Then he reflected that this might be natural in a woman older than Tom who was absorbed in her work. At least she had given Tom a temporary inspiration, while Agnes would permanently benefit by the fresh current of life and of interest Miriam had brought with her.

CHAPTER III

MEANTIME as the other three walked up the path to the farmhouse Agnes hurried ahead a little toward Miss Ballington, who stood in the doorway to welcome them.

"Is the baby all right? How was he during the evening?" she asked anxiously.

"He's asleep now, dear. I rocked him off once or twice."

Agnes kissed the faded cheek. "It was good in you to give me this nice evening, Aunt Margaret," she said. "I'm very grateful."

"I've a little lunch for you in the dining-room," Miss Ballington responded happily. "Eliza wanted to go out and I let her, but I got a tiny little lunch myself."

"Eliza ought not to have left you," said Agnes with surprise and displeasure in her tone. "But never mind, it was lovely in you to get something ready for us."

They all went to the dining-room, Miriam accompanying Miss Ballington and entertaining her with an account of their boat ride. "I wish you might have been with us," she said as they sat down to the table.

Miss Margaret's pride in her own unselfishness expanded beautifully under the general appreciation of herself and her repast. She beamed upon each in turn and gave an ornate and detailed account of the way in which she herself had spent the evening. She had been reading her favorite poem, "In Memoriam," and she gave a florid and stately little eulogy on friendship and its power in the world.

Ferdinand listened with his smile of superiority. He had heard Miriam speak slightingly of the poem once, and it was with the consciousness of saying something agreeable that he began in his turn to disparage it. He also took occasion to comment with indulgence upon his aunt's impossible ideal of friendship. Friendships were utilitarian; pure, disinterested friendship was a bird of an extinct species. He glanced toward Miriam during his remark with the comfortable assurance of having one appreciative listener. Somewhat to his disappointment their guest did not seem to be listening to him, but Agnes recognized in her friend an expression she had come to know. It meant that

Miriam's usual tolerance of all men's opinions had fallen from her like a veil, leaving bare a nature as hard and unyielding as flint.

As a matter of fact Ferdinand's remarks about his wife that afternoon, to which Tom had taken exception, had been rankling in Miriam's mind ever since they were spoken. They had given the last touch to an antagonism which had been instinctive in Miriam five years before, the first night she had ever seen Ferdinand, and which had been steadily becoming fixed. Her unfailing tact of manner toward her friend's husband had been achieved only by a persistent effort of will.

After the conversation had drifted away from the dangerous topic to a harmless discussion of Stevenson and South Sea Island scenery, and Agnes was breathing free again, Miriam trusted herself to look toward her host as she addressed a remark to him. As Miriam's gray eyes crossed Ferdinand's steady blue gaze, Agnes was conscious of a flash such as springs from the clash of flint on steel, while Ferdinand, too, felt an unwonted sensation, an instant's recoil.

"You ought not to talk about the South Sea Islands till you have been there, or, at least, you ought to be sure of the source of your information," Miriam said, smiling. "Your friend's criticism of Stevenson is ridiculous. I have been there. And now, since it is my last night," she said, with more graciousness than she so far had been able to assume, I am going to take an old friend's liberty and dispute with you. A little while ago you were talking about friendship in the same way that you have just been talking about the South Sea Islands."

Her slight shrug and gesture of differential disapproval pleased Ferdinand—it was so feminine.

"I doubt if you know what friendship is," she continued thoughtfully, her manner changing. "I sometimes think it isn't as common as it once was—we say so much less about it than our great-grandfathers did. As for me, I owe the best part of myself to your wife here. You and I are something alike, Mr. Ballington. We both need to be educated in things of the soul." Miriam rose as she spoke, but paused with both hands on the back of her chair, looking steadily at her host.

Ferdinand watched her closely, wondering at the expectancy with which he awaited her next words.

"You don't like to yield a single point, Mr. Ballington. Neither do I. We are hard people. I have the hardness of the jesting Sadducee, you of the upright Pharisee. Our friend here," and she turned with inexpressible tenderness to Agnes, "is neither a Pharisee nor a Sadducee, but a Galilean, and we can no more resist her without damning ourselves than this world can resist her Master. She is broader than you or I ever will be, sees deeper into life. She is doing for us both what no other influence ever can do. The friendship of such a soul is the greatest blessing in the world."

Ferdinand was uncomfortably conscious of an inexplicable melancholy stealing through the atmosphere, a repetition of the mood which had fallen upon the party on the lake after Agnes' song. He wondered if he caught the drift of what Miriam was saying.

There was a moment's silence; then Miriam took her hand from the back of the chair, smiled at her host, said good-night, touched Aunt Margaret's shoulder lightly, thanking her once more for her hospitality, and, without speaking to Agnes, turned and went toward the door. The instant her back was turned her smile vanished, and as she went up the stairs to her room she struck her right hand into her left palm, "If God should do it," she thought, "it would be all wise. If I should, it would be murder in the first degree. God appears to have gone hunting, or peradventure He sleepeth."

A few moments later Ferdinand followed Agnes slowly up to their rooms. He found himself watching his wife with unaccustomed interest, trying to discover what there was in her to call forth Miriam's late eulogy. He was rewarded by a fresh zest in her physical appearance.

"You're looking very well again, Agnes," he said, feeling a pleasurable prick of novelty in complimenting her. For the first time in weeks, he felt something of the old attraction.

Agnes looked up at him gravely, and went over to arrange the baby in his crib. Then she turned back to him. "I'm going to stay with Miriam tonight," she said. "I don't know when I shall see her again, and there is much I want to talk about." She went over to him and kissed him good-night, as usual.

"Don't stay awake too long," he said, the flash of interest already faded.

Then he entered his own room, while she went down the hall to Miriam's.

CHAPTER IV

AS Agnes opened Miriam's door she saw her friend kneeling before her trunk, while Miss Margaret sat near the open window talking to her. The light breeze was grateful to the little lady's flushed cheeks as she discussed in an animated monologue, interrupted by occasional appreciative interpolations from Miriam, some of the things which were nearest to her heart. Soon after Agnes entered, however, and began to help Miriam fold and pack the soft and mellow toned fabrics strewn upon the floor and chairs, Miss Margaret rose and wished the younger women, as was her wont, a good night's sleep and pleasant dreams.

Miriam and Agnes filled and locked the far-traveled trunk and portmanteau, and then put out the light and sat for a time on the window-sill, looking into the starry and moonlit heavens and over the gently rising country to the dark promontory where Winston College stood. They spoke of memories, living for an hour or more entirely in the past.

At last, Miriam stood up and turned away from the window. "It's very late, Agnes. We must go to sleep." But they began to talk again as soon as they had gone to bed.

A broad stream of moonlight falling across the room to the foot of the bed filled the room with light.

"If I were you, Agnes," said Miriam at last, calling her thoughts resolutely to the present, "I should get rid of Eliza. I've been thinking a good deal about it lately. This second girl your mother sent up from Kent isn't going to be able to live with her. I don't believe anybody could but you and Aunt Margaret. It will be easier for you to have two good girls than one Eliza."

Agnes sighed. Then she spoke with decision. "I intend to get rid of her, Miriam, and soon, but it's not easy to dislodge an old servant. Eliza has been here ever since Ferdinand was born. He says it's only women who can't get on together peaceably in the same house. He thinks Aunt Margaret's to blame, and he even suggested boarding her at Miss Matcham's boarding house. Of course, that would kill Aunt Margaret. Ferdinand and I must go out of this house if necessary, but never Aunt Margaret. It's her home."

"Another thing I've wanted to speak to you about, Agnes," continued Miriam, "is the music. There is no reason why you shouldn't do much with your voice. You are young and strong, and even when the children are little by practicing carefully you can keep your tones. Then, too," she added earnestly, "there's nothing like it to soften the harsh things of life. For that reason I live with a musician in New York. I never model so well as when she is playing. I noticed when I came here four weeks ago that you were despondent, fagged in mind and body, and now that you have gone back to singing again you have back your youth."

Agnes waited a moment, then replied slowly, "'Twasn't the music that was the matter with me, Miriam. I had something on my mind."

"That's just it," commented her friend. "If you had kept right on singing you could have sung your cares down, as the good brothers and sisters used to sing down long winded talkers in revival meetings back in Vermont. You'll have something on your mind again some time. Sing it down!"

"Miriam," said Agnes with resolution, "my conscience is troubling me."

"Well, so does everyone's," Miriam answered sadly.

"But mine has good reason," Agnes continued. "Miriam, I've always felt that I was guilty of my father's death."

There was a startled silence.

"During my mother's absence I neglected him. We had no girl and Aunt Mattie couldn't cook. Beatrice Mott was visiting in Kent then, and I was carried away. I don't think it expresses it too strongly to say my father was starved."

"Have you ever told this to anyone else?" asked Miriam abruptly.

"No. I thought it would hurt my mother too much. If I should tell anyone, it would be Ferdinand. I've tried to be honest with him."

"Well, Agnes," said Miriam gently, "it may be true that you neglected your father during the last of his life, but I've never heard that spinal meningitis is the result of starvation. Nor would it ease your father's spirit for you to tell Ferdinand that you killed him."

"But this same negligence and incapacity have shown themselves again and again in other relations," Agnes went on with a self-control that would not have been possible from her four weeks before, "I never seem to know how to grapple with a situation until it's gone by. I didn't treat my mother rightly, and I think I have lost my chance to influence my husband on serious questions. I was ignorant and hysterical when I married, and you know how hard it is to gain back a good opinion once lost."

"These are things we all have to face," said Miriam. "We may count ourselves happy if we find out how to grapple with a situation after it has gone. Most people never do that."

Agnes' voice fell lower and became more tense as she continued. "My husband has told the truth to me ever since we were married. I have wished many times that he wouldn't. For some time past now I've been overwhelmed with shame in contrasting my attitude toward him with his toward me. For a year now, I have deceived him continually in one respect. I needed some money a year ago, and, in order to get it without his knowledge, I falsified my housekeeping accounts. Since then I have sent things home several times without his knowledge which he supposed I was buying for his own house. Now my books are far from right. It's the same old story, beginning with a little theft and drifting on. I tell you," she said with bitter scorn, "I know how these absconding bank clerks get into it. Here's poor old Aunt Margaret, who hasn't any more head for figures than a chicken, she ran the house honorably for twenty years; and my father's daughter—"Here she suddenly stopped.

"Of course you had a reason for it," Miriam interrupted hastily. "Never mind telling me what it was. How much are you behind?"

"Four hundred and thirty-seven dollars."

"Well, I think you were very economical," said Miriam, with what Agnes considered ill-timed levity. "You must let me replace that money and keep it as our private arrangement. After that see to it—"

Agnes took her friend's hand affectionately. "That's like you, Miriam, but the only decent thing for me to do is to confess the whole thing and start in fair and square. There must be perfect honesty between husband and wife."

Miriam hesitated. Should she leave Agnes naked and innocent in her arduous paradise, or should she be the serpent of worldly wisdom in her friend's tree of life, clothe and send her out into a darker but more real world?

"That is the right spirit, Agnes," she said at length, "and I'm glad you have it."

She was going to stop there, but the other impulse was too strong. She continued energetically, "I'm very glad you have it. But a woman must have something more than the spirit of making confidences with the very best man who ever lived. Men seldom are as confiding to their wives as wives think they ought to be to their husbands. You say Ferdinand never has hesitated to tell the truth to you. Is it because he is honest, or because he isn't ashamed of it? Has he ever told you what he considers to be one single weakness in himself? of one mistake? of one error?"

Agnes was silent.

Miriam continued, "I thought not, and I must say that in this particular he has shown himself wiser than you. I don't believe the man ever lived who was not forced to confess to himself sometimes that he had done the wrong thing. It doesn't follow that he ought to rush up on the housetop and proclaim his fault, nor even down into the house and tell his wife about it—that is, provided he rectifies it. Someone says that more trouble has been caused in domestic life by morbid confession than by deceit."

Agnes was shocked.

Miriam continued unmoved. "I know it's a hard doctrine—too hard for the wicked. They ought to confess every time. Only the righteous ought to hold their tongues. I beg you not to tell Ferdinand about this money, nor about any other peccadilloes you may be guilty of. I tell you, Agnes, you will make an irretrievable mistake if you undertake to tell anybody in this life everything you do. Don't commit any faults, but don't tell about them if you do. He never will forget them, and the time will come when you will wish he didn't know."

Agnes was silent, thinking drearily that they were not peccadilloes, but sins, and therefore she must tell Ferdinand, although she knew that she would suffer for it. There was but one path for her, one of perfect integrity. There must be no deceits behind. Concealment of her past faults would be cowardice and lack of will-power, the same things which had led her into them. The only hope of a fortunate outcome of her life with Ferdinand lay in the development of a controlled and wisely directed will, a power in her which he could recognize and respect as he did his mother's memory.

As she did not reply Miriam continued: "Why do you allow Mr. Ballington to deprive you of financial equality, Agnes? If you were the active wage-earner would you not recognize him as participating in the right to dispose of your income?"

"Yes."

"Doubtless you think that self-sacrifice in this matter is better than what seems to you a vulgar insistence for a separate purse." Miriam spoke in a matter-of-fact tone. The matter so personal and sore to Agnes had long been one of liberal and impersonal interest to her friend. "But let me tell you," she went on more earnestly, "if this were a question of spiritual liberty instead of material, you would see at once what is your duty. You are hurting your husband as well as yourself by failing to assert your just claims. It is no more moral to condone a material wrong than to submit to a spiritual wrong. We submit to injustice not for ourselves only. That's the point. We strengthen tyranny everywhere when we falter before it ourselves. If you won't assert yourself against injustice in money matters or any other tangible affair, you will be forced some time to face it in something more momentous. Moreover, you will come to that final struggle without prestige against an opposing force accustomed to dictatorship."

After a considerable pause Agnes answered, "I know that the sordid and material forms in which spiritual questions clothe themselves confuse and get the best of me. I do not think it cheap or vulgar to meet them, but I am afraid of the consequences which direct grappling with them may bring to me. They will raise very large problems for me, larger than you realize, and I cannot yet see clearly how I ought to solve them."

The silence which followed was rich in mutual understanding. At length Miriam broke it: "To go back once more, Agnes, to a pleasant topic—your old friend Professor Stoddard is going to start a summer conservatory up here, to be a permanent thing, I believe, and I've no doubt that he would be eager to obtain your services as an assistant teacher. He never has forgotten your voice, always asks after you every time I see him. You had better seize every opportunity of a musical kind. We never know what is going to happen to us in this world. There are two reasons why a woman of your talent ought not to be a mere house keeper. One is that Mr. Ballington might lose all his money and die of the shock, leaving you with a family to support. There is your mother doing it. It is happening every day. The other is that the great goddess Nature will revenge herself upon an unthankful debtor. For my part, I consider that the moral obligation imposed by an undoubted gift should be perhaps the determining factor in marking out a woman's life. I never should feel right myself to marry. I feel that I have another work lying closer to me. You are happier than I am in having your children, but you are also encumbered. If the time ever comes when your burden gets too heavy, if you are called upon to sustain losses of any kind,"—she spoke the last words slowly and Agnes understood what lay behind them, "then I want you to remember that I am free and able to help you and that you are the nearest thing to me."

A thrill of energy and hope tingled along Agnes' nerves. An unlooked-for power had placed itself behind her. Defeat vanished from the perspective of the future. If it came to the worst, she might begin over again, and in Miriam's vocabulary there seemed to be no "too late."

After a time she responded in a tone of high resolve, "You have put new life into me. Life is going easier from now on. It gives me infinite rest and peace to think of you behind me in the battle of life. I shall remember what you have said."

When the town clock struck two both were asleep.

CHAPTER V

WHEN Tom arrived at the station the next morning to see Miriam off for New York his eyes fell upon Ferdinand's neat suit-case, ready for travel, standing near Miriam's on the floor. "What's that?" he exclaimed suspiciously, his ready color rising, as he looked at Agnes for an explanation.

Miriam interposed. "Mr. Ballington is going to make the trip down to New York with me," she said, and then handed her umbrella to Tom, remarking, "I've been trying for ten minutes to snap the strap together and no one has offered to help me."

Tom bent over the refractory clasp silently, his heart heating like a trip-hammer with rage at this move of Ferdinand's.

"Yes, I'm going on through to Washington," explained Ferdinand, magnanimously making Tom the confidant of his plans. "I had to go, anyway, and I thought I could see to Miss Cass' luggage."

Tom glanced at the umbrella with an insane impulse to lift it and smite Ferdinand to the earth.

"He is going down to see about his patents," Agnes added. Tom pulled himself together and chatted moodily until the train came in. Then he pushed Ferdinand aside as the latter was stooping to pick up Miriam's suit-case. "You have your own to carry," he said grimly. He assisted Miriam into the car, arranged her comfortably, gave her a couple of the latest magazines and a newspaper, lifted his hat formally and left her. Ferdinand was waiting to enter the seat.

After the train had gone, Agnes and Tom rode down together to the city, Agnes talking affectionately of Miriam and what her friendship meant. The station was situated on a hill overlooking the town; they drove down slowly, and before they reached the car-shops Agnes had communicated her spirit of bravery to him. He went into the office, hung up his hat, opened his big ledger, eyed it as though it were a battlefield, and began his campaign.

Agnes, too, was entering, she knew full well, on a struggle which would tax her to the uttermost. Whither it might lead her or what might be its outcome it was futile to forecast.

Two obvious necessities confronted her at the outset: one of them Eliza's dismissal, the other the confession of her deceit to Ferdinand. Now that she had determined to make this confession she was anxious for Ferdinand's return, that it might be over speedily, and she waited somewhat restlessly as the days passed and his short notes and telegrams announced a still further delay. She had determined to leave Eliza's discharge until her husband's return, in order to vindicate herself from the cowardice which tempted her to get rid of the Irishwoman while he was away, and thus to avoid a collision with his will.

Each day, however, seemed to increase by geometrical progression the domestic friction. Eliza took advantage of Ferdinand's absence to tyrannize over Miss Margaret, while she sulked before Agnes' face and threatened behind her back. After a week of it, Agnes resolved to put an end at once to what would be soon an impossible situation.

The crisis between her and the old servant came suddenly one day.

When it was over Agnes went into Miss Margaret's room and shut the door. "Aunt Margaret," she said quietly, "I have discharged Eliza."

Miss Ballington began to tremble. She had felt this coming, and, much to Agnes' perplexity, had striven painfully to prevent it. At last Agnes knew the reason. Her altercation with Eliza had brought out several revelations, one of them explaining much that had seemed curious in Miss Margaret's relations with the cook. Sympathy with her aunt followed swiftly upon the discovery.

"She says, Aunt Margaret," said Agnes, going over to the couch and taking hold of her aunt's hand, "that you owe her some money. Is that so, dear?"

Agnes could feel the little form quiver as Miss Ballington looked up with a supreme effort to retain dignity and self-control. "The little Flynn baby had no milk, Agnes. They all were starving."

"How much is it, Aunt Margaret?" Agnes asked, with a slight pressure of the feverish hand.

Miss Ballington did not answer. Agnes repeated her question gently.

Miss Margaret raised her distressed face once more, and said with more assurance, "Donald always gives me money on my birthday, and perhaps Sarah would buy my camel's-hair shawl. She always has wanted it."

"But it must be paid now, dear. Eliza says she won't go till she gets it. You must let me know and I will pay it out of the house-money."

Miss Margaret drew her hand away spasmodically. "But then Ferdinand would know!" she said breathlessly, and she added with a frightened whisper, "I daren't have him know."

Agnes waited a moment, thinking.

"Is it really nearly two hundred dollars, as Eliza says?" she asked at last.

She read an affirmative answer in her aunt's face, and then she realized that the loans had been going on, perhaps, for years. This had been Miss Margaret's way of surmounting financial stringency, as falsifying accounts had been her own.

The two women set to work to find some solution, and though Agnes insisted for a time that Ferdinand should be told, she knew in her heart from the beginning how it would end. What she was prepared to meet for her own misdoing she had not the heart to put upon the only survivor of the old generation of Ballingtons. Moreover, there was an added reason. Flynn's case was a notorious one. He was a skilled workman who had insisted in disregarding one of Ferdinand's pet regulations at the shops and whom Ferdinand had made it a point to force into submission by way of example to the rest. To his surprise and mystification, Flynn, with a large family dependent upon him, had managed to exist through a hard winter, and had just succeeded in obtaining a better position in a new steel plant. There was no telling to what lengths Ferdinand might be incensed against Aunt Margaret should he learn that she had been supporting Flynn's family during the late unpleasantness.

"Never mind, Aunt Margaret," Agnes said at last, "we are losing time talking here. You can easily get the money, and there's no reason why you shouldn't. I'm going to ask Donald to lend it to you."

She went to the telephone, hesitated, then wrote a note instead, and carried it out to Sam at the barn, telling him to deliver it at once. As he was leaving she said to him, "See that you give it to Mr. Donald Ballington himself, Sam."

The man tipped his hat and went off.

Within an hour he came back with a package, which Eliza brought upstairs to Agnes. The inflamed little eyes of the Irishwoman had a canny look as she handed it over. Agnes tore it open with indescribable relief. Donald had sent the money for her aunt with a single line saying, "Thank you." She at once paid Eliza, and took a receipt.

To her surprise the Irishwoman, who at first had insisted that she should remain until Ferdinand's return, now announced that she should leave before dinner. Some hours later they heard her thumping down her trunk, a stair at a time, without Sam's assistance, from the third floor to the kitchen. She left the premises in sinister taciturnity late in the afternoon.

The uneasiness which Agnes felt in seeing the hostile figure go off through the garden was dissipated, as she turned back to the kitchen, by the cheerful face of the strong second girl from Kent.

"I've got the dinner almost ready, Mrs. Ballington," the latter said, in the tone of one who was giving a blessing from the Lord. "And if you like, ma'am, I'll send up to Kent this afternoon for my sister Joan to come."

Agnes went at once upstairs to her desk and wrote to Ferdinand of the change that had taken place in the house hold.

Then she sat still with her pen poised in the air. It would be better, while she was about it, to clear her conscience at the same time. The pen dropped to the paper, and she wrote out plainly the unhappy story of the diverted money and the tampered accounts.

She was about to add Donald's wedding gift to the confession, but stopped, feeling that she had no right, having accepted it, to involve him in difficulty because of it. So she wrote this to her husband:

There is one other thing I should like to tell you, and if it concerned myself alone I should. It happened before we were married. My chief regret concerning it is that you could not know it. As it is, I cannot gratify my desire to tell you more than this.

When she sealed the letter she held it in her hand an instant. "This means untold shame to me," she reasoned clearly, "but at last I am square with the world, and I can start again." After dinner she mailed the letter.

Five days later Ferdinand returned.

The trip south had been satisfactory to him in a business way, and it had been a recreation as well. He occasionally allowed himself these relaxations from his methodical and disciplined course of life, having the comfortable conviction that only those can enjoy who prepare themselves for a few golden hours of pleasure by months and even years of industry and sobriety. While in Washington he had gone around with a couple of spirited and accommodating political friends, and when the time came for leaving he was permeated with a glow of content. He had learned how to combine two characters generally considered antagonistic, those of the Stoic and the Epicurean. He had left business without haste, and he was returning without regret, and on the whole he reminded himself of Huxley's "calm, strong angel," who plays the chess game of life with less able opponents.

During his absence from home he reflected off and on in moments of leisure upon Agnes' returning spirits, and her ability to hold the respect of such a woman as Miriam Cass.

He had found himself unable to get on a more confidential footing with Miriam when he was alone with her during the journey than he was when Agnes was present. He had tried to resume conversation about Agnes and about himself, but, without realizing how she did it, he was conscious that she parried his beginnings and directed the conversation to impersonal topics. He acknowledged at length that she intended to speak intimately with him where his wife could hear her, or not at all. His irritation toward Miriam was counter-balanced by his admiration of her wisdom, and it was with the latter sensation uppermost in his mind that he turned his attention away from her.

Along with his reviving hopes in his wife had gone a disquieting sense of his neglect of her the last year. He wished that he had put through without interruption his original plan for conducting their marital relations; not that he had overstepped a man's privileges unduly, but he was above the ordinary man's privileges, and he had started out upon ideal lines laid down by enlightened masculine reason.

It was at such a moment of reflection that he received his wife's letter. The announcement of Eliza's discharge, astounding as it was to him, was dwarfed in importance as he passed on to the confession at the close of the letter. Surprise and anger that for so long a period such subterfuges had been employed without his suspicion were speedily swallowed up in another emotion. He dated the receipt of the letter and then put it up carefully in a private notebook. With the exception of her half-confidence, he would consider his score with his wife balanced, and upon his return they would both of them, as he expressed it, "begin over." The half-confidence, however, rankled in his memory.

He half expected to find Agnes waiting for him at the train, was disappointed to find Sam alone, and was surprised at his own eagerness for his wife as he rode home.

As he entered the house he heard the children's voices in the library, and went there first, expecting to find their mother.

"Where is Agnes? he asked of his aunt, who was holding little Stephen in her lap.

"She went up to her room this very minute, dear," answered Miss Margaret, noticing the brilliance of his eyes.

He left the room, went upstairs, knocked at his wife's door, then opened it without waiting for an answer.

Agnes was waiting for him, apparently unoccupied. He noticed, too, that she wore the maroon dress in which he especially liked to see her. She looked at him anxiously, but did not speak.

Ferdinand crossed the room, bent down and kissed her, told her he had come home earlier than he had intended, that he had hoped to see her at the station, that he had looked for her first in the library, and that Estelle had wanted to follow him upstairs. Then he talked to her a little about the possible future for his invention.

To all this she responded with nervous acquiescence.

At last he broached the matter of her letter, limiting his discussion to the financial part of it.

"Why is it that you shrink from my advice on business matters, Agnes?" he finished. "I am a business man. It is absolutely useless to try to help Pleasant Mabie if you allow him to manage his own affairs. You have thrown all that money away. Anyone will tell you that I am an unusually successful financier, and it's because I won't be worked on by my sympathies to chuck money into the stove. Experience has taught me what I know, and you should be willing to accept facts from me."

"I am willing to do that, but I could not consent that my sister should become your hired help," said Agnes, disappointed and worried that Ferdinand took no note, apparently, of the ethical side of the question.

"The only thing which need concern hired help is that it does its work well," said Ferdinand imperturbably.

Agnes met his eyes seriously. "How could she do her work well? You would not be satisfied with what Helen could do. You would demand as much from her as though she were a stout German peasant woman."

"It was her own choice to marry a farmer. I am sorry for her; but, of course, that doesn't mend matters."

As she did not speak, he took up the conversation again. "It seems curious to me," he said, scrutinizing her, "that you always have felt such reluctance to my knowing how you spend your money. I have no such feeling with regard to you."

"You can decide for yourself how you wish to spend it. I have to submit to your judgment." Agnes spoke gravely, knowing that the inevitable consequences of the stand she had decided to take would soon be upon her. Ferdinand's ignorance of the seriousness of the crisis between them intensified her own earnestness.

"I furnish you with all the comforts of life," said Ferdinand, glancing around the room, and then touching lightly the rich gown she wore.

"Except liberty," said Agnes briefly.

"Certainly. It is the husband's prerogative to decide matters for his family." The persistent failure of his wife to affect his mood as he had a right to expect after an unusual separation, also her refusal to appreciate the full extent of his magnanimity, were beginning to irritate him.

"Would you permit another person to make your decisions for you?" asked Agnes thoughtfully.

"No. It is a man's privilege that he may make his own," said Ferdinand, who was at last aware of something behind all this.

Agnes was silent for some moments. Then she said slowly, without raising her voice, but with the hereditary note which had rung through Kent ever since Dr. Sidney first brought his wife there to live: "Ferdinand, I wrote to you that I was going to make a new start. It remains with you to decide just what that start will be. Henceforth I must have a definite sum of money to use as my own. Will you give this to me?"

"What are you going to do about it, if I do not?" asked Ferdinand coldly.

"I hope you will not refuse. If your sympathies were as well developed as I hope they someday will be, I should not demand this. But I want—" She was about to say, "I want to help my mother occasionally without your feeling at each little gift that she is dependent upon you." She prudently checked this impulse, however, remembering that Ferdinand had casually remarked upon several occasions since Pleasant's letter, "I am already supporting three families, and now my wife's brother-in-law has applied to me." She feared that his next allusion to the subject might include her mother as the fifth family.

"Well?" inquired Ferdinand, waiting.

"If you do not give it to me," she answered, "I shall earn it."

"How?"

"I shall ask Professor Dimmock for students to coach. I shall apply for a position in Westminster choir, and next summer I shall become an assistant, if possible, in Mr. Stoddard's summer school."

"What about the children? You are forgetting them, are you not?" said Ferdinand in a hard voice.

"I have considered the children," Agnes answered.

"This alternative of yours implies a threat," he said after a moment.

"It states a determination," she answered very low.

"Very well. I will consider it." His glance met hers with what might have been courtesy or might have been hate.

With a sudden change of feeling, she reached out and took his hand. "If you knew how miserable this makes me!" she cried earnestly. "I can't bear to have you leave me like this, although I know I am right. Only listen to me a moment. To us wives our position seems unjust. I know that hysterical women always say what I am going to say, but it is true that we take our lives in our hands when we marry. We stake everything we have. If it were merely a business transaction, it would be the highest-priced position open to human beings. The reality is that if our husbands give us anything, it is called a 'gift,' and if they give us much, they are called 'generous.' Is it right that mature and reasonable beings should be dependent upon gifts after they have given up incomes?"

Ferdinand suffered his hand to remain in hers till she had finished. Then he withdrew it. "Are you ready to go down to dinner?" he asked.

They went down together, each silent and cold. Miss Ballington in her frantic efforts to make the meal pass pleasantly put the finishing touches to the discomfort of the other two.

Ferdinand, contrary to his habit, put on his hat and went out directly after dinner. He wished now that he voluntarily had offered to do for Agnes what she had demanded, but he revolted at being forced to change his methods.

Agnes told her aunt with humiliation and disappointment the result of her effort to obtain an allowance, part of which was to have been given to her. Miss Margaret's face fell at the news, and she went off crying.

Agnes put her baby to bed, then spent the evening in the library trying to read, but tormented with apprehension as she saw approaching near her the necessity which she had hoped against hope might be diverted. She went upstairs before her husband returned, and lay long awake thinking of her mother's needs for the coming winter, of the inevitable sickness and pain in store for Aunt Mattie, of Helen expecting her sixth child—and of Ferdinand, accumulating capital and fifty thousand a year.

When Ferdinand returned he came into her room. "Are you asleep, Agnes?" he asked softly.

"I am awake, Ferdinand."

"I have considered your request and decision. I cannot disarrange my entire system of management to accommodate your whim. At the same time I will not refuse you money to a reasonable amount for any purpose which upon careful consideration seems to you sufficient ground for spending it. I say you may do this whether it meets with my approval or not. But you must confer with me first."

There was a short unbroken silence.

Then Agnes replied. "Ferdinand, your condition is a denial of my request. I will not accept it. I am sorry to offend you, but I shall be more independent if I can my own money."

"You persist in your determination then?"

"I do."

"Then I have nothing more to say. I might, of course, request Professor Dimmock and the trustees of the church to disregard your caprice, but I have more consideration for your feelings than you have for mine. You are, therefore, at liberty to pursue your own course of action. But"—he paused, then continued as though he were reciting a formula—" I wish to impress it upon you that you do this in distinct opposition to my wishes, with the knowledge that you diminish my affection and respect for you, that you take upon yourself the responsibility of any harm which may befall the children when you leave them. That is all. Good night."

He waited a moment for her to speak, but she said nothing. Then he left the room and closed the door between their apartments.

Agnes when alone once more questioned herself closely as to what she had determined to do. "Why should I hesitate to take this step? My mother would not hesitate if she knew her motive was justifiable. It doesn't worry her what other people think. But what if something should happen to the children? Something might just as naturally happen while I was out driving with Ferdinand. He doesn't go to church himself, and it is no more than fair that the father should bear their responsibility for one day in seven. After all, will he respect me less for taking a self-respecting stand in our mutual relations? I am inclined to think he will respect me more."

She did not sleep that night, but, hour after hour, watched the heavy vibrations of the dark, watched the dawn creep under the curtains and slide nearer and nearer her bed, touching into grim prominence as it came the different objects in its path— her desk, her table, and the other reminders of her daily work. It was not the first time she had been of those who watch for the morning, but once she never would have believed that a night in which she gave up once for all long dreams of youth could have contained for her also so much of courage and energy and hope. For that night, whatever its agony and its renunciation, put an end forever to the melancholia which had threatened in the last year to engulf her. As she dressed for breakfast she felt a sense of relief. She no longer had anything to hide, and she had dared to act for herself. As she went downstairs she told herself that the fresh start was made, and that it was good.

The deeper question to which this move of her was soon to lead did not confront her yet. Other wives had fulfilled a double duty. Unsympathetic as Ferdinand was, she nevertheless believed that with wisdom she could be both wife and wage-earner.

CHAPTER VI

IN July, Beatrice Sidney was summoned by telegram to New York. She arrived barely in time to see her father alive. The old General had gone down to the seashore, as he expressed it, to "set 'em up with an old friend." It was a hot day and the enthusiasm of the cocktails lifted the burden of years, so that he proposed going into the surf. The two joyful old blades went down together into the sea. It was soon noticed by the other bathers that General Mott was behaving strangely, and he presently was forced out of the water by the bathing guard, sank upon the sand insensible, was carried back to the city and never regained consciousness.

Beatrice's mourning for her father was vehement and sincere. For weeks, she was subdued beyond her wont. Then her old restlessness began to revive. One day in November, she informed Fred that she was going over to Winston to have Thanksgiving dinner with Agnes. "You can have Aunt Kate and Aunt Mattie and Quinn here with you," she said genially when leaving. "I've ordered all kinds of things, and Aunt Kate can see to them. There are some Thanksgiving presents from me in the escritoire. Hand them around during dessert." She gave Fred a couple of French kisses and hurried away from his expostulations.

Thanksgiving eve she walked in upon Agnes and Ferdinand as they were eating dinner, drew up a chair beside Aunt Margaret at the table, spoke to the waitress, who had once worked for her in Kent, telling her to bring back a bit of fish only, that she didn't care for the soup, and then fell to talking heartily of Mrs. Sidney and Fred and Dr. Quinn and other Kent people Agnes knew.

"Tomorrow, Aunt Margaret," she said, wheeling around to Miss Ballington and pinching her knee under the table, "you and I are going to have a good time. We'll go to the—football game!" she finished, her eyes twinkling across the table at Ferdinand. Tom was the only member of the Ballington family who approved of football, Ferdinand considering it a game for rowdies.

Beatrice stayed with Miss Margaret most of the evening, offering cordially to occupy her room with her at night which plan the little lady accepted, pleased that Beatrice enjoyed talking with her.

Before they went to sleep that night, Beatrice had learned all that Miss Margaret had to tell of Miriam Cass and of Tom's devotion to her. "I don't think they can be exactly engaged, dear," Miss Margaret confided, "but Tom is certainly in love with her—deeply."

Miss Margaret no sooner had made the announcement than Beatrice started humming with great spirit a tarantelle, snapping her fingers in the air for an accompaniment of castanets.

"Do put your arms in," said Miss Margaret nervously. "You'll catch cold in those lace sleeves. One of them is torn, too. You aren't snapping your fingers at Tom's being in love, are you?" she continued confusedly.

"'E non che sono poco vezioso!'" sang Beatrice with abandon. "Not a whit, not a whit, Aunt Margaret. Why, who knows better than I do how Tom falls in love?" A moment later she put her soft, dark hand over Miss Margaret's eyes. "You go to sleep, pet," she continued authoritatively.

Beatrice herself did not sleep, however. She drew her lace-covered arms in close and lay still and straight, as she generally did in those private sessions with herself wherein she reviewed unpleasing situations.

"Two things to do," she thought darkly, a swarm of recollections and anticipations rioting in her brain. "First, treat Ferdinand so he won't object to my coming here when I like, and it will be the hardest thing I ever did, too. Second, look after Mr. Tom. He has been neglecting me for a long time. If he won't come to the lake house, I'll come here. Miriam Cass is too old for him."

When she had organized her plans, she shut her eyes, mumbled over a baby prayer she never had neglected since her mother died, and then went resolutely to sleep.

In the morning she was up and dressed before even Miss Margaret, whose early rising was a family nuisance, and Agnes was awakened by the sound of the two playing and singing old ballads in the green room downstairs. Miss Margaret's ghost of a voice was drowned by Beatrice's strong alto, save now and then on the high notes, where the thin voice came out with piercing shrillness in its effort to keep the key, while Beatrice frankly fell off a quarter of a tone.

After breakfast Beatrice went around with Aunt Margaret inspecting the various new things in the house. Then she announced that she would go out marketing with her, saying that she always learned so much from seeing Aunt Margaret buy.

Miss Margaret was so pleased with this compliment, whose irony was lost on her, that she straightway ordered the carriage without remembering that the stores were all closed on Thanksgiving Day.

"Never mind," said Beatrice dauntlessly; "I'd just as soon hear you talk as see you market. We'll ride, anyway."

"It's so sweet in you to want to go with me," said Miss Margaret all in a flutter. "I'm afraid it's selfish in me. You'd have a much nicer time with Agnes."

"My dear," said Beatrice in a half-whisper, "I feel as if I were with my grandmother when I'm with Agnes, while you are just my age."

Miss Margaret was in imminent danger of losing her head over this continuous adulation, but she conscientiously strove against it.

"Poor Agnes isn't old, dear. She isn't very fresh always. Ferdinand was saying just this morning that she didn't look very fresh. He thinks these church rehearsals are too much for her. She's been up nights a good deal with Stephen, too, lately."

"I guess Ferdinand must be losing his eye-sight," said Beatrice satirically. "Agnes looks better than she has any time the last three years. Getting used to being married, I guess. Fred says all Winston is going to church again just to look at her sing. Here, let me hold that funny little shawl for you!"

"Dear me!" said Miss Margaret, dropping into a chair, "I've got it folded wrong again, Beatrice. This is the third time. The sides without the fringe on are always the ones that get on top."

"Rip off the fringe then and sew it on the other two sides," volunteered Mrs. Fred Sidney, whisking the shawl out of Miss Margaret's lap and shaking it open with a resounding snap. "I'll help you. We'll begin at the two ends and sew toward the middle. There, I've got it all right now. Come along downstairs."

As they opened the door into the library they found Agnes reading aloud to her husband. Beatrice went up behind her and looked over her shoulder. "Patent records!" she exclaimed. "Well, I declare! Ferdinand, you picked out your wife just as shrewdly as you do most of your business."

Ferdinand rose irritably and went to the window. Then he said something which he previously had made up his mind to say as soon as he had heard that Miss Margaret and Beatrice had ordered the horse. He addressed Miss Margaret, but there was a significant warning for Beatrice in his tone. "If you are considering driving to Aunt Sarah's, Aunt Margaret, I must request that you don't stop at the shops and disturb Tom. He is doing extra work today and will be held closely to his time."

Miss Ballington looked over at him in surprise, but Beatrice's eyes instantly grew hard and bright. "Oh, ho!" she cried. Then she made a wide circle around Miss Margaret in an elaborate minuet step, and, still circling, approached nearer and nearer to Ferdinand, as though she were weaving some incantation.

Ferdinand did not move from the window where he unwillingly watched her implacable approach. He always had hated those strong and flexible curves, and now she was coming with a mingled leisure and abandon which repelled him doubly because it showed off her figure to such undeniable advantage.

When she reached him, she made an eighteenth century courtesy. "So Tom's followed Fred's example and turned clerk! Well, one's enough for me. We'll leave him alone!"

She watched him a moment with a look of great satisfaction at her successful acquiescence, then turned back to the other two. "Come on, Aunt Margaret. Sam's waiting," she said in high good-humor.

As she reached the door she paused and turned back to Ferdinand, who had not taken his eyes from her. Lifting her hand to her right temple, she gave a salute. Then she whirled around and vanished after Aunt Margaret.

"How much longer is your cousin expecting to stay here?" asked Ferdinand of his wife when the outside door had closed.

"I don't know," said Agnes, picking up her book again.

"She has pretended to come to see Aunt Margaret and you," said Ferdinand crossly, "but of course you know she comes to see Tom. I don't know that you can expect anything better of old Mott's daughter, though," Ferdinand continued contemptuously. "That man's funeral was a disgrace to the community. A regiment of women he had married off to his tenants were there, weeping and wailing a good deal more than they would have done for their husbands."

Agnes found the place where she had left of reading. "Shall I begin at section four?" she asked, looking up inquiringly. "Or wait—the second paragraph of section four."

"Before we begin again there is another matter I want to speak to you about," he said. "Mr. Bucher was in town yesterday. It seems he lent your mother four thousand dollars last winter and took a deed of her home. Were you aware of this?"

"Yes," said Agnes, closing the book and looking at him. "The simpler way to state the fact is to say she sold him the house for four thousand dollars."

Another care she had been bearing in secret for almost a year was out at last.

"Hardly," returned Ferdinand, smiling slightly. "It was not an unconditional sale. Bucher promised not to dispose of the place under two years, when either she or Dr. Quinn expect to buy it back—a woman's piece of business."

"I can tell you the facts," said Agnes, "if you care to know them?"

"Yes. I should have been glad to know them before this," replied Ferdinand.

"Pleasant has been running behind more than anyone knew. My mother knew nothing about it till she went out there when Helen was sick last winter. Then she found out that he had been borrowing money and that my father's friend, Dr. Clisdale, had signed notes with him. Mother insisted that everything be settled up then and there. They were pushing Dr. Clisdale hard."

"That was his own lookout," commented Ferdinand.

"You know my mother never would let him suffer for Pleasant's sake. The result was that she sold her own home and paid the notes."

"How about Mabie's farm?" asked Ferdinand.

"The mortgage was foreclosed."

"I thought you had paid up the interest for two years out of my money."

Agnes flushed scarlet. "He paid the interest for only one year out of what I sent and asked the man to wait for the other year's interest. He went into some fancy poultry-raising with the rest of the money."

"You acknowledge then that I was right about sending money to Mr. Mabie?"

Ferdinand could not conceal his triumph at this vindication of his sagacity. "Yes."

"How does your mother expect to buy back her property?" he inquired after a moment, and he could not forbear adding humorously: "Out of your church-money? Or will she live out at the farm she has made such a point of keeping?"

"Dr. Quinn expects to buy the place," returned Agnes, not noticing the latter part of his remark. "Mother intended that he should have it. He is going to let her have her home there always, and he is going to give her an interest in his invention besides."

"There's no telling whether his invention will ever amount to anything," said Ferdinand dryly. "It will be a long process if it does. He can't afford to push it. He made his mistake when he declined my offer."

Agnes made no reply.

Ferdinand opened a drawer in his desk and took out a document. "What are Mr. and Mrs. Mabie going to do?" he asked.

"They are going to run the farm on shares for one more year. Pleasant has promised mother that if he doesn't succeed then he will come East."

Ferdinand opened the document and handed it to Agnes. "I have relieved Bucher of the old place," he said.

Agnes half rose. "Mr. Bucher sold you our house!" she cried involuntarily. "He has sold it after he promised—"

"Yes. He is hard up, and he seemed gratified when I offered to take it off his hands. I'm inclined to think he may go down as Balch did. The condition your mother imposed burdened him, but I told him that of course I should regard that condition also."

Agnes hesitated. She felt that she and all her family were caught in a net. Indignation at Mr. Bucher and at her husband prevented sane thought or speech for some moments. But at last she pulled herself together.

"Ferdinand," she said earnestly, "I cannot understand how Mr. Bucher came to do this unless you led him to suppose that he was doing my mother a kindness. He must have thought that you would be generous with her. Now I want you to be generous with her. Give my mother her home." She had risen and approached him as she spoke.

"It is useless to give to your mother," said Ferdinand judiciously. "She always will scrimp herself for the Mabies. It would be wiser to let her scrimp in order to get back the house. Besides, who knows what she can get for it from Quinn?"

"But, Ferdinand, you don't realize how severe mother's scrimping is," insisted Agnes. "She works too hard for a woman of her age. She will break down."

"Hasn't that aunt of yours any blood-relations?" asked Ferdinand speculatively after a moment of reflection.

"Yes, but none who can or will help her."

"They won't, of course, so long as your mother does. That woman will outlive your mother. They are a long-lived pair, however," he finished. "If your aunt's family won't help her, the State will provide for her."

"Ferdinand!" exclaimed Agnes, outraged by his words.

"Or she might go to the hospital," continued Ferdinand, feeling that perhaps he should have made more allowance for the fact that he was speaking to a woman. "Your father worked to get a hospital in Kent for just such cases. Your family should have the benefit of it."

"Don't say another word, Ferdinand! My mother never will desert Aunt Mattie, so long as she has a crust for herself."

Ferdinand sat down, opened the record book, and handed it to her, as he said with an air of finality, "When the last crust is gone, you will find me ready to talk with you again. You were at the words, 'patented by T. Robertson.'"

Agnes also reseated herself and took the volume. Her voice trembled as she began to read, but before long she had it under control.

The reading continued for some two hours, until the others returned.

"Here we are!" cried Beatrice, pushing her companion into the library. "Put up your books, good people. Thanksgiving!"

"We had such a nice time, said Miss Margaret brightly, "and do you know, whom should we meet but—"

"Old Miss Sewell!" interposed Beatrice, suddenly throwing all her wraps in a heap on the lounge. She went on volubly recounting all that Miss Sewell had said, while Miss Margaret collected the heap of garments from the sofa and carried them out into the hall.

As soon as she was outside the door Beatrice stopped, "I guess you two don't want to be interrupted," she said, with a breath of relief at the narrow escape from having it disclosed that they had met Tom on the street and that he had been driving with them. "I'm going up with the children till dinner." Then she followed Miss Margaret into the hall.

Ferdinand picked up a marked newspaper and handed it to Agnes. He had been admiring her persistence and self-control in reading to him during her recent agitation, and it was with a conciliatory manner that he said, "Senator Balfour's speech of yesterday is the finest thing of the year." He knew that this would please her, for Senator Balfour had been her father's roommate at college, and both Mrs. Sidney and Agnes had followed the statesman's career with interest and pride.

"I am glad," said Agnes simply, taking the paper.

"When he comes up to this part of the country we will make a point of meeting him," continued Ferdinand.

He gathered up the papers as he spoke, with the comfort able feeling of having accomplished a good deal during the morning. Even Beatrice seemed tolerable. Agnes had been as reasonable as she could be about the sale of the house, had acknowledged her folly in sending money to Pleasant, and, take it all together, the official thanksgiving which was annually forced upon him was less disagreeable than usual.

CHAPTER VII

BEATRICE made flying trips to Winston all through the winter, but her coming did not seriously affect the regularity of life of any of the Ballingtons except Miss Margaret. Agnes wondered at the conciliatory attitude Beatrice maintained toward Ferdinand. On his part he paid little attention to her when she came. He was absorbed in his invention, which he was just patenting in America, and which he expected to introduce on the Continent during the next summer.

Agnes was even more surprised and delighted at Tom's poise under his old comrade's attentions, at his faithfulness in the routine of business and his wistfulness and earnestness whenever they talked together of Miriam. Her correspondence with Miriam took on pleading for Tom. She begged her friend to reward the efforts which had been inspired by her.

It seemed hard to Agnes when Miriam answered unswervingly, "I am happy at what you write me of your cousin's life, but his reward will be what he achieves in himself. Respect for one's own soul, not anything another can give, is the only starting point for a successful life. I hope your fears for Tom are groundless, but I have known those who develop only through mistakes, perhaps sin. If his conscience does not keep him from these, I could not really help him spiritually, even though I might direct his course of action. You use your husband's parents as a case in point. Doubtless Estelle Landseer did, as you say, preserve the first Tom Ballington from fatal indulgence. Did this preservation make him the stronger and better man? There are too many protected children in the world. We need self-reliant men and women."

The latter part of February Tom planned a business trip to New York. Both Donald and Ferdinand guessed the reason for it and made characteristic comments to Agnes. Donald's was solicitous. "Do you think it can do any good for him to go on thinking about Miriam? She never will marry him. Would it not be better for him to forget her?" Ferdinand's remark was more sententious. "Miss Cass' friendships with younger men, I suppose, vary the monotony of art."

The night Tom left he went to see Agnes and confided to her his intention to call upon Miriam. "You are the only one who knows it," he said, pleased with his own secretiveness.

Agnes responded cordially, but she had been thinking over Miriam's letter, and the fear lest Tom might be disappointed sobered her words. "You must remember that Miriam is older than we are, Tom. She is less egoistic, more self-sufficient. I know better than anyone else what her friendship means. The best part of it is something you don't guess."

Tom felt a note of warning in her voice. "What is that?" he asked.

He was struck with the unconscious power of her face and manner as she rejoined, "It is a confirmation of one's own soul. Her friendship is straight and sound and so clear sighted in its fullness of feeling that when she gives it, it comes as a crown of glory. She never gave it to anyone who had not first deserved it except me. She gave it to me because she knew I never would stop trying to be worthy of it. She will be doubly sure before she ever gives it to a man."

They spent a quiet evening together, singing and talking. Tom unconsciously was coached by Agnes in topics which she knew to be of interest to Miriam, and he finally started off in an optimistic state of mind.

He reached New York in the morning, but he held himself to the firm's business during the day.

When evening came he stopped at a florist's on the way uptown and bought a bunch of violets. Then, with a high-beating heart, but with a sense of self-respect in the knowledge of what his life had been since their parting, he sought the apartment on forty-third Street, where, much to Mrs. Silas' consternation, Miriam was living with a musical friend a little younger than herself.

Tom found his way to her door. He felt a palpitation of the heart as he saw the double card inscribed,

MIRIAM CASS.
ETELKA RAVACZY.

He listened before he pressed the bell. It was quite still. Immediately after he had rung, however, a peal of laughter came from the rooms inside, striking him almost as an answer to his ring. In a panic of embarrassment he thrust the violets into his pocket, crushing them as he did so. Their odor penetrated the air as he heard the sound of footsteps within. Another moment and he was facing a tall girl with coarse black hair, oblique eyes, and straight brows. In spite of her simple manner, Tom felt abashed by a bizarre power in her. She looked at him with courteous inquiry.

"Is Miss Cass at home?" he asked.

"She is. Will you step inside?"

The girl stepped back, drew aside a curtain behind her, disclosing a group of men and women within, and called lightly, "Miriam!"

Tom stood on the threshold trying to compose himself. At first, he did not see Miriam. He took in the general appearance of a large room. The walls were rich but plain in tone. A shelf ran all the way around the upper part, on which a row of steins and curious and barbaric jugs and vases were thickly 'ranged. A grand piano stood in one corner, with iron lamps each side the keyboard. Against an old tapestry curtain a number of daring clay models were hung. A marble bust of Stevenson done from the life stood in front of it. Curios from all over the world, rich old cloisonné from Japan, Benares brass from India, mosaics from Italy, Chinese ivories, temple-gongs from Tibet, a teak-wood cabinet filled with rare Chinese pottery, covered the walls. In one corner there was hung, wreathed about with great sprays of coral, a trophy of walrus tusks, an enormous swordfish's weapon, harpoons, Esquimau and Malay fish spears, and many curious implements of nameless use collected by Captain Cass on all the shores washed by the oceans.

Opposite was sitting a man whose face was well known to the public as that of a rising politician. In the center of the room, seated around a card table, were four persons. Two tall candles diagonally opposite each other across the table, their flames reflected in the polished mahogany, lighted up the group. Tom's gaze fell upon Miriam, who was seated with her back toward him, her mass of black bronze hair vivid in the candle light. Next to her a square, stocky figure, nerved with the "rigor of the game," stooped over the table. A hale, despotic old face, featured like Miriam's and crowned with thick, grizzled, black-bronze hair, proclaimed him Miriam's father, the much-wandering Ulysses of the sea, Captain Cass.

As Miriam heard her name she laid down her cards, rose as she made a laughing remark to her father, which called forth a vehement protestation from that gentleman, and, without waiting for him to finish, turned and came toward Tom. The captain raised his voice and pursued her with words which were intended to bring her to reason. Miriam's eyes were full of merriment as they fell upon Tom, but their expression instantly changed, as she recognized him, to one of surprise and pleasure.

"Why, Tom," she exclaimed, "have you snowed down? Come in. If Providence provides another, we can have a second whist table. I'm so glad you're here to meet my father."

Tom laid aside his hat and coat and followed her into the room as she talked. She led him at once to Captain Cass.

"Father, this is Mr. Ballington, from Winston."

"How do you do, sir?" said Captain Cass in a business-like way, wheeling around in his chair to face Tom. He did not offer to get up, and, as he shook hands with the newcomer, instinctively turned his cards face down on the table before him, as a safeguard from the perfidious eyes of his daughter.

"She says I might as well play with my cards wrong side out," he continued discontentedly, explaining to Tom the ground of his recent controversy.

"These are our friends, Professor and Mrs. Whitney," interposed Miriam, nipping off her father's harangue with experienced promptitude. Captain Cass gave an unwilling grin, and winked at Tom as much as to say, "I'll finish it in a minute."

Professor Whitney rose to shake hands. He was a tall man with a scholarly head, keen eyes, and polished manners. His wife, a weary-looking woman who was slightly deaf, responded to the introduction with a bow only.

Miriam then drew forward the foreign girl who had been waiting a little behind her, with the words, "Etelka, Mr. Ballington. Miss Ravaczy is my violinist-comrade."

Then, turning to the politician, Miriam added, "Mr. Strong."

"I see I am interrupting your game of cards," said Tom. "Go right on with it."

"I am relieved at the interruption, Mr. Ballington," said Professor Whitney, still standing. "I am just beginning to learn whist. I either have a hand that a way-faring man though a fool couldn't help playing, or I have one that would make the wisest man on earth sit down on the ash-heap."

Miriam laughed under her breath, but before she could speak, the captain broke in.

"Sit down! Sit down, Whitney!" he exclaimed, fanning the air irritably with his free hand in the direction of the Professor. The young gentleman wants us to go on. Strong and—the young lady over there aren't playing." The Captain felt his inability to pronounce Etelka's name, and with a motion of his hand he waved Tom toward the settee. "Your play, Miriam!" finished her father briefly.

"Mr. Ballington is from out of town, father," said Miriam remaining by her father's chair. "You will excuse me—"

"Sit down! The game is almost done," repeated the Captain peremptorily.

"Let me take your hand, Miss Cass," suggested Mr. Strong, coming forward. "I have been watching the game."

The Captain leaned back in disgust, while Miriam gave Strong her cards and retired with Tom and Etelka to the seats by the wall.

"How is Agnes?" she asked at once.

"She's very well and sent her love to you," said Tom, the conventional words making him feel formal and ill at ease.

"Is Mr. Ballington the husband of the Mrs. Ballington of whom I hear so many things?" asked the musician, looking at Tom gravely.

"Not a married man yet!" answered Tom, more and more discomforted. "I'm a cousin of Ferdinand Ballington. I see you have Agnes here," he added brusquely, nodding at the farther wall where he had noticed several studies of his cousin's head.

"Yes, I did those from memory. Do you think they are like her?" Miriam's eyes followed his critically.

"Exactly, when she looks that way. It's a pity she doesn't look that way oftener." Tom had intended to give a compliment, but Miriam's sudden smile made him conscious of the fact that he had done the opposite.

Without attempting to mend matters, he changed the subject. "You have a lovely room here," he began diffidently. "May I go round and look at the things after a while? That sea corner over there," and he pointed with animation in the direction of the coral, "has an Arabian-Night spell for me. Coral is my fetish."

"I like the room, said Miriam, "best of all when Etelka practices here. I have my studio in beyond there and I can hear her when I'm at my work. Perhaps she will play for us tonight."

"I will play if you wish it," replied that young lady seriously.

"Meantime, look around if you like," Miriam said kindly, turning to Tom. "You may go in the studio, too, if you care to."

Tom rose feeling constrained and unhappy. This was the world he had hungered for in his teens, the world he had found in books and in imagination while his youth slipped away from him in the ugly treadmill he was born to. Now he was out of place in both worlds. As he walked through the room with Miriam at his side explaining the different objects, his undisciplined admiration of the beautiful collections was struck through with rage and bitterness for his lost years. Anger at his mother, Donald, Ferdinand, his dead father, contempt for his own weakness in letting his life be controlled by others, surged rebelliously within him. What good had these months of hard work in the office been to him? He never would arrive at companionship with Miriam through such smothered existence.

They were interrupted by laughter and the shoving of chairs back from the card-table. Captain Cass' look of complacence announced that the game had gone to suit him. "You're coming up, Whitney!" he said, drawing back his arms to stretch his back and shoulders.

Then he swung toward Tom. "Glad to see you, Mr. Ballington. Very staunch woman, your mother-in-law. Miriam made me call on her last summer when I went through Kent."

"This is Tom Ballington, father," corrected Miriam, "a cousin of Agnes' husband."

"Poor relation of his!" added Tom, looking squarely at the old gentleman. He was infuriated by this second confounding of himself with his detested relative. Miriam must have been talking a good deal about Ferdinand.

"You live on the old stamping-ground of the Iroquois Indians?" asked Professor Whitney courteously. "A most interesting region. I am working up a paper on the origin of their political ideas, and I went over the ground very carefully last summer."

"Yes. We have an Iroquois necropolis in our backyard," answered Tom, feeling easier. "Don and I used to dig there."

"There are legends to be heard, no doubt?" asked the Professor, raising his eyebrows a trifle.

"Oh, yes, there's a great yarn," said Tom, brightening up. "There was a chief of theirs who—"

"Whitney!" broke in the yarn-satiated old seaman, addressing his friend, "that Dawson was a fool. I told him so to his face, after the lecture. He stood up before his audience and got off that old gag about defying the law of gravitation when he raised his arm. I told Miriam that was all I needed to know of him."

"Why didn't he defy the law of gravitation then?" exclaimed Tom bitterly. "He overcame it by his muscle." He did not forgive Captain Cass for quenching his attempt to take part in the general conversation.

"You'd better read Huxley, young man," said Miriam's father good-humoredly. "Well, Miriam, I'll go out on that business now. Good-night, Whitney. Good—"

"Won't you stay a little longer, father?" asked Miriam.

"—night, ladies. Good-day, Mr. Ballington." And with an abrupt bow, Captain Cass left the room.

The politician, whose easy silence Tom had resented, looked leisurely toward him now and inquired if he were staying long in New York.

"No. I expect to leave tomorrow. I am here on business," Tom answered.

He looked at Miriam as he spoke, and the look pierced her sympathy. She put a warm friendliness into the smile she gave him in return, which started Tom's heart throbbing. He forgot art and science. After all, she was a woman as well as an artist and a scholar. He tried to think of some of the subjects he had talked over with Agnes, and said at a venture, "You have become interested in Hungarian literature, Agnes tells me?"

"Indeed!" exclaimed Mr. Strong, turning toward Miriam. "You hadn't mentioned that to me."

Professor Whitney let his fine eyes rest upon his wife as he said, "In my old age I am affording much amusement to my family by learning to play cards and to read novels. I have just discovered that nothing so illustrates racial differences as the novel."

Racial differences! Tom gave an inaudible groan. Had he started this? Once more he was left on one side by the current of conversation, which flowed busily on in a comparison of the Russian, Hungarian and English novel. Whitney was interested in the philosophy of fiction, strong in the politics, Miriam in the genius and the social theories of the authors.

Tom, who always read for the story, felt childish and foolish and sank into a despondent silence.

Miriam seemed to realize his mood, for she presently broke off and went to the piano. "Etelka has promised to play for us," she said, smiling at her friend.

Tom's hopes revived. Here, at last, Fate was affording him an opportunity. Nature had done well by him in one respect; she had given him a voice. While Etelka was tuning up her violin he cleared his throat quietly, preparatory to his Rubinstein songs. As she settled the instrument under her chin and questioned it with her bow before beginning, Tom leaned back in comfortable anticipation of the "Cavatina" by Raff, or the "Legende" by Wieniawski, or possibly Handel's "Largo."

A moment later an ear-splitting discord, insisted upon fortissimo by piano and violin alike for several bars, galvanized him into an erect position. The discord resolved itself into a melody so exquisite and far away that it fell like balm on his soul and tears rushed to his eyes. Almost imperceptibly the music drifted into a dance-rhythm, and he was drifting away with it when he was stunned by a recurrence of the discord, and Etelka took the violin down from her shoulder.

Embarrassed by the unexpected close, his eyes involuntarily sought the clay models on the wall and he examined them anew in the hope of discovering what influence such music as this had on Miriam's work. He was concluding that there was something of the same abrupt energy, daring, and grace in both, when Etelka began playing again. This time the music was massive, grand, somber—a fugue whose classic counterpoint was unintelligible to Tom. He soon gave up trying to follow the ever-complicating voices, and looked hopelessly at Miriam's face kindling into exaltation as she played on with ever-deeper feeling and humility; while Etelka, on the other hand, seemed to dilate and blaze before their eyes like some genius of the elements, struggling heavenward through the network of sound.

Tom felt his last hope leave him as the music stopped a second time, and Strong sprang up, went to the piano, and began turning over the leaves of music as he discussed with Miriam and Etelka in turn of this and that passage and expressed unqualified delight in a composition which was to Tom one long excruciation.

After Etelka had repeated one or two phrases at Strong's request, she put up her violin and came over to Tom. "Now it is Mr. Ballington's turn to sing," she said in a matter-of-fact way.

"I can't sing," declared Tom, looking across at Miriam, despair in his heart. A gulf had opened and was momentarily widening between him and somebody he had thought he knew. Some way the artist and the woman were one. They could not be separated. What was in the fugue was in her. Tom felt dimly that it had to do with the whole of her, mind and soul. His refusal seemed a signal for the company to ply him with urging. Tom looked around upon them and his mood changed to one of defiance.

"Very well, I will sing!" he said, rising and seating himself at the piano.

His eyes darkened and a dull color came into his cheeks as he mechanically went through one of his little Rubinstein songs. All his faith in its beauty had been destroyed by Etelka's fugue.

When he had sung it to the bitter end he turned around doggedly, but took care not to meet Miriam's eyes. He could have thrown himself on the floor and sobbed, as the group of listeners thanked him.

Presently there was an odor of coffee, and just as the hostesses were beginning to serve a salad, the door burst open and Captain Cass returned, red in the face and out of breath. He swung himself out of his greatcoat and cap and rubbed his hands together briskly before joining the company.

"You should clear your decks before you begin action, Miriam!" he said, kicking aside a fox rug and placing his chair upon the bare floor. He ate from the table. The others held their plates in their laps.

"That is the third time Blackwell has told me that he would be at home when he wasn't," resumed the Captain grimly, after a pause. "When I finally catch him, as I shall, he will wish he didn't have any home."

Tom eyed the speaker with swelling resentment. How was it that he was so at home in this circle? He had no business to be. Yet he assumed equality with the casts on the wall and the music on the rack. His kind of energy and daring outraged his daughter's, and neither he nor she appeared to know it!

After the intermission there was more music, but Miriam could not persuade Tom to sing a second time. Presently he rose and said good-night.

"We shall see you again, I hope?" said Miriam as she followed him to the door.

"I think not." Tom paused. "I shall leave in the morning."

"Won't you stay over another day? I will take you to see the relief I have just hung in the Academy of Design."

Miriam understood his look and urged him cordially.

Tom knew a stab of happiness. She wanted him, after all. He was about to accept the invitation when Miriam turned to Mr. Strong and added, "We will postpone our engagement till the day after tomorrow." Then she turned back to Tom expectantly.

He replied instantly, "It is impossible for me to stay." The last vexation was too much for him. He wanted to control himself here, but habit was too strong. The words were uttered before he could check them, though he cursed himself for a fool as he spoke. "Good-night," he finished abruptly.

He bowed, took his hat and coat, and went away without one backward look.

Miriam had her hand on the door to follow him. She felt Agnes' eyes urging her to do it. But she dropped her hand and turned back to her guests. Tom was going off like a willful child in unreasonable despondency. He should have stood up to it like a man. It was inevitable that he should have been ill at ease during the evening. It would not be well for him if she should obliterate the discomfort he had experienced. She believed he had the strength of purpose to translate that memory into persistent effort. Agnes' letters had proved that he was under her friend's influence and guidance, and, in that relation, he would run no danger of sentimental complication. Hitherto he had been treated as a child. In no way could strength come so surely as in facing discouragement manfully. She had learned her own greatest lessons so, and victory, hardly achieved, brought with it a supreme happiness. To leave the field clear for such a victory, in spite of her sympathy, she felt was the best she could do for Tom.

But who can count upon the feverish impulses of the human spirit? Miriam had underestimated Tom's disappointment and overestimated his strength of purpose.

The next morning Tom took the early train for home. All the way he found it impossible to call up the picture of Miriam without a sense of mental distance and overwhelming loss. He dozed off in the afternoon, and woke up when the train slowed up at a station. Through the car-window he saw the statue of an Indian, tomahawk in hand. It was Kent. A temptation attacked him. Beatrice was waiting for him there—she liked surprises.

A wild craving for outlawry was accompanied with the thought that there would be no doubt of her welcome.

With a muttered oath he snatched up his valise, ran out of the car, and jumped to the platform at Kent.

CHAPTER VIII

THE following summer, as he had planned, Ferdinand left for England and the Continent, to be gone till fall. He spent the summer introducing his patent to the attention of railroad men across the water. It was always his motto that a man must see to things himself if they were to be done thoroughly.

During his absence Agnes was free to live her own life. She made her plans before Ferdinand left. She obtained a position as teacher in Mr. Stoddard's summer music-school and sang at the Conservatory concerts as well as in church. She spent many days In Kent with her mother and aunt. She caught eagerly at the privilege of reliving that short period of her life after her father's death wherein she had been her mother's chief support. It seemed a good omen to her that Fate had reconsidered for once, not only given back a vanished opportunity, but given her ampler power to utilize it. She was earning what seemed to her mother and Aunt Mattie a large income, and it was most grateful to her to use it chiefly in relieving the pitiful economy of her mother's family. Then, too, however brave a face Mrs. Sidney had put upon her expedients, Agnes realized as she never had done before that the last five years had told heavily upon even that indomitable will and vigorous physique.

The separation from her husband offered Agnes another opportunity which she seized as earnestly as she did the one to regain elasticity and independence. This was a chance to put before Ferdinand, without being interrupted or forced away from the subject, certain questions which demanded settlement: first, the moral education and the individual rights of the children, together with her own rights; another concerned Ferdinand's plans with regard to her mother's home; still another, Aunt Margaret's right to an allowance. Her husband's replies were disappointing. He answered her letters kindly but evasively, and his own were filled with absorbing accounts of his business success. As they came, one by one, she watched with anxiety the developing passion in her husband for financial power. Every step toward that but increased his impatience for more. She saw more clearly than she ever had seen how consuming his ambition was. His cold and self-contained nature seemed voracious for sympathy in one respect only, and that was this lust for money-power.

As the bright, full days of summer passed swiftly on toward fall, and Ferdinand's letters followed one another unmoved by the reiterated appeals in her own, the reconsideration of fate for which she had been so thankful began to take on a grave significance for Agnes. It grew upon her that, unless she could make some impression upon him while he was away, her husband's return must be the crisis of their married life. The eagerness and hope of June had passed gradually into persistent argument through July, and by the middle of August she found herself facing alternatives of action, either one of which must bring with it renunciation.

There were no services the last two weeks of August in Westminster Church in Winston, and Agnes took occasion to go to Kent and stay over Sunday with her mother. She talked late with her mother Saturday night and overslept Sunday morning in consequence. She came down the stairs of her old home late in the morning, and paused a moment in the front doorway looking out into the quiet street. The inhabitants of Kent were in church, and the sounds of hymns and Gregorian chants came from the Presbyterian church near at hand and the Catholic church further away. The sun was hot and the air full of the stifling moisture of the newly-sprinkled street. Agnes listened until the music ceased, then turned and looked through the downstairs rooms, calling Mrs. Sidney and Aunt Mattie. There was no reply, and not finding them in the kitchen she went out to the back door and looked into the garden.

At the farther end she saw her mother expostulating with Aunt Mattie, who was endeavoring to spray a rose bush with the garden hose. Mrs. Sidney was arguing that the Sabbath was not a day to use the hose, while Aunt Mattie replied that any day that dried up flowers was a day for spraying. The little enclosure of fruit trees, garden vegetables, and old fashioned formal flower beds was dripping from its late shower bath, and birds were diving and fluttering and chirruping with almost June-like abandon in the wet grass.

Agnes' eyes traveled in delight along the cinder walk which pursued its economical way close to the high board fence in whose shade vegetables could not well grow. At the farther end of the garden, however, the walk swerved to the left, passed under a grape-arbor and ended at the barn door. The spicy perfume of nasturtiums was in the air, and a florid mass of dull-red dahlias flaunting in front of one of the posts of the arbor completed the mid-summer fullness, the cessation of eager, aspiring effort, the rest and leisure which hung over the scene.

For a moment Agnes yielded to the nirvana which stole back over her with drowsy memories of other Sabbath mornings when as a child she had looked upon those same scenes idly and wished she could lie under the grape-arbor and dream instead of going to church. A moment later she called out, "Mother, are you staying home from church to take care of your rose bushes? Why didn't you call me?"

The two women at the other end of the garden looked up, and Aunt Mattie's crippled hands, slipping on the wet hose, sent an unexpected jet of water against Mrs. Sidney's shoulder. It broke and dispersed in spray over the rest of the ample figure, and, with an exclamation of dismay, Aunt Mattie dropped the hose, sending an aimless stream of water hissing into the sod.

"Turn off the water up there, Agnes!" Mrs. Sidney called in a carefully controlled voice; and then, turning to her deprecating companion, she said in a half-vexed, half-humorous tone, "That's the fourth time you've done that, Mattie. I did think when you turned the hose on me the third time last Wednesday that would end it." Then, shaking the drops from her clothes, she took Aunt Mattie's arm and assisted the cripple toward the house. Agnes noticed with amusement that her mother had by no means lost the power of enjoying a joke at her own expense, while Aunt Mattie looked unnaturally humble.

"Well, I guess I'm well punished for staying at home," said Mrs. Sidney when they reached the steps. "I thought, since you didn't have to sing in church today, that I'd just let you sleep and have a late breakfast. Meantime Mattie nearly killed herself getting out here alone to water this yard. She turned the water on and did the whole thing herself."

A gleam of pride and triumph transfigured for a moment Aunt Mattie's humility, confirming Mrs. Sidney's assertion.

"I had just gone out there to help her into the house when she turned the last drops on me," Mrs. Sidney finished as they reached the porch.

Agnes descended a step or two to assist in getting Aunt Mattie into the house.

Then Mrs. Sidney insisted upon the other two women sitting upon the front veranda while she changed her waist and put breakfast on the table. A little later her cheery voice called them to the dining-room.

Agnes sat down to the table with an exclamation of delight.

"I tell you, mother, nobody but you knows how to get up a breakfast like this. You have fixed places for yourself and Aunt Mattie, too. I'm glad you waited for me."

"Yes. You can't muzzle the ox that treadeth out the corn," her mother returned, as she sat down with a long sigh of relief.

The three chatted fitfully for a few minutes! then Mrs. Sidney asked with gravity:

"Has Tom Ballington given up caring for Miriam Cass, Agnes?"

"No, mother, I think not," returned Agnes, uncomfortably.

"Well, he is acting as though he never cared for any decent girl," Mrs. Sidney went on. "It won't be long before Fred Sidney's wife will be involved in a scandal. If he cares for Miriam Cass, why don't you get her to use her influence with him?"

"She has used it, mamma, but Miriam is never going to marry. Tom knows that she never will marry him."

"How does he know that?" demanded the old lady, leaning back in her chair.

"Mamma, you wouldn't have Miriam marry Tom the way he is now, would you? Not that he's bad," Agnes added hastily.

"No," Mrs. Sidney assented, "I suppose she is too good for him. But a young woman ought to use her influence for good, and I don't like this new-fashioned way girls are getting of thinking they're above marrying. What is her reason for never marrying?"

Agnes looked thoughtfully at her mother. "Miriam feels that she has a gift in carving which she ought to exercise. She says that sooner or later the necessity for it, if she should marry, would interfere disastrously with her domestic happiness. She might have married either of two men whom she respects highly and who have brilliant futures before them, but she feels that she must work her own way."

"Well," replied Mrs. Sidney decidedly, "Harriet Beecher Stowe wrote 'Uncle Tom's Cabin' while she rocked a cradle. However, although I don't agree with your friend, I must say I think it is better for a woman to stay out of it than it is to go in and blaspheme it. There is Beatrice, who has been married longer than you have, with no children, and carrying on without any conscience about home or husband. It is a bad situation when a self-willed woman holds the purse strings."

"Yes," assented Aunt Mattie, "only self-willed men should hold the purse-strings."

Mrs. Sidney glanced quickly at her sister-in-law, then at Agnes, and with an effort suppressed something that she evidently wanted to say.

Aunt Mattie continued. "General Mott always kept a liberal establishment at home and then went and did as he liked elsewhere. Beatrice keeps up her house well, too, and Fred could have as much of her money as he wanted, if he'd take it. He is in a much better condition than Mrs. Mott was, and, if he would give up the bank, Beatrice says he never would have another thing to complain of in her."

"Mattie, I'm ashamed of you," said Mrs. Sidney, considerably stirred up by this impartiality. "Sometimes it seems to me as if your sitting around and looking on at things had turned you into wood. You ought to be afraid of passing lightly on moral matters the way you do. One would think to hear you talk that General Mott was an exemplary man, and that if Beatrice is like him that excuses her for anything she takes it into her head to do. If you don't use your moral sense in judging situations, Mattie, you won't have any moral sense pretty soon. If I didn't know what a good wife you always were to Stephen's brother," she added more amicably, "I'd think you didn't have any idea of the sanctity of marriage. Marriage isn't a thing of money."

"Neither Walter nor I ever found it so," reflected Aunt Mattie.

Mrs. Sidney looked at her a few moments with many things to say and no way to say them. Then with an effort she brought her mind back to Beatrice.

"If Beatrice had some children to take care of," she began again, "she wouldn't have time or energy to throw away on Thomas Ballington."

Agnes looked across at her mother for a moment. "Mamma," she said at last, "ever since I married I've been trying to decide just what is a wife's duty. You can't just say children are from the Lord. We all know that the Lord doesn't have anything to do with a good many little waifs. I believe with you that Beatrice would be better off if there were children in the family. I am most thankful for my own. I believe that children should be sent to families who can care for them and that it's a sin to refuse the parental responsibility of marriage. At the same time, mamma, look at Helen. We all know that Pleasant could hardly take care of himself alone. Helen might have taken care of a small family. I could take care of my two. But what can she do with six?"

"Well," said Aunt Mattie impersonally, "she can care for six a good deal better than she can care for ten a few years from now."

Mrs. Sidney hesitated, then valor got the better of discretion, and she replied dauntlessly, "I thank the Lord that my children don't shirk their duty. The mother of the Wesleys had eighteen children."

"How many of them grew up?" interposed Aunt Mattie with interest.

Mrs. Sidney withered her with a glance, but did not offer to answer the question. "Mrs. Wesley was a wonderful woman and she was well rewarded in the lives of her sons. If Helen lives to have ten children, the older ones will by that time be able to help support the family. All the children will be trained to thrift and unselfishness."

"It's a pity that Pleasant can't be trained, too," said Aunt Mattie regretfully.

"Mattie," demanded Mrs. Sidney, roused to sweep her antagonist from the field and put an end to these irritating interruptions, "do you want all women to do the way Beatrice is doing?"

"They couldn't," said Aunt Mattie simply.

"I asked you," repeated Mrs. Sidney with fire in her eye, "if you wanted them to?"

"No," replied Aunt Mattie placidly, not properly realizing the ignominy of her defeat.

"Well, what do you want?" said her now thoroughly exasperated sister-in-law.

"I don't know," replied Aunt Mattie with unprejudiced candor.

Agnes could no longer control a desire to laugh, and this was the last straw laid upon her mother's forbearance. She was at last goaded into saying something which she never had allowed herself to think before, much less to express, and for which she never forgave herself afterwards.

"Well, if you had had some children yourself, Mattie, you'd be a good deal better off than you are now. You're like all the other critics who find fault with people who are doing the best they know how. If you were doing something yourself you'd have more right to talk. Meantime, I'll trust the Lord's plan of running the universe rather than yours. He, at least, knows what He's about, if we don't."

"I hope He does," replied Aunt Mattie doggedly. "He was the one who decided I shouldn't have any children and that I should be a helpless burden on you, Kate."

Mrs. Sidney's wrath instantly cooled. "That was a wicked thing for me to say, Mattie, and I hope you'll forgive me. I was carried away because you blamed Helen for setting her shoulder to the wheel. She's had a pretty hard time, but she's raising her children well. They're a good deal better off than the single child of rich parents."

"Well," Aunt Mattie returned, ignoring the late personal turn of the conversation, "I should be better satisfied if Helen was setting Pleasant's shoulder to the wheel."

Agnes divined in her aunt's tone that her thoughts were not altogether upon Helen's situation any more than her own had been. The conversation had but made objective the complications which she herself must face at no distant time. The unsuccessful correspondence with Ferdinand had brought home to her the knowledge that her summer's position of compromise between wifely duties and financial independence could not be permanent. She knew her husband was bitterly although tacitly opposed to it, and she now clearly saw that he looked forward to the time when it would become untenable. He expected to demonstrate to her that in the course of nature she could not be a normal wife and an independent wage-earner. At the same time he would make no concession in the way of settling an allowance on her. She knew him well enough to feel sure that he was waiting for unconditional triumph.

In short, her brief assertion of personal rights had already broadened into the gravest possible issue. This issue involved nothing less than the alternative of living with Ferdinand and bringing up an increasing family in entire dependence upon him, or with at best short intervals of partial independence when she might be able to resume outside work; or the no less serious alternative of leaving him and living an independent life with the knowledge that he would obtain and keep control of the children as soon and for as long a period as the law would allow. There was no middle course. When it came to the point of leaving Ferdinand, and she now knew that he would force the issue to that point, Agnes' mind staggered. Grave as were her accusations of her husband, could they justify the breaking up of his family?

After she had finished her breakfast, in obedience to Mrs. Sidney's peremptory request, Agnes helped her aunt out to the veranda and stayed with her a few minutes. Then she excused herself on the plea of writing some letters, and went to her room.

Once up in her own room Agnes sat down to her table, but, instead of writing, drew toward her and opened a leather case full of old letters which she had brought home with her. She took out one of the letters and glanced at the indorsement. "To my daughter Agnes, to read when she is about to decide on marriage. S. S." Her eyes lingered a little on the familiar handwriting, then with a sigh she drew out the letter.

It was but a few words one single sheet of paper:

MY DEAR DAUGHTER:

In making one of the most far-reaching decisions of your life I want you to remember the greatest facts of life. Love is underneath and above us all like the everlasting arms. The law of love is the law of God. But love is something more than you know yet. It takes years of suffering to make us understand it. Don't follow your imagination in making this decision, but remember that all the great souls who have loved most in this world have also endured most. You will have trials and wearinesses and disappointments. Choose none but a man you can trust and honor, and having married him forgive seventy times seven. Marriage is for life and death, and there is only one way to live and die. Our Master knew what it was. "And I, if I be lifted up, will draw all men unto me." If we would be loved all our lives, we must sacrifice ourselves all our lives. Only so can we draw.

God bless you.

YOUR FATHER.

Agnes knew the letter by heart, and now, as she read it for the hundredth time, her eyes unconsciously rested long on the sentence, "Choose none but a man you can trust and honor." There was the rub. She could not hide from herself the fact that she did not trust or honor Ferdinand. Yet her situation was one she had brought on herself, and when she did so she solemnly had vowed to love, honor and cherish her husband so long as they both should live. She had made the promise before she knew what it involved, and she had mistaken the man whom she had married, but these were not excuses a person of her Puritan training could conscientiously plead. It should have been her business to find out what she was doing before she married.

She leaned her forehead on her hands and endeavored to think clearly. It was not the sacrifice of herself that she shrank from in going back to Ferdinand's control. The whole force of her early education and later training, of her mother's example, and of her own observation, bore with overwhelming insistence upon the one point, the necessity of self-sacrifice in the life that was to be lived for the highest good. What she dreaded was giving up the privilege of helping her mother and sister, sinking to a powerless position in her own home, strengthening Ferdinand's arbitrary will—and behind all these, doing violence to the principles of liberty and justice in themselves. Was it possible that the law of love, which is the law of God, required submission to injustice?

Agnes had asked herself many times during the summer just passed what it was that was meant by the word "love," so vital to the marriage ordinance. She had been aware for a long time that Ferdinand and she interpreted it differently and that he considered her grudging in its fulfillment. To him true wifely love appeared to entail, besides the primal duty of bearing and raising children, a constant concurrence with the husband's will, a satisfied recognition of his reason, a grateful response to his affection, and ready sympathy with his needs. This summed up her moral obligation. Very soon after her marriage Agnes had struck out from her own conception of marriage—love the concurrence with her husband's will; sometime afterwards she had removed the conviction of his reason; her affection and sympathy had changed gradually in character. Now she found herself considering the responsibility of the most elemental of wifely duties, "the primal duty of bearing and raising children." The seriousness of the question at stake made her quail. She felt that she had reached the crux of her dilemma. All society was built upon this relationship, and, in return, fortified and protected it. No other relationship went so deep or extended so far, as this which meant the perpetuation of the species. All the others existed for it or grew out of it. How dared she consider breaking it?

Along with self-distrust, and directly challenging it, there came to her troubled mind some words of Miriam's: "You do not submit to injustice for yourself alone. If you evade the material struggle, you prepare defeat for yourself in the later spiritual struggle." If Ferdinand refused justice, what right had she to evade the issue?

With a heavy heart she returned to her father's letter. "Marriage is for life and death," he said. This, Agnes' own experience corroborated. Ecstasy, confidence, respect, all gone, she nevertheless was aware in her contemplation of her marriage of something which made it irrevocable and eternal. It was not duty, nor was it the existence of her children. Neither was it love, as that word is commonly interpreted. It was a bond which to the pure in heart is indissoluble.

This bond her father knew. Miriam did not. The Scriptural text about a man's leaving father and mother to cleave to his wife was not arbitrary. It was founded upon a law of nature, and she was being pushed to the conclusion that to that law she must bow. Violence to the marriage bond meant ruin to society, violation of the soul. She must bear a less wrong to avoid committing a greater.

With the tears running down her cheeks she put the letter back in the case and drew toward her the unfinished sheets she had begun the night before for Ferdinand. "I must draw my husband. I cannot drive him. My father is right. We must sacrifice ourselves all our lives if we would make men better."

As she quoted her father's lines, the gentle and saintly spirit that had written them seemed close to her, understanding her struggles, sympathizing with herself-renunciation, sustaining her faltering courage, leading her with unswerving steps along that ever narrower and steeper path whose end was hidden in darkness.

Darkness! for she had accepted a paradox, that the law of God required what was unjust.

CHAPTER IX

FERDINAND arrived in New York the day before Senator Balfour was to make the long-deferred visit to Kent, and Agnes telegraphed her husband to meet her at her mother's home and go with her to the reception for the Senator afterwards. As this reception was to be given at the home of Fred and Beatrice Sidney, Agnes was relieved when the answering telegram came acquiescing in the plan.

Nothing but his long friendship with the Sidney's would have brought Senator Balfour to Kent. The heterogeneous company who had been invited to meet him in Mrs. Fred Sidney's parlors did not know this fact, however, and there was not a cloud upon the civic pride which beamed upon him from every countenance. Beatrice had asked Mrs. Sidney to receive the guests with the Senator, and, buoyed up by his companion's hearty pleasure in introducing him, the bored old statesman felt a prick of interest himself. Between the introductions, they talked together.

Rather late in the evening he asked abruptly, "Who is that just greeting your niece?"

Mrs. Sidney's eyes followed his, and she exclaimed with unaffected satisfaction, "Well, there they are at last! That's Agnes and her husband. Ferdinand looks as though England had agreed with him. He's just got home today. He's been patenting his new invention. Doesn't she look like Stephen? I tell her if she behaves as well as she looks, she won't disgrace her father."

Senator Balfour did not reply. As the daughter of his old friend approached him he was stung by the realization of lost youth. There is no death's-head so startling as a young face that smiles at our age with eyes that answered our own just so forty years ago. The keen, elderly face watching Agnes approach reflected something of the emotion roused by her appearance. The ironical mouth that the funny papers found so easy to caricature changed its expression suddenly as he went to meet her.

He held her hand in acknowledgment of the introduction, and then, instead of the commonplaces he had been uttering all the evening, he ended a few moments' silent scrutiny, as he released her hand, with the phrase, "The face that launched a thousand ships."

His eyes wandered over the pearl satin of her gown and the opals on her neck, and he thought that both seemed to reflect her vivid flush, as she replied at once,

"'The Scythian Tamburlaine?
Whose fiery eyes are fixed upon the earth,
As if he now devis'd some stratagem.'"

Balfour laughed aloud with the joy of one who discovers that his fine carbuncle is a royal ruby. "My dear young lady! I supposed that I was one of the very last cave-dwellers who still read Marlowe. Your father and I used to spout those lines forty years ago. Is it possible that you have read Tamburlaine—or did you cram beforehand, knowing my weak point?" His shrewd eyes twinkled through the shaggy eyebrows he drew down over them suddenly.

A string trio began to play in one of the windowed recesses. Senator Balfour remained by Agnes' side, conversing with her interruptedly, while the group around them changed continually.

As Ferdinand paused in one of the doorways to glance through the rooms, Mrs. Sidney came up behind him and touched his arm. "Ferdinand, I want you to notice Agnes."

"I have been noticing her all the evening."

"Then notice Senator Balfour, and remember that he is a statesman. Then I want you to remember something I said one time that you contradicted. Another time I want you to be more careful about contradicting an old woman who knew a statesman before you were born."

Ferdinand was amused by his mother-in-law's triumph. "Agnes is now the social peer of a statesman. She could not have interested the Senator like that when I married her, however. She has developed, you must remember."

Ferdinand was conscious of a listener behind him, and, turning, saw Fred Sidney.

The newcomer spoke at once. "Have you time to come into the den a moment, Mr. Ballington? There's a matter I want to talk over with you." His manner and voice were unusually friendly to his cousin's husband, but his eyes were burning.

"Certainly," replied Ferdinand, wondering what Fred Sidney could want to see him about, "I'll come now."

They went upstairs to the smoking-room, and Fred closed the door.

"Will you smoke?" asked Fred, going to the table without glancing at his companion.

"No, thanks."

Fred motioned Ferdinand to a seat, while he himself remained standing, his hands thrust deep into his pockets.

"I hope," he said, still in the friendly voice that contrasted oddly with the hostile eyes, "that you can forget for a little while that you are an inventor and capitalist and that I am a bank clerk."

"I don't know why you say that, Sidney," replied Ferdinand flushing slightly; "I never thought the less of you for being a bank clerk."

Then he noticed Fred's haggard face with its fever spots, and a light broke upon him. The words "bank clerk" recalled Beatrice' s habitual jeer at her husband's occupation. Ferdinand had already satisfied himself from his cross-examination of Agnes, on the way to Fred Sidney's house, that Beatrice and Tom were again entangled and that the quarrel between Fred and his wife on the subject of the bank was becoming acute.

"I imagine I know what you want to say," he began again in an altered voice. "You have no idea of taking all that talk about your business to heart, I hope? I have admired your cool persistence, Sidney. When your wife loses—" The last sentences were fairly amiable. Fred doubtless was about to ask him for advice.

"It is your wife and not mine I want to talk about," Fred interrupted.

"I don't care to discuss my wife with you or any other man," returned Ferdinand instantly.

Then be half regretted his words. Suspicion entered his mind that Fred had some disclosure to make. His irritation against him was somewhat allayed.

Fred's next words continued the assuaging process. "Agnes was my cousin before she was your wife. We were brought up together, and she is just the same as my sister. During the summer she has been up here several times and I have become worried about her."

"Do you mean she is working too hard?" asked Ferdinand. "It's her own doing."

"No," returned Fred quickly; "her work has given her more happiness than anything she has had since her marriage."

Ferdinand maintained a dignified silence.

"Agnes is unhappy," Fred went on distinctly. "Something is troubling her. I know all the marks of concealed misery."

Ferdinand's eyes became watchful.

After a slight pause he said carelessly, "Your solicitude is unnecessary, Sidney. The first years of married life are always hard on the wife. There's the physical strain and the mental one of readjusting herself to a new environment, but that is a morbid idea you have about concealed misery. She is getting on better than most young wives. She will drop this new fad herself, in time. I haven't hurried her. She has had every opportunity to develop. Instead of worrying, look how she has improved the last few years. She wanted only time and opportunity to become what she has. She has had both."

Ferdinand had not intended to say so much when he began, but he was thinking, while he spoke, of other things.

Fred's next words gave him a start. They were spoken in a high and hard tone. "A person wants only time and opportunity to die. I don't know what you call hurrying! You have forced what you call her 'development' to the limit of endurance. First thing you know there will be a snap. You needn't think she has been talking matters over with me," he added as another thought struck him. Then he stopped, passed his hand across his forehead, and tried to quiet his mind.

The long strain of his difference with Beatrice was telling on his nerves. He warned himself that this was not the way to gain consideration. He was rousing anger. Ferdinand had risen and was about to leave the room without a word. Fred bit his lip, then stopped him. "Wait a moment, Mr. Ballington. I did not intend to use this tone toward you. I was betrayed into it and I beg your pardon."

There was no response from the man watching him.

Fred continued with an effort to conciliate, "Agnes has developed as few women do. She gives great promise for the future. I am glad you see it and want her to realize it. I am glad you have let her follow her own bent, too. If you let her have the liberty she has had this past summer, for a year or two longer, she will get back her youth and add to it the vigor of maturity. You must see what the last months have meant to her. If you can't see it, for God's sake take the word of anybody who has known her!"

Ferdinand turned to the door.

When he reached it, Fred spoke again from the middle of the room. He had turned white and his voice shook. "God! You ought to be shot dead before you leave this house!"

Ferdinand neither hastened nor retarded his steps. He left the room without a glance behind and closed the door quietly after him. There was an unusual color in his cheeks and his eyes roved impatiently as he went down into the lower hall.

Agnes was singing in the music-room. It was a song whose long notes gave her cello-like voice full sweep and grandeur. Her late training told magnificently in the purity and control of the notes.

Ferdinand went to the door and stood watching her. His recent conversation with Fred Sidney had but touched his pride and sense of ownership—had put an edge on gentler feelings. His eyes followed his wife as she left her place and crossed the drawing-room with Senator Balfour. For an instant Ferdinand saw her pause and look up at her escort. He caught the soft light of her hair, the splendor of her eyes, the gleam of satin, and the changing flash of her opals. Then she disappeared from his sight.

The evening had become wearisome to him and he wished to go. He went into the parlor, passed around behind the guests, and sat down on a window-seat. Scraps of conversation reached him from different parts of the room: Tom's voice, gruff and sulky, refusing to sing; the Reverend Mr. Carter's flowing placidly and monotonously along as though he were in the middle of the "long prayer"; a jovial question from Beatrice to her husband, asking if he thought she were Job that he didn't pay any attention to what she was saying.

Near him a voice which seemed to continue the song sounded intermittently, answered by the whimsical inflections of the Senator. Agnes certainly had succeeded in arousing the famous guest's interest, and Ferdinand was struck by the different way in which her remarks were received from the indifferent responses he himself had drawn from the Senator earlier in the evening.

He looked at his watch impatiently, then rose and made his way in the direction of Agnes' voice.

She saw him coming and raised the cordial glass she was holding in her hand, touched her lips to it, and elevated it still higher in mute salutation. The Venetian glass cast an amber light on her bare arm and neck. "We have missed you for some time," she said with the Sidney smile, which ended in sadness.

"Let us go," he replied briefly. "It is very late."

She arose at once, said good-bye to her friends, and went to the dressing-room.

"Mrs. Ballington is going," said several voices as she came down the stairs with her long cloak hanging open from her shoulders, and a group of her friends gathered in the hall.

Ferdinand stood waiting till she had passed through the door and then he followed her. She paused in the vestibule for a last good-bye.

"Don't forget us, Agnes," called Fred from the hallway. It cost him an untold effort to choke down his emotions into those words.

Senator Balfour gave a slight sigh as the door closed and then turned back to Mrs. Sidney.

As husband and wife went down the steps a gust of wind rushed by them heralding the approach of a storm.

It grew darker and sultrier, the horses plunged going down the hill, and just as they reached the little hotel where Ferdinand had insisted on passing the night, on the ground of not wishing to cause Mrs. Sidney unnecessary trouble, the thunder began rumbling restlessly and the raindrops seemed to burn here and there as they fell.

Ferdinand took the cape from Agnes' shoulders when they had gone to their room, while she stood looking through the window-pane into the night. After he had laid it across a chair he came back and stood beside her, putting his arm around her shoulders. "What a rest it is to get home again," he said with a sigh of relief.

They stood so for some time, each pursuing a line of thought.

Presently the storm increased, drove the rain fiercely against the window, then passed on into the north on the wings of the bleak and melancholy wind. In the lull they turned instinctively to each other.

"It is like the night we became engaged—wind all night," said Agnes. Her voice was low and anxious as she continued, "I've been remembering and thinking how beautiful first love is. There's something less of earth in it than in what comes after. What comes after is deeper, more vital, but—" She hesitated, broke off.

After a moment he said, with some constraint in his voice, "You have been writing all summer, Agnes, that there were certain things which we could no longer postpone deciding. I have answered you that, so long as you hold your present views, further discussion between us on these disagreeable subjects can do no good. I will tell you now, however, that upon many points since our marriage I have found that time and natural development were all you needed to open your eyes to reason, and that I am still waiting until time and experience shall have convinced you of my wisdom in those respects wherein we are still at variance." He added more slowly, "I am sorry that you could not have learned from our relations in the past to trust my judgment where you have had no experience." He paused on the last sentence, and then continued with the methodical patience that had become one of his mannerisms, "I wished to spare us both domestic unpleasantness and the gossip of the town, but if you must find out everything for yourself, there is nothing for me to do but to continue to wait."

Agnes told herself, while Ferdinand was speaking, that the supreme moment had come, and it was with difficulty, so great was her perturbation, that she kept her attention upon his words and followed him from sentence to sentence, considering each one conscientiously as it passed. Unless she could succeed in reaching Ferdinand's sympathy, and through that his will, the things she most dreaded would come upon her. As an ignorant and volatile girl she had allowed her father to pass his last days without care. That had been an unwitting crime. During these summer days at her old home, among his books and papers, her renewed grief in recalling it had expressed itself now and then in her letters to Ferdinand. He had been puzzled by these stray allusions to her girlhood and to some cause which she had for remorse. Now, however, Agnes was realizing the second and bitterer tragedy. In taking up her duty as a wife she must be prepared to give up for the most part her salaried positions and be content to see her mother in age again uncomplainingly take up the burden that would have staggered her in her prime. Cleaving to her husband meant literally forsaking her mother, and she must forsake the second parent with all the agony of full knowledge, and witness the inevitable results. Nor was this all. She must impotently see her children misunderstood and made to suffer struggles dangerous to their intellectual and moral equilibrium.

When he was done she stood still for a moment, grateful for the support which the window casement unobtrusively gave her. Outwardly, she was calm, but in her heart she felt forlorn and weak. Long before her husband's arrival she had arranged logically what she had to say to him. It had seemed that no reasonable mind could fail to be convinced that her pleas were just. Now, however, she felt her confidence going; nor did she know any longer where to begin to answer her husband. He seemed impregnable. In addition to her natural reluctance to oppose Ferdinand, she was distressed by the seeming ungraciousness of pressing such a conversation at such a time. They were both weary and he was just back after a long absence and a long journey, but she knew that her chances of winning him were greater at that moment than they could be again.

"Let us sit down, Ferdinand," she said, meeting his look with a half-frightened, half-pleading expression, but at the same time she motioned him to a chair with one of those swift, firm gestures he knew and had once admired. "There is a good deal to say, and it must be said now."

"If you insist upon further talk, had we not better defer it till we reach home?" asked Ferdinand. He still stood, although Agnes had seated herself near a small table and he could see by her clasped hands resting upon it and by her dilated eyes that she was making ready to begin. "You forget how late it is."

She unclasped her hands and drew the vacant chair nearer her. Her husband's reference to, their home accentuated in her mind the sense of fitness she already had felt in having such a conversation take place in a hired room, a place of accommodation, a caravansary, a spot around which no man's memory clung.

"Sit down, dear, please," she said. "I know you are tired and I am sorry to keep you, but it will be better for us both."

He took the chair in resignation and waited with the dim resentment he always felt when he knew his wife was going to push him to saying in plain words what he thought and what he was going to do. He realized that, baldly stated, his views sounded brutal. It was dignified to say that a father should train his children to obedience, that a husband should protect his wife, that the head of the family should pay all family expenses; but to make him say that his arbitrary will about the children's education could not be questioned, that his wife must ask him for every dollar she spent, that his aunt who had brought him up should be absolutely dependent on his bounty, and that no consideration could change his decision on these points, was irritating. He was not to blame that nature and society had given him brains and made him master in his own house. He resented bitterly Agnes' repeated demands for explanations and reasons that ended ultimately in the simple, dogmatic statement, "I do so because I think best," and the equally simple reply, "How do you know what is best?"

"Well?" he urged as she did not begin. "Let us be as quick as possible about it."

He took out his watch, looked at it, shook it a little, and held it to his ear.

Agnes rested her arms upon the table and leaned a little toward him, speaking in a gentle tone which yet somehow struck Ferdinand as in accord with the renewed ticking of his watch. It was equally exact, dogged.

"Ferdinand, I intended to talk about only those few points upon which we must think and act alike at once or see our home suffer. But I see I can't begin on those. I must go back to our relations in the past."

Ferdinand stirred and was about to speak, but she checked him instantly.

"You make it necessary for me to go back when you say that because I have changed since I married you, because, under your influence, I have come to think differently from what I used to, that therefore I ought to defer to your judgment in matters where I am still unchanged." As she continued, the pleading in her eyes crept into her voice and her whole attitude underwent a subtle change from reluctant determination to appeal. "I know I was ignorant and bigoted and uncontrolled when you married me. I am wiser now, more rational, and I hope that I can control myself better, but we have not grown together, Ferdinand, as you seem to think. We have grown apart and the distance widens every day. You must see this fact with me, and help me to alter it—if it can be altered," she added almost under her breath.

Ferdinand listened to her without changing his position. Into his face, however, a watchful alertness was coming.

"You are making dangerous statements, Agnes," he said quietly. "If you are speaking hastily, I would advise you to reconsider."

"No, I am not speaking hastily, Ferdinand. It has taken me all this time to know myself and trust myself to speak. The reason I have not done it earlier is because I have been too confused, too cowardly, too conscious of my own short comings and sins, and, besides all this, because I have loved you and clung to what love you have for me, dreading to lose what was left of it by angering you." She dropped her hands from the table to her lap, where they fell wearily as she added, "Yet I have known for some time that this must come, that I was wronging the love I promised you by putting off talking through these things to the end."

Ferdinand waited during the pause that followed her last words. "What is it you feel we must talk through to the end?" he inquired at length, wishing to get it over as soon as possible.

"Ferdinand, I cannot have the respect you think I owe to your general view of life, nor can I acquiesce in the way you live that view. Since I do not and cannot think as you do, considering the parental responsibilities we share alike, we must arrive at a working compromise between your theories and mine."

"What are yours, at present?" asked Ferdinand in the tone of endurance that he had persevered in since his wife began talking.

There was a scarcely perceptible pause, after which Agnes went steadily on.

"You and I differ primarily in our attitude toward the rights of others. This would not matter so much if we were not both under responsibilities to the same people; Estelle and Stephen first, my mother, Aunt Margaret."

"Since when have Estelle and Stephen developed so much individuality?" interrupted Ferdinand with covert satire. "What philosopher have you been reading this week?"

Agnes went on without noticing her husband's question.

"I think we should recognize that the children have individual rights. I think we should not be arbitrary in our decisions. I think they should be treated with the same self-control and reasonableness which we exercise toward our equals. If Estelle is frightened in the future as she has been in the past when she has committed some little fault, she will become hysterical, and Stephen sullen and sly." A note of anguish in Agnes' voice marked off the last statement from the preceding ones. She was putting an almost intolerable memory into words as she continued, "I can, as you know, understand from my own experience both of these states of mind. It required all my mature courage and will to extricate myself from the sin of deceit. How can I expect my little boy to resist it when you put an equal strain upon him? You will give him no sympathy yourself, and, if I do, you say I am training him to disregard you. You force me to leave him without it, or to give it to him behind your back, or to let the children see that we disagree."

Ferdinand rose and stood before his wife, looking down upon her. "If my children have had the misfortune to inherit hysteria and slyness," he said, roused to the short, metallic voice which the men at the shops dreaded, "I do not intend that it shall be fostered by environment. I refuse to listen longer to your womanish whining. You are carrying it too far."

Agnes, too, rose, fighting down the grief and despair in her heart. Her hand rested upon the table with the knuckles pressing hard against the pine boards.

"I think, too, that our children must have some religious training, Ferdinand. I had it, and, if your mother had lived, you would have had it. How can you think it right to let our children grow up unguided in their most vital development while you coerce them severely in other respects. I do not ask that they receive sectarian instruction. I couldn't give it to them any longer if I would. I am an agnostic, as you profess to be." The last phrase caught Ferdinand's attention and he listened unwillingly as she went on, "In reality you are not an agnostic. You are"—she waited a moment, and then said slowly, as though the words hurt her— "a materialist. Your mind is on material pleasures, material duties, above all, on money, and what money can buy. You don't ask what is true, first of all, Ferdinand. You only talk about facts. You interpret the deepest and most spiritual relations of life by the hard and narrow philosophy based on the few facts that you will see. How superficial and false that philosophy is only a true agnostic could tell you."

Ferdinand was further angered by this nice distinction of terms and he interrupted her cynically. "I always have supposed that the agnostic dealt with facts as opposed to windy theories, but perhaps I am wrong there as well as in my other views."

Agnes made a supplicating gesture. "Ferdinand, don't break my heart. I and our children are something more than mouths to feed, bodies to clothe. We want room to grow in, we want a husband and father to whom we can go with those longings that are farthest out of sight in our souls because they are too sacred to show to any but the noblest and best. I married you believing that the outer union was but the step to that. Did you never feel the longing to get away from buying and selling, and live"—she made a hesitating step or two nearer to him— "with me and our children in love and perfect comprehension? Doesn't it sometimes come into your heart to give yourself to me as you never have, to give up to something stronger than desire? We all have something back of passion in us. We have a deeper instinct to give instead of get, to get away from ourselves to something beyond us. Shall we never love each other so, away from ourselves?"

Ferdinand looked at her as she spoke, heard the voice rise and fall, felt the old subtle glow and exaltation stealing over him. A faint wish to yield to the unknown power she described passed across his mind. Then he scorned his weakness. He picked up his evening coat and hat and moved toward the door leading into the adjoining room. "It is nearly one o'clock," he said when he reached it.

"Will you say nothing more than that to me, Ferdinand?" Agnes said in a trembling voice.

Without speaking her husband entered the second room, leaving the door open. The room was dark and Agnes lost sight of him as soon as he passed the threshold.

She remained where she was, erect and motionless. Then she shivered, reached for her cape, drew it around her shoulders, sank into the straight wooden chair by the table, and clasped her hands tightly over her eyes. She had done all that she could, and had lost.

Presently Ferdinand appeared again in the doorway. As she heard his step she was instantly on her feet, holding the cloak together with one hand at the throat. Her head was poised with that upward lift and statuesque stillness hunters are familiar with in wild creatures surprised by the chase. Her hair was pushed back from her face like a boy's, and she looked at him with the boy's self-unconsciousness.

"Where are you going?" asked Ferdinand, startled.

The uncertainty in his tone flashed a last hope into Agnes' brain. She caught at it at once. She had failed utterly in telling bare facts to him. She had meant to be tactful. Instead of that she had antagonized him—had not appealed as she might have done to those emotions which she had felt all the evening were awake in him after their long separation.

"You think that I may be going, Ferdinand. You realize, then, that I might be driven to it. You can't see all that hangs on your decision tonight, however. If you did, you surely would answer me differently. We have been apart for months now. Absence has made this meeting like a beginning of life together. We have made mistakes in the past. We both know how and when. We never shall have this chance to start right again. If we go wrong now, in the light of past experience, it never can be rectified. Something, the rarest and noblest in us both, will perish. Give me freedom to live as your best and closest friend. Give me light and air. God knows I'm not begging for myself so much as I am for our children. How can I be a mother to them if my heart is crushed and my hope and faith chained like slaves? I can't love you as I long to, past the injustice that threatens to push in between us. You don't realize this. There is just one way for a man and woman to live together and be happy. They must trust each other and give each other liberty. Only so can marriage be anything but a yoke too heavy for any but the best and the worst of women to bear. I know you will see this some time—I believe you have come back to tell me that you realize it now. Our first imperfect marriage will be but a dream to the power and the glory of this. We are two souls, two wills. Nothing but willing union can make us one. Give me free will. Give me power to be a wife. You have come for that—you cannot have come for anything else. You have been thinking of all we were to each other once, and of all that absence has taught us we may be to each other again if—if life is not lost on us."

Her voice caught, almost broke, on the last phrase. She had drawn near him, step by step, under the stress of passionate pleading. She paused after every sentence, searching his face for a signal of encouragement, and when it did not come, she hurried to the next, as though fearing he would break in.

The beseeching in her voice became almost unendurable to Ferdinand, and when she paused to gain control of her emotion he profited by the opportunity to put an end to the painful scene.

"Let us spare ourselves any further conflict on these points, Agnes. You yourself are my best argument for refusing your own request. Whatever sorrow our marriage has caused you has but made you better and wiser than you would have been without it. There may be, as you say, two souls and two wills in man and wife. I've never attempted to deny it. All I have contended for, and still insist upon, is that the husband and father is the head of the family. I shall do my best to be conscientious in the fulfillment of my duties. I am sorry we cannot see things alike, but I have enough faith in you to believe, as you do, that we yet will. Meantime, I must request you to give up all expectation of a change in our financial and domestic arrangements."

His wife looked at him without moving, and Ferdinand's eyes wavered from hers and passed almost reluctantly over the somber red of the cloaked figure. Then he compelled himself to meet again her gaze, through which was emerging a great obscure force which he dimly knew to be tragic. An answering impulse flared up within him, defiant, hostile. It was the instinct Fred had aroused earlier that evening, to crush, if need be, that which threatened him in her.

He went up to her, put down the half-protesting, half supplicating arms, bent the dark head forward to his breast, and held it there. After some time he said, "Agnes, this is my first day home. Have you nothing else to say to me?"

She raised her head, drew up her hands, and put them against his breast, pushing him back a little so that they could see each other. He found himself looking into two strange eyes, as fathomless, as quiet, as the night.

"What?" he asked, bending his head as though she had spoken.

"Forsaking father—and mother—rich—or poor—in sickness—and in health—till—death—us do part," she said.

PART V

CHAPTER I

THE short fall was followed by a bitter winter. Old inhabitants of Winston fell into a reminiscent strain about a winter back in the forties when the water had frozen on the dinner table and old Silas Ballington had lost half an ear walking from his kitchen door down to the cow-barn.

Ferdinand had put a new furnace into his home and speculated in coal early in the winter. He made enough by the latter device not only to pay for his heating plant, but to present Agnes at Christmas time with a set of sable furs, Miss Margaret with mink, Estelle with a coat and cap of Tibet lamb, and the two-year-old Stephen with a long, straight garment and cap of sealskin. He ordered for himself at the same time an otter ulster with seal trimmings and cap. When he presented these, he asked Agnes to collect all the old furs of the family, and these were sent for later and taken away by the town furrier. Improvements were also made in the house.

Agnes, on her part, had started in their new life together with a determination to make a persistent effort to touch and broaden her husband's sympathies. She told herself that if she were patient enough and tactful enough she must wear away his resistance. This course of hers was so quiet, so free from feminine heart-burnings and moods, that the current of their home life moved more smoothly than it ever had done before. Superficial vexations there were, but Agnes' purpose in life now moved too far below the surface to be disturbed by any but profound emotions.

She had come almost to believe that she never again could feel the extremity of torture to which she formerly had been sensitive, when she was forced to experience another of those shocks which seemed to threaten the springs of life. It happened in February after the expiration of the two-years' grace granted Mrs. Sidney to redeem her home. Agnes knew that some weeks before Ferdinand had received a letter from Mrs. Sidney explaining that the winter had made unexpected demands upon her purse, offering to pay him a part of the money, and asking for another year in which to pay the rest. Dr. Quinn had written also, corroborating Mrs. Sidney's statement, and adding that he would be able in a year to buy the home from her, and that at the same time he would allow her life-residence there. Agnes never had been able to get a frank expression from Ferdinand as to what he intended to do with her mother's home. She knew that he had not answered her mother's letter, and when she saw him preparing to go to Kent instead of writing she began to worry. She did not, however, receive any satisfactory answer to her questions, and it was not till Ferdinand's return from Kent the following day that the subject was plainly opened between them.

He spent part of the afternoon at his office, so that her anxiety had time to grow, and when she met him in the hall upon his arrival it was with great apprehension that she asked at once, "Is it all right—about the house, Ferdinand?"

He put away his cap and ulster before he replied, and then said, with satisfaction in his voice:

"Yes, it is all right. Come into the library and I will tell you."

Agnes followed him into the room with misgivings, and although he offered her a chair, she stood waiting for him to speak.

"I have been able to do better for your mother than I expected," he announced. "I have sold the house for two thousand dollars more than she herself asked Dr. Quinn for it."

Agnes had expected that if Ferdinand should insist upon selling the house she would at least receive warning of his intention. It was, therefore, in a dazed and uncomprehending voice that she began to reply. You have sold the house? But Dr. Quinn—"

Then the blood rushed into her face and she did not finish her sentence. She put her hand on the back of the chair and steadied herself against a dizziness that came over her. The utmost that she had allowed herself to think had been cruelly exceeded. The roof had been sold from over her mother's head in winter when she had a crippled relative to care for. Where would they go? To Beatrice's, to Pleasant's, to the little farm which her mother always had held in reserve, but which was unfit for a home? The thought that it was her husband who was filling her mother's last years with needless sorrow, with implacable determination piling burdens upon that failing but still cheerful spirit, while she herself could neither hinder him nor help her mother, came upon her with full weight of meaning. She tightened her grip of her chair, refusing to credit the situation.

"I am not sure that I understand, Ferdinand," she said. "It has come on me so suddenly. Do you really mean that you have sold my mother's house—away from her?"

"For two thousand dollars more than she herself asked Dr. Quinn," repeated Ferdinand.

The expression of business complacence on his face began to be qualified by something else—a subdued but grim satisfaction at having requited Quinn for the slight the latter had put upon him in refusing his patronage of the doctor's surgical invention. He had managed his mother-in-law's business so as to gain two thousand dollars, which he had determined to use toward her support, and at the same time, he had taught Quinn the lesson that poor men could not afford to be independent.

Agnes sat down and began to sway slightly back and forth in her effort to control herself.

Ferdinand feared the result of the tumult of her feelings, but he did not attempt to touch her "Don't, Agnes," he urged gently. "This transaction means at least two years' support for your mother. The house is a poor investment, and getting worse all the time. She is well rid of it. She took the matter reasonably, as you do not."

As he spoke Agnes grew quiet. Her eyes wandered away from him around the room without seeing any outward object. She was calling up in memory the little house in which she had been born, and in which her father had died. She saw the office as it used to be, open on a spring morning, with flowers where her father had placed them on desk and window-sill. She saw the grape-arbors he had made, the flower-beds he had planned, the blue myrtle-blossoms in the grass about the steps. Each neat and well-kept room of the house passed before her mind as though in farewell.

Then her thoughts returned to the one who would suffer most in leaving that home. It was some time before she could trust her voice to ask, "What did my mother say when you told her?"

Ferdinand was relieved at the question. It indicated returning reasonableness. "She took it very sensibly," he said. "I think the first thing she did was to ask for a month in which to move." He felt that his mother-in-law's conduct, whatever may have been her lack of discipline in the past, in this transaction had been exemplary. Like any fair minded person she had refrained from foolish complaining and had realized the validity of his motives—at least she had not questioned them. He went on considerately, "Of course I told her she could have all the time she wanted."

He waited, half expecting Agnes to come to herself.

As she made no reply, he proceeded to explain the advantages of the arrangement. "It isn't only the money I was thinking of when I did this. You see it really relieves your mother in many ways. Your aunt's own relatives will be compelled to look after her now, a thing they should have done long ago if I could have had my way. I am going to make suitable arrangements for your mother to spend the remainder of her life in some good family, and I intend the two thousand dollars to go toward her board. She won't have the care of a house, and she will be looked after herself when she needs it. I told her that you and I would talk that over together. I want to please you in the place we select. Perhaps the Talbots will take her," he said reflectively. "You said they were old friends of both your parents."

Agnes looked at him so curiously that he thought she was going to say something, but she did not. Instead, she walked over to the window and looked out.

He occupied a little time straightening up some papers on the table, and, as she still did not speak, he turned to go out into the hall.

Instantly her voice arrested him.

"You have not told me yet to whom you sold my father's house."

Her mind had leaped forward from her memories of the house to speculation upon its future possessor. Who was there in Kent besides Quinn who wanted the old place, and wanted it enough to pay so much for it?

Ferdinand turned back to her. "It is a man who has written me several times about it. His name is Malthus. He is a doctor."

There was a pause. A look of abhorrence and incredulity came into Agnes' face. The name Malthus had been associated in her mind all her life with everything that was shameful. As it grew upon her that the one man in their native place whom her father would have been glad to disgrace had gotten possession of Dr. Sidney's office and home, and had done this expressly because it was Dr. Sidney's home and would cast a cloak of respectability over his own name, all her pride and self-control were merged into denial of the intolerable truth.

"No! No! Ferdinand!" she broke out. "Please—not that! You don't know what you are saying. Indeed you can't know. A good doctor can't—I can't bear it! I can't bear it!"

She went up to him and seized his hands, wringing them as she stammered on. He thought as he looked at her that her face had withered and grown old, while the eyes vaguely alarmed him.

"My father's life was spent for his profession," she said brokenly "All Kent will tell you that—the honor of the profession. No man living has disgraced it more than Dr. Malthus has. My mother will not speak to him. Ferdinand, I cannot live to see him go into my father's house."

She slid down to his feet and held herself there, choking down sentence after sentence as they fought for expression. Ferdinand was thoroughly disturbed, and tried to help her up. But she shook herself free with a cry of anguish, and then lay huddled up, absolutely still.

"We all know your father was honorable, Agnes," Ferdinand said presently in a voice which he thought was soothing. "His honor hasn't anything to do with the house."

She caught her breath, but did not look up. Then she corrected him with strained emphasis. "Two thousand dollars' worth!" she said laconically.

After a moment's silence she rose to a half-sitting, half-kneeling posture, and continued, "Why do you think Dr. Malthus was willing to pay so much? You often have spoken slightingly of my father to me. Since you have found out that his name is worth something you should treat it with more respect."

Agnes' words struck Ferdinand. He was conscious that he did think more highly of Dr. Sidney, and he was vexed with himself for not having paid a higher tribute to his father-in-law's memory by placing an additional thousand or two value upon it. As he looked down at his wife he saw that her mood had changed and that he had lost the chance of granting her appeal since she would not renew it. The change in her hardened him and he drew away from her. Agnes glanced at him, and then turned her eyes away as she rose once more with difficulty to her feet.

"Ferdinand," she said a moment later, distinctly, "I see at last that I deserve this. I have made a mistake that is now irreparable. Your return from England was the turning-point in my life. I outraged my reason when I went back to you. You have taken advantage of me, as you have of everyone else, every time you have had me in your power. You were glad when my condition made me give up my salaried positions. You were glad to gratify your resentment against Dr. Quinn by selling—my father's—and—my mother's house. I ought to have left you when you came home from England. I lost that opportunity also! I shall not have many more to lose."

She ceased speaking for a moment, then wild recklessness rushed up within her. "Before our betrothal you led my mother and me to think you other than you were. Since our marriage you have robbed me. If you had not, my mother need not have lost her home, nor would we be at your mercy now."

She could not look at her husband after she had spoken, but turned away and walked with difficulty, as if she were freezing, out into the hall. She had, too, the instinct of the freezing to thaw herself out with the cold. It seemed to her that her slow hands never could get the front door open and let in the air. At last the bolt yielded and a gust of wind brought her back to life. It stung her blood into action and with her blood her shame. She waited a moment, then closed the door and went back to the library.

Ferdinand was standing where she had left him, with that careful absence of expression in his face which accompanied unusual emotion in him.

She approached him and stood looking fixedly at him. He did not move nor return her gaze. They stayed so, without speaking, long enough for a woman who had been entering the yard when Agnes closed the door to come up the front steps, ring, and be admitted.

Neither of them heard her enter the house and she was opening the library door, when Ferdinand at last found his voice to say, "Because you feel it so, I will do what I think it unwise to do." He had been realizing that her mental state might react disastrously upon his wife's physical condition, and he had made up his mind to say the most generous thing he ever had said to her.

He was interrupted at this point by the unceremonious opening of the door, and some inflamed thing seemed projected into the room. He saw the wind-reddened face of Beatrice.

She pulled off her huge gloves and flung off the furs in which she was enveloped, as though she were flinging away all restraint with them, and her bold beauty took on insolence as she turned towards Ferdinand and began to speak.

"Your friend Malthus up in Kent says your papers aren't signed yet, so I've come down here to strike a better bargain with you. Aunt Kate never would let me buy the house, but I guess you will if I pay enough. I understand you are telling around that you are selling the house for your mother-in-law's sake. Now, then, I'll pay you as much as you want to ask on those terms. If you refuse, you prove yourself a lying scoundrel."

She held her check-book in her hand and was looking over the table for a pen. As she picked up one she glanced over her shoulder at Agnes and said, "Why, in Heaven's name, do you live with—" She made a motion with her hand toward Ferdinand instead of speaking his name.

Ferdinand's face hardened at the insult. He was keen enough to see the dilemma in which Beatrice's wit had placed him, and he revolted at being coerced by her. There was a moment's silence. Then, in words which were as ominous to himself as to Agnes, he said, "The house is sold."

As soon as he had spoken he attempted to pass the unbidden visitor and leave the room, but all that was good and all that was bad in Mrs. Fred Sidney was aroused now, and met in her hatred of Ferdinand. Her whimsical but staunch love for Mrs. Sidney had become a passion with Beatrice. "In spite of you, I'm going to see you through, Aunt Kate," she had repeatedly declared, and General Mott's daughter had a free hand where her affections were touched. She had come to Winston with the determination to see Mrs. Sidney through. Now, as she looked at Ferdinand, the grudge which she with difficulty had held in abeyance swelled into full virulence again. She was not only Mrs. Sidney's avenger, but her own. As he took the first step toward the hallway she divined his intention to escape, and to thwart it she sprang into the open space between him and the door.

Agnes was too appalled at what followed to comprehend what Beatrice said. A confused reminiscence went through her mind of things she had heard about General Mott's blasphemy when he lost his temper. It must have been from the father that the daughter had learned the copious vocabulary she was using with more than masculine dexterity. Insults and vituperations fell like a whip of scorpions upon her husband, and Agnes watched with dazed horror the effect upon him. His face changed and took on an expression of fury and violence such as she never had seen.

Beatrice, too, caught it. An exultation in her power urged her to a still more daring outburst. "Now that you've done your best to leave your mother-in-law without a roof over her head," she said, backing toward the hall, "Agnes will realize that she's married a pawn-broker. You speculator in other people's goods! Put up the three balls over your front-door! I've heard you talk about my father, but I've heard him talk about you. He spent his money where you make your profit. You're not fit for a decent woman to live with, and if your wife hasn't found it out yet I'll open her eyes!" She was out in the hall as she finished. There she turned to Agnes and cried discordantly, "Come to us, Agnes! You've got to go somewhere soon enough. Then your mother will come, too."

She reached the door, flung it open, and went out, drawing it to with a jar behind her.

A moment later it was violently thrown open, and she stood once more on the threshold.

"Ferdinand!" she cried.

His face was livid as he strode toward her. He reached the door and was forcing it shut on her.

"I forbid you to set foot in our house again, and everyone shall know that I've done it. I hope I may never see you again"—she braced herself and grew purple in the face—"till I see you in Hell!"

She withdrew suddenly, and the door shut, almost dislocating Ferdinand's shoulder with the shock. Agnes shrank back, thinking that Beatrice must be injured.

But the next moment they heard her voice, as she went down the steps outside, singing out of tune.

Ferdinand did not look at Agnes as he turned away from the door and went upstairs to his room.

She returned to the library, and sank into a chair, her mind dizzied by the license and blasphemy of Beatrice's outburst. A fright for Fred took possession of her. In this case, Beatrice's passion had been generous in its origin, but its excess appalled her. Should her evil passions be roused and the cause her own, nothing could stay her from plunging herself and all she controlled to ruin. At that moment, Agnes could hardly tell which seemed more terrible to her, the relentlessness of Ferdinand or the lawlessness of Beatrice.

Presently she heard her husband coming downstairs again, and rose with a sickening heart to meet him; but he did not glance at her as he took his hat and went to the door. She noticed that he had written a telegram and was going out to send it, and the bitterest moment of her life accompanied the realization that the last hope of saving her father's house was gone.

CHAPTER II

FERDINAND'S manner to Agnes was oddly guarded and taciturn during the days following his announcement of the sale of her mother's home. He never once referred to Beatrice's intervention, but a week later when Agnes told him she was going up to Kent to help her mother pack her things, although he did not demur to the visit, he concluded a long series of instructions about protecting herself from the cold by saying briefly, "You understand, of course, that there is to be no more intercourse between us and your cousin's family."

There was, no one to meet Agnes at the station, for her coming was unexpected, and she walked alone through the familiar streets of Kent to the home which was her mother's no longer.

When she reached it she stood still, looking at it for some moments, the only figure in the quiet street, too profoundly stirred to trust herself to enter. The day was very still and everything seemed motionless except the feathered flakes of snow which wavered down and poised irresolutely as if loath to add their ethereal weight to the already laden trees and buildings. Drifts of snow buttressed the Sidney homestead, cut through by exact and clean paths from the street to the office door and to the front door. Evergreen trees had been cut and placed against the house as usual as a protection against the cold, but little of the green could be seen beneath loads of snow and the crystal ice-casings which imprisoned what the snow could not, and which hung in transparent pendants from the tip of every bough and spine. The house itself was hooded with a mass of white whose purity and beauty would have seemed a gentle covering had it not been for the fringe of ice which hung in carved tracery from the eaves down to the chamber windows. Not a living thing was in sight. The only flowers and shrubs now to be seen through the office windows were white and delicate fronds in frost. The whole scene, beautiful and silent as it was, to Agnes was a scene of death—but death freed from decay, arrested life.

At last, she went up the steps to the office door and entered. Dr. Quinn was not in, but the slate on his open desk announced his whereabouts and time of return. Agnes walked through the two offices and the sitting-room into the downstairs bed room, where she found her mother hard at work, while Aunt Mattie, propped up in a rocking chair, was watching her. Mrs. Sidney was leaning over a half-filled wooden box, rearranging its contents to better advantage. She turned at the sound of footsteps, and then at sight of Agnes, exclaimed a welcome which her daughter instantly interpreted as an expression of relief as well as of greeting. The involuntary tone told Agnes that her mother had been suffering for her, and that she was comforted to see her daughter well and self-controlled.

Agnes went up to the kneeling figure, took Mrs. Sidney's face between her hands, looked into the clear old eyes, and then kissed her mother silently. Then she turned with a word or two of tenderness to Aunt Mattie.

Mrs. Sidney began to explain in a cheerful voice just how and where she was going to move her household goods. Agnes entered into the preparations without comment, sorted the well-remembered chest of linen, and packed it with the ample supply of blankets and patchwork quilts that bespoke her mother's New England thrift. Mrs. Sidney praised her common sense in not mourning over what could not be helped, with many fine old Biblical phrases, and with the allusion to Job's troubles and their happy period that has helped many saints in sore distress to keep their courage and their faith unbroken.

Aunt Mattie was clearly living upon a lower level, for she was heard to let fall these words after Mrs. Sidney's fervent epitome of the patriarch's story: "I suppose Job never mourned over his dead sons and daughters. He was perfectly satisfied with the new ones the Lord gave him. I'd be just as fond of those old patriarchs if they hadn't been so easily comforted with new wives, too. His old wife was a good woman."

Mrs. Sidney warned her sister-in-law of heresy, but in a more indulgent way than was her wont. Aunt Mattie was not to be judged like other people.

"Why do you hurry so with the packing, mother?" asked Agnes late in the afternoon, as they were finishing their task.

"I want to be on my own property," replied her mother decisively. "I shan't be contented till I get on Stephen's farm." Then she laid her hand for a moment on Agnes' shoulder and added gravely, "I'm glad Stephen doesn't have to bear this. These things don't mean so much to me. Did you ever notice, Agnes, that the Lord never sends trials to anyone who can't stand them?"

"There was a man who taught his horse to eat sawdust," soliloquized Aunt Mattie, "and just when the beast had learned, he died."

"You needn't be afraid of dying yet, Mattie," replied Mrs. Sidney. "Now, Agnes, we will go into the parlor and rest awhile before I get supper. Quinn has insisted upon running a big fire while I've been packing and it's nice and warm in there."

They moved in Aunt Mattie in her chair, and after they were comfortably seated Mrs. Sidney took up some sewing while she continued to controvert her sister-in-law's danger our skepticism. Agnes noted her aunt's quizzical gray eyes, and suspected that there was a kindly motive for her policy.

Suddenly Mrs. Sidney dropped her sewing in her lap and pointed to the window. "There comes Beatrice; and, yes, that's Thomas Ballington with her again. Run to the door and call them in. I want to see those two together."

Agnes rose instinctively, but hesitated, and just then the sleigh, with its tufted horses and Cossack-looking driver, turned toward the house. In its simple seat, a snug nest of furs, were Tom and Beatrice, ruddy with the cold. As they passed the house Beatrice swung back behind Tom, straining her eyes to look into Mrs. Sidney's windows. Mrs. Sidney promptly answered the look with a vigorous gesticulation summoning Beatrice to turn back and come in. Agnes saw Beatrice lean forward to speak to the driver, and then the horses turned and came to a standstill.

Agnes exchanged a glance with Mrs. Sidney, who spoke at once. "You needn't think to stop me, Agnes. The Bible says that after you've taken your friend by himself in vain, to call in another. Thomas Ballington is the one to call in."

She hurried to the door, opened it, and called out just in time to prevent the driver from starting on again with Tom: "Thomas Ballington, don't go away! I want you to come in here, too."

Beatrice laughed back at Tom over her shoulder. "Come along, Tom. Face the music." Then she ran up the steps and enveloped Mrs. Sidney in her furs. "Here he is, Aunt Kate!" she announced a moment later as Tom entered, closing the door behind him with sullen civility.

Beatrice pushed open the parlor door which Mrs. Sidney had closed to keep out the cold. Agnes rose to meet her with the memory of the scene when they had last parted in her mind. But Beatrice came in buoyantly, pulling off her cap, "to cool her head," she said. Her face, which had been contorted with passion the last time Agnes saw it, was now good humored and laughing. Her eyes were bright, her hair, roughened and matted by the cap, was damp and glossy about her face. "Hello, dear!" she cried heartily to Agnes. "Hello, Aunt Mattie!" And then she turned back again to Mrs. Sidney.

"Sit down, Beatrice," said Mrs. Sidney, taking off her glasses and wiping them. "Sit down on that cane chair, Thomas Ballington. I have called you both in here, Beatrice, to talk to you from the Lord. You are my niece and you know well that I love you, but that shan't hinder me from telling you that you are behaving like a lost woman. I don't say you are such or that you intend to be. But your ways are evil. You are young and gay and headstrong, and I think you don't know the end of the course you've entered on. You've got money and good looks and health, but these aren't going to last always. They are bound to go, and what then?"

Beatrice smiled at Mrs. Sidney, at Tom, at Agnes, at Aunt Mattie, who had succeeded in getting out of her chair alone and now hobbled painfully out of the room—but said nothing.

"What then?" repeated Mrs. Sidney sternly.

"Why, then I suppose I'll grow old, Aunt Kate," replied Beatrice, supporting her elbow on her knee, her chin on her hand, and returning her accuser's gaze with one of impregnable cheerfulness.

"And what then?"

"Then?" Beatrice gave a shrug as though apologizing for being forced to introduce an unpleasing vision. "Well, humanly speaking, I'll die."

"*And what then,*" finished Mrs. Sidney in stentorian tones.

"Why, after—"that Beatrice hesitated, but she was determined to carry this through with spirit. Accordingly, she winked at Tom. The temptation was too much for her. "After that, Aunt Kate, I expect to work, to shovel coal for a living."

Beatrice's sides were shaking as she made the answer, but this time she had miscalculated upon that sense of humor which was one of the enduring links between Mrs. Sidney and herself. The old lady's face clearly showed her disapproval and grief at the stale and ill-timed flippancy.

"You are grieving God's Holy Spirit, Beatrice," she said warningly; "you are laughing at the eternal ruin of a soul. You wouldn't have talked this way two years ago. You are getting callous. But there is worse to follow. Think of the rich man lifting up his eyes to Lazarus.”

“I’d never be as bad off as that man, Aunt Kate,” said Beatrice, reaching over to lay her hand reassuringly on Mrs. Sidney’s knee.

“Why not?” demanded Mrs. Sidney involuntarily.

“Because I’d look up and see you in Abraham’s bosom. You wouldn’t go back on an old friend who had seen better days. You’d get that drop of water down to me. Don’t I know you would, bless your heart!”

The genuine love that rang through the reckless speech strengthened Mrs. Sidney’s purpose. She turned to Tom.

“Thomas Ballington, I want you to give me your word of honor that you will use your influence with Beatrice to go back to her husband and home.”

“She’s never left her home,” sulked Tom, crimson with humiliation and eying the floor. “Besides, I haven’t any influence, if she had.”

“I don’t ask you to use any more than you have,” returned Mrs. Sidney directly. “You can get a good deal more by keeping away from Kent and going to work. You are a millstone about your brother’s neck, young man—an idler in a world that is going wrong for lack of workers.”

“I have my work,” said Tom, choking down his anger.

“What is your work then? What have you done today?”

The questions impaled the young man promptly, and he squirmed in silence.

“Thomas Ballington, what have you done today?” repeated Mrs. Sidney.

“Tom played a game of—“

“I’m not speaking to you, Beatrice.”

“I know you’re not, Aunt Kate. But I see Tom has a dumb devil, and it isn’t polite for you not to be answered. Tom played a game of checkers with me this morning, and wrote some letters this afternoon.”

“Played a game of checkers! Wrote some letters! And you call that work. That’s just punctuating idleness.”

Beatrice burst into appreciative laughter at the words. Mrs. Sidney turned to her instantly, holding up her hand.

“Don’t, Beatrice!”

The old lady’s voice had a ring of pain that subdued her guest’s levity. She continued in a lower tone.

"Beatrice, I'm not the only one who is noticing you, even if I am the only one who yearns over you enough to face you in your iniquity. You are demoralizing this town. Many things that are going on now and are winked at by good society would not have been tolerated ten years ago. You are a rich woman and a leader. The young people look to you for all the latest fashions in clothes and manners. You give liberally to the fashionable church, and, I will say, that you give liberally everywhere else, too. The point is that you've a good deal of influence and that you're using it to tear down safeguards that are already too weak to keep idle people out of mischief. You ought to be an example and a help to the hard-working and self-denying. Instead of that, you make life harder for them by scoffing at their old-fashioned virtues. Such people as you will be the ruin of this country if you can't be brought to your senses. You will destroy public morality. Besides, Beatrice, there is only one end to all this. You're not the kind to stop in time. Some day you will find yourself an outcast."

"Not as long as I give good dinners and theater parties, Aunt Kate. There are just two people in Kent whose good will can't be bought. Those two are you and me. We are a good deal alike, after all. The only difference is, you are good and I am bad."

"It isn't your money that keeps good people's doors open to you. It's Fred Sidney's name. It's an honorable name."

"Well, three cheers for Fred Sidney! I've told you a million times I've no grudge against Fred, Aunt Kate."

Then Beatrice sat up in her chair and squared her shoulders. "But see here! Who gave me my money and position in the first place? My General. We all know he wasn't any saint, but he was an easy man to live with. He lived the way he wanted to, and didn't lie about it. He wanted everybody else to have a good time, too. He left me all the money there is in our family. When I married Fred I expected him to let me provide for him. If he'd had the money he'd have thought it all right to provide for me and he'd have been mad enough if I'd insisted on keeping a kindergarten to earn my own clothes. But there he sticks in that bank, an underpaid clerk! He won't take a cent from me. We can't go off anywhere together except for two weeks in summer, when it's so hot we'd shrivel up on the way. I have to go around alone. I'd like nothing better than taking Fred with me, but he can't leave. If there was any sense in it, it would be a different matter. But it's nothing but his picayune pride. He's tying us both down here to satisfy that. My father never expected it, and I didn't expect it. Now, then, since I must stay here, I'm going to get as much pleasure out of this place as is to be gotten, and if he doesn't like it, he knows how he can stop it."

Mrs. Sidney was about to rejoin when Beatrice cut her off.

"Oh, you don't know what I've had to bear. I've lost all my moral sense lying about things in order to take care of him properly. Just last week I wanted to get him an overcoat. He ought to have furs. He wouldn't take them. Then I forgot myself. There were some hot-house berries on the table and I told him he might just as well take the coat as to be eating those. He never ate another one. Since then he has taken his luncheon downtown at that miserable temperance eating-house which can't nourish its rats—and he starves himself when he's at home." Her voice softened, she paused, then finished, "I don't want to hurt your feelings, Aunt Kate, and I'm going to leave this minute. Come along, Tom!"

She caught up her cap and gloves and put them on swiftly. She wanted to kiss Mrs. Sidney good-by, but she knew it was wiser not to delay, and she was already at the door, when Mrs. Sidney's voice held her.

Beatrice's revelations had indeed made their impression upon her aunt, but Mrs. Sidney was not to be put off from the main point under discussion.

"Beatrice Sidney," exclaimed Mrs. Sidney, rising and approaching her, "if you were my daughter, I should put you in a house of correction."

"So you would, Aunt Kate," Beatrice called back. "You're the very salt of the earth, but the Lord knew who was best for my mother. We mustn't rebel. For my part, I don't see why you shouldn't be satisfied with Agnes."

Tom strode after her with a black face. The two went out of the front door, and soon there was a jingle of bells as the sleigh drove away.

Mrs. Sidney went back to her sewing with a look of distress which pierced Agnes' heart.

"Mother," she said, going over and kneeling by her mother's chair, while she held the busy fingers still a moment, "do not bear too many burdens. Nobody can direct Beatrice."

"If I'd said the right words, Agnes," her mother responded sorrowfully, "I could have reached her. She has a good heart, but I don't know how. Stephen always did."

Agnes leaned her face against her mother's shoulder to hide the tears which she could no longer keep back. She controlled her voice carefully, however, as she replied gently, "You have more influence over Beatrice than anybody else has, mamma. I realize that every time she and I talk together. If it had been possible to influence her, you could have done it. She appreciated that it was hard for you to say what you did, and honored you for it. She knows you love her, but there's something underneath in Beatrice's nature that even you can't deal with. She is just as impregnable in her way as Ferdinand is in his."

Agnes was thinking as she spoke of the scene when Beatrice was last in Winston, of those few moments of unbridled passion when both she and Ferdinand had dropped every pretense and faced each other, each self-absorbed, irreconcilable, with invincible defiance. Again Agnes recalled with curious wonder that it had been Ferdinand whose defiance had been tinged with fear, and she felt instinctively that Beatrice was somebody whom even Ferdinand could not manage. This accounted to her now for Fred's passivity in dealing with his wife and for his own set refusals to yield to her. He, too, had hardened in his course, giving up the hope of influencing her, and she had given up persuading him.

Agnes stayed over another day with her mother, and then with a heavy heart left for home. She felt that it was her last visit to her old home, that she never would enter it again. Her mother's persistent cheerfulness was almost more than she could hear when Mrs. Sidney called after her as she went down the walk to the gate, "In the summer we'll have you all out to the farm. You tell Estelle and Stephen they shall have pigs and chickens and all the pets they want. It's a shame for children not to have pets! You can play the little organ in the country church there, too. Your grandmother used to sing there. How glad old Mr. Jewell will be! You are bringing up your children to keep the Sabbath, aren't you?"

"I'm trying to."

"That's right. Blessed is the man that keepeth the Sabbath from polluting it."

Agnes went alone to the station. There was a wind blowing, and she made her way against the unfriendly gusts with flagging steps. As she drew near the red building she saw a man with gray hair standing outside as though waiting for someone. He looked at her carelessly. Then they started toward each other with mutual surprise.

"Why, Fred, I didn't recognize you! How good this is of you! How did you get off so early?"

"Bucher let me out. There's a quarter of an hour yet. The train's behind, as usual. Let's walk out this way. Does it tire you to walk? You were coming so slowly that I didn't know you till you got right up to me. That hat makes you looked different, someway."

The cousins linked arms and paced along the platform to the little station yard. They turned into it, and Fred led the way to the iron bench in front of the empty fountain basin. They sat down and Fred asked sympathetically after his aunt.

"I left her with a smile on her face, quoting a verse from the Bible after me. She's a wonderful woman, Fred. Why can't I be like her! I can't tell you how I feel about this sale of the house." Agnes rose to her feet impetuously and started to walk away, then turned and came back again.

Fred felt a recurrence of his old rage against Ferdinand. Agnes realized it, and said, as she so often had said to herself of late, that one person must not judge another. No two think alike. Her husband was a business man, who had, as he thought, made an advantageous bargain.

Fred did not reply at once. When he did it was with an abrupt announcement. "Agnes, Bucher advises me to get a divorce from Beatrice."

She started and turned a stupefied face to his. Something dreadful must have happened to make a conservative man like Mr. Bucher advise divorce. She well knew that he would be the last man to countenance it, and that this fact, coupled with the long relation existing between him and Fred, would lend great weight to his opinion.

Hard upon her astonishment there crowded a disquieting memory. Her husband had said more than once of late that Sidney was a tame fool, otherwise he would get rid of his wife. It was a coincidence, too, that just now Ferdinand and Mr. Bucher were having business relations. But she shook off the unwelcome thought.

Fred continued with a colorless face, "I'm going to tell her tonight."

"Is this because of—Tom?"

"Yes. I went home last night and found them drinking champagne. We had a talk before he left. He promised to keep away from Kent, but he can't. You see she should have married him, not me. It has taken me a long time to see through that. There is nothing for me but just to cut loose—is there?"

He put the question with anguish. Agnes well knew that the deepest tragedy of life never comes in earthquake or fire, but in the horror of great darkness, where a man may lie down and die beside his own doorstep, thinking himself a thousand miles off on the plain. Was the world all gone wrong? Had they made some fatal error in their own conduct? Could they, perchance, have touched the right springs of action—he in the wife, she in the husband? Could it be possible that if they only put out their hands in the right direction now, they could touch the portal of safety and happiness?

Fred waited a moment, and then repeated the question.

Agnes turned to him, leaning forward as she said with one of her old restless gestures: "I shouldn't do it, Fred. Remember it was for better or for worse! and she never loved Tom. Don't allow that thought to stay in your mind. She did love you. Bucher is wrong. Somebody—something has misled him. This isn't love that Tom and Beatrice have for each other. It is a kind of possession. They both want something else."

Her face kindled. She struck her hand forcibly on the arm of the bench and her voice had a ring of courage as she continued quickly, "There is splendid stuff in both of them. You can't give up. Try to compromise. Take all you can that she gives you, and love her for it. You have been too proud. She has a right to do for you. In time, she will come to see that she must give up some things, too. Don't talk to Bucher. Talk to her. Come! Bucher and you and I have no sort of backbone. Look at my mother. That is the way to face life."

Fred looked at her with a spark in his eyes. It died out in a moment, however, but his face brightened. They both looked more like themselves, and involuntarily their minds reverted to their old life together. Agnes felt a recurrent rush of the old delicious faith in the world with God in His Heaven over it all. She smiled at Fred with sudden brilliancy.

"That is the way to face life," she repeated, "to settle every little question as it comes up with good-will and finality. Treat little things wisely as though they were serious and large. Let others have their rights in the little things, too. You haven't given Beatrice hers. You ask her to give her life to you and you won't take her money. If you take the real thing why not take its symbol? Oh, Fred, it's wrong to refuse to share with her because you're a man. It's as wrong as—" She checked herself, then continued in a different tone, "My father and mother were co-workers. Each lived according to his own conscience, and when they did not agree they came to a mutual understanding of how much each must give up. You want Beatrice to meet you spiritually. Show her that you are willing to meet her where she craves union. Take your good things together. Make your sacrifices together. Your money and your travels and your work will be the accompaniments of a spiritual union."

"Agnes," said her cousin, "you make me feel like old times. I feel as though we only had to look up to see Uncle Stephen drive old Peggy up to the platform. Some good people have lived after all. It ought to count when a poor cuss does as well as he can, even if it is pretty poor." He stopped, then made a motion as if to speak and stopped again. Presently the words came: "It's hard for me to do it, but I will try to follow your advice and see what comes of it."

A whistle announced the approaching train and a rumble and clanging bell jarred the air around them.

They rose and went over to the cars. "If you yield some and talk only to her, I think she will yield, too," said Agnes urgently.

When the train rolled out Fred stood watching it out of sight. Then, with new endurance in his heart, he turned and walked home.

CHAPTER III

MRS. SIDNEY stood by her bedroom window and looked out into the back garden. It was eleven o'clock of the last night that she was to stay in the home to which the doctor had brought her a bride forty-five years before. The house itself had changed but little, but she remembered, as she looked out, how bare the garden had been when they first came. He and she together had planted the trees, the grapevines, and the rose bushes. The one tall poplar that now overtopped all the other trees Stephen had stuck in the ground as a mere whip once when they returned from a country ride. He was lying now out there to the west, past the spires of the Catholic church. Further to the west, her baby was mistress of a home of her own, and way on beyond where the land grew level Helen was waiting out her lonely pilgrimage. Upstairs Aunt Mattie was asleep in a cot. In the office, Dr. Quinn was patiently at work on his accounts.

Mrs. Sidney turned away from the window and knelt down by her bed. She waited there for a long time for prayer to come, as she had waited night after night previously, but at last, she pulled her heavy body up again, took up the lamp, and went out to the office. When she opened the office door Dr. Quinn turned in his chair. She started as she saw him.

"Is there anything the matter?" he asked in friendly apprehension.

"No, Quinn, I started to come in here to speak to you, but just as I turned the knob of the door I thought I was going to see Stephen here at his desk. I guess I haven't been sleeping enough."

He knew this, and he asked with half the physician's and half the friend's gentleness, "Can I do anything for you?"

"Yes, Quinn. I can't seem to get hold of myself. I have been trying to have family prayers. Stephen and I had prayers together the first night we passed in this house. Perhaps if you should come in and sit with me a little while I might come to."

Dr. Quinn shoved away his books and followed her into the sitting-room. They sat down by the table, and after a little while the old lady said, "What do you think is the 'secret place' of the Most High, Quinn? I've been saying that over and over to myself, 'He that dwelleth in the secret place of the Most High shall abide under the shadow of the Almighty.'"

The doctor opened the big Bible that lay in its accustomed place on the table, and after some searching found the passage he desired and turned the book toward her.

But Mrs. Sidney made a little motion for him to keep it. "You read," she said, "and then perhaps I can pray." And she leaned back in her chair and let her eyes close.

Dr. Quinn watched her for a few moments. He felt an involuntary inclination to reach out for her wrist. But as she presently opened her eyes enough to question him with them, he turned back to the book and began to read. He was slow of speech, but one could see in his reading the mind moving along with the words, like the finger of a child, from line to line. Tonight Mrs. Sidney's mind moved laboriously, too, so that she was glad to sit still with her eyes shut and have time to think what each word meant.

And the doctor read, choosing his passages:

"He bowed the heavens, and came down; and darkness was under his feet. *He made darkness his secret place*; his pavilion round about him was dark waters and thick clouds of the sky."

"I will lift up mine eyes to the hills, from whence cometh my help. My help cometh from the Lord, which made heaven and earth. He will not suffer thy foot to be moved: he that keepeth thee shall not slumber. Behold, he that keepeth thee shall neither slumber nor sleep."

"Like as a father pitieth his children, so the Lord pitieth them that fear him. For he knoweth our frame; he remembereth that we are dust."

Mrs. Sidney opened her eyes when he had done, and they both knelt down. Dr. Quinn was still thinking from the look of his friend that she was a little confused in mind and mistook him for her husband, but as soon as she began to speak, he knew that her mind was clear.

She began with the Lord's Prayer, saying the words in a full, clear voice, whose meaning was such that the doctor felt he never had known the words before.

He knew that she would go on presently, and so he waited until she did.

"I have come back, O Lord, and I am ready to stay and work in Thy vineyard as long as it is Thy will. I am not afraid any longer. I will dwell in the secret place of the Most High. O God, cover with the shadow of the Almighty my two little girls. They are Thy own children. We gave them to Thee when they were born. I put it to Thee, O Lord, to take care of them. And bless this young man who is to take Stephen's place here. Fix him like a nail in a sure place. And now I lay me down in peace to sleep, for Thou, Lord, makest me, to dwell in safety."

Dr. Quinn helped her to rise, and they stood for a moment facing each other, she with her hands on his shoulders. He saw that it was well with her in her heart, and he did not say what he had wanted to about his own inability to buy the house.

"I trust you, Quinn," she said, giving him a mother's smile. "You will keep up the doctor's name here. God has been very good to send you here."

He stooped and kissed her, and she knew that he understood all that she meant, and, if he had been a man who could talk, that he would have answered.

Then they spoke about some little duties that were left between them, the bandages she had made for him out of the old sheets, the doctor's clothes she had given him, the use of the books. She brought him some milk to drink, and then they said good-night.

Dr. Quinn went back to his books and finished the task he had set himself, but before he lay down to sleep in the back office he walked softly to the door of Mrs. Sidney's room, which was left ajar. He heard her regular breathing and knew that her soul was satisfied and the weary body at rest.

CHAPTER IV

AFTER Mrs. Sidney left her home and settled on the Sidney farm some fifteen miles out of Kent, Agnes did not go to see her mother.

Mrs. Sidney had been there a fortnight when the Mabies arrived to make their permanent home with her. Pleasant had at last exhausted all the devices for losing money his fertile brain could hit upon, and Mrs. Sidney as a creditor was clothed with more authority than she had been able to wield as a mere mother-in-law. Helen broke up housekeeping simultaneously with her mother, and the bitterness of her grief was incalculably augmented by the thought that Pleasant had been responsible for the loss of both homes.

When Ferdinand learned that the Mabies were coming, he experienced the disagreeable sensation of the general who thinks he has captured his opponent's position, only to find he has taken but the outer entrenchments. The opposing general, meantime, has withdrawn into his stronghold, massed his forces, and, being well-provisioned for an indefinite siege, indifferently refuses to consider terms. Ferdinand had expected to arrange Mrs. Sidney's future sensibly for her, and to be able at last to dictate his shiftless brother-in-law's method of life. He had upon several occasions tried to obtain possession of the little farm, and, failing that, had watched it run down with philosophic approval. It had seemed to him an impossible refuge for his mother-in-law. He would not acknowledge to himself the irritation he felt when Mrs. Sidney turned her sturdy back upon him and gathered the prodigal Pleasant with his inexcusably large family under her own roof. Ferdinand's chagrin was not at all lessened by a shrewd suspicion that he never again would be able to get a finger into his mother-in-law's affairs. Pleasant was doomed to walk in Mrs. Sidney's ways, and the whole family would continue to live in that self-willed and wasteful manner from which he had been able to rescue only Agnes.

It was with a grudging but uncontrollable curiosity to see how they got along that he suggested one day to Agnes that they should go down to see her mother and greet the Mabies. To his surprise Agnes quietly declined; and when he expostulated with her upon not being filial and sisterly, her clear look made him awkwardly conscious that she knew all that was in his mind, and thought it beneath him. Nevertheless he went alone, and apologized with undiscouraged civility to his mother-in-law for Agnes' failure to accompany him, on the ground that she was not able to make the journey.

He was caught and made resentful by a satirical twinkle in Aunt Mattie's eyes, which bore a disagreeable resemblance in an aggravated form to the penetration of his wife's expression before he left home. Ferdinand was so incensed at the latent sagacity of this crippled old cumberer of the earth that he took occasion later, when all the heterogeneous family were present, to remark casually, "I suppose your sister-in-law expects to make her home during the large proportion of the year with her own relatives? The house seems small for so large a family."

That remark proved to be the turning-point of Pleasant Mabie's career.

Pleasant was just ripe for this turning-point, too, because of certain influences which had been working upon him quietly for some weeks past. Upon his arrival at the farm where he had found in Aunt Mattie one more helpless than himself, the instinct which in the past had led him to buy up and take care of all the sick and disabled animals he could get hold of took a new direction. This was fortified by a brow-beaten remorse for his own responsibility in the family disasters which in secret had preyed upon his soul ever since he had received a letter from Ferdinand earlier in the winter. The two emotions combined to rouse him to a humble and pitifully dogged effort to take as much of the burden as he could carry from the women of the household.

This letter of Ferdinand's had contained a full and detailed summary of all Pleasant's business career, and had closed with a scathing analysis of the methods which a man of so hopelessly futile a character as Pleasant's ought to pursue at once in order to make as little trouble as possible for the future. Ferdinand had pointed out to Pleasant that he never again must think of doing anything whatever unless some superior mind advised him. In conclusion, the writer stated indifferently that in consideration of his wife's relationship to Helen Mabie he himself would consent to take the burden of Pleasant's guardianship from now on.

The humiliation and resentment which this letter had caused Pleasant, along with the letter itself, had been carefully concealed from even his wife. He had destroyed the letter as soon as he had read it, and he had relieved his mind many times since by composing grandiloquent answers which even he could not help realizing would cause only amusement, and which he accordingly tore up regularly twenty-four hours after they were written.

Upon this hopeless and weakly desperate mood Aunt Mattie had acted with unexpected stimulus. The spring of pity and incongruous joy which welled up in the able-bodied but shuffling man when he first realized Aunt Mattie's condition created an oasis in the desert of life. He established himself at once as a kind of lady's-maid to the cripple, and Mrs. Sidney acknowledged before he had been twenty-four hours on the farm that Pleasant saved more steps than an invalid-chair would have done. He carried Aunt Mattie up and down stairs, saw that she had an airing regularly, and had her on his mind from the time that he awoke until he went to sleep.

At first Aunt Mattie had been harassed and humiliated by these unremitting attentions from a man to whom she always had felt an instinctive antipathy, but her canny mind soon saw that here was an opportunity, not indeed such as she would have chosen, to establish a beneficent despotism over Helen's invertebrate husband. To this end she feigned a dependence she was far from feeling, and it was out of consideration for this that Pleasant's quixotic chivalry considered itself bound to carry out all her suggestions. Thus already, before Ferdinand's visit, Aunt Mattie had managed to supply Pleasant's willing energies with brains.

The unexpected turn of affairs had filled Mrs. Sidney and Helen at first with incredulity, then with relief and thankfulness; while Aunt Mattie, for her part, and to her own surprise, was experiencing the first eagerness and interest in life she had known for years. She was finding a grim pleasure in mortifying her spirit by managing Pleasant, and a gentler pleasure in becoming the boon-companion of the children. Kitty read to her. Dan laid all sorts of objects at her feet and listened enthralled while she discoursed to him about them. Each of the small children, too, found in the laconic, humorous cripple some phase of intimate companionship. Thus, much to the surprise of everybody concerned, the center of gravity of the household seemed actually shifting and promised in time to adjust the weight somewhat evenly between Helen and Mrs. Sidney and Pleasant and Aunt Mattie.

It was just as the dawn of this new possibility was becoming apparent that Ferdinand made his call and very unexpectedly witnessed the full sunrise of the new era for Pleasant. Nay, he even acted as the Apollo who guided the chariot of the ascending luminary above the horizon.

When he made his carefully calculated remark about the smallness of the house, with the accompanying supposition that Aunt Mattie probably intended to live elsewhere, a sudden change was visible in Pleasant Mabie. The universally addressed apology which had been apparent in the droop of every dejected muscle of his frame for weeks past disappeared. His mild and plaintive voice took on a ring which startled Mrs. Sidney so much that she put on her glasses to look at him.

"If this house is too small, my boys can sleep out in the barn with me, and we will, from now on. We're the ones to get out. I allow I'm not a shining success in life, but I ain't got down yet to turning women out of doors because they're old and crippled and only related to me by marriage."

There was a dead silence after this unequivocal speech.

At last, Pleasant had succeeded in giving expression to the meaning of the grandiloquent letters to Ferdinand which an instinct of true literary criticism had forbidden him to send. He was conscious even as he spoke of the difference between the literary style and the vernacular, and he regretted bitterly the lack of dignity and impressiveness which necessary haste demanded. If he only could have remembered those few good sentences which in calmer moments he had been able to cull out of the diffuse body of his late literary labors! The consciousness that he was not fully rising to the opportunity Fate had granted him made him much more uncompromising in facial expression and bodily demeanor than he otherwise would have been, and so, all innocently, he demonstrated the true value of rhetorical composition. He was perfectly clear upon what he wanted to say and had gone over all the ways in which it ought not to be said. At last, what he had been toiling to draw out suddenly burst forth of its own accord, rampant, unattended by the rosy graces and the flying hours.

Helen heard and flushed, then turned white. Mrs. Sidney stared as though Pleasant had become a specter. Aunt Mattie was carefully measuring the distance between her chair and the door, deliberating whether she could make it alone or not. Pleasant instantly rose, with a flourish of fury and loathing in Ferdinand's direction, and said with genuine solicitude to the cripple, "Come out into the kitchen, Aunt Mattie. You can stir the samp while I'm setting the table."

Mrs. Sidney made a motion as if to rise, but Helen stopped her with a sign, and Pleasant and Aunt Mattie made their exit in state, closing the door after them.

Shortly after this untoward interruption, Ferdinand brought his call to an end and left the house to return home.

It was with a feeling of intense dissatisfaction that he turned to give a last look at the dilapidated place as he drove away. Kitty Mabie stood in the doorway looking after him. The only emotion apparent on her face was one of curiosity at his spring coat. She regarded him no more than she would have any other stranger who had made a passing call. Her straight young figure was disagreeably suggestive of a reincarnation of her grandmother, and Ferdinand's last impression as he went around the curve of the road was one of family defiance which would one day be younger and stronger than he was. As he passed through Kent, Ferdinand told the driver to take him by Agnes' old home. This, at least, he had been able to dispose of to the advantage of the unthankful.

As he neared the place, he at first failed to recognize it. The new occupant had painted it, taken away the fence, and built on a wide veranda. The blinds had not been rehung. The evergreen which had banked the house had disappeared. Ferdinand noticed these changes with approval.

As he was about to continue on his way he was startled by the appearance of the next house. He cast a bewildered look about him to get his bearings, thinking he had made a mistake in locating Agnes' old home. He had made no mistake—Malthus' sign over the door was proof of that—and yet right alongside, just across the alley, stood what seemed to be an apparition of Dr. Sidney's old home, with all its familiar features unchanged. It was as though, with the arrival of Malthus' veneered personality, the spirit of the Sidney home had gone over to the next house, taking the external characteristics of its accustomed abiding place with it. There were the Sidney evergreens thriftily stacked in a corner of the yard, there were the old Sidney blinds. Ferdinand noted with chagrin the similarity in shape of the two houses, while, to complete the resemblance, Dr. Sidney's original sign was hung out on the wing corresponding to the office of the old house. Under Dr. Sidney's name, in modest letters, he read the legend:

Marcus Quinn.

It was several seconds before Ferdinand realized what had taken place. An old-fashioned buggy, drawn by a familiar horse and driven by a familiar figure, at this moment drove up before the gate and hastened in him the discovery that Quinn had merely moved into the next house, taking all the doctor's prestige with him along with the evergreens and blinds and horse and buggy. As he looked more sharply at the stolid figure sitting in the buggy an unpleasant sensation of recognition was aroused by the sight of an appreciative grin upon a face which he now knew to be that of Quinn himself.

Quinn ducked his head, and then began to climb heavily over the wheels of the buggy. Ferdinand touched his hat, and sharply ordered his driver to start on.

As he passed Quinn the possibility of the doctor's purchasing this new but unmistakable Sidney home flashed upon him. His incorrigible mother-in-law and her insane and pig headed accomplice, Quinn, could not be broken in. After all he had done they still managed to get the better of him. Ferdinand, who calculated not on sentiment, was unaware of the loss and grief weighing down the hearts of those who loved every timber of the old house, and who found the new one but a dreary substitute.

Ferdinand looked at his watch and hurried up the driver. He had another call to make before going to the station, and his time was short. He was in a bitterly discontented frame of mind.

As he passed the bank, and, looking in, caught sight of Fred Sidney's bent head, it reminded him of another annoying thing. He no longer heard any talk of Fred's getting a divorce from Beatrice. Ferdinand did not acknowledge to himself that there was any malice in his desire to have the separation go through. He would have been incensed at anyone's daring to suggest that he had desired and sought to bring about so unequivocal an acknowledgment from Fred Sidney that his marriage had been a mistake, or that he would have been still more glad to humiliate and socially ostracize Beatrice Sidney. He had not asked himself why he had been so ill-humored at his wife's and Donald's persevering efforts to break up the relation between Beatrice and Tom, nor why this ill-humor had deepened into settled irritation at Tom's interrupted but on the whole growing attempts to get back again into business habits.

"Is it up this street, sir?" asked the driver, who was unacquainted in Kent.

Ferdinand roused himself to answer in the affirmative, and, as his eye caught sight of the Bucher residence a little up the side street into which the carriage was turning, his thoughts took a new and pleasanter direction. He spoke amiably to the driver as he left the carriage and turned toward the old-fashioned mansion. "There's a livery three blocks to the left. Go down and wait there for a half hour." Then he opened the wicket-gate and went in.

Ferdinand's call upon Mr. Bucher was ostensibly a business one, merely one of the periodic conferences which had been taking place for some time between them.

The long acquaintanceship between the two families had become a personal relation between Ferdinand and the banker ever since the former had begun to lend the bank money. This relation dated from the time when Ferdinand relieved Bucher of Mrs. Sidney's home. Ferdinand's surface amiability, which he not uncommonly employed in financial dealings with outsiders whose prospects for the long run were good, was in Bucher's case colored not only by far-sighted policy, but by personal motives into which even he himself never inquired too curiously. From the first, he had measured his man, and he took with the Kent banker an exactly opposite method from that by which he had hastened Balch's ruin in Winston. He had advanced Bucher small sums of money upon several occasion, taking desirable security, and he had shown such patience and consideration as a creditor that Mr. Bucher never could be convinced that the rumors of Ferdinand's severity with Mrs. Sidney were true. There must have been something behind it all, he said.

The crisis of the old gentleman's obligation to Ferdinand had occurred recently, and it was one which had descended upon him so suddenly that he hardly realized the danger he had met and passed till it was over and he found himself practically in Ferdinand Ballington's control. Ever since the marriage of Beatrice Mott to Fred Sidney, the Kent bank had had the use of a share of the Mott wealth. Dealings had commenced with the General himself and had been continued by Beatrice. It struck dismay to the anxious banker when some weeks before, following the sale of Mrs. Sidney's home, Beatrice Sidney, with much talk, direct and indirect, had withdrawn the Mott funds from Bucher's bank. The blow, coming as it did at a time of financial depression, would have put an end not only to Fred's clerkship but to Bucher's business existence, had not relief providentially been sent from an unexpected quarter. No less a friend than Mrs. Sidney's much-defamed son-in law came to Bucher's assistance and saved the bank from going under. "I would not be disturbed by anything Sidney's wife can say," Ferdinand remarked reassuringly to the worried and conscience-stung old friend of Dr. Sidney's. "She's going the same way her father did."

Ferdinand would not have allowed himself the indulgence of foiling Beatrice had he not thought himself financially safe in his venture; but of this he was assured. Bucher was getting old and he had his hands on a good deal of very desirable property, which might just as well pass into Ballington control as into a stranger's. Ferdinand consequently had permitted himself to carry over the harassed banker, and during the process, he had obtained a marked ascendency over the older man's mind. The good but obtuse German, who through his prime had unconsciously been guided by his friend and neighbor, Dr. Sidney, now as unconsciously fell under the influence of his old friend's son-in-law. How much financial dependence aided in the banker's failure to read Ferdinand he was himself unaware. He was loaded down with anxieties, first among which were his unmarried daughter and the large family of growing children left him by his second wife, and after them the hard-working Kent men and women who had trusted him with their savings.

As Ferdinand entered, the banker rose, coughing, from a lounge drawn up before the fire and came forward to greet his visitor.

Mary Bucher, who sat sewing near her father, also rose and quietly left the room. She never remained when Ferdinand called, and he not infrequently had felt dimly that the mild and motherly girl who managed the banker's home was as instinctively distrustful of him as her father was instinctively subservient.

"I have been out to the farm to see Mrs. Sidney," said Ferdinand, accepting the banker's invitation to sit by the grate, "and I had a half hour to put in before returning to Winston."

The tone of domestic intimacy gratified Mr. Bucher, and he responded by encouraging his guest's confidence. There was some talk of the family on the farm, then of Fred Sidney, and at last, as was usual, of Beatrice.

At mention of her name, the banker's face clouded. He never had approved wholly of Beatrice or of his daughter's friendship with her. He had been surprised at her engagement to Fred Sidney, and never knew that his repugnance to the marriage was partly because he, like Mrs. Sidney, had drifted into the conclusion that some time his own daughter Mary would marry Dr. Sidney's nephew. He had seen and feared Beatrice's social influence in Kent, and had known better than anyone else, what Fred had suffered in his home. His German sense of what was a woman's duty in life had long been violated by the way in which Beatrice Sidney conducted herself, and lastly there was his perturbed consciousness of the lawless woman's open defiance and injury of himself. It was with real apprehension for Fred, as well as with a subconscious recognition of righteous retribution coming upon Beatrice, that he listened to some new disclosures which Ferdinand now made.

When the half hour was up, Ferdinand left the house with a feeling of satisfaction. He knew from the banker's face what was in his mind, and he was reasonably certain that any new indiscretion on the part of Beatrice would decide Fred's employer to advise and once more set forward the divorce which Sidney himself so weak-mindedly had let lie.

He arrived at the station just in time for the train and made his way home without incident.

CHAPTER V

THE grudgingly told news which her husband brought back from the farm convinced Agnes better than any willing account would have done that Ferdinand's plans for her mother's and sister's families had miscarried. A feeling of hope and returning energy was born in her with the realization that the family fortunes had touched their lowest point and were beginning to rise. Her relief assisted her to make a determined effort herself to fight against the despair of her own situation. She refused to succumb to her growing physical disability, and even made its enforced leisure tributary to her mental development. She had been writing for some time and had been undiscouraged in her attempts to gain recognition. It had seemed, too, like a confirmation of the legitimacy of her desires that this winter for the first time bits of verse and one or two prose articles had been published in the magazines and were winning favorable comment. The letters from her mother and sister were regular and hopeful. Miriam, who was in Paris studying, was sending a weekly budget of stimulating comment upon men and events in the French capital.

This contact with the larger current of life kept Agnes from brooding too much upon her individual eddy. Impersonal rumors of war, of international jealousy, of diplomatic intrigue, that appeared in the newspapers took on a vivid and dramatic interest at the touch of Miriam's pen. She had met this German prince and that French diplomat at a soirée which came off after the long secret interview where they had decided the fate of an oriental kingdom, and she told in her whimsical way how all the company were agog to read in the inscrutable social masks which the famous men put on with their decorations, which of them had been worsted, or if it were true that a challenge had been offered and accepted during the heat of the interview. On the margin or at the head of a page might be a sketch of the unofficial Papal legate, whose fixed smile and drooping eyes proclaimed more eloquently than words the Papal attitude toward the republic. In close juxtaposition to the diaphanous Italian would stolidly stand the sluggish, fat, fez-topped inertia of the last Turkish envoy-extraordinary sent over to beg off for burning some French consular establishment anywhere between the Red Sea and

Macedonia. There were apologetic criticisms of the last opera and the last play, and dogmatic assertions about the salon pictures and statues. All this served to keep so much of the full-resounding roar of the great world constantly in Agnes' ears that she was able to submerge the insistent throbbing of her own single string in the great sea of sound.

But there came hours in the silence of the night when the great world seemed swinging far off in space around its prescribed orbit while she was but a wandering fragment belonging to no world—lost in chaos. Strive as she might to lose the consciousness of herself in the care for others, she could not keep out of her mind her spiritual loneliness and that ever present question: "Am I winning or am I failing?"

Except in the night, however, Agnes did not have much leisure to search her own soul. In one direction her forebodings had been fully realized. She was kept constantly occupied making intercourse possible between her husband and their children. Ferdinand's inability to realize the immaturity of mind and disposition in the children made him cruelly harsh in his treatment of them. His rules were so many, and the infringement of them consequently so inevitable, and Estelle and Stephen lived in a kind of peon age, slaves to a constantly renewed penalty. Then, too, much as she loved Aunt Margaret, the latter's furtive and well-meant indulgences often forcibly recalled to Agnes' mind Estelle Landseer's solution of her similar dilemma. Ferdinand's mother had taken her child and gone away for a time. Unfortunately, no such course was open to Agnes.

In one respect, however, Agnes' personal endeavor seemed slowly tending toward success. In conjunction with Donald, she was encouraging Tom's wavering alienation from Beatrice. She could not work upon Beatrice directly on account of Ferdinand's command that there should be no intercourse between the families, and even Tom she could not see as often as she wished because of Ferdinand's and his mutual dislike. Donald she saw often, and the seriousness of their common object sometimes made her ignore and sometimes blinded her to her husband's cynical toleration of his business partner's visits. It had been a great relief to her that Fred had tacitly dropped the subject of divorce, for she realized that time seemed to promise everything now. She began to look back with increasing hope to that early conversation she as a girl had with Beatrice, wherein she had been convinced of the latter's affection for Fred.

As spring advanced, the willows bordering the lake slowly brightened into yellow flame. A green mist gathered about the gray branches of the trees, and the air grew balmy. Agnes spent much time out of doors with her children. She never had been so poignantly grateful for the spring, and day after day the little group traced the almost imperceptible arrival of the flowers and foliage and birds. These were the friends Agnes was teaching her children to live with. Each day they eagerly brought her new blossoms, and, every night before she put them to bed, they lingered long at the nursery window watching the home-coming of the birds through the lengthening twilight. A pair of robins had made their nest in the poplar tree outside. A shy catbird lived somewhere in the garden shrubbery, but they never had been able to find its nest. Under the eaves of the old barn dwelt a colony of swallows. Stephen knew the robins and swallows, and Estelle could recognize them all on the wing, and while they watched for the dark flitting spots coming swiftly homeward through the sunlit air of evening, their mother told them of the wooing and loyalty of the little aerial families.

It seemed to Agnes that her emotions were more and more withdrawing themselves from the social world, and that she was drifting, with her children, into a life where the sweet and kindly instincts of nature ruled with wise harmony. But one day, late in May, a shock precipitated her back into the chaos created by human passion. A messenger boy brought her the following letter from Fred Sidney:

MY DEAR COUSIN:
At our last meeting I promised to tell you before I committed myself irrevocably to the course of breaking up my home. Accordingly this is to acquaint you with my decision before I put it into execution. It is impossible any longer for me to ignore my plain duty. Bucher advised me some months ago, as I told you, to arrange a divorce, although he believes that divorce should be a last resort.

It seemed to me during the past weeks as though my wife were trying to put up with me and the bank, but an interview I had with her last night put an end to hope of compromise.

I had a talk with Bucher yesterday afternoon, which was occasioned by Tom's visit down here last Sunday, and he very reluctantly told me something which confirmed what I had heard before, but had forced myself to disbelieve. Bucher said he had proof that Tom and Beatrice were originally engaged, and he told me what had broken it off. I don't believe the latter, nor do I trust the source from which I believe it came to him, but it was something that may become true any day if I do not give my unhappy and desperate wife the release which she craves.

Beatrice has told me in the past that she wished she had married Tom. I went home and asked her if she would seriously make that statement, or if she would retract it. She became angry, said that she would not retract it, and, more than that, that the next time she would say it in a way I could not misunderstand. I then told her that I would relieve her from that necessity by getting out of her way—in other words, by "deserting her." When I said this, she insulted me by telling me that I might as well speak out plainly and say that I wanted to marry Mary Bucher. Nothing that I could say diverted her from this interpretation of my motive, and I can only conclude that she put it forward as a pretext to further our alienation.

I left my wife's house yesterday and am now leaving town.

Do not imagine that my own affairs keep me from thinking often of you. I hope you are well and brave, and that some time in after years when we have fought our struggle to the end and have forgotten somewhat its agony we shall, doubtless, talk life over and find that it means something good after all.

I haven't worried Aunt Kate with my matters.
Your affectionate cousin,
FRED SIDNEY.

As she dropped the letter in her lap Agnes realized with terror that hours had elapsed since Fred wrote it and that Beatrice's passionate nature would be likely to have expressed itself at once in some reckless and irrevocable deed. Her instant thought was to get to Beatrice to make her wait. She realized at once with a woman's instinct the hurt pride and furious disappointment which lay behind Beatrice's taunt. She knew, too, as Fred did not, although

Beatrice did, that Mary Bucher had loved him. She was dismayed at this talk of Beatrice's long love for Tom, and wondered at Fred's confirmed blindness.

Much as she wanted to see Beatrice she was not able to make the hurried trip to Kent, and after a moment's hesitation she decided to get Beatrice to come to her. She knew that it would be no easy task to overcome Beatrice's objection to re-enter Ferdinand's house, and she also knew that Ferdinand would attempt to turn her out if he should find her there. But too much was at stake not to risk embarrassing consequences.

Agnes went to the telephone, asked to be connected with Kent, and waited in an agony of suspense after ringing up Beatrice. If she were not in her home, where would she be? Agnes' heart went out to her cousin's wife, who, with all her money, was alone in the world. Mrs. Sidney was no longer in Kent, and she well knew that Beatrice's proud spirit would seek counsel or sympathy from nobody else.

Agnes' heart was beating so as almost to suffocate her when she heard at length Beatrice's well-known voice. She was evidently calling to someone in her own hall. Agnes heard her say, "No, no, not that one. My suit-case, the tan suit-case. It's all packed."

A moment later there was a sharp and stern "Hello" through the receiver. It was followed by an ominous silence when Beatrice learned who was speaking to her. Then came the laconic question, "Well, what can I do for you?"

Agnes' voice trembled, but she answered at once: "You remember the last time you were here you told me to come to you if I was in trouble. I am in very great trouble. I cannot get to my mother and I want you to come to me at once. You must not refuse me this. It's a life-and-death matter. I'm not able to come to you or I would. You can just catch the next train."

She paused and held her breath for the answer.

There was a wait; then the same laconic voice inquired, "Are you sure it's me you want?"

"Yes. You have just time to get the train."

There was another pause.

"All right. I'll get it," came the answer, and there was the clang of the receiver hung up.

With a revulsion of feeling almost too great to endure, Agnes left the telephone, ordered the carriage to meet the train upon its arrival, sent Miss Margaret out for the afternoon, and then dispatched a note to Donald, telling him to detain Ferdinand at the office until six o'clock that afternoon. Then she composed herself to wait as best she could.

An hour later the doorbell rang. Agnes answered it herself, although she knew it was too soon for Beatrice. Strange things of all kinds were ready to happen. This would be one. It was a note from Donald, and a few sentences, simple as they were, made her feel that his anxiety was as active as her own.

Ferdinand will be detained tonight by a necessary inspection of the shops. Crowell was hurt today. Tom quit work before noon. He has been strange all yesterday and today. There is a telegram from Kent waiting for him at the office now.

D.

Agnes read the letter twice, then burned it. A new fear leaped into her mind as she put together Beatrice's remark about the packed suit-case and the waiting telegram to Tom. What did it mean? Would Beatrice really come to her at Winston as she had promised? Where was Tom?

A moment later she rang up the shops and tried to speak to Donald, but learned that both he and her husband were with the mortally injured Crowell.

Agnes went back to her watching, wondering what would happen next. It seemed as though her preternaturally active mind might have prophesied poor Crowell's disaster before the news had reached her. The minutes at length brought round the hour when Beatrice should arrive. Still Agnes looked through the green-room window minute by minute for an hour over time. She would have given up hope of Beatrice's coming had it not been for the fact that the carriage had not returned. That meant that the train was late. Oh, why should it be late today of all days!

Suddenly the telephone rang furiously. Agnes answered it, and Donald's voice, clear and low, spoke to her. "The gentleman has just left for home. It was impossible to keep him longer. I must find Tom."

Agnes hung up the receiver and leaned against the wall to steady herself. In twenty minutes Ferdinand would be there.

At the instant of this realization she heard the sound of the returning carriage. She hurried to the door, threw it open, and saw Beatrice coming up the steps. An overpowering relief and gratitude to the loyal friend surged over Agnes. Her fears had been groundless, she thought, but a moment later they came back augmented. Beatrice kissed her feverishly, and her first words were a strange mingling of tenderness and excitement.

"I can stay here only twenty-five minutes, Agnes. I have to get the next train. Be quick and tell me what has happened."

An intuition flashed like lightning upon Agnes with the words. "She has already seen Tom somewhere on her way to the house," she thought.

CHAPTER VI

AGNES reached around Beatrice and closed-the door. "You were good to come," she said twice, not with nervousness, but with a kind of solemnity. Then she pushed open the door of the green room and motioned Beatrice in.

They looked at each other silently, both standing. During the journey, Beatrice had run over many possible situations in her mind, but they all pointed to the conclusion that Agnes had determined to leave Ferdinand, and she now scrutinized Agnes with a sharpness which haste rendered unequivocal. Agnes, on her side, returned the searching look, and she found herself even more moved than she had expected to be by Beatrice's appearance. Beatrice's face was pale, haggard, grim, and an uncontrollable anxiety showed in every movement. Agnes felt distinctly that her cousin's wife was at her wits' ends and ready to do any reckless thing which might come into her head. The girl-fondness she had felt for Beatrice, the long and silent gratitude she had given her mother's friend, and the late womanly sympathy which she had repressed with difficulty, came over her now, together. Emphasizing all these was the look she saw growing in Beatrice's eyes. Agnes wished to take this friendless woman to her heart while she pled with her, and now she saw in Beatrice's eyes the same maternal yearning encircling herself— a yearning so unwonted there, that Agnes, her faculties on edge by reason of the graveness of the situation, thought the look incongruous, even grotesque. A quick reaction, however, softened her heart with pity for Beatrice, for herself, for all poor failures, made not by crime but by lack of vision. It was some moments before either of them spoke. Then Beatrice wiped her eyes, turned resolutely to the lounge, sat down and reached instinctively for her chatelaine. She thought she knew why she was there, and she was valiantly endeavoring to collect her faculties and bear the brunt of that conversation to which she had been summoned.

"I knew it would come some time, Agnes," she said, unclasping the network of gold that hung from her girdle. "It's better over with. I wish to God it had come before. Things might—but perhaps it is just as well. Sit down, dearest. How many you have left who really love you. There's your mother and your sister and your aunt—" She halted, then went on. "There's Fred, too.

He thinks the world of you. Now listen. I've got everything all planned. I want you to go right to my house and stay with Fred. Here are the keys." She pressed the ring of keys into Agnes' hand with the unconscious whole-heartedness which characterized her whenever she was giving.

Agnes saw in her face a kind of fierce comfort which softened temporarily its reckless expression. The thought that Beatrice with entire self-forgetfulness was feeling a happiness because she was able to help Fred, whom she was leaving, and also Agnes, who had tacitly, at least, cast her off, filled Agnes' heart to overflowing. She saw, too, that in undeceiving Beatrice she would take away the only comfort left to her. Yet it must be done.

While she waited, Beatrice went on. "I stopped down town and cashed a check. The bank was closed, but old Tompkins cashed it for me. I'm going to leave half with you. We can settle about the future, later. It's too late for you to go to my house to-night. Go in the morning,"—she drew a deep breath and finished with disguised bitterness— "and at last I guess Aunt Kate will come there, too." Then she checked her thoughts from dwelling upon her long disappointment over Mrs. Sidney's persistent refusal to live with her, and repeated gently the question she had asked on entering the house, "Tell me what has happened."

Agnes passed by the question and took up her cousin's words. "I have made up my mind that I shall come to your house, but it shall be to see you as well as Fred," she said earnestly. "Beatrice, why do you say 'to stay with Fred'?"

"I said we would plan about the future later," returned Beatrice restlessly. "I'm going off on a trip. There isn't time to talk about that now. I'll write."

The packed suit-case, the telegram to Tom, his sudden disappearance, Donald's worry, and this prospective trip of Beatrice's confirmed Agnes' fear. If she was to accomplish anything, she must do it at once.

She clasped her cousin's hands with infinite pleading. "It hasn't been right for us to be separated as we have been. I never shall let it occur again. Oh, Beatrice, things have been going wrong—all wrong—wrong for everybody. We all have been to blame. But it isn't too late yet. That's why I sent for you. I couldn't come to Kent, or I should have done so, but as soon as I'm up from this—"

"What are you talking about?" interrupted Beatrice brusquely. Then suspicion for the first time entered her mind. "Aren't you going to leave

Ferdinand?" She turned threateningly as she put the question. The tenderness went out of her face, and left it sharp.

"No," said Agnes slowly, not releasing Beatrice's hands.

There was a flare of color in Beatrice's face and eyes, and her voice rang ominously.

"Then why did you send for me?" She was on her feet and stood poised waiting for the answer as for a signal.

Agnes' fingers closed with no uncertain grip over the arm she still held. "You have a right to be angry with me, Beatrice, but you're here and you must listen to me. Fred and you both have been wrong, but you are going to ruin yourselves now—and needlessly, needlessly. Fred has loved you always, and he does still."

"What do you mean by getting me down here to meddle in my business!" cried Beatrice passionately, trying to free herself from Agnes' hold. "Look at your own!" She was as rough as she dared to be, but apprehension for Agnes compelled her to hold down her fury.

Agnes drew Fred's letter from her dress and forced it before his wife. Beatrice sprang back from her violently as she felt the hold on her arm loosen, and the paper fell on the floor between them.

"You must read that letter before you go! It is that which made me send for you!"

The agony of insistence in Agnes' voice checked Beatrice. She glanced down at the paper, recognized Fred's handwriting, and with a gesture of refusal turned instantly to the door.

"Fred is not doing this! Other people are forcing him! Mr. Bucher is one! You don't know what is going on!" Agnes' voice was strained and tuneless as she raised it in a forlorn hope.

Beatrice's hand was on the door. At the name of Mr. Bucher, her face blazed vindictively. "Bucher's always had Fred. He can have him in the bank to all eternity. Besides, do you think I am made to live with a man who is influenced by his employer against his wife!"

She turned the knob. Agnes rose. A faintness passed over her and left her face gray. Her lips opened, but she said nothing.

Beatrice put out her arm to support her. "Who is here to take care of you? Where's the bell? I'll ring."

"Wait, Beatrice!" said Agnes. She shivered. "Ferdinand has done this. He is using Bucher to ruin you. Oh, do not let him!"

Beatrice stood quite still. Then she turned around and leaned her back against the door, her hand behind her still on the knob. "*So!*" she said. At last, another person had said in plain words the truth about Ferdinand, and this person his own wife. A new expression was coming into her face. A new current of passion had struck across her wild resentment toward her husband, and momentarily she was adrift between the two. Agnes' heart began to beat heavily with hope. There was a glimmer of returning attention in Beatrice's eyes, a suggestion of struggling will-power in her voice when a moment later she said quickly, but in a low tone, "Tell me what you know!"

"This is what I believe," said Agnes, pale but unflinching, "and Fred's letter has confirmed it."

Beatrice's eyes took on a steadiness and glitter.

"Since mother's house was sold Mr. Bucher and Ferdinand have been in very close relations. There is nothing in which Ferdinand's opinion does not direct the old man. Hear what Fred writes." She stooped suddenly and picked up the discarded letter.

Beatrice waited without stirring, and Agnes read aloud: "It is impossible for me any longer to ignore my plain duty. Bucher advised me some months ago—"

Beatrice stirred impatiently, and Agnes hurried on, skipping here and there. "Bucher said he had proof that Tom and Beatrice were originally engaged, and he told me what had broken it off. I don't believe the latter, nor do I trust the source from which I believe it came to him."

Agnes' hand dropped to her side, but her eyes met Beatrice's unwaveringly.

"There can be no doubt," she went on, "that 'the source' is Ferdinand."

Rage flamed in Beatrice's face.

"Of course it's Ferdinand!" she cried in bitter scorn of her husband. "And I told Fred all about this long before Bucher did, but he believes Bucher's version."

"No! no!" interrupted Agnes.

"He believes it of me, now! He has told me so. It's a pity he should be disappointed. When Ferdinand slurred me to Tom, Tom came straight to me and asked me to marry him. He knew what to believe about me. That's the difference between him and Fred. I refused Tom because I didn't want him, but since I've lived with Fred I've come to appreciate him better. I could have made something of Tom. I'll do it yet. Fred shall see!"

"Beatrice!" cried Agnes, "don't you see you are going to do yourself what Ferdinand has tried to bring about, and failed? Ferdinand hates Fred almost as much as he hates you. I don't know why. He wants to break up your home."

Beatrice gave a short laugh, stopped. A thought flashed into her mind. She then looked keenly at Agnes.

"You want to influence me to go back home. There is one way you can do it. Put on your things, come back with me, tell Fred what you have told me and make him leave Bucher. That will square me off with Ferdinand, I guess."

As Agnes returned the gaze, she saw dawning in Beatrice's face an expression of triumph. She connected it with Beatrice's threat to Ferdinand the last time she was in his house that his wife should come to her. At last she was seeing her way to accomplish it.

"Beatrice," Agnes implored, "do you wish to break up my home as the price of preserving yours? You offer to go back for hatred and revenge. What kind of a reunion with Fred will that be?"

Beatrice clicked her watchcase and turned to the door.

"Good-bye," she said.

Agnes stepped forward. The determination to say what she was going to say gave a meaning to her gaze which Beatrice respected by delaying.

"If you take this step, you give the world grounds to say truly what Ferdinand has said falsely. More than all this,"—Agnes came still nearer as she spoke,— "it means life-long suffering to you. You wanted to make Fred happy, and might have made him happy—I know you loved him!"

"Love!" said Beatrice furiously. "Fiddle-de-dee! Love hasn't anything to do with our real selves or with the right and wrong of things. You loved Ferdinand, and it made you idiot enough to marry him. You could get on a good deal better with Donald, couldn't you? I dare say you've thought about that. Well, so can I get on better with Tom than with Fred, and I've got sense enough to do it!"

The reckless words, with their sharp question to herself, shocked Agnes momentarily into silence.

Then she said steadily, "It *is* true there is something which can overmaster a man and woman when it has little or nothing to do with the real life of the mind or spirit. But that is not love. Love suffereth long and is kind. Oh, Beatrice, the only way to know any happiness in this life is in self-sacrifice. It seems as if we each must give up just the thing we want to keep the most. I know Fred is unyielding. I know how disappointed and how hurt you have been, and how you've tried—"

The tears rushed to her eyes as she spoke. Beatrice saw them and she put her hand up to her throat, but her eyes were dry.

Agnes struggled on. "I know that when we're hurt so much—when things we long for—feel we must have can't be ours—it's so hard—we give up trying to be good. We sin."

Her voice was low, no longer strained, but broken rather by suffering, self-revelation, a beseeching so intense that every other feeling was lost in it.

"So great a sin as this can bring to a woman like you only unending woe. You have tried to do right, but, if you have been unhappy doing that, no words can tell what you will suffer in sinning. There's no other torture so terrible as the consciousness of guilt. You think you are going to live now, but life will be less than nothing to you. I know this, and I would willingly die if I could save you and Fred and Tom from this frightful mistake."

Agnes' voice shook and stopped on the last word. As the two looked at each other, the recklessness of Beatrice was dominated by the endurance of Agnes. The dark face quivered and broke into agony.

Agnes leaned forward, trembling, to catch the words of self-conquest which she knew were coming. The glory of salvation was almost upon them.

It was checked by a sound outside. Someone was coming up the front steps. They heard the sound of a key in the lock, the opening and shutting of the front door. They still looked at each other, but their faces changed as they stood listening.

Ferdinand's step came down the hall, hesitating now and then. Apparently he looked first in the library; then he re-entered the hall and approached the green room. An instant later, the knob turned and the door struck against the figure of Beatrice.

With a faint lifting of the eyebrows at Agnes she moved aside, and Ferdinand entered the room.

He glanced from Beatrice to his wife, on whom his eyes rested for some moments before he spoke. Then he asked, "Is this visit with your permission?"

"It is at my request."

Ferdinand turned to Beatrice. "In that case, I have only to say to you, Mrs. Sidney, that you may consider your call at an end."

"Not until I have finished talking to her, Ferdinand," said Agnes, laying a detaining hand upon Beatrice's arm. "She must not go yet. Either leave us here, or I shall take her to my room."

Beatrice did not speak, but her brows rested over her eyes as she looked at Ferdinand. At the sight of him, the old defiance rose again, gained possession of her and turned the full tide of her new emotions away from the vision of renunciation into a permanent and dangerous enmity.

There was something terrible even to Ferdinand in the daring, the malignity, and the power of her pose and expression. Everything else had sunk into the background as she found herself thus unexpectedly face to face with her foe. He knew that if she could once get an advantage over him she would use it mercilessly. Agnes' astounding move in inviting her to his home, coupled with his wife's open opposition when discovered, seemed giving Beatrice this dangerous advantage. On the very verge of domestic and social ruin old Mott's daughter had turned into a formidable menace to his own home. Hitherto in his differences with Agnes he had felt assured of his authority and ultimate success. Now, however, Agnes seemed uniting with the rebellious nature whom he always had the instinct to crush and thrust out of the way. His anger against Agnes was extreme.

He made up his mind at once, and he replied instantly, "I forbid you a single word more with this woman. Go up to your room alone."

There was a moment's dead silence.

Then Agnes said in a voice equally clear, "Very well, then. Since you compel me to address her only through you, I must ask you if you ever told Mr. Bucher that Beatrice married Fred because you had broken off relations between her and Tom? If you do not answer, I shall telephone at once to Mr. Bucher and ask him."

"I shall not allow you to excite yourself, either over a conversation with me, or by telephone with Mr. Bucher," answered Ferdinand. "Mrs. Sidney must leave this house peaceably at once, or I must compel her to leave." The impulse toward brute force was rising within him.

Beatrice's lip curled. She turned with dignity to Agnes.

"Agnes, I'm going, but it's not because I'm afraid. If you will come with me, I will go home with you. I will give you a suitable income and back you up in whatever you see fit to do. You will be sorry if you don't take my offer." She said the last words slowly and meaningly. A pause followed them. Ferdinand looked at his wife steadily and opened the door. Agnes understood the mute reiteration of his demand upon her. In a flash she saw the intolerable consequences of both alternatives. If she only could know her duty she would do it! Instincts inherited from her ancestry seemed crying out that she must stay. Her passion to save Beatrice wrestled with them, but though Beatrice and Ferdinand both waited for her decision, she did not speak, would not speak, till, word by word, her reason directed what she should say.

"As soon as I can, I will come to you, Beatrice."

Ferdinand's voice struck in on the last word. "If you are going, why do you not go now?"

Agnes turned toward him. "Because," she replied at once, "I believe you would use it against Beatrice. If I go, I shall go by myself for reasons which are independent of others."

Beatrice stopped her with a passionate gesture. "Always talk! Nothing but talk! You Sidney's are all alike. You stick by the things that ruin you. You insult and throw away what tries to be good to you. Now, by God! I've done with the lot of you!"

She rushed out, slamming the door. Agnes called to her and started to follow, but Ferdinand stepped between her and the door, barring the way. Agnes seized his arm and strove with all her strength to fling him aside. He was immovable. They heard the front door torn open, and Beatrice's stumbling steps hurrying down the walk.

Both knew that she was going to Tom.

CHAPTER VII

AGNES went to the dining-room and poured herself out a glass of wine. The fear that she might faint and so lose the chances that were left to her to save Beatrice made her move slowly and carefully, but she did not blunder.

When she returned to the hall she found Ferdinand near the telephone. He anticipated her intention, and spoke to her at once as she came up to it. "Considering your state of mind, I forbid you to use this telephone."

She turned away from him, rang the bell for her maid, and ordered the horses.

As the girl was leaving, Ferdinand stopped her.

"You need not give that order," he said incisively. "You may say instead that my horses are not to leave the barn today."

The girl looked blankly from the mistress to the master of the house.

Agnes again turned without comment and went upstairs to her room.

The summons to dinner came while she was gone. Ferdinand disregarded it, and silenced the maid when she came a second time.

Presently Agnes came down dressed for the street. Ferdinand was waiting for her in the lower hall. This time she spoke first. "You have gone as far as you can with me, Ferdinand. Do not attempt to stop me from leaving this house. When I come back we will talk things over finally."

"You shall not leave the house today. You are unfit to in every way." The determination of Ferdinand's voice was unmistakable.

Agnes came up to him and stopped. "I shall leave the house at once, Ferdinand. You must let me pass—"

For answer Ferdinand threw his right arm about her, seized both her hands in his left, and half-carried, half-forced her to the stairs.

As he put his foot on the first step, Agnes spoke to him. "You hurt me. Let me alone and I will go up quietly."

He released his hold with a feeling of relief that the turning-point had come, supported her up the stairs and to the door of her room.

As she entered his hand felt for the key; then he remembered that one of the children had lost it a few days before and that it had not been replaced.

Agnes stood in the center of the room watching him.

As his eyes met hers he spoke deliberately. "I want you to give me your word of honor that you will not leave this room tonight."

Agnes bowed her head, "I will stay."

Ferdinand looked at her a moment longer; then he started to go out. As he was closing the door he turned back, "I will send up your dinner, and if there is anything that you desire I will see that you have it."

He waited for an answer. There was none.

As he went down the stairs the excitement which had possessed him for the last half hour faded, and an anxious foreboding which he never before had known settled upon him. He went into the library, leaving the door open, picked up the evening paper, glanced it over, then went out to the dining-room.

The children were already at the table eating, and the maid apologetically explained that it was past their dinner hour and that Miss Margaret would not be home till later. Ferdinand sent Agnes' dinner up to her. Then he and the children ate in silence.

He observed a puzzled expression on the maid's face when she came downstairs, but he attributed the girl's manner to her mystification at the events of the afternoon.

After he had finished dinner, he sent the children up to bed, and returned to the library. He had been reading some time, when he heard a carriage drive up to the door. Thinking it was Aunt Margaret returning, he read on for a half hour or so. Then his attention was caught by the sound of a second carriage stopping in front of the house.

He laid down his paper and went uneasily to the door leading into the hall. An unsteady hand was fumbling with the latch-key, the carriage drove off, and presently the door opened and his aunt stood on the threshold.

"I'm sorry to be so late, dear," she began, conscious of sin as usual, "but Agnes told me to stay as late as ever I wished."

Ferdinand turned without replying and went back to the library. Who had come in the first carriage and entered without ringing? Agnes had gone out while he was at dinner!

While he stood collecting his thoughts for a renewal of the struggle between them, the maid came and tapped timidly at the door.

"Mrs. Ballington wishes to see you at once, sir," she said, and withdrew as soon as she had spoken.

Ferdinand stood a moment longer, then, with a look of determination, turned and went upstairs.

As he pushed open the door, he saw Agnes sitting before her desk as though she had been writing. The window back of the desk was still open, although the warm spring air had taken on the chill of night. The faintest odor of apple bloom was in the air. As Agnes turned in her chair and looked across the room at her husband, he was aware, as he met her still gaze, of the same coolness and the same faint sweetness in her that seemed to permeate the room. The beauty of outline of her face was conspicuous now that her color was gone.

"Ferdinand," she said, after a moment during which she had been silently regarding him, "I have sent for the doctor and the nurse to come. I also have sent to Kent for my mother and Dr. Quinn. Miss Elmore ought to be here soon. I wanted to say what I have to say before she comes."

"You broke your word and left the house while I was at dinner."

Ferdinand made the statement like an automaton.

Agnes considered him curiously. "Yes," she said, as though it were a matter of no moment, "I had to go, and there was no other way."

Ferdinand's anger rose at her indifference. "Agnes," he said sharply, "your repeated lies, disobedience, and deceit have become insupportable. What such a man as Fred Sidney cannot tolerate in his wife I certainly will not endure in mine. Your conduct to-day can be condoned only on the theory that you are not responsible now. But I tell you, once for all, that no such excuse will serve you in the future. Where did you go after leaving the house?"

"I went to the livery-stable and hired a boy to drive me to Donald Ballington."

Ferdinand's face flushed.

"The man who has repeatedly given you money without my knowledge."

"Once only, Ferdinand," she corrected him, without emotion. "It came to me in such a way that it seemed as though I must take it. I used very little of it for myself. It was a wedding-gift to me in my father's name."

"This is a surprise," said Ferdinand cynically. "Eliza told me of a sum Donald gave you when she left. How do you reconcile that with your statement that he has given you money but once?"

"The second sum was not for me. It was borrowed by Aunt Margaret. She has nearly paid it back."

"How much more have you had from him?" persisted Ferdinand brutally. "And what have you given in return? A good deal has passed between you. I believe that you asked him to keep your husband away from home long enough for you to entertain his brother's mistress."

Still Agnes regarded her husband with a grave serenity which galled him inexpressibly. Nothing he could say seemed to reach her. "I said Donald has given me money but once," she replied. "I never have done anything for him. I wish I had."

Ferdinand took a step nearer to her. His voice sank to a menace. "Since we are started, you may as well make a clean breast of it. You have several times dropped covert hints, both in your speech and in writing, of things in your past which you could not tell me. In view of what I have found out myself, I insist upon knowing the rest."

Agnes waited a moment; then she said slowly, "I am willing to tell you everything now. Donald's gift was one of the things I could not tell you. The other is this. I have always considered that my neglect and giddiness while my mother was away from home were responsible for my father's death."

Ferdinand waited for her to go on. When she did not, he continued. "Putting together what you have confessed and what I have discovered, the fatal results of your giddiness as a girl, your intimacy after marriage with an old lover, your falsified accounts of household money, your shameless deceit and open defiance of this afternoon, and your unequivocal lie this evening— these things, taken together with a perpetual course of politic equivocation, by which you have attempted to baffle me in my control of my own aunt and children, and a swarm of petty swervings of the truth on every conceivable occasion, have brought me to the point at which I can no longer place any reliance upon what you say. Nothing but lack of money has kept you from being a second Beatrice Mott. If you had had her liberty you would be where she is."

When he stopped, Agnes looked at him as though waiting for him to continue. When he did not, she said, without a tremor in her voice, "I know that for just so much as I have sinned I must answer."

Then a certain exaltation came into her face—her father's look. "I have done at last with all that falsehood and equivocation. I never have been what you say I have, but it is true I have sometimes lied. I always have wanted to be as sincere as my father and as honest as my mother. My marriage with you entangled my relations with everybody so that in order to be true with myself I would have had to injure my mother, my children, my sister, Aunt Margaret and more than one of my best friends. It seemed to me selfish to prefer my honor before their well-being. No one knows what I have suffered. I thought it was inevitable. I see now that my own blindness caused the situation."

"You have been blind a good deal of the time since I married you," said Ferdinand when she stopped a moment as though considering.

"Yes," she answered gravely, and paused again. She was listening to another voice than Ferdinand's, which was saying: "You will live in that world more and more, and, though in a different way than you think, I doubt not with me." Far as she had traveled from her father's creed, how irresistibly had she journeyed home to him in that spiritual progress, which now seemed to be the whole of life.

After a moment she went on again in the same quiet voice:

"I cannot live with you and be true to anything. There is just one thing we must live our lives for, and that is truth. It isn't joy, no matter how much the soul longs for it, and it isn't love, no matter how dark the world is without it. Nor is it hope or faith, no matter how desolate the life may be that never has found them. With all these things, but without truth, life is a failure. But without all those, and with truth, life is triumphant. What is done, is done. I know now how to do better."

Scorn was in Ferdinand's voice as he interrupted, "What is this theatrical announcement for?"

Agnes stood up with an effort, shut her desk, and leaned against it for a few minutes, her face away from him.

He knew that she was suffering intense physical pain, and for the first time under such circumstances he felt no sympathy with her. When at last she turned toward him again, he noticed with the same absence of emotion the exhaustion in her face.

"The only possible way I could have helped you was to have left you. I have done the worst thing for you as well as for all the rest of us by living here. I have attempted to palliate and neutralize what I ought to have renounced, and you have hardened in the course which I accepted. Loyalty is a duty, but only when harmonious with truth and honor. The time has come when I must make my duty square with my conscience. If you had changed, or if I had helped you in any way, I should know that I ought to stay."

She hesitated. She was studying his face for the last time, and, as she did so, suddenly another face grew out of it—the face of Estelle Landseer. How different might have been the course of her husband's life if had not been cut off in infancy from that strong and conscience-ruled mother-love. What miracle might not a mother's love and wisdom achieve if it were allowed space to work!—and a third face, that of her little Stephen rose before her.

An infinite yearning came into her eyes with the revelation at last that Infinite Love is also infinite justice, that He does not express Himself in paradoxes or issue conflicting demands. Her belief was as strong as ever that neither law of man nor death itself could annul the bond of marriage, but she believed, also, that the faithful fulfillment of the law of love demanded not that she stay with her husband, but that she leave him.

Her next words fell gently, but finally. "I shall have to stay here, Ferdinand, until after our last child is born. Then, to be true to you as much as to myself, I shall take the children and go away."

"Where do you intend to go?"

"To my mother's farm. Afterwards I shall get work."

Ferdinand laughed, but it was a mirthless laugh. "Don't you know, Agnes," he said, "that a woman who leaves her husband has no claims whatever upon him? He can divorce her."

"I know that you will divorce me."

"I can keep the children, too."

She did not move or speak for some seconds, and Ferdinand would have felt that at last he could dictate to her, had it not been for the absent expression of Agnes' face. Her eyes were resting on a bunch of early dandelions which filled a little mug that stood on the desk. He knew that the children had placed them there that morning, and he noticed that the flowers were shut up for the night. Presently he saw her reach out and touch the closed blossoms gently, but he did not know that the sight of them had carried her mind out beyond the walls which sheltered the sleeping children to the wide, quiet fields where the flowers considered not, yet were watched and fostered by that deliberate and infinite Power which makes forever for beauty and righteousness. Her fingers closed over the buds involuntarily, as she lifted her eyes again to her husband's.

"I am not so sure of that," she said. "I shall be able to support them, and my reputation is good."

She withdrew her hand abruptly, made a slight gesture, half of pain, half of dismissal, then crossed the room slowly to the bed and sat down near the foot.

"You forget that my reputation is also good," said Ferdinand harshly. "How will you support my children?"

She did not look up.

"I asked you," he repeated, "how you intend to support my children? Have you consulted Donald?"

She lifted her head and they faced each other. Ferdinand felt a start of alarm as he caught sight of a glitter in her eyes. It seemed struggling with a darkness which was slowly blotting out intelligence, to leave in her look only the fright of mortal pain. He understood that she was making a supreme effort to keep her mind clear, and he wondered if she had heard or realized the full insult of his question.

The cloud wavered, receded, and Agnes' spirit gathered itself in a brightness so intolerable that Ferdinand glanced away.

"I have thought it through to the end!" she said in a voice that shook with a triumph and freedom as unendurable as was the brilliance in her eyes.

Ferdinand compelled himself to meet her gaze again, and after a moment of torture under the supernal radiance that streamed into his shrinking sight, he was conscious of relief. The light in her eyes went out, she looked at him a moment longer, unrecognizing, unseeing, with the wide eyes of the dying, then her head dropped upon the hands which gripped the brass pillar of the bed.

CHAPTER VIII

MIRIAM finished her work in Paris and started for the French coast with a feeling that her future was assured. During the hard-working term of serious apprenticeship in New York her friends had seen that her progress was sure and swift, but she herself had not indulged in many hopes as to her professional career. She had paid quite as much attention while she worked to her father's blunt criticisms as she did to those of her masters. During the period in Paris there seemed to come suddenly an ability to make the clay take the shapes she had been possessed to create ever since childhood. Only time and strength were needed now—the power of creation in marble and metal was there. She chafed at delays necessary to give her body rest. But it was with a different feeling that she turned her face homeward in the spring. The holiday was well earned, and all that she most wished was waiting for her, a sailing trip across the Atlantic with her father, a class reunion at Winston during the summer-school session, and then a quiet month with Agnes.

There were three days before Captain Cass' schooner was to reach Brest, and Miriam took the occasion to accept an invitation from some Russian friends to stop in Finistere and visit the governmental laboratories. Professor Kolensky, who had been busy all winter at the Pasteur Institute, was to have charge of the summer-school at Roscoff, and the chance of seeing once more at first hand something of the scientific investigation which always had held her interest, decided Miriam upon the roundabout trip to Brest.

The Kolenskys met her at the station, and they drove together in the diligence down the long road to the little Breton town crowded on a point of land jutting out into the English channel.

"This is about the last place in the world to which I ever expected to come," Miriam said as she looked out at the few rows of little stone houses, and then up at the big whitewashed building called "La Maison Blanche," at which they were alighting.

"We are very Parisian here, though," one of the Professor's daughters returned in her mellow French, "and we are to have a table d'hôte in your honor tonight which will be something magnificent. Here comes Madame Julie now."

They went up into the large dining-room whose wooden walls were decorated with old china, seaweed, and shells, and Miriam looked with delight at the peasants in their dark suits and blue sashes.

As they sat down at the table reserved for their party, a man who had been eating alone at a distant table rose and left the room. He did not look toward them, but Miriam caught sight of his back just as he was passing through the door way, and started. "Who is that?" she asked involuntarily.

The Kolenskys smiled. Professor Kolensky explained that the man was an American who had gained such an eccentric name for himself in the few days he had been there that Madame Julie had been jesting with them about bringing another American into the house.

Miriam heard their courteous after-remarks about Americans, abstractedly. When she left the table and walked across the road to the terrace where coffee was being served, she began to look nervously among the guests seated at little stands under the pavilion which stretched across one side of the garden.

At the very last table at the other end of the terrace, her eyes found the American. He was sitting with his back toward the others, his coffee and brandy apparently untouched on the little table before him. He seemed to be only half conscious of his surroundings as he looked at the sea.

Miriam watched him as she sipped her coffee and heard the Kolenskys eagerly discuss an octopus hunt that was to take place the next morning. After a time she turned to the Professor and said, "I believe that man is someone I know. I am going down to speak to him."

"Ask him to go octopus hunting with us tomorrow," said the naturalist kindly, in his monotonous treble.

Miriam walked swiftly down the terrace. Before she reached the end of it she had lost the sense of strangeness and anxiety that she had been feeling as she had watched him a few minutes before. That excitement had changed to one of eagerness. She was going to see him, was going to hear of Agnes—and now, instead of waiting six weeks. All the longings she had been holding off ever since she left Paris began to rush in upon her, as she stopped just before his chair.

"Tom!" she said.

The man made a spasmodic shove back from the table and turned around.

If Miriam had the advantage of Tom in not being taken off her guard, it was more than made up for when she saw his face. She had remembered Tom Ballington's look with pleasure. Whatever shortcomings he had, they had not been registered in his face. That was frank, responsive, and lovable. But she wondered, as she looked at it now, whether it contained more ugliness or more woe. All the ruddy look which she had liked so much seemed to have blackened, and now as the blood rose from his neck, it blotched the skin with purple.

Tom put up his hand and loosened his collar.

"Where did you come from?" he blurted out, shaking the glasses as he backed against the table.

"I came from Paris this evening."

"How did you know I was here?" he continued. "I did not know it. I saw you just as you were leaving the dining-room." She added after a moment, "Can we not go somewhere and talk?"

Tom looked out at the ocean again. "I walk along the shore every night," he said.

"Let me go with you. I will explain to the Kolenskys."

Tom took a step forward to stop her. She noticed it and looked at him inquiringly. "They are the Russian family I am visiting," she said, as he did not speak.

"Don't mention my name to them," Tom said huskily.

Miriam looked at him earnestly.

"I am registered here by the name of Pond," he added, and an agonized expression came into his sullen eyes, which he forced to meet hers.

Miriam bowed gravely.

When she returned to him he had collected himself somewhat, but his embarrassment was still so great that it affected her also.

"You might not like to be seen walking with me," he said, hesitating to make the move toward the gate.

Miriam made it herself, and he followed a step or two behind her. They went down to the shore without exchanging a word.

Then Miriam inquired, "Which way do you walk?"

"Out to the right," Tom answered. "Nobody else goes that way. That is Santa Barbara Church way off on the bluff there."

Miriam turned to the right. When they had gone some little distance she asked, "How long ago did you leave Winston?"

"Two or three weeks."

"What brought you here?"

He made no reply.

Miriam stopped and looked at her companion with mingled anxiety and sympathy. "What is it that has happened?" she said earnestly.

Tom looked down and kicked the stones at his feet. How could he tell this woman, of all the world, what had happened?

She saw his extremity and began to walk again, instinctively climbing the bluff. He kept by her side.

Presently she stopped. "Let us sit down here." Her eyes went out over the twilight sea as she spoke. The slow sweep of the revolving light on the Island of Batz drew her attention to the left. How many ages that stubborn cliff had defied the hurricanes of the Atlantic, to be touched with infinite melancholy by its association with the fugitive wandering of Mary Stuart! As her companion seated himself beside her, her eyes traveled from the island to the rugged promontory on which the town was built. The after-glow lingered on the fine bell tower of the fifteenth-century church, tinged the little white houses with pink. Miriam followed the zigzag of the main street which rose out of the breakers, and pursued the ridge until it faded out above the town. The promontory lifted itself higher into lonely desolation, swept around behind them like the wall of an amphitheater, jutting out into the sea again on their right. Crowning the summit of the second cliff was the little chapel, Santa Barbara, as white and still as a brooding seagull.

Tom watched Miriam like some dumb animal, and when she turned again she saw the old look of wistfulness emerging through the blind despair of his face.

"I wish you would tell me what is troubling you," she said. "Perhaps I could help you," she said again.

He began to tremble and drawing away put both his hands up to his face and sobbed. Miriam never had seen a man give way like this. She waited, alarmed at the violence of his grief. But the physical spasm spent itself at last, and when he took down his hands and left the swollen features exposed, he seemed to have wept out some of the brutality that had stained his face.

Miriam continued as soon as she saw that he could listen.

"I am going to America on my father's schooner. I wish you'd let him take you back, too. Whatever it is, it would be better to go back than to run away. You have only begun life. If it's begun wrong, there is time for you to begin over again. Will you go back?"

"I can't." The answer came instantly, but after a considerable pause, he said again, as though the reply were the result of thinking, "I can't go back."

Miriam reflected.

"Does your brother know where you are?" she asked at last.

"No."

She was still watching him earnestly, and a dim memory impelled her to put a question to which she dreaded to hear the answer. "Are you alone?"

Tom did not change his position. He raised his head and looking at Miriam full in the eyes said, "I came here with Mrs. Fred Sidney."

For several seconds they looked at each other, then simultaneously turned their eyes away.

"Where is she now?" asked Miriam.

"Out there!" He pointed to the island in the ocean. "She was through with me before we left the steamer. I've followed her here town by town, not to be with her, but so she won't be alone. She can't go any farther unless—" He gave a short gesture toward the water. "I'd follow her there, all right. Most women snatch a little happiness out of being ruined. She didn't get even that."

After a silence, Miriam spoke again: "Has she no one who can come to her?"

"Nobody."

She waited again, then said simply, "I will go to her."

Tom turned a look upon her which Miriam instinctively shunned. It was too piteous an unveiling of his soul.

"I will make some suitable arrangement with her," she added hastily, steadying him with the commonplace words.

Tom sat rigidly upright. "Miriam," he said, "you once offered me your friendship. I tried to deserve it for a while. Under other circumstances, God knows I would have tried for more. I gave up all trying that night in New York. The only thing that makes your kindness bearable to me, now, is the fact that you're not doing this for me. I know now that your friendship does not demand greatness. You'd do it for anybody. Oh, God! if I only had stayed even what I was then!"

The last words burst from him in a choked scream. He leaped to his feet, stumbled a few steps away from her, and turned his back.

Miriam's eyes were fixed upon him. Then she said shortly, "Look out there in front of you. Those fishermen down there fight the ocean all their lives. What! will *you* give up at your first shipwreck?"

The bitter kindness of the words lashed Tom to a last struggle for self-control. He forced himself to face his companion again.

"All right," he said between his teeth. He looked at her with shamed and beaten but unflinching eyes. Miriam's face changed slowly. "Miserable sinners all of us," she said at last, scarcely realizing that she had put her thought into words. At first, Tom did not take in their meaning. Miriam's look was a revelation to him. His mind was irresistibly drawn away from himself. He repeated her words half comprehendingly, and his thoughts turned to the myriads of blind and suffering beings who were hating and loving and ruining each other, and through it all were groping toward the light—all but the woman before him. She was above it, clear-eyed, untouched, yet she pitied and comprehended. The first faint impulse toward regeneration, tragic and hardly to be won though it was, stirred within him—that inevitable instinct which drives the spirit of man upward, not for hope, nor for reward, but for existence.

Miriam withdrew her eyes from him and, leaning over abstractedly, arranged the pebbles at her feet. As Tom watched her, a memory out of his childhood came back to him, and he quoted, as in a dream, "He that is without sin amongst you, let him first cast a stone. And again He stooped down and wrote with His finger in the sand."

Miriam's hand paused. She raised herself. Tom's eyes rested upon her head, but she looked off to sea. The stars were beginning to come out. The distant monotone of the ocean was a background for the silence. The memory of that Figure writing in the sand filled their souls.

"Miriam," said Tom, "can I ever become good?"

"Yes."

"I want nothing more."

A strange peace fell about them while the stars came out thicker in the sky and the low thunder of the ocean rose with infinite power and victory.

When they stood up to go, Tom held out his hands.

"Good-by till we meet again," he said, "if we ever do."

They clasped hands and then he turned abruptly. She saw him run with his head down, along the lonely shore to the right, straight into the oncoming dark and the incoming ocean. There was a narrow rim of shore-line between the bluff and the sea. But she saw that though he would be wet before he reached the point, yet he would reach the edge of land from which the little chapel, Santa Barbara, sent its ever-constant beam of light out over the rocky shore.

A line from Dante about a runner came into her mind:

"And he seemed as those who conquer, not those who are defeated."

CHAPTER IX

SIX weeks after Miriam's meeting with Tom at Roscoff a group of girls were waiting nervously in the reception room of the Kappa Phi Society House of Winston College. There was a college reunion, and they were expecting the arrival of their guest of honor.

"Is that the carriage, Lou?"

A tall girl standing by the window, who looked composed enough in the back, turned over her shoulder a scared face to answer the question. "I didn't hear anything," she replied, then leaned over the sill and stared down the curving driveway.

"I wonder if she looks at all as I remember her," queried the first speaker. "I never shall forget those stories she used to tell us through the college fence. We were all afraid of her, but we couldn't resist her stories."

I have still a little clay head she modeled for me one day out of one of my mud-pies, and to think now that she carves statues for the crowned heads of Europe! I read in the College Art Journal that the whole French Academy went down on their knees before she would design caryatides for the new gallery."

"You ought to have seen them!" a full ringing voice interrupted from the doorway.

The girls gave a start and gazed with a frightened fascination at the newcomer who announced herself so unceremoniously.

She entered the room, drawing off her long, gray gloves, and tossing her plumed hat on the lounge, as she continued, "There was Monsieur O., with all his honors thick upon him, and an imperial that made him an animated souvenir of the Second Empire as he knelt! there was M. le Professeur G. on his right, and on his left the absinthe drunkard cartoonist, L. Behind him the rest of the Academy filed in and knelt, and last came the famous but somewhat aging Hermes, who didn't want to kneel, but I pointed to the floor and he sank. Then they all began in concert, "We, the unworthy painters of France, beseech the glory of America to vouchsafe to carve two of her immortal figures of fame for the entrance to our Art Gallery. If she will not, we perish!"

Miriam's eyes shone with a mixture of mirth and pleasure as she sank into an easy chair and surveyed her disconcerted hostesses.

The tall girl, Lou Allen, was the first to recover herself and to come forward with heightened color. "We have been wondering ever since we received your telegram, Miss Cass, how we can show you that we appreciate the honor you do us in accepting our invitation. You mustn't be surprised if your fame has been somewhat twisted in coming so far to get here. May I introduce some of the girls? Frances Marshall—she is our Nestor, always dropping wisdom. Ruth Grant—plays the banjo. Sally Tracy—basketball. Roddy Random—valedictorian and whistler, Alison Drew—my chum—aims to sing in opera. Polly Hedges—paints. Go bring your portfolio, Polly. Miss Cass will like to see them."

Polly turned crimson as the others broke into sudden laughter. "Never painted anything but chairs in my life, Miss Cass. They're just trying to guy me."

"Yes, she has, Miss Cass. Here's the portfolio."

Polly flung out desperate hands. "You devilish girls!" she exclaimed. "Don't, Miss Cass!"

Miriam caught the note of agony and laid the portfolio unopened on the table. "Let us talk over all that has been going on since I left college. Come! who will begin?"

There was an intimacy and freedom in Miriam's manner that set the girls' tongues in motion. They perched around her and began one of those anthems of youth where many voices take up the theme, "You are great and we are proud to be near you." Miriam leaned back while her burnished head turned slightly to this one and that one as they checked and chaffed and interrupted one another under the excitement of the older woman's smiling and luminous eyes. There was a sense of restlessness in the air. With them it was the exhilaration of talking with a famous woman. With her, it was the re-living of youth. She was waiting through all their chatter for the sound of a well-known, eager footfall which would bring back the one enduring charm of her girlhood, the one friendship that had been unsullied by time. Her cheeks began to burn with unwonted color, and the mood of the girls rose to a bacchanalian hilarity.

Presently, under cover of the mirth awakened by an anecdote of her bohemian life, one of the girls leaned over to whisper to another"

"She can't have been such friends with Mrs. Ferdinand Ballington. That was like the rest of the alumnae gossip."

The whisper seemed to have conveyed a subtle suggestion to Miriam's mind, for she sat up and drew a long breath. "Well, girls, this has made me years younger, so that I am beginning to feel the uncontrollable hunger of infancy. Let us eat, drink, and be merry. Then I must leave you and go to spend the evening with a friend I have looked forward to seeing, as you will look forward to seeing one another when you have had Academies and Salons littering up your floors with their renowned knees."

"Happy woman!—who is she, Miss Cass?—is she coming up here?—may we meet her?"

Miriam's eyes laughed at them kindly. "Certainly you may see her, but you must not keep her long. It has been three years since I saw her, and much as I love you on three quarters of an hour's acquaintance, you must make way for your elders. I telegraphed her to meet me here. It is Agnes Sidney—you know her, of course, as Mrs. Ferdinand Ballington."

The girls looked at her, dropped their eyes, sat quite still.

Miriam's manner suddenly changed. Her brows settled over her eyes. "Has anything happened there?" she asked, as though they were strangers.

They looked at each other with furtive glances, but there was no escape from those imperious eyes.

Frances Marshall finally found voice to say painfully, "It can't be possible, Miss Cass, that you didn't know—that you can't have heard how Mrs. Ballington—about the unfortunate—" She stopped in a panic.

The color had faded out of Miriam's cheeks. "I have heard nothing," she said, so rapidly as to be scarcely intelligible. She drew a quick breath, as though to ease her heart. "Tell me what has happened. Be quick about it!"

"Mrs. Ballington died over two months ago."

Miriam's hand left the arm of the chair, hung poised in the air a moment, and then dropped back. The girl who was "aiming at opera" knew that the hand had tried to ward the dagger from her heart, but had been too late. The girls turned away and busied themselves in aimless ways about the room. Three of them stole out through the door behind her. Miriam did not move.

One of the girls who remained sat down on the lounge in a dark corner of the room, buried her face in the pillows, and began to sob noiselessly. Still Miriam did not stir. What was passing in her mind only those who have felt that mortal thrust know.

When she spoke again her words sounded like the burial service. There was no passion, no personality in the tones. "Be kind enough to tell me the particulars."

Two of the girls came forward. The third left the lounge and fled from the room.

"Mrs. Ballington had been apparently in perfect health, Miss Cass. She was down street the day before she was taken sick. I saw her and she bowed to me, although I remember I wondered if she recognized me, she seemed so preoccupied. She was not looking well then, but I had seen her frequently about the city before that, and she had been looking particularly well."

Miriam's gray eyes were looking through and beyond the speaker and she seemed hardly conscious of her own words as she asked, "Were you ever close enough to her to see if—if her hair—"

She broke off as her mind went back and divined the cares and griefs and struggles in her friend's life that must have undermined her strength.

Frances Marshall waited for her to finish.

"Go on, please," said the voice.

"I often noticed Mrs. Ballington's hair, Miss Cass. It was not gray at all. She did not seem to age like other women, only to grow richer and sweeter in mind and body."

Frances' voice stopped huskily, but after a moment she went on.

"The occasion of her illness was a premature birth. There were several physicians. Dr. Quinn came down from Kent, but only in time to see her die."

Miriam looked at her as though she were still speaking. Presently she glanced away to the window. After a long silence she drew another quick breath and rose. "If you will find my hat and gloves, I think I will go. It was a very pleasant visit until—and I thank you all—but I see they have gone. I have given you a very bad half-hour, my dear. The reason I heard nothing was because I came over from France in a schooner. Whatever letters I have were written me there, and have been forwarded to her home, where they are waiting for me. I will go down and get them before I leave the city."

She put on her hat and stood idly fingering her gloves. Frances Marshall's eyes began to sting and presently two tears burned their way down her cheeks. Miriam looked up, glanced around the room, and started for the wrong door.

"This is the way out, Miss Cass," said the girl brokenly. "If you care to come back, you can be alone here."

Miriam turned. She touched Frances' tear-wet cheek with a gentle finger. "Good-by."

She followed the old lilac-bordered path curving round to the gate. Overhead the locusts hung heavy with honey and bees. Beside her walked a phantom girl in white with a Roman sash and vine-leaf hat. They reached the gate, the girl stayed behind, smiling her old brilliant, eager smile, kissing her hand in farewell. With eyes of agony Miriam saw her fade into the pine trees, and turned to go down the street.

Then she was conscious of another presence, older and sadder, still more beautiful, and thrilling with love and longing. She felt the gentle hand steal into hers, and with a face that made the few passers-by give her the whole walk she went down into the city, listening to words that would never be spoken to her again.

There was a jar, a break-off of the familiar voice. Miriam looked up with blind fury at the interruption, to see a man standing in front of her hat in hand. It was Donald Ballington.

"I was just coming to find you, Miss Cass," he said eagerly.

Miriam put out her hand mechanically.

Donald waited a moment, and went on. "My mother is away, and I am living down at the hotel on the lake during the summer, but the house is open and I wondered if you would not like to go there rather than to—" He did not finish. "You can be quite alone or not, as you like."

The last sentence was a refuge to Miriam. If she could be alone for a while, she could pull herself together. She was still holding Donald's hand as though they were girls together, when she replied, "Thank you, Mr. Ballington. I should like to spend the night there. In the morning I shall go back to New

York. When I am a little used to it, I will come back to Kent to see Mrs. Sidney."

Donald turned and walked beside her in silence. He divined that she was not thinking of him.

"I suppose you came on to see the children," he ventured at last. "Aunt Margaret telephoned me you were to be here."

"I came on to see Agnes."

Donald started.

Miriam added, "I heard she was dead only half an hour ago."

Donald's heart swelled within him. They reached the gate of his house. He opened it and stood aside for her to enter.

"Mr. Ballington, I wish you would come in a few moments," said Miriam; "I want to ask some questions, and I have something to tell you."

Donald followed her up the walk with a foreboding heart. As they went into the hall, the twilight struck cold to his fancy; their foot-falls echoed through the empty house. They sat down in the drawing room, and Miriam placed her hat on the table beside her.

"I wish you would tell me very particularly about the last weeks of Agnes' life. Her letters told me much, but we do not write the things that affect us most. In this case death anticipated what might have been said."

Donald told all that he remembered. He said little about Ferdinand, much about Agnes and her cheerfulness in the face of physical weakness. He recounted a conversation he had had with her, in which she had sent upstairs for a packet of Miriam's letters, neatly docketed and tied with a purple ribbon, and read him passages here and there.

Miriam's head sank upon the table in a spasm of grief. Donald hesitated and stopped. She thought it was because she troubled him, and, after a little, she raised her face and wiped her eyes, "Don't mind me, Mr. Ballington. This is just what I want to hear."

Then he began on the story of Tom and Beatrice. Miriam looked at him searchingly and, once, when he halted, urged him gently, "Tell me everything just as it was."

The slow anger of the righteous was in Donald's soul as he continued. "Ferdinand was aware of the situation, Miss Cass, and he was glad of it. He always hated Tom and Beatrice both. He hates me because I did some things for his wife that he wouldn't do; and more than that, because I told him that I thought he couldn't and wouldn't make her happy. He stopped her by force from getting any message to me or Fred of what Tom and Beatrice were doing, and she had to lie to him and creep out of her own house like a thief finally to get to me. She drove around to find me in a hired carriage, with her heart breaking because she had been detained so long. She was dying when I talked with her. She left the carriage, walked out of hearing of the coach man, but she could scarcely stand. He killed her, and that is all there is to say."

Miriam sat outwardly controlled as Donald went through the rest of his recital—his last interview with Agnes, his fruitless pursuit of the fugitive pair as far as New York, his return to find Agnes dead, the dissolution of partnership between him and his cousin.

When he was through there was a silence; then she said, with a self-restraint which Donald felt to be more terrible than any outburst of passion, "I saw your brother before I left France and had a talk with him. I also saw Mrs. Fred Sidney."

Donald's face flushed crimson.

"They had separated," Miriam went on, "and both were wretched."

Donald listened with strained attention to Miriam's words of Tom. When she had finished he waited a moment to get control of himself, and then said in a husky voice, "I once hoped Tom and you might marry. Perhaps you have helped him more than if you had." He waited, then said still huskily, "Tell me about Beatrice."

Miriam considered. "I cannot repeat the conversation. She was reticent and told me nothing of what I have learned from you. We spoke of her future, however, and she is now with friends of mine in Paris. I am in communication with her. I have with me a letter from her for Agnes."

Another pause followed, then Donald fulfilled his last commission from his cousin's wife.

"I have a letter for you, Miss Cass. It is from Agnes and it is postmarked the day before she died. As you see, she directed it to be returned to me in case it did not reach you."

Donald rose as he spoke. Miriam held out her hand unsteadily for the letter, and then went with him to the door.

After he was gone, she asked to be shown to her room. Later on when the maid took up a tray upon which a delicate luncheon had been arranged, Miriam answered her rap at the door at once, and the letter was in her hand still unopened. It was late that night before she broke the seal.

CHAPTER X

WHEN Miriam came down to breakfast in the morning she stopped at the foot of the stairs and looked down the wide hall she had entered for the first time eight years before with Agnes. Through the open doorway she could see the pillared veranda and below it the well-kept walk and driveway. Presently she turned and went into the music room. The piano was open and a book of songs still rested on the rack. She crossed the room wondering if it were the Rubinstein song Agnes had sung that first night, but the music was open at Lassen's "Es war ein Traum." As she read the words she seemed to hear Tom's voice singing as they drifted on the lake, while Agnes sat in the stern of the boat trailing her fingers in the water. Miriam turned away to the dining-room with the memory of that last day and night with Agnes around her, and as she walked the letter which she carried next her heart lay with insupportable weight upon her.

She found a note from Donald on the breakfast table, saying that Mrs. Sidney was coming in from Kent on the morning train and that if she wished she would be able to see her a few minutes at the station before her own train left. There was also a time-table with her train marked on it. "Mr. Ballington left word that the carriage is at your disposal," supplemented the maid who served her.

As she ate her breakfast Miriam remembered Donald's saying that Ferdinand had been out of town several weeks and that Miss Margaret and the children were out at the lake where Mrs. Sidney was to meet them. She decided to go for any letters which might be held at the farm for her, and after breakfast ordered the carriage. Having packed her few things, she left a note for Donald thanking him for his kindness, and started off for the deserted house which she had come to visit with such hope and eagerness.

As the double row of clipped cedars came in sight, Ferdinand's spirit seemed to challenge her, and two sullen spots of red began to glow high up on her cheeks. She left the carriage at the gate, and as she went swiftly up the walk to the house she noticed that the great front door stood open. She was scarcely conscious of what she did as she went up the steps and entered without ringing.

There was the green parlor with the door shut. "They carried her out from there," she thought. After a moment, she turned to the library. "No more flowers here now." Down the hall the door into the dining-room was open, and Miriam caught sight of the tall iron lamp and the old-rose shade.

With a sense, of desolation she turned to the stairway. As she went up the letter in her bosom seemed to burn into her the sentence in which Agnes had stated without emotion the way in which she for the last time had struggled up those stairs— "When I reached home I could no longer stand; I think I must have come up to my room on my hands and knees."

Miriam paused a moment at the top of the stairs, and then turned toward Agnes' room. Her heart beat heavily as she put out her hand to the door. After a moment's hesitation, however, she turned the knob noiselessly, and the door swung open.

The white curtains at the windows blew gently toward her with the current of air that drew through the room with her entrance, and they subsided again as she closed the door behind her. There was a flicker of sun and shadow on the shades as the trees outside swayed in the breeze.

Miriam stood still until her eyes accustomed themselves to the twilight. She noticed that the door into Ferdinand's room was ajar and that a rim of light outlined the opening. Upon the wall opposite the door was hung the portrait of Estelle Landseer, and Miriam wondered why it had been brought from the green parlor. Agnes' desk had been moved from its old position over to one of the front windows where it stood open with a chair in front of it as though someone had been writing there recently. Miriam turned away with a feeling of strangeness to the bed. That, too, was differently placed. Then her eyes passed quickly over the other objects in the room, and she discovered that the pictures on the wall alone remained as she remembered them.

A passion of homesickness, an uncontrollable desire to have things as they were, came over her. It was intolerable that this one place of all others, which should be the shrine of her friend's memory, should be desecrated by change. Scarcely thinking what she was doing, she went swiftly over to the desk and shoved it across the room.

As she did so she saw that a late picture of herself hung framed in one of the compartments. A mist of tears, the first she had shed, blurred her eyes as she turned away.

A moment later, she had replaced the chairs as they used to be, and then there was the soft rumble of the bed rolling around on its castors.

When it was in its old position Miriam stood looking down at it. "Agnes!" she said under her breath. Then, as if in a dream, she put out her hand to touch the pillow, but it stopped an inch or two in the air above it. Then her hand began to pass slowly downward toward the foot of the bed, always a few inches above it, now higher, now lower, as though it were following the curves of a recumbent form. Then Miriam straightened herself and stood motionless, her eyes fixed upon the little space of air an inch or two above the pillow.

There was a sound of steps in the adjoining room, the door was pushed open, and a man's figure paused in astonishment on the threshold.

Miriam neither heard nor saw.

Ferdinand's eyes glanced quickly around the room and took in at once what the sound of the moving furniture had meant. "What are you doing in here?" he exclaimed angrily, taking Miriam for the servant.

There was an instantaneous change in the motionless figure by the bed and Miriam wheeled toward him.

Still Ferdinand did not recognize her across the room in the dim light. He was conscious only of a dark and hostile presence that filled him with something he would not confess to be dread. He waited a moment for a reply, then crossed the room, and sent one of the window shades with a snap to the top of the sash. Then he turned and recognized her.

"I did not hear you come in, Miss Cass. Have you been here long? No one told me you had come."

Miriam stood looking at him. All the night before she had struggled with passions that had taken a form which only the strongest can feel without mental and moral shipwreck. Love, grief, hatred, and vengeance had scarred her soul. Now as she stood face to face with the man she considered her friend's murderer a stillness of mood succeeded the tumult. It seemed to her as though she were standing in the presence of the dead, and when she spoke she felt herself to be pronouncing the epilogue of a tale that is told.

"No one heard me come in, Mr. Ballington. The door was open and I did not ring."

He did not know how to break the silence that followed, and waited for her next words.

"What are you going to do with the children?"

There was a well-modulated surprise in Ferdinand's voice as he replied, "I shall keep them here in charge of Aunt Margaret."

There was a pause that lasted until it became embarrassing to Ferdinand. He moved uneasily and opened his lips as though to speak, when Miriam anticipated him.

"It may be that I never shall have another chance to talk with you. Mr. Ballington, when I was here before, we did not talk seriously. Perhaps no one but Agnes ever talked so to you."

As Ferdinand met the gray eyes that were steadfastly upon him, something in him flinched. They searched him as the eyes of his mother's portrait searched him, and he could neither baffle them nor meet them unconcerned.

"Let us go downstairs," he said with studied courtesy, turning toward the door. He felt an overwhelming reluctance to talk with her in this room.

Miriam stayed where she was. When he reached the door and turned back to her, she said:

"If you will stay I would rather talk here. It will be only a few moments."

Ferdinand hesitated, then came back to her.

"Mr. Ballington," asked Miriam directly, "what killed Agnes?"

The unexpected question confused Ferdinand. He replied after a moment, "I believe the immediate cause of death was heart-failure."

An intuition of what was coming brought with it a dread which was inexplicable to him. He could not shake it off, and he could not rise above it. Her next words roused him to strained attention.

"You and I know the real reason."

As they continued to look at each other Ferdinand's memory began to stir. He found himself seeing as Miriam would have seen long-vanished expressions of his wife's face. When they occurred he had scarcely noted them, or worse, had commented on them impatiently—expressions of weariness, of quickly-disguised pain, of disappointment, of bewilderment, of fear, of anguish, of hope fading into endurance. As they passed before him there thronged into his mind the words that had accompanied them. When they were spoken he had heard them with indifference, with indulgence, with anger. Now he heard them as they would have sounded to Miriam, and the recollection troubled him more than he ever had been troubled before. He was at a loss, too, how to reply to her last curious remark, whose meaning was by no means clear to him.

"I don't understand you," he replied stiffly, without withdrawing his eyes from hers.

"If you did not and could not understand me, it would take away my only excuse for talking to you. It is on the chance that you do and can that I venture it. Surely you must have suffered, or at least been shocked, in losing your wife and baby. You must have thought then, and since, things that you never had thought before." Miriam spoke quietly but without hesitation.

"It is not necessary for us to talk over my thoughts," interposed Ferdinand.

Again he turned to go, but her statement once more held him. "Agnes wrote me a letter the night before she died."

Ferdinand waited half-warily, half-contemptuously. As she did not continue, he returned shortly, "Well?"

He was watching her intently now, but her face might have been made of stone, he told himself bitterly, so free was it from the self-revelation to which he had been accustomed in Agnes. There was not a tremor either of friendliness or of hostility in the fine, strong mask against which his fixed gaze struck and glanced idly off.

"The facts I know are inconsequent, except in so far as they enable me to talk to you understandingly. Mr. Ballington, you had given to you the daily companionship of a soul that tried to live the spiritual life. You could not see what was your most precious possession. You looked at Agnes' mistakes, her weaknesses and her failures, and blamed them, not knowing that it was only these that made and kept her your wife. That finer and truer Agnes, the steadfast soul that learned through weakness and failure to lay hold of courage and power, you more than blamed, you hated and tried to crush—but all you could do was to kill her."

Miriam's voice broke. Ferdinand noticed it instantly. After all she was but an over-wrought woman, he considered, her loss of control atoning for what she had said. But the break was momentary. Almost immediately she resumed.

"Mr. Ballington, the world is going another way, from yours, no matter who or how many will to stop it. You have pinned your faith to what you call hard facts, but there are spiritual facts that you never have seen. Sooner or later, however, spiritual facts enter into your world of hard facts and they never demonstrate themselves so irrefutably as they do when a man like you, refusing to believe in them, himself unwillingly proves the opposite of what he set out to prove."

Ferdinand now had himself well enough in hand to indulge an ironical smile. Agnes' school-friend had one feminine gift at least, that of oratory.

"What did I set out to prove?" he asked.

There was a short silence broken by the twittering of a nest of young swallows under the eaves over the window. Then Miriam replied: "That selfish interest is the determining force of life. It has not been with the strongest people you have known: not with Dr. Quinn, who preferred Mrs. Sidney's friendship to yours: not with Mrs. Sidney herself, who sold her home to rescue her daughter's family, although legally another man was responsible for Mr. Mabie's debts. You would have let the other man pay them. Mrs. Sidney burdened herself with a crippled relation who had nearer claims on other people. You advised turning her over to them. Agnes followed your guiding principle, although she did not do it legally, when she falsified her house accounts. She took what she considered was hers, although it happened to be in your possession. She repudiated your theory when she confessed to you. She continued to repudiate it from that time till she died. Now look at results!"

"I trust that you are satisfied with results," commented Ferdinand.

"Relatively speaking, yes. Dr. Quinn never will be a rich man, but he will live the life he wants to live. Mrs. Sidney, in spite of loss and bereavement, has an old age rich in love and gratitude. The cripple has been something better than an encumbrance, she has been an encouragement and a comforter. Agnes' death proved that she was right and you were wrong, for it proved that it is impossible to reconcile the life of the soul—and that is the life of the race—with your hideous creed that would stifle the soul and hence the race. When you killed her you proved that. There is no coming to terms with you or your kind. You must be abandoned. You tried to ruin Beatrice Sidney through her weaknesses and those of her husband and Tom Ballington. Selfishness and recklessness blinded them so far. Then the higher nature awoke and, instead of ruining, you have truly saved all three. They see, at last, and they forgive. Since it has been demonstrated, you should acknowledge that you have been wrong. Until you feel uncertain of yourself and what you have lived for, you are a lost soul."

Ferdinand stood without moving through all she said. He looked at her unwaveringly, but there was a curious veil over his eyes. Whether he heard her or not, Miriam could not tell.

She paused a moment, then, when he did not move, she turned and went to the door.

Glancing back at him a moment before she left him, she saw him looking after her with the same inscrutable quiet. With a sigh of farewell to the room she never might enter again, Miriam went out and closed the door after her.

Ferdinand stood where she left him. Anger and bitterness darkened his face. He heard her leave the house, heard the carriage roll away. Then he went over to his wife's desk, sat down impatiently, drew some sheets of paper to him and picked up a pen. In order to free his mind from the unwelcome thoughts Miriam had called up he was about to write a business letter. He raised his eyes a moment preparatory to starting the letter and found himself looking at his mother's portrait on the wall opposite. Agnes had asked a short time before her death that it be brought to her room in order that her children might have its constant companionship. He turned his eyes away from it instantly, rose and touched the bell. A few moments later the maid tapped at the door. He told her to order the horse to be saddled, and dismissed her curtly. As he heard her receding footsteps the silence and emptiness of the house grew upon him. He went back to the desk, and, as he was shutting it, saw Miriam's picture looking at him. With an exclamation he picked it up, pulled open the little drawer, threw it in, and shut the drawer violently. Then he closed the desk and stood frowning at it abstractedly. How oppressively still the house was! The children were coming home from the lake that night, but the thought gave him no pleasure. They shrank away from him, and it seemed to him that even his aunt was beginning to do the same. Donald had left the office. Tom never again would be conveniently present to point his morals. Whispers against himself that had started when he sold his mother-in-law's home had touched his reputation in Winston. He fancied that people treated him differently since his wife's death, and he wondered uncomfortably how much they knew. Miriam Cass had insulted him, and he could not reply. How still the house was since she left! Would anything ever fill the emptiness again? All his successes began to seem dreary, the world to seem mechanical. A sentence he had heard somewhere came back to him. "Have you never wished to get away from this world of buying and selling to live,"—he started into full recollection as the sentence completed itself "with me and the children?" The passionate appeal he had denied assailed him once more, no longer beseeching but condemning, terrifying. The sound of horse's hoofs on the gravel outside roused him. He passed his hand over his eyes trying to shake off a question which began to prey upon his self-assurance. Dropping his hand, he turned determinedly to leave the room. Once more his eyes rested upon his mother's portrait. Ferdinand was conscious of a thrill of fear, for the still gray eyes met his own with the same silent question he felt henceforth would challenge his soul.

Had Agnes been right?

CHAPTER XII

AS the horses stopped at the station Miriam stood up in the carriage and looked back down the slope to the city resting on the shore of the lake. It seemed a mass of green, with roofs showing here and there among the trees. Several spires rose above the green, one of them lifting the outlines of a cross against the sky. The waters of the lake in the distance looked still and blue, but the noise in the great trees near at hand brought the sound of waters to Miriam's ears and she closed her eyes for an instant as in memory she walked with Agnes along that curving shore.

Then she heard Donald's voice speaking to her, saying that Mrs. Sidney had come, and she turned and let him help her from the carriage and take her where Mrs. Sidney was waiting. Donald left them together, saying that he would return in a few minutes to put Miriam on her train.

The two women looked at each other in silence with inexpressible thoughts speaking from their eyes.

Miriam was recalling, as she looked at the steadfast old face, the time when as a college girl she had watched Mrs. Sidney and the doctor in church and had made a sketch of them, calling it "Fate and Aspiration." Now she was seeing the faith and the humbleness which illumined and softened the strong features. Her heart ached with the unconscious pathos of the sturdy figure. It asked so little and gave so much; it had lost so uncomplainingly and suffered so dauntlessly; it had struggled so faithfully to subject its headstrong instincts to the law of gentleness and renunciation; it so persistently transformed defeat into victory.

When at last Miriam spoke, it was half the artist in her that said the words. "The most wonderful thing of all, Mrs. Sidney, is your face."

Miriam's own face had been indescribably changing as she looked at the older woman. The sternness went out of it, leaving exposed for the time being the Miriam whom Agnes had known. It was a self-unconscious, spiritual face that looked up at Mrs. Sidney. All that Miriam had meant to say was leaving her. Mrs. Sidney's face meant victory. It did not ask consolation.

Agnes' mother put her hardened hand over Miriam's beautiful one. "Miriam, you look good. Be good," she said earnestly.

Miriam felt a pain in her throat.

"If he smite thee on one cheek, turn the other. If he take thy coat, give him thy cloak also!" continued the uncompromising voice. Miriam saw that Mrs. Sidney meant the words she had quoted. She had been driven step by step to the logical conclusion of the Christian philosophy, and like her Master, she had accepted it.

"Take up thy cross and follow me," the voice went on. "Did you ever think what was the end of that journey, Miriam?"

"Yes."

Mrs. Sidney sighed as if to ease the tenseness of her body, letting it relapse as she did so. A smile whose radiance was not of this earth transfigured her face, as she continued, "But after the agony of Gethsemane and the cross, we shall see the great white throne, and there shall be no more death, neither sorrow nor crying, neither shall there be any more pain, for the former things have passed away."

Her eyes fell to the lifted face of her daughter's friend, and her smile changed and became one of human warmth and encouragement "It's a journey of love, Miriam," she said tremulously.

"To the strong like you, who make it so," Miriam replied.

Mrs. Sidney thought a moment before she spoke again.

Then she began to speak of something which she never had expected to mention. "Something happened to Agnes before she died, Miriam. I saw that as soon as I went into the room. I'd seen that same look on Stephen's face. When I asked her about it, she told me that if she got well she'd tell me, but that there was no need for me to know if she should die."

Miriam did not say anything.

She was thinking that it was a mercy that Mrs. Sidney had been spared the truth, when the old lady added quietly, "But of course I knew what it was." She looked keenly at Miriam and asked, "Perhaps you know, too?"

Miriam did not trust herself to speak. She saw by her friend's face that Mrs. Sidney was re-living the last scenes her daughter's life, and Miriam felt a hunger to live them with her. "What was the look you mean?" she asked, forcing herself to call up Agnes' face with mortal struggle upon it.

Mrs. Sidney seemed to have been waiting for the question. "*It was a look of mighty deliverance,*" she answered in a full, triumphant voice.

Miriam was startled. She felt herself sustained above her grief, as she had been lifted when she first saw Mrs. Sidney's face. Then she remembered that Agnes must have been dying when her mother arrived and that the look her mother had seen was that with which Agnes met death.

"I knew she would die so," she said presently.

"I do not mean death, Miriam. I mean incorruption and power. She would have lived on so, just as her father did, if she hadn't had heart failure. The death doesn't matter one way or the other. That was only an episode. She wasn't thinking about dying. She was thinking about living."

"Didn't she know she was going to die?" asked Miriam in surprise.

"She wouldn't give up hope till she had to. Quinn says he never saw anybody make such a fight for life. The nurse asked her once if she didn't want to make some preparation for the next world, and she said, no, she was ready for that any time, but that we must concentrate all our energies on keeping her in this."

"Right! She was like you!" broke in Miriam poignantly.

Mrs. Sidney still held to the purpose she had had in bringing up this conversation. She went on, undirected by Miriam's cry:

"She said to me once, 'I have just learned how to live, mother.' That seemed to be why she most wanted to get well. But when Quinn told her there was no hope, she acquiesced."

"Death meant little to her," said Miriam gravely. "She had fought her fight and kept the faith. She had won her point, that was the main thing. She refused to compromise."

"That is so," assented Mrs. Sidney thoughtfully. "She had learned to accept a good many sorrows and at last she learned not to fret herself because of evildoers. When I saw her, she was not troubled any more about Ferdinand. He that is unjust, let him be unjust still; and he that is righteous, let him be righteous still. She had no more to do with his way of life, Miriam, than I have or you have." Mrs. Sidney looked at Miriam as she said the last words, and then added, "The way to live is to be holy. Those who are not, we must forgive, for they know not what they do."

The whistle of the train was heard from the distance, and a plume of smoke could be seen nearing them from round the bend of the road. Both women rose.

"Agnes is safe now and happy," said Mrs. Sidney bravely, "and when one has accepted all in this life, it doesn't come so hard to accept death. She did the very best she could and she has gone to her reward. She had some troubles, but a good many good things, and her children are going to grow up and call her blessed. They will have their troubles, but what is their mother in them will come through it all the way she did. When I think of Stephen, I don't think of the hard times he had, but of what he was, and his daughter was like him."

Miriam placed her hands on Mrs. Sidney's shoulders. "When Agnes' children grow up," she said earnestly, "they will not be left alone to struggle with their father's will. You and I will tell them their mother's story, and her death will drive the story home. They never will forget what I shall tell them. They shall not suffer if they are disinherited of his money, which is all he has to give them and which he will hamper with conditions. I can give them enough, as their mother would give it, freely. They will come to me for it, too—for that and the chance to live. It is only a little while to wait."

The train drew into the station, and Mrs. Sidney saw Donald coming toward them.

"The last words Agnes spoke were to the children," she said. "She seemed very well just then. I heard her ask them to say a verse after her and to remember it always because it was true. She said it twice, and Estelle and Stephen said it after her. 'Blessed are the pure in heart for they shall see God.'"

Miriam stifled a sob.

Mrs. Sidney had one more thing to say, and she said it briefly. "You are a good friend, Miriam. God bless you for it. But friendship isn't all God meant women to have. Remember that Agnes' married life is the exception. The doctor's and my life is the rule. I have heard that you have said you will not marry. Do not set yourself up against the laws of nature. Nothing but trouble can come from it."

Miriam smiled affectionately at her companion. It pleased her that the old lady's mind continued to cope with other people's difficulties as well as with her own. Grief had not broken her down, and fortune had done her worst.

"You are quite right," she said. "Far be it from me to set myself up against a law of nature. But that is not the only law of nature."

A gleam of her old humor came into her eyes for a moment. Then she changed the subject.

She put two envelopes into Mrs. Sidney's hand. "Donald will explain," she said. "One of them is for your nephew from me. The other is from Beatrice to Agnes. She sent it by me and I know Agnes would have given it to Fred. I believe that after reading these, he will wish to see his wife again. Then I shall come to Kent."

As Mrs. Sidney glanced down at the letters, bewilderment, then relief and thanksgiving unspeakable, quivered in her face.

"To think this, too, is about to come out right!" she said brokenly. "Goodness and mercy have followed me." She could say no more.

Miriam leaned over and kissed her friend, then went aboard the train with Donald. Mrs. Sidney waited outside under the train window.

Donald arranged Miriam's packages for her, and then handed her a book. "Aunt Margaret found this book lying open in Agnes' room and gave it to me for you. It must have been the last one she read."

Miriam recognized the volume as one of her own gifts to Agnes, and accepted it silently.

They clasped hands, and then he turned and left her, his eyes wet.

The tears were in Miriam's eyes, too, as she leaned from the window for a last look at Mrs. Sidney.

"God bless you, Miriam— good-by," said the doctor's wife. The train began to move. "I shall see you again soon. Trust the Lord and put your faith in Him," she continued, walking along by the window, "and remember this about all the things we have talked of and things we haven't talked of, that now we see as through a glass darkly, but then—"

She stopped. A mist of tears clouded her eyes and rolled down her cheeks. Miriam saw her expression change into that look which tells that the well-beloved has gone. There was a moment of wavering, then the unconquerable spirit rose once again, resumed control, and just as Miriam was losing sight of her, she called after, completing her sentence— "but then we shall see face to face!"

The trees, the roofs and spires of Winston, the still blue lake, passed out of Miriam's view. For some time she did not change her position, but continued to look through the window at the green world below and the blue dome overhead.

"But then we shall see face to face?" she repeated thoughtfully to herself.

Her eyes dropped to the book Donald had given her, which had fallen open in her lap. Agnes' pencil marks drew her attention to the page, and she read the underlined words: "Here, however, I touch a theme too great for me to handle, but which will assuredly be handled by the loftiest minds, when you and I, like streaks of morning cloud, shall have melted into the infinite azure of the past."

9 781396 320927